THE BADMAN

Ron Eckert

Carol,
Thank you
for your support,
Ron Eckert

I dedicate this novel to the Lord Jesus Christ,
who came to seek and to save the lost.

PROLOGUE:

How I Came to Know and Write About The Badman

Dime store novelists have written, and poets have told, of the Badman and his exploits, sketching a portrait of a legendary gunfighter, the fastest, meanest shootist ever to roam the West. Skeptics have questioned the veracity of these sensationalized accounts and dismissed them as tabloid bunkum designed to sell books to eastern greenhorns hungry for pulp.

I, too, was a skeptic, until my perspective was suddenly and forever altered by my personal encounter with the truth. An author by trade, I had been paid a princely sum to ghostwrite the autobiography of Lord Lawrence Dunvale, a robber baron descended from the English aristocracy. It was early fall, and I was a passenger aboard Dunvale's train. I was there to listen to stories from his life, which I was expected to fashion into a larger narrative. I was to be a court historian. Dunvale told me the purpose of the book was to improve his public image and reputation, which meant magnifying his achievements while overlooking his shortcomings.

The train chugged through the night, over hills and rivers, through canyons and meadows, in the still darkness of the midnight hour. I had written most of the manuscript, which I placed on the dining table in the Pullman palace car. A few loose ends remained, necessitating a meeting, after which I could finish the book and receive my long-anticipated bonus, due upon publication. I had already secured a publisher in Chicago, our destination.

Dunvale's hounds traveled with him, and they were then in the process of devouring strips of fat falling from their master's table. Dunvale was in full form, languishing on a red velvet cushion, arms outstretched across the table, bragging about the role he had played in winning the Civil War. He smiled, relating how he had financed the Kansas Red Legs, an irregular company of Union soldiers known for their brutality, in exchange for certain concessions from the United States government after the war, including the granting of precious right-of-way for his trains.

"I picked the right side. My Red Legs showed Sherman how to fight…dirty," he said, while he downed a Scotch poured by his personal butler.

Lightning flashed outside, followed by a sharp peal of thunder, rocking the train. Dunvale turned to me and grinned. He saw the concern in my eyes.

"You have nothing to fear, young fellow. This train was built with the sturdiest steel from Pennsylvania and designed by the finest engineers from London and New York."

His smug expression vanished when the rear window of the palace car suddenly shattered. Shards of glass littered the floor. A man clad in sable reached through the broken window, turned the lever of the car door, and stepped inside. He threw a Navy Colt pistol toward Dunvale. It landed on the table next to his Scotch glass.

The intruder's face was shrouded by a peculiar bandanna. He said nothing. I caught but a fleeting glance at his eyes, piercing blue. Dunvale's eyes dilated with terror.

"I don't want to die, Mister. I'm building the West."

The outlaw gestured to the gun without saying a word. In desperation Dunvale reached for the Colt with his shaking right hand. Too slow, and too late. Two shots roared from the outlaw's Schofield, drawn in a black blur, in less than a heartbeat. Dunvale collapsed, writhing in pain, murmuring profanities between muffled coughs of sputtered blood. The outlaw walked over, placed his boot on Dunvale's nose, spurred his face, and stared down at his dying victim. He spoke soft and low. What he said I'll never know.

I cowered, my fingers trembling, my lips mumbling a prayer. I pondered my next move. If this outlaw were in fact the Badman, I knew I had moments to live, as it was said that he never left any witnesses behind. My thoughts turned to escape, however improbable. I crawled toward the rear of the car as quietly as possible. I moved my hand to the handle and tried not to make any noise. Then, my heart racing, I snapped the lever, opened the car door, and leapt off the train. There were no shots. Behind me I heard a terrible laugh.

I landed on an iron rail, fracturing my right leg. Despite the pain I scrambled on hands and knees toward the underbrush skirting the train tracks, inching toward the safety of the shadowy woods beyond. I glanced back at the departing train and was relieved to be leaving it behind. Then, I heard the sound of hooves thundering through the night.

"Badman's comin', boy!" he yelled through the pitch of night as I continued to crawl, hoping against hope I might reach the woods and find a good hiding place. The outlaw tied a magnificent black stallion with a beautiful white blaze to a nearby oak and retrieved something from the saddlebag. That something turned out to be my unfinished manuscript. In my haste, I had left it on the train. Now it was stained with Dunvale's blood. The outlaw threw it at me. It landed on the ground in front of my face.

"Ar…are…are you really the Badman?" I asked. "Are you going to kill me?"

"In just a moment, I'll let you know."

The brigand lit a candle, picked up the manuscript, and began to read. After several moments, which seemed like eternity, he put down the papers and shifted the candle, so that it lit up my face. He watched me… studied me. Why?

"Not if you promise not to use so many adverbs when you write my story. They interfere with the flow. And only if you burn this abomination, for it portrays the recently departed in a false light. And if your book veers in the slightest from the truth as I tell it, I'll feed you to the buzzards."

Over the course of the next few months, we met for hours and days on end. Between bank and train robberies he told me about his life and about how and why he had become the Badman. What follows is the only authentic biography of the Badman ever written. He wanted me to assure the reader that what follows is the truth about his life, to correct the lies and misunderstandings previously told and published. Now grab those reins and hold on for dear life. Get ready for a wild ride!

Book I: The Birth Of The Badman

Sunday Morning, April 27, 1862
Paint Rock Village, North Alabama

Miles Collins walked to the podium with purpose. He was a preacher who farmed. He held a weathered King James Bible in his large right hand, given to him by his grandfather Patrick, an Irishman who came to America in search of land and freedom.

Miles Collins was in his fifties, his hair graying but not quite yet a solid silver. His eyes were steely blue with an intensity not forgotten once encountered. He was over six feet tall, broad-shouldered, and was known for his physical strength and virtuous character. He considered himself a preacher first and a farmer second, though it was farming that made his living. He never drew a salary from the church. He loved everyone he met and gave everyone a fair shake. So, when he spoke people paid attention.

Miles began:

"Today's lesson is "do not kill." There's been a lot of talk lately about war and killing. There's been some of our own boys out there shooting at Yankees from behind bushes even, which, aside from being wrong, seems cowardly.

They say in this war it's brother against brother. Not too much different from the first murder recorded in human history. Cain killed his brother Abel, you might recall. As a result, he had to leave his people and his homeland, exiled to the Land of Nod. As far as we know, he spent the rest of his days away from his mom and daddy. He also had to wear a mark on his face. The mark of Cain.

Then later on, after God delivered the Israelites from Egypt, He gave Moses the Ten Commandments, the sixth of which is "Thou shalt not kill." I stand here today to urge you to live at peace with all men, so much as it is possible to do so. Each of us may soon be required to choose between war and peace. My fervent hope and prayer is that you make the right decision, even when those around you do otherwise. Choices beget consequences, and you do not want to wear the mark of Cain. It won't wash off. And once you're in the Land of Nod you might not be able to come back home again. So, remember, everyone, do not kill. Peace before violence. Love before hate. If we choose brotherly love over brotherly hate, maybe we can live at peace with our brothers from the North."

The sermon did not go over well. Some members got up and left before it was finished. One pointed his finger at Miles.

"Don't forget where you're from, preacher! Whose side are you on, anyway?"

Scanning the pews, Miles was surprised to see his son Gene sitting on the back row. Gene had not been to church in at least a year. On the Sunday after his eighteenth birthday, he had declared his religious independence and stayed in bed while his family went to church.

Though brokenhearted, Miles believed in the freedom of choice he preached and refused to force his faith on Gene. He thought Gene would come around eventually and felt his presence at church that morning was a good sign.

After the invitation and closing prayer, Miles, with wife Diana, walked arm-in-arm toward the back of the church. Their seventeen year-old son Johnny followed behind them.

Miles whispered to Diana, "We have a special visitor today. See him back there?"

"Gene!" Diana rushed toward him. "Son, it's so good to see you. You've just got to come out for lunch. I've even made your favorite – sweet potato pie. It'll be just like old times."

Gene smiled and hugged his Mama.

"What are you doing here?" Johnny asked. He slapped his older brother on the back.

"I don't know, I just got homesick."

"Mama, I have to share the sweet potato pie with him? He'll eat it all, just like he used to," Johnny said.

"That's right," Gene said. He thumped Johnny in the back of the head. "I can't wait, little brother. I'll meet ya'll there."

Gene untied his horse from an oak tree and mounted.

"Just like old times," Miles said.

Miles, Diana, and Johnny climbed into the wagon and rode to the farm with Gene behind them. It was a sunny spring day, and the birds were singing beautiful songs to each other.

Gene tied his horse and walked inside just behind his family. Finding his old seat at the family table, he smiled at the variety of foods his Mama kept bringing to the table.

"Thanks for the invite. I sure miss your meals, Mama. You're the best cook in Alabama."

"It won't be long before you're back home again. What were you thinking moving into town? You're a farmer, not a store clerk. Living in a one-room shack in the back of Bailey's General Store? That's no life for my boy."

"I know, Mama, but I just wanted to try something new."

"Well, you're over eighteen. You can do what you want, but we miss you. Anytime you want to come back home you're welcome."

"Well, I might just take you up on that someday, but I'm learning so much from Mr. Bailey. He's a smart businessman, and he's taken me under his wing."

"Are you sure he's teaching you the right things, son?" Miles asked. He stared at Gene with intent. "I hear he's training young guerrillas."

Gene looked out the window to avoid his father's gaze.

"The war's coming, Pa, whether you like it or not. You can't stop it. Whose side are you on?" Gene asked with a challenging voice.

"The Lord's side," Miles answered.

"Is that so? And whose side is the Lord on?"

"The side of peace. But enough of this political talk," Miles said. "I have an announcement to make. Great news! Johnny's going to be baptized on Friday, May 2, 1862, in the Paint Rock River."

"Congratulations, Johnny," Gene said. "On Mama's birthday? I wouldn't miss it for anything."

"I hope you'll be there, Gene," Miles said.

"Well, boys," Miles said, "if you'll excuse me, I've got to work on a sermon. It sure was good to have you back home, Gene."

He shook his son's hand, then wrapped him in a typical Miles Collins bear hug.

"Wish you'd stay. We could use some help on the farm."

"Thanks, Pa, I might just do that someday."

Gene crossed the room to his mother.

"Thanks for the meal, Mama," Gene said kissing her forehead. He turned toward the door. "Good to see all of you. I better be on my way. I'm going hunting with Luke. Later, Pa."

Gene walked out the door.

Johnny followed him onto the front porch.

"Johnny, can you keep a secret?" Gene asked.

"Sure."

"I've been reading my Bible a lot lately. As much as I hate to admit it, Pa's sermon really got to me today. Would you mind if I joined you next Sunday?"

"Well, of course, Gene, but you already said you'd be there at lunch."

"No... what I mean is would it bother you if I got baptized with you. I'll let you go first."

"Gene! I don't mind, I'm thrilled! Everyone's going to be so excited. Wait 'til I tell Mama and Pa."

"No, don't tell 'em. I want to surprise 'em. So, you and Pa wade into the river, and just before he takes your confession, tell him to wait just a second, and I'll wade in behind you and tell him the news."

"I can't wait," Johnny said.

"Hey Gene, where are you hunting tonight – can I join you?"

"That's one of the reasons I'm here, Johnny. I wanted to invite you to come along. I can't tell you where we're going or what we're doing. It's a secret."

"No secrets between brothers, Gene, and besides, I can keep a secret, remember? You just told me one, a pretty big one."

"Okay, we're hunting Yankees, and we're going to rendezvous at Miller's Cave. That's where we plan our raids."

Fear suffused Johnny's face. "Raids? Yankees? That sounds dangerous."

"What are you, Johnny, some kind of chicken or something? You're the best shot in Alabama. Why, one time I seen you shoot a deer through the heart from three hundred yards away with Pa's Sharps. Johnny, we need your help."

"To do what, kill people? I don't believe in killing, Gene. You know what I want to do when I grow up."

"I know. I've heard it all before. Pa's your hero, and you want to grow up to be a preacher just like him, but times are changin' and war's comin' – you and Pa can't bury your heads in the sand and pretend you can preach both sides into peace."

"Let me spell it out for you Gene. N-O. No. I'm getting baptized because I believe in love, not war. And just like Pa I'll preach peace, out of faith, not fear."

"But Johnny, you can't hide your gift with guns. Too many people know about it. Not just the guerrillas. The regular army, too. And they'll expect you to enlist when you turn eighteen. They'll be awfully sore with you if you refuse."

"I'd rather offend them than God, or my conscience."

"Well, I'll tell everybody I tried, anyway. I tried to tell 'em you were mule-headed and wouldn't do it, but they told me to give it my best shot."

"Who's they?"

"Just about every teenage boy in Paint Rock – guys you grew up hunting with, fighting with, and yes, going to church with, even the Thompson brothers, our cousins."

"Bill and Charlie are involved in this?"

"Yeah, they've been spying on the Yankee soldiers and bringing us ammunition. They're awfully proud of their brother Luke for standing up for Southern values. I guess you don't feel the same way."

"Gene, I've always looked up to you, you know that, but it's a matter of faith. I don't think I could ever kill

13

another person. Remember the sixth commandment? Thou shalt not kill. I just couldn't do it. Gene, have you done it?"

"Not yet, but Luke has. He got his first Yank the other day, picked him off a train from a hundred yards away. Shot him from behind a stump. Billy Yank never knew what hit him."

"So, Luke fired first?"

"Yeah, in this war it's kill first or be killed."

"Sounds like murder to me, when you shoot a guy like that."

"It's not murder if it's war, Johnny. You think the Yankees believe in civilized warfare? I've heard some interesting stories about what they are doing to Southern civilians."

"Really? Like what?"

"I've heard about a real hard case who'll do anything. This guy rides with the soldiers, but he ain't one of 'em. He don't wear a uniform. He shows up sometimes to fight guerrillas. If there's been a guerrilla raid, and he can't find the raiders, he just burns the closest town. Everybody in that town either dies or moves, 'cause his soldiers torch everything in their path--houses, farms, livestock."

"Everyone?"

"Yeah, even people like you and Pa. This guy's cruel. Luke told me a story about him, supposed to have happened in Georgia. He had caught some guerrillas and was asking them some questions. They wouldn't answer, so he took a blazing poker and branded each of them in the face with the letter 'C'."

"Why the letter 'C'?"

"No one knows – some think it stands for 'coward' and others say 'Cain,' you know, from the Bible."

"Aren't you scared, Gene?"

"Not really, Johnny; it just makes me want to kill him before he can do it to anyone else. If they win, we're all goners."

"Well, Gene, when I turn eighteen, I'm gonna head west, find a small town, and be a farmer and preacher. I don't want to get caught up in some war I don't believe in."

"Some people will call you a coward and a traitor, Johnny."

"Yeah, I know. What will you call me, Gene?"

"Brother – always," Gene said.

"Good luck, Gene. See you at the river."

"Later on, Johnny."

Baptism of Johnny Collins
May 2, 1862
Paint Rock Village, Northwest Alabama

Baptisms in Paint Rock were always special, especially so in spring when flowers bloomed, and tree blossoms perfumed the air with a blissful fragrance carried by soft southern winds to honeybees searching for nectar. Squirrels frolicked through the hickories, and cardinals flew from pine to pine, their wings waxing red against the cerulean sky. The animal world teemed with life, much of it new, from scampering bunnies to curious fawns still with their spots, rising and falling, learning how to walk.

Most of Paint Rock village had gathered on such an idyllic spring day to witness another form of birth: the baptism of seventeen year-old Johnny Collins, their beloved hometown boy. Johnny was exceptionally handsome with azure eyes, thick brown hair, dimpled cheeks, and skin bronzed by the sun. He was over six feet in height with broad shoulders and powerful arms. He possessed a keen intelligence and was well versed in the classics and the Bible, having been tutored in both by his father, whom he resembled and adored.

Johnny had a carefree, adventurous demeanor. He was usually smiling, and often laughing. He wanted to be a preacher like his father. He dreamed of founding a church in the West, a world outside the South, a world untouched by civil war.

Northwest Alabama was a simmering cauldron of hate, and, judging from the thousands slain at Shiloh just a few weeks before, a bloodbath was coming. Johnny wanted no part of that. While he disagreed with slavery and supported the Union, he also opposed the War on religious grounds. To Johnny's way of thinking, "do not kill" and "turn the other cheek" were divine commands to be obeyed. They weren't optional. Miles felt the same way.

Of course, Johnny understood that other, well-intentioned people felt differently including some of his friends and family. Even his brother Gene, who had joined up with a group calling themselves the "Southern guerrillas" against Miles' wishes.

Miles and Johnny began walking toward the river amid laughter and joyful banter from Johnny's family and many friends. He heard the gentle, happy voice of his mother, Diana, somewhere behind him. The warm noonday sun cast its golden rays against the glistening water. The water mirrored a moving reflection of a father and son walking in harmony together.

"Pa, I'm so happy. I've waited a long time for this."

"I know, Johnny. I still remember the day my Grandpa baptized me. There's nothing better in the world than the feeling you'll get when you rise up out of that water."

As Miles spoke, Johnny looked around for his older brother. Gene was nowhere in sight. Unknown to their parents, Johnny and Gene had planned to surprise everyone and get baptized together, on their mother's birthday, in the Paint Rock River, the river that meant so much to them. The river where they had fished, swam, and skipped rocks.

Reminiscing, Johnny was lost in reverie, daydreaming while walking, realizing that somehow somewhere along the way the ground beneath his feet had turned to water. Suddenly, Miles stopped. He turned and faced his son.

"Johnny, do you believe with all of your heart, soul, and mind that Jesus Christ is the son of God?"

Johnny couldn't and didn't answer. All he could think about was Gene. Where was he? Johnny surveyed the landscape in vain for his brother. How could Gene miss their baptism?

Johnny looked back at Miles, who repeated the question. Just as Johnny was about to say "yes," a sound like rolling thunder disturbed the calm waters. Gunfire sounded, and bullets whizzed overhead and thudded against the riverbank. Johnny turned to find Federal soldiers on horseback, rifles raised. Miles pushed Johnny into the river, and they swam underwater toward the riverbank. Using roots as handholds, they climbed out of the river.

"Johnny, Diana, let's go!" Miles yelled as he mounted the family wagon and led the team toward the village. He saw Jake Thompson, his best friend and brother-in-law.

"Jake, tell everyone to meet at the church. We'll make a stand there!"

Several wagons and teams of horses raced toward the church. Their occupants jumped out and arranged their wagons in a circle and prepared to defend themselves. They gathered what guns and ammunition they could find. Miles told Johnny to remain inside, to hide in the closet behind the altar.

Instead, Johnny grabbed his Pa's Sharps rifle when Miles wasn't watching and left the safety of the church and wagons. He climbed a tree on a hill overlooking Paint Rock not too far from the church. Scanning his surroundings, Johnny saw two Confederate guerrillas on horseback, with their hands tied behind their backs, being led by Federal soldiers toward the river. Johnny could not identify the guerrillas given the distance. Looking the other direction, he saw Federal troops approaching the church. On the lead horse was a man dressed completely in black.

The man in black gestured to the bugler who sounded his horn. With a stentorian voice that Johnny heard clearly from twenty-five yards away, the man in black boomed. "We mean you no harm. We are here

19

only to deliver a message. This message shall be delivered at the tall oak tree near the river bridge, the tree you people call 'Goliath.' If you go to the bridge, you shall not be harmed. If you stay in the church, you shall surely perish."

Johnny came down from the tree. Instinct told him to warn Pa about the prisoners he'd seen. Thinking the Yankees might shoot if they saw him with the Sharps, Johnny left it in the bough of the tree and circled back to the church. Johnny was too late. He saw the dust from the departing wagons headed toward the river bridge. The man in black was still near the church though, talking to two soldiers. Johnny crept closer, hiding behind a tree only fifteen feet away.

"Take what you want from the town, then burn it. Don't leave one building standing, not even this church. Return to Huntsville. We'll meet you there after the hanging."

After barking his orders, the man in black mounted his horse and rode toward the river as the soldiers lit torches and threw them into the church. Johnny's eyes grew cloudy as he watched the church burn. So many memories, gone forever.

Johnny raced back to the tree, grabbed the rifle, and ran toward the river. He climbed a tall oak about a hundred feet from the river bridge to see what was happening. Looking toward the bridge, Johnny saw the two guerrillas were being led on horseback down to the riverbank. Two nooses had been slung from Goliath's sturdiest branch.

Johnny was now close enough to identify the prisoners: his cousin Luke Thompson and his brother Gene. Now it all made sense. Gene had been captured, and now he would hang. Johnny had to stop it, but how?

The man in black rode up to Goliath, dismounted, and began to speak.

"Citizens of Paint Rock, I'm glad you could make it to the party. I am here to punish the actions of your misbehaving youth, who call themselves guerrillas. We call them cowards and bushwhackers because they prefer to shoot from behind bushes than to fight face-to-face like real men. We only caught two of these cowards, but I know for a fact there had to have been at least ten or more. Since they won't come forward and confess their sins, I have no choice but to hold the community collectively responsible. Today I will burn the town of Paint Rock to the ground, as just punishment for their sins. Every house, every barn, every storefront shall see the torch. Not one stone shall be left upon another. All livestock shall leave their pens, for they shalt surely be destroyed. Be thankful I spare your lives. If I have to return, I shall not be so lenient!"

After finishing his speech, he gestured toward a sergeant, and the sergeant approached the prisoners, his intentions apparent.

Rage and guilt mingled in Johnny's mind. If only he had joined Gene on that raid, he could have saved his brother. Gene had told him that in this war it was kill or be killed, that it was a mistake for Johnny to believe he could preach both sides into peace. Was Gene right? What had the people in Paint Rock done to this madman? Nothing. The image of the burning church returned to his mind.

From his vantage point, Johnny saw the sergeant struggling to place Gene's squirming head in the noose. Gene didn't have much time left. Johnny had to do something, but what? Kill? Wasn't that against everything he'd been taught – to kill a man in ambush? But what about his brother? If he did nothing, Gene would hang.

Several times Johnny raised the rifle only to put it down again. Time warped to a slow crawl. Gene's screams grew louder, more urgent. The soldiers were slapping him as Gene resisted and shouted. One of them hit Gene with his rifle butt, and Gene's cries morphed into yelps. Johnny heard the wails of a brokenhearted woman. Diana Collins ran toward the man in black. She prostrated herself at his feet and begged for her son's life. The man in black turned his back and motioned to the hangman.

Standing in the bough of the tree, his hands shaking, Johnny cradled the rifle in a V-shaped fork in the branches. He prayed, aimed, and fired. The bullet struck the would-be hangman in the neck, killing him and showering those nearby with his blood. The man in black jumped behind Goliath preventing Johnny from getting a clean shot.

After the first shot, it grew easier for Johnny. He shot every soldier who tried to approach. The Sharps rifle was a wonderful weapon, and Johnny, after much practice over the years, had become an incredible marksman. If Johnny had a passion other than religion, it was guns. He loved to shoot, and he spent hours practicing. He was generally regarded as the best rifle shot in Paint Rock, if not all of Alabama.

Johnny had also learned how to load and reload fast. He had once matched Sharps' own record of fourteen shots in a minute.

Johnny shot twelve times; a dozen men were dead. Nothing unsettles an army like a sniper. Panic spread through the Union ranks. Some soldiers deserted never to be heard from or seen again. From behind the tree, the man in black shouted to his men. He commanded them to remain in their ranks.

Johnny shouted from the tree. "Pa, I've got you covered. Cut them loose!"

Miles unsheathed his Bowie knife and ran toward the tree. The man in black sprang out from behind Goliath's thick trunk, tackled Miles from behind, and grabbed the Bowie, which he placed against Miles' throat just hard enough to break the skin.

"Rebel sniper, I've captured your father. I will slit his throat should you fire any more shots. Do I make myself clear?"

Two soldiers approached the captives to finish the hanging. Before the noose tightened, Gene yelled. "Avenge me, brother! And I'll see you in Heaven!"

"I doubt it," Johnny said.

He watched Gene swing from the tree, his tongue contorting outside his mouth, writhing and twisting until it stopped. Johnny's eyes narrowed into slits.

"But vengeance shall be mine, brother," Johnny said with the hiss of a snake. "Vengeance shall be mine."

§§

"So that was your boy up in the tree?" the man in black asked. "And that guerrilla is yours, too? Just what is it you do for a living to raise boys like that?"

"I'm a preacher."

"A preacher?" The man in black laughed. "Did you hear that, boys, that's the best joke I've heard since I came down to Dixie. Preacher? How could a preacher raise two boys like that?"

He looked at his men. They were trying to act brave.

"Men, fan out and scour the countryside. He's out there. Find him. We're going to have us another hanging when you do. I'm about to deliver a sermon to this preacher while you're gone."

The man in black grabbed a black quirt hanging from the side of his horse.

"Remove thy shirt, preacher. It's time you learned a lesson about discipline. It was wise King Solomon who once said, 'Spare the rod and spoil the child.' Why have your sons become monsters? I'll tell you. Because you didn't whip them when they were young. I think it's only just, then, that you get the whipping they missed."

The man in black drew back and swung the whip with all the force he could muster. He strafed Miles' bare back with a powerful blow. Blood streamed in rivulets to the ground. Miles cried out in pain, before regaining sufficient composure to speak.

"So just what is it you do where you're from?"

"I'm a preacher," the man in black said.

Miles chuckled despite the agony. "A preacher? Did you hear that, Jake, that's the best joke I've heard in a long, long time."

Jake Thompson was the father of Luke Thompson, the boy hanged with Gene. He was also Miles' brother-in-law having married Miles' sister.

Enraged, the man in black lashed Miles again, this time in the shoulder close to but not quite touching the right ear.

"I whip you today for disgracing our profession," the man in black said. "How could a true preacher own slaves?"

"I don't," Miles said.

"How could a true preacher oppose the Union of free states?" the man in black asked.

"I didn't and don't. I have always preached against slavery and supported the Union. You, sir, are the true disgrace--violating every rule of war and every law of humanity, while claiming to be a man of God."

"Preacher," the man in black said, "it's obvious you haven't read your Old Testament. Don't you remember how Saul was commanded to slaughter the Amalekites, man, woman, and child? He died because he refused to obey the Lord's commands."

"I don't see any Amalekites around here," Miles said. "And I certainly don't believe you've received any divine revelation. There's a darkness in your soul, and we know where that comes from."

Dumbfounded, the man in black smiled.

"I'm going to enjoy watching you die. I was going to let you live, but you will die for what you just said to me – for calling the arm of the Lord the arm of the devil."

"No," Miles said, "you're going to die for killing my boy. The blood of my son cries out to Heaven, and his cries will be heard. Vengeance is mine, sayeth the Lord, and I'll leave it to Him to take care of you someday."

The man in black whipped Miles once more, this time across the mouth.

"Maybe that will stop your sermons for a while."

"That's enough!" Jake charged the man in black with a Bowie knife. Three soldiers stepped forward to block his advance. Jake looked around at his friends and neighbors, furious.

"Why won't you help us? They can't stop us if we fight them together."

"Because they're cowards, just like your son. I had thought you would have stayed with the women, but I'm glad you stepped forward. You need the same sermon, I'll warrant."

The man in black whipped Jake until his face was red pulp.

§§

A company of soldiers rode up.

"Any news? Where is that sniper?" the man in black asked.

"Colonel, we can't find him. He knows this country better than we do. He fell down from the tree where he was shooting, and we almost got him, but he got away. We haven't been able to find his trail."

"Look for caves. That's one of their favorite hideouts, I've learned. Keep searching. Search until sunset, then we've got to leave for Huntsville."

Motioning toward Miles and Jake, the man in black told a private to tie their hands behind their backs.

"While you're searching for our young sniper, I'll be taking a scenic tour of Paint Rock. I feel the need to burn something, starting with the farms owned by these two. Who'll tell me where they live?"

Silence.

"Okay, let's try this again. Who'll tell me where they live? I'm going to shoot someone in the next ten seconds unless I have a volunteer."

Mr. Bailey stepped forward.

"Don't shoot, mister. I'll show you anything you want to see. I'll tell you anything you want to hear."

"I bet you will. I can see it in your eyes. Fear. I like that look. And for coming forward I'll spare your farm and livestock. Let's ride!"

Jake spit at Bailey as he walked by.

"Don't you just love a Judas?" the man in black asked. "I never could tolerate one myself. I'd shoot all of them if I had the chance, but they sure do come in handy in wartime when you need information."

"I'm not a Judas, mister," Bailey said.

"Shut up, imbecile, you are what you are, now lead the way."

Bailey led the man in black and his soldiers toward the Thompson and Collins farms, which were within a mile of each other.

§§

After the hanging, Johnny sat for a while in shock. How could this have happened to him and his family? Where was God? How could He have allowed something this terrible to happen? Johnny thought of Job, who endured the death of his family and other hardships but refused to blame God. Johnny resolved to do likewise, but his faith had surely been tested, shaken to its core.

But now he was a killer. He had shed human blood. How could he be a preacher now?

With unsteady feet, Johnny came down from the tree. He snagged his big toe on a small branch and tumbled. He landed with a thud.

As Johnny rose up, a Federal soldier dashed through the underbrush toward him. He ordered Johnny to drop the gun and come with him. Johnny darted through the woods in the other direction. The soldier drew a pistol and fired, narrowly missing his target. Johnny ran through the woods, his mind racing, thinking of a place to hide.

Miller's Cave, that's where he would go. Johnny hoped the man in black had not caught Gene and Luke there. If he had, the cave would likely be guarded, and he could be running into a trap. Gene and Luke had come from the opposite direction near the train tracks, and so he hoped the cave was safe. He didn't have many options.

He found an old deer trail, known only to Paint Rock natives, that led to Miller's Cave.

Miller's Cave got its name from an eccentric named Henry Miller, who lived there in the early 1800s with his Cherokee wife. He owned a farm in Paint Rock, and made a decent living, but never built a house and never went to church. He chose to live in the cave instead. Henry never talked much about anything, keeping speech to a bare minimum.

One day he left his wife in the cave and never came back. He took one horse and left all of his tools and other livestock behind. Years afterward, following a heavy rain, some Paint Rock boys had gone spelunking through the cave's labyrinth of interior passageways. They discovered the skeleton of the Cherokee woman with Miller's knife nearby.

Miller's Cave was near the top of a large hill overlooking Paint Rock. It was not plainly visible from town, though, and could be seen only from certain angles halfway up the hill. It was an excellent hideout.

Johnny moved from tree to tree up the hill, looking for soldiers. He heard a sudden movement, and his heart raced. Just a whitetail doe enjoying the spring foliage. She looked at Johnny with sad brown eyes, then scampered away.

Johnny stopped at a grove of trees ringing the cave's mouth. He stared at the cave and wondered whether soldiers would be waiting inside. Behind him Johnny heard rustling in the grass. He ran inside. The cave was empty.

How long would it be before they found him here? Soldiers climbing the mountain would eventually spot it. He had two choices: explore the cave to worlds unknown and potentially dangerous or hide in the mouth of the cave.

Johnny had heard stories of people dying inside the cave. And not just Miller's Cherokee wife either. Some kids had gone exploring and gotten lost. They went in but never came out. After a flood, several small skeletons washed up to the mouth with jagged fracture lines of unknown origin.

After weighing his options, Johnny chose to hide in the mouth and to take his chances in the inner recesses only if necessary. To find him his pursuers would have to locate the cave first. Johnny thought he might be able to hide it.

He went outside and tore tree limbs and branches from several trees. He stretched them over the mouth. Inspecting his work, Johnny felt the cave would be hard to find. His new abode looked more like a rat's nest or thatched hut than a cave. It might buy him enough time to escape come nightfall.

§§

About an hour before sundown, Johnny heard a whinny outside the cave followed by a human voice.

"Wait here, Blackie."

Johnny looked outside to see a Federal soldier facing the opposite direction, urinating. He saw a young black stallion tied to a tree. Only one soldier. He heard other noises, but they seemed to be farther downhill.

Johnny rushed over, raising his rifle. He hid behind the horse, waiting for the soldier to finish. The soldier fastened his trousers and turned around to find Johnny's rifle barrel in his face.

"Come with me, mister. One move and you're a dead man."

Johnny wondered what he should do with the horse. If he shooed it downhill, it would attract attention. He left the horse where it was tied. The stallion had plenty of grass to eat.

Johnny directed his captive into the cave and ordered him to disrobe. Johnny put on the Federal uniform, a little big for him but only slightly. Johnny tore off part of his long johns and used the strips to tie the soldier's hands and feet.

"Who is this man in black?"

The soldier refused to speak.

"Tell me who he is and where he comes from."

The soldier remained silent.

"Do you see this gun? Were you at the hanging? If you were, you know I won't hesitate to kill you. Now tell me what you know, or I'll shoot."

"Okay, boy. The man in black is named Hawk, Colonel Julius Rubicon Hawk. He was sent by General Sherman to stop the guerrillas."

"Where is he from?" Johnny said.

"Lawrence, Kansas. They say he's a preacher there."

"A preacher?"

"I don't know. I've seen him pull some pretty cruel tricks on you Southerners. When we look at him funny afterward, he just says he's the arm of the Lord come to punish the wicked."

"He killed my brother today."

"One of the bushwhackers?"

"Yeah. Tell me how Hawk captured my brother."

"A couple of weeks ago, some bushwhacker popped up from behind a stump with a rifle and shot one of our men. Killed him. We never could find him. He disappeared into the woods. Hawk was called in at that point."

"So, what did he do?"

"He forced some Confederate prisoners to wear our uniforms and get on the train. We put on their uniforms and rode through the woods where the bushwhackers had been."

"What happened?"

"When we fired at the train – we aimed high so not to hit anything – two young men came out of nowhere. They had rifles and ammunition – thought we were Rebs. They tried to shake Hawk's hand. Hawk smiled and said, 'It's good to meet you, boys, glad you decided to turn yourselves in.' The boys were shocked."

"Pretty sneaky," Johnny said.

"Yep. After we caught the boys, Hawk told us to build a fire. He put a poker into the fire, until it was red hot."

"Then what?"

"He walked over to the boys and said, 'Tell me where your parents are. I need to visit with them.' They wouldn't answer, so Hawk started burning their feet. Finally, one of the boys broke down and told him his Pa was at the Paint Rock River for his brother's baptism, and he was supposed to be there to get baptized with his brother. He begged Hawk to let him go to the river. He wanted to get baptized."

"What did Hawk say?"

"Hawk told him he was an infidel – said there were not any true Christians in the slaveholding South, that he would go to Hell before the day was over. Then we rode down to the river."

"Is that it?"

"Yeah. Please don't kill me for what he made us do. He's a terrible man, but he'll do the same thing to us if we don't follow his orders."

"One more thing," Johnny said. "Where is your base, and where is Hawk staying?"

"Huntsville. Hawk stays in the officers' quarters in the hotel."

"Tell you what I'm going to do," Johnny said. "I'm going to leave you here, bound and gagged. Eventually you'll work yourself free and make your way back to Huntsville."

"Thanks for not killing me, boy. I've got a wife and kids."

§§

It was about a half hour before sunset when Johnny left the cave. What should he do, and where should he go, he wondered? Home. Home to Mama. She would make things better, somehow, like she always did.

Growing up, Diana Collins had always taken care of her boys, tending to their every need. She made their food, washed their clothes, and taught them how to read and write. She was an active part of the farm, helping plant and harvest the crops. Johnny's parents owned a small family farm, which they sarcastically called "Our Plantation," a not-so-subtle dig at the large plantations and wealthy planters. The Collins were not part of the Southern plantocracy. They were self-sufficient, not relying on a team of slaves to do their work. Diana had become the driving force behind their farm. Johnny marveled at how many tasks she could complete during the day but remain energetic enough at night to read the Bible and sing gospel songs to her children.

Johnny imagined how she must have felt watching her son die a horrible death. He remembered a verse from the Bible, 'Cursed is he who is hanged on a tree' or something like that. Was Gene cursed? He died before he was baptized, and Diana had told Johnny that Gene had never adopted the Christian faith. Was Gene in Hell?

But then Johnny pondered Gene's last words, "I'll see you in Heaven." Had Gene seen angels as he was dying? Was he actually in Heaven? Wherever he was now, he had left behind a brokenhearted mother, and Johnny wanted to console her if he could.

To get to the Collins farm, Johnny had to ride back through Paint Rock. He rode through its smoldering ruins; his eyes grew misty. As he neared the church, the wind picked up blowing ashes through the air like a thick fog. Johnny coughed. Where the altar used to be, Johnny saw two human corpses burned beyond recognition. He stared at their charred remains in disgust.

Johnny found Thompson Trail and rode toward Collins Hill, a small slope overlooking the Collins farm. He rode just off the trail to avoid detection. Cresting the hill, Johnny sat up on his horse and searched vainly for his home place. Thick smoke rose where it once had been.

Johnny saw his father and his Uncle Jake on horseback with their hands tied behind their backs. Where was Mama? He found her not far from where the front door used to be. A Union soldier was grabbing at her. She broke free of his grasp. She tried to run, but he caught up and forced his arms around her.

Johnny raised his rifle, but there was nothing he could do. He was too far away. As good a shot as he was, he might miss, and who knew what Hawk would then do to his father and uncle in retribution. Just then, help came from an unlikely source. Hawk drove the molesting soldier away with a long, black quirt. Hawk put his arms around her to shield her. He gestured with his hand, and the army marched away.

Once the army was out of sight, Johnny rode to his mama. About fifty yards away, he heard gunfire and felt a bullet whiz over his head. He looked in the direction of the shot. Charlie Thompson with a rifle.

"Charlie, it's me, Johnny, don't shoot!"

Charlie put down the gun.

"Johnny? We thought for sure they'd got you."

"They almost did."

At the sound of her son's name, Diana looked up with newfound hope, in time to see Johnny dismounting.

"Johnny?" I'm so glad you're alive," she said between sobs.

"Yes, Mama." He walked over and gave her a big hug.

"Oh Johnny, they killed Gene! And they burned him! Not even a Christian burial."

"What?"

"The man in black told his soldiers to throw him and Luke in your Pa's church, then they burned it and the rest of the town to the ground."

Johnny recalled the remains in the ruins. He remembered the horrible smell of death, and the swirling ashes scattered by the wind.

"What's going to happen to Pa?" Johnny asked.

"I don't know. They took him and your Uncle Jake. They tied them up and put them on horses. I don't know where they're going. Nobody knows where the troops are stationed."

"I do," Johnny said.

Then Johnny told Diana and Charlie about his harrowing escape to Miller's Cave, and what the soldier had said.

"I'm scared, Johnny," Diana said. "I think they're going to kill your Pa and Uncle Jake. They were bound and on horseback just like Gene and Luke were. Poor Gene." Diana began to cry again. "I don't think he was saved."

"Now Mama, there's something I want to tell you about Gene. It was a secret between brothers, but I know he'd want me to tell you now."

"What is it?"

"Last Sunday after lunch, Gene told me he'd been reading his Bible and had come to believe that Jesus was the Son of God. He asked for my permission to be baptized with me. We were going to surprise you and Pa."

"Oh Johnny. Really?"

"Yes, Mama."

"That makes me feel better, but I regret he was never baptized."

"I guess we'll have to leave that up to God, Mama."

"Thank you for sharing that with me. I hate that man in black. What did we ever do to deserve this?" she asked. She pointed to the ruins of their home.

"He's killed my son, burned my house, destroyed our crops and livestock, and now he's about to kill your Pa. Why?"

"I don't know, Mama. But he's not going to kill Pa, not if I can help it. If I can get there in time."

"I've already lost one son. I'm not going to lose another. You're not going anywhere."

"Mama, you don't understand. Gene was right about one thing. In this war it *is* kill or be killed. If we don't get there in time, they'll kill Pa and Uncle Jake, and they don't deserve to die."

"But Johnny, how can you do anything about it? It's

you against the Union Army."

"No ma'am, it's not just him," Bill Thompson said. He'd been eavesdropping. "Charlie and I are going too, Aunt Diana. We've lost our brother, and they've taken our Pa. We've suffered the same losses you have."

"That's right," Charlie said. "We're in this together."

Bill and Charlie Thompson were a year apart, Bill being the older brother. Johnny was a year older than Bill. The Thompson farm was adjacent to the Collins' property, and Johnny had grown up with Bill and Charlie. They were his best friends. They were also family. Naomi Thompson, Bill and Charlie's mother, was Miles' sister. That made Johnny, Bill, and Charlie first cousins.

Walking over to the group, Naomi said, "Diana, I don't think we can stay here. We've no place to stay and no reason to."

"I guess you're right," Diana said. "We've got to leave. We really don't have any choice."

§§

Johnny looked at everyone. "I've got a rescue plan."

"Let's hear it," Bill said.

"You see this uniform I'm wearing? That's my ticket in. We'll ride to Huntsville; I'll walk through town and find out where they are."

"What if they've killed them already?" Diana asked.

"Then we're already too late. But we'll find their trail

and follow it. Maybe they're still alive," Johnny said.

"What do we do once you find them?" Naomi asked.

"Bill and Charlie will start some fires near the building where they're being held – create a panic. When the guards come out, I'll take care of them. I'll get Pa and Uncle Jake. Mama, you and Aunt Naomi will have the horses ready. Bill and Charlie will meet us at the horses, and we'll ride like thunder."

"One thing. Where are we going to find horses?" Diana asked.

"Good point, Mama. I hadn't thought about that. My plan won't work without horses, and I guess the Yankees killed or stole them all."

"No, they didn't," Bill said. "When you all rode back to the church, I rode home with Charlie. We'd heard stories about this guy, and how he burned people out, including their livestock, so we came home, rounded up our best horses, and herded them over to Cherokee Point."

"How many did you save?" Johnny asked.

"Six – made two trips before the Yankees got here. I saw you riding down the hill in that uniform, and I got worried. I drew a bead on you, but you were riding too hard. I couldn't get a clean shot. I rode up just in time to see Charlie miss."

"It's a good thing for me it was Charlie shooting," Johnny said. He laughed and slapped Charlie on the back.

"Boys," Diana said, "if we're going to do this, we'd better get started. We don't know how much time they've got. They could be dead already."

"Let's ride," Johnny said.

Johnny led the way back down Thompson Trail where Bill found the soldiers' tracks. They followed the trail toward Huntsville.

§§

Huntsville was a day's ride from Paint Rock, and the soldiers had a head start. They would arrive several hours before Johnny and the others unless their progress was delayed by the thunderstorm developing ahead.

The storm began with a few isolated lightning strikes and some distant rumbling of thunder. It grew with every minute. Torrents of rain smacked the ground, the horses, and their riders. They rode low in the saddle with their arms outstretched to shield their heads from the hail. Behind them Johnny heard a loud noise. A tree creaked and fell just twenty feet away, struck by a lightning bolt bright enough to light up the woods. Concerned, Johnny led them to a thick grove of trees. They tied their horses and took cover to wait out the storm.

Alabama was famous for its spring storms. As the rain poured down in silver streaks, Johnny recalled how he, Gene, and Pa would sit on the back porch and watch the storms roll in. Those were some of the best times he'd ever had with Gene and Pa. Now Gene was dead, and Pa probably would be soon.

"Gene never should have gotten mixed up with those guerrillas. We wouldn't be here if he had just listened," Diana said.

"Well, Mama, Pa and I never joined the guerrillas, and look what's happened to us. And what about the other innocent people in Paint Rock, who lost everything? They hadn't joined the guerrillas, either. I rode through Paint Rock on the way back from Miller's Cave. There wasn't anything left. Hawk burned everything."

"I don't think he'd have done that if the guerrillas hadn't started shooting at those soldiers," Diana said.

"Who knows, Mama? We didn't deserve what happened to us. And a couple of days before he died, I asked Gene if he had killed anyone, and he said he hadn't."

"After we get your Pa, Johnny, we're going to ride away somewhere. Escape this war."

"I hope you can, Mama, but I promised Gene I would avenge his death."

"So you can die too? Do you think Gene would want you to die?"

"It's a matter of honor and justice, Mama. We can't let Gene's death go unpunished. An eye for an eye, and a tooth for a tooth, doesn't the Bible talk about that?"

"Maybe in King David's time, Johnny, but a Christian believes just the opposite. Love your enemies, turn the other cheek, do good to those who persecute you. Do you remember when the soldiers came for Jesus in the Garden of Gethsemane? Peter wounded Malchus, the High Priest's servant – cut off his ear. What did Jesus do? He healed the soldier and left without resisting."

"What happened to Peter?" Johnny asked.

"He went on to become a great apostle and preacher."

"Even after he cut off the soldier's ear?"

"Yes, son."

"Mama, wasn't it Peter who also denied Jesus?"

"Yes, son. Three times."

"Wasn't Peter defending Jesus' honor when he cut off the soldier's ear?"

"I guess so."

"And Peter wasn't punished. You just said he went on to be a great preacher."

Diana paused.

"Johnny, you have an interesting way of looking at things, but I don't agree. Peter's punishment was the healing itself. It was Jesus' way of saying that's not how I do things. That's not right. I stand for something new; I stand for grace, something quite different than the old system of 'eye for an eye.'"

"Mama, I never could win any arguments with you,

but then neither could Pa, and he's a preacher."

"That's right, Johnny. Mama's never wrong, don't you forget that. Now go to sleep. You need to be alert tomorrow." They decided to make camp, if not for the night, for a few hours, so everyone could get some rest.

Soon they were all asleep, exhausted by the day's horrific events. Johnny slept a few hours in the grip of an intense nightmare. His father was hanging from Goliath, eyes bulging, saying, "Cursed is he who hangs from a tree. I will soon join your brother in the land of the dead."

"No!" Johnny bolted upright in the darkness.

Diana heard Johnny's shout and rushed over. "It's all right, son. It was only a nightmare."

"Come on, let's go," Johnny said. "They'll hang them unless we get there soon. We need to make up for lost time – we've been here at least two hours, maybe three. Bill, Charlie, get up, let's ride."

In minutes, they were riding hard for Huntsville.

§§

The Federals encountered the same storm, but Hawk made them ride through the rain. The hail was hard on the soldiers, but brutal for Miles and Jake. They rode hatless, with their hands behind their backs, and the hail beat down on their bodies. All they could do was close their eyes, and bend forward, keeping their heads down as much as possible.

45

"Brimstones and hailstones. Divine judgment coming upon you, Preacher Man," Hawk said.

Miles remained silent. The hail began to subside. Then it stopped.

"And all because of slavery. Your people brought this upon themselves. Abolitionists like me are just like the Hebrews of old. We are driving the heathen from our midst."

"Maybe you didn't hear me, Mister. I don't own slaves, and I have preached against it."

"So you say. But your son was a guerrilla who fought with the slavers. How do you explain that? Are you a hypocrite, preaching one thing in public, another in private? I saw a Negro on your property. Don't try to tell me he's not your slave."

"He's not. I freed him after my father died. He earns fair wages."

"I don't believe you. When we get to Huntsville, your case will be brought before the Vigilance Committee jury of twelve persons, and you can plead your case."

"A jury of my peers, I'm sure. And which law will apply?"

"God's law as found in Exodus Chapter 21, verse 16. Shall I recite it for you. 'Anyone who kidnaps another and either sells him or still has him when he is caught must be put to death.' I don't believe you freed that slave; I think he was being held against his will. And I

46

have to tell you, Preacher, I will be your jury foreman."

"I'm telling the truth, but you'll learn that one day."

"When will I learn that?" Hawk asked.

"Judgment Day, when you stand before God and answer for the wicked things you've done."

"My conscience is clear. Anyway, there'll be a great chasm between you and me. I'll be in Heaven, and you'll be in Hell. I'll be in the North, and you'll be in the South, so to speak."

"So, when do I get my day in Court?" Miles asked.

"When we get back to Huntsville. Your execution will serve as a lesson to the good people of that community. No one is above the law, not even a preacher."

"I see, that's why you haven't hanged us already. We're part of your sermon – an illustration."

"You're smarter than you look."

"I think I've had my last conversation with you," Miles said. "I'm not going to beg for my life if that's what you're after. You've already reached your verdict."

"Very well, Preacher Man. I still control how you hang, fast or slow. You'd do well to remember that."

§§

Weary, Miles fell asleep. He dreamed about Gene and wondered what Heaven would be like. He hoped Gene would be there to greet him. The horse moved forward through the night, without assistance from its rider.

Jake had overheard the conversation and realized his life would soon be over. Just a few weeks ago, Luke came home bragging how he'd shot a Federal soldier on a train from a pretty good distance. His eyes lit up when describing the shot as though he'd killed the biggest buck in Alabama. He was proud of the kill. Jake had discouraged Luke from joining the guerrillas. Jake supported the Confederate government but did not believe in irregular warfare.

Jake and Miles had fought the Mexican War under the rules of limited engagement taught by West Point. Their commanding officer was a West Point graduate who taught that guerrilla warfare was wrong. War was to be fought between regular armies, not by guerrilla fighters waging a private war outside of a chain of command.

After the killing, Jake had talked with Luke about those rules of war, and how bushwhacking was not honorable. Luke stormed out of the house and moved in with Gene in the apartment behind Bailey's General Store. Naomi had cried every night since, and Jake suffered in his own quiet way.

Miles and Jake went to Bailey's one night to visit their sons. Jake was disturbed by what he saw. To get into the boys' apartment, one had to enter through Bailey's back door, then climb some stairs up to a loft. Walking in, Jake saw rifles, revolvers, ammunition, and

48

even a small artillery piece stored in the back room. The boys wouldn't tell their fathers what Bailey was doing with the arsenal. Miles and Jake cornered Bailey the next afternoon. Jake recalled the tense conversation.

"What are you doing with all those guns, Bailey?" Miles asked.

"None of your business, Preacher. I like guns is all."

"It is my business if it involves my boy. Now out with it."

"No sir. I've sworn an oath of secrecy. You understand, Preacher, it would be wrong to break an oath."

Jake grabbed Bailey's arm.

"Bailey, if my son gets hurt, I'm going to kill you. You have my word on that."

"If you men are so concerned about their safety, why won't you help us? We need men who can use a gun."

Miles and Jake had declined the invitation. Now Jake felt guilty. If he had joined, he would have been there to watch over the boys, to keep them from doing something stupid. He might have kept them alive.

Unbeknownst to Jake, Miles felt the same way. Maybe he should have been there with Gene to serve as a better mentor than Bailey. Maybe the man in black was right. If he had been more involved in Gene's life, things might have turned out differently.

But Miles also questioned the morality of a nation

that would unleash the man in black upon a civilian population. What happened to the Bill of Rights? To freedom? What right did this man have to burn an unfortified town? Why was this war really being fought, and by whom?

To Miles the Union had always held the high ground because of the "peculiar institution" in the South. It was wrong for one man to own another. Oh, Miles had heard the arguments from his neighbors for years. Slavery was legal, and slaves were private property whose ownership was protected by the Constitution. The New Testament commanded slaves to obey their masters. In the Old Testament, the Israelites, once slaves themselves, took slaves of their own after the Exodus to build King David's palace.

Despite enormous peer pressure, Miles refused to budge. He preached against slavery. He freed his father's slave and paid him a fair wage. This arrangement offended the planters, but Miles was widely respected, and his views on slavery were not hidden.

How had America rewarded Miles for his patriotism and loyalty? With the burning of his church, his town, his home, his farm, his barns, and the hanging death of his son. Miles felt a bitterness swelling inside as he drifted in and out of sleep. He sat up in the saddle, fully awake. He needed to talk this out. Jake was a good listener.

"Jake, I think I made a big mistake."

"How's that?"

"I should have been there for Gene."

"Yeah, I feel the same way about Luke," Jake said.

"If we had only been there, maybe we could have kept them alive. Surely Gene would have listened to me," Miles said.

"I don't know, Miles. He was headstrong just like his Pa. And so was Luke."

"Jake, we've got to survive. We've got to save our other boys."

"Yeah, Miles, I don't see how, though. I overheard your conversation. I think we're going to swing."

"Not if we pray, Jake. When it's His will, there's always a way."

§§

Johnny wondered what else could go wrong. They had survived the thunderstorm and the hail. Now they fought hunger. They hadn't eaten since Sunday breakfast, and they were all dizzy and grouchy.

Johnny had been searching for game, as had Bill and Charlie, but it was not until dawn the next morning when Johnny spotted a doe three hundred fifty yards in the distance. It was a long shot. Johnny leaned against a nearby maple for extra balance, sighted the Sharps, and fired. The deer fell with a bullet through the heart. Everyone marveled at the shot.

"Is that what you intend to do with those guards, son?" Diana asked.

"I don't have a choice, Mama. It's either them or Pa. They won't negotiate. I saw you try that with Gene, and it didn't work."

"I just wish there were some other way."

"I know, Mama, but I'm the only one here who can do the job. It sure isn't Charlie – we all know how he shoots." Johnny laughed to defuse the tension.

"Hey, if I shot any better, you wouldn't be here," Charlie said.

Now everyone laughed. The boys dressed the deer while the women built a fire. They gorged themselves on the venison. The protein gave them new energy. Johnny whistled *Dixie*. Diana looked up. She had never heard that tune from Johnny before.

"On to Huntsville," Johnny said. "I figure we've got about an hour left. We'll camp outside town in the thick brush where they won't find us. I'll walk into town, wearing the Union blue, and find out where they're being held. I'll come back on foot and give you a report. Then we'll decide where to tie the horses. It will have to be somewhere close to where they're being held. They'll be coming after us, and we'll need to get out of there as soon as we can."

§§

Huntsville greeted Hawk and his men around dawn.

"Lieutenant Edwards, take these prisoners to the railway depot and hold them there with the other prisoners of war. You will assume command of the jail. Give them a good meal tonight. I believe the condemned should have a good last supper."

"Are they condemned, sir?" Edwards asked.

"Not yet, Lieutenant...but I have a strong premonition," Hawk said. He grinned. "I smell a conviction coming on. I will select a jury this afternoon to decide their fate."

"Where will you find this jury, sir?"

"Lieutenant, I'm the one who asks the questions around here, do you understand that?

"Yes sir."

"Very well. I also give the orders, and you have yours."

"Yes sir."

Lieutenant Edwards escorted Miles and Jake to the railway depot, which served as the temporary holding cell for prisoners of war. Many of the men would be sent to military prisons in the north for the war's remainder.

"Sir, I overheard your conversation with Colonel Hawk," Edwards said to Miles. "Are you really a preacher?"

"Yes, Lieutenant."

"Our men spoke with the Negro on your farm, and he confirmed your account. He is a free man, as you say. He said you freed him years ago."

"Did you tell this to Colonel Hawk?" Miles asked.

"Yes, sir."

"So, why am I still a prisoner"?

"He didn't believe the Negro was telling the truth. Beyond that, I don't think he likes you, and I think he wants to hang you because he couldn't catch your other son. You're the closest thing. If he kills you, it will kill your son, not physically, just emotionally."

"What do you think, Lieutenant?"

"Your dying is a bad thing. Your son is an amazing marksman. Our killing you will cause him to use those skills against us, and many a soldier will die an unnecessary death. I don't think you should die. But Hawk is a hard man. He believes in what he calls "the hard hand of war." And he believes he is that hand."

"Anything you can do for us, Lieutenant, I'd appreciate. I think I could persuade my son not to kill you and the other soldiers if I were still around. I'll tell you this about Johnny. He is the best rifle shot I've ever seen. He could shoot you from three hundred yards away and you'd never see it coming."

"I believe you. But I don't know who I'm more scared of, him or Hawk. I'll give it some thought."

"Thanks, son. Where you from anyway?"

"Ohio."

"Where's Hawk from?"

"Lawrence, Kansas."

"You call him colonel, so why doesn't he wear a uniform?" Jake asked.

"He's on special assignment. He wears black because that's what he preaches in back home. I've heard him say he's doing the Lord's work, and that's why he fights in those clothes."

"What was his other occupation?" Miles asked. "I know firsthand that preaching doesn't pay enough to raise a family."

"He was a schoolteacher. There's a famous story he tells of how he went to Missouri and set up a school under false pretenses. He opened the school and taught there for two weeks, just long enough to see who owned slaves. Then he left for Kansas and returned with a militia regiment. They burned many farms and homes. A lot of them were owned by the parents of his pupils."

"I imagine this behavior made him very popular in Missouri," Miles said.

"Yes, sir. Hawk brags about how much they hate him there, and how Quantrill desperately wants to kill him."

The lieutenant looked around to ensure no one was listening, then continued.

"You know that story reminds me of how he caught your sons. About a month ago one of our soldiers had been shot and killed while riding a train. The shot came from the south, and someone saw the smoke from the rifle, but we never could find the shooter. Because of this incident, Hawk was dispatched to our district, to thwart the guerrilla fighting."

"So how did he catch our boys?" Jake asked.

"He put some Confederate prisoners on the train wearing blue uniforms. We traded uniforms with some Rebels. Wearing the butternut, we fired at the train. After the gunfire, your boys came out of the woods, rifles in hand, shouting hooray."

"So, Hawk tricked them?" Miles asked.

"Yes sir. Your boys never saw it coming. They were shocked when Hawk ordered us to tie them up. We changed uniforms again and rode for Paint Rock. Your son told us about the baptism, how he was going to surprise his parents and be baptized with his brother that day. He begged Hawk to let him get baptized before he died."

"How did Hawk respond?" Miles asked.

"He told him no but made him lead us to the river. You know what happened next."

The lieutenant stared at the two fathers, his eyes misting.

"I have two sons of my own in Ohio. What do you want for supper? The colonel wanted you to have a nice meal."

"Steak and potatoes," Jake said.

Miles nodded in agreement.

§§

When he walked into Huntsville, Johnny was several hours behind Hawk and his men. The journey had been difficult. Johnny led his party off trail to avoid detection by Union pickets. They fought through dense undergrowth, thickets, and swampy conditions left by the previous night's rain. The boys hacked through the underbrush with knives to forge a path through the woods. Just outside of town, Johnny decided to walk. He didn't want to attract attention. He would drift around, listen, and observe.

Johnny was concerned. He was trying to grow a beard to look older than seventeen, but he was young and there was no hiding it. For some reason older men always picked on younger ones. How would he avoid trouble?

He also worried about his accent. It was hard to hide a Southern accent, especially one from Alabama. He was trying to pass himself off as a Yankee. What would he do if people spoke to him? He'd agonized over the quandary and discussed it with the group.

They decided it would be best for Johnny to feign illness, to use a deep, exaggerated cough to discourage conversation. If approached, Johnny would cough, point to his throat, and whisper, "I'm sick – better not get too close."

They climbed a small bluff overlooking Huntsville to discover a town crawling with Union soldiers. Johnny hugged his Mama. She led a prayer for Johnny's safety. She hugged him tight.

"I love you, son. I need you. Don't get yourself killed."

"I won't, Mama. I'll be back real soon to tell you what I've learned." He looked at the other boys. "Bill, Charlie, take care of Mama if something goes wrong and I don't make it back. Stay out of sight until I return. Don't follow me, whatever you do."

§§

Miles and Jake spent the afternoon with the other prisoners, many of whom were malnourished. They came from various backgrounds, but their stories were similar. Hawk had burned their homes, their farms, and killed or kidnapped their loved ones. Several had sworn oaths of vengeance against him.

"Does he have any conscience?" Jake asked.

"Conscience? Sometimes to animals, and often to slaves and women, oddly enough," a tall Georgian answered. He continued. "I saw him whip a soldier once for mistreating a horse. There's been times I've wished I was a horse. At least they get food and water every day."

Miles and Jake told the soldiers about their own experiences and how the Vigilance Committee would be deciding their fate.

"I hate to tell you this," the Georgian said, "but I've never seen them return a not guilty verdict. Every time they've met it's been death – death by hanging."

"He as much as told me that on the way here," Miles said.

"I just can't get my mind around that," Jake said. "Many of you were just like us. Why has he decided to kill us?"

"That's easy," the Georgian said. "Your son made him look weak, which is the one thing he won't tolerate. He's hanging you for what happened to his men at the river. To him it's eye for an eye, tooth for a tooth. He's got to avenge the lives of the soldiers who died. That's where you two come in."

"I just wish he'd get on with it," Jake said. "I don't like knowing, and I don't like waiting. I'd rather die when I didn't expect it."

The lieutenant walked in with a tray of food: steak and potatoes as promised. Miles watched the eyes of the other prisoners widen at the sight of the feast.

Miles suspected the public presentation of the supper to Miles and Jake was Hawk's way of punishing the other prisoners. Famished, Miles and Jake began to eat, but Miles stopped after a few bites. He gave the leftovers to the gaunt Georgian and several other captives who scarfed them down like wild dogs.

Watching from across the room, the lieutenant was moved by Miles' act of charity. He gestured for Miles and Jake to join him for a private conversation.

"The verdict was guilty," the lieutenant said. "You'll hang tomorrow at noon, barring some unforeseen escape of course. I've thought it over. I'd like to help you, but only if it doesn't implicate me. I'll be back in a few hours to hear your thoughts on the matter."

The lieutenant left the depot. Jake's face brightened with hope. He turned to Miles.

"Got any ideas?" Jake asked.

"I'll cogitate on it," Miles said.

§§

Johnny headed to the general store. He had been there several times through the years. Hunter's offered more of everything than Bailey's, and it was a real event to go there. Now it was nothing more than a reference point for Johnny as he began his mission.

Where should he go for information? Johnny thought of two places: the saloon and the barber shop. He would try the barber shop first because he remembered where that was. On their trips to Huntsville, he, Pa, and Gene always got their hair cut at Bo's. Bo didn't say much or tell many jokes, but he had a way of getting his customers to do it, and the atmosphere was always electric with laughter.

They were supposed to have come to Huntsville the first week of June to get their summer haircuts. It was strange to be there now, a month early, for different reasons.

If anybody would know what was going on, Bo would, but Johnny wondered whether the barber could be trusted. Would Bo betray him?

Not intentionally, Johnny thought, *but what if he calls me by name?*

Johnny had to assume Hawk knew his name by now. Any mention of his name in public would ruin everything.

What were Bo's political beliefs? His arrangements with Hawk? Was he still cutting hair during the Union Army's occupation? Bo never talked much, but his eyes had always spoken kindness to Johnny. The young man followed his instincts and prayed everything would be all right.

Bo had a bench outside the shop for waiting customers. It was empty. Johnny walked over and sat down. He kept his face hidden from the patrons inside.

Johnny looked into the shop. Colonel Hawk was sitting in the barber's chair. Bo stood behind the colonel with a pair of shears. Bo looked through the window straight at Johnny. His initial smile gave way to a concerned grimace.

Bo knows something all right, Johnny thought.

Johnny's hand was on the butt of a Colt revolver, the one taken from the soldier in the cave.

This is too easy. I'll kill him on the way out.

He slid to the end of the bench nearest the door. It

was open. He could hear almost everything.

"You don't talk much, do you, barber?" Hawk asked.

"No, sir."

"Did you hear about what happened in Paint Rock?"

"Yes, sir."

"What exactly did you hear?"

"Heard you hanged two bushwhackers. Some sniper shot some soldiers."

"That's not all of it," Hawk said. His self-satisfaction was evident. "We captured the sniper's father. We'll hang him tomorrow. What do you think about that, barber?"

"I don't think much, sir. I just cut hair. Hair's the same, North or South."

"I like you, barber, but I bet you know a lot more than you let on. I bet you feel a lot more than you show. But as long as you do a good job with my hair, you're all right with me."

"Yes, sir." Bo snipped a while. "Colonel, mind if I ask a question?"

"Out with it."

"Who'd you catch?"

"A preacher. Name of Miles Collins. And his brother-in-law. Do you know Miles Collins?"

"No, sir, don't reckon I do."

Johnny looked at Bo; they shared a faint smile. Bo motioned with his eyes for Johnny to leave, but Johnny remained with his hand on the gun.

"How does that look, Colonel?" Bo asked. He swiveled Hawk around in his chair to face the mirror.

"Perfect. Just perfect," Hawk said. He smoothed the side of his hair. "Just perfect."

Hawk paid for the haircut and started to walk out the door. Bo came to the door.

"Gonna walk out with you, sir. I need some fresh air," Bo said.

Bo stayed between Johnny and Hawk. Bo shook Hawk's hand and watched him walk down the street.

Johnny had cocked his gun and was ready for action, but Bo wheeled around.

"Think of your Pa, Johnny. Isn't that why you're here?"

Johnny lowered the hammer.

"I guess you kept me from making a mistake, Bo. I thank you for that. Do you know where my pa is?"

"With the other prisoners of war at the railway depot. It's not too far away, about 500 feet north of here at the west end of town."

"Thanks, Bo," Johnny said. He'd walked several paces when Bo called.

"Hey, Johnny?"

"Yeah?"

"Do you want one last haircut? People might think it strange us talking out here without you coming inside. I'm not known as a talker, you know."

"Good point, Bo, but I don't have any money."

"Don't need any, Johnny. It's on the house."

Johnny sat in the familiar chair and reminisced. He recalled how Gene and Pa would always go first. During their cuts, he would listen to the snip of the scissors and watch their hair fall in swirls to the floor. The floor was black and white tile like a chessboard. Johnny would always imagine kings, queens, bishops, and knights jockeying for position. Johnny loved chess. He had grown up playing it with his father. He delighted in the strategy and had become a formidable adversary. After beating his father, Johnny was the reigning family chess champion.

Sitting in the chair Johnny realized war was like chess. Every move required forethought and preparation. Moving on impulse could get you killed.

Johnny had almost killed Hawk. Without Bo's intervention, he would have. The likely result? The soldiers would have killed his father, uncle, and probably him, too. Checkmate.

He would have to treat war more like chess. He would have to plot each move carefully, anticipate his opponent's likely response, and never underestimate his enemy's intelligence and resourcefulness.

"Thanks, Bo," Johnny said.

"Good luck and God bless, Johnny. If you need anything, let me know."

§§

Johnny walked out, alive with confidence. He headed toward the depot. It was a brick building with a solitary window. Rugged iron bars guarded ingress or egress. Johnny saw two sentries posted outside the jail. He wondered whether there were others inside.

Miles was discussing escape plans with Jake. He looked out through the bars and glimpsed a young Union soldier coming his way. The lad had his cap pulled low, but there was something familiar about the way he moved. Miles watched as three older soldiers approached the young one.

Johnny saw them and began coughing. They were undeterred. The ringleader started talking – loud and boisterous. "What do we have here, boys? I bet he thinks he's something. I bet he thinks he's a real ladies man."

Number two said, "This boy's too smooth, too slick. I think we need to roughen him up a bit, what do you think?"

Without warning, the first soldier smashed Johnny with a right cross to the face; Johnny fell. The second man kicked him in the gut. The third spit on him.

"I haven't had this much fun in a long time," the leader said. He looked at Johnny. "Sonny, no squealing to any officers or the next time will be worse."

Johnny thought about shooting them, but he realized it would be wiser to take the beating and stay quiet. No need to attract more attention.

Miles watched the assault. When the bullies sauntered off, the young soldier dragged himself up to a sitting position, then got to his knees. After a while the boy stood and continued walking, though a tad wobbly. Miles recalled a time when a younger Johnny had been beaten up by some older kids, and how he had walked away with that same, determined step.

"That boy reminds me of Johnny," he said under his breath.

The soldier disappeared around the corner, and Miles returned to his planning.

Johnny's jaw was sore; his ribs ached. But his mind was still sharp. He had studied the jail and its surroundings; he knew where the outside guards were posted. He had spotted an ideal sniper's nest: the northwest corner of the roof of a dry goods store on the same side of the street as the depot, about a hundred yards southeast of the depot's front door. There was a climbable drainpipe leading up to the roof. Behind the store was a dense grove of oak trees.

Johnny figured he could steady his rifle against the building, shoot the guards, run to the depot, free his father and uncle, and cover them as they ran for the horses. The horses could be tied to some trees in the woods around seventy-five yards from the depot. Meanwhile Bill and Charlie could set diversionary fires, creating generalized panic in the Union ranks. The ensuing chaos would delay Hawk's pursuit and give Johnny and his family time to regroup and ride away – if all went well.

Johnny's mind returned to the game of chess. Those were their moves, but what about Hawk's? What would the colonel do? Guesswork wouldn't suffice. Johnny had to get it right.

The best way to anticipate an opponent's moves was to know him, his tendencies, habits, and character. Johnny had known Hawk for just a few days, but it was long enough to know he was cunning, ruthless, and never to be underestimated.

With this in mind, Johnny calculated the time, distance, and speed elements involved with the jailbreak. At most, it would take a few minutes for Bill and Charlie to set the fires and sound the alarm.

In the ensuing panic, the guards inside would rush out of the jail and leave their prisoners unattended. Johnny would have to shoot them when the commotion was loudest. The chaos would cover or at least mask the source and direction of the rifle fire.

By Johnny's estimation, he would have a little over five minutes to shoot the guards, free the prisoners, and make it to the woods to the horses. Any delays – game over.

A successful escape was a long shot. Surprise would

be critical. If they caught Hawk and his men asleep, in the middle of the night, amidst the fire and resulting chaos, it just might work. The fires might delay Hawk's pursuit and allow Johnny and his family to ride west to the safety of the Confederate lines. Any rescue effort would be risky, but Johnny had no choice. He owed it to his Pa and Uncle Jake.

§§

Avoiding soldiers, Johnny walked back to camp, where his prolonged absence had been causing concern.

"What's taking him so long?" asked Charlie.

"I haven't heard any shots, so I think he's all right," said Bill. "He's just being careful. You know Johnny."

Diana was kneeling, hands folded in prayer for her husband and sons.

"I'm fine," Johnny said, walking into camp. "Are you ready to light up the town?" When he got closer the firelight revealed the damage to his face.

Diana's hands flew to her mouth. "Johnny, what happened?"

"It's a long story, Mama. I'm all right – just aches a little."

Johnny sat by the fire and related the afternoon's events.

"They're still alive. They're being held in the railway depot. I walked past the depot and checked it out. Best I can tell, there are two guards posted outside the depot.

Probably more inside."

"Johnny, what happens if we escape? Won't they just hunt us down and kill us?" asked Bill.

"They'll sure try," Johnny said. "But I figure if we can put some miles between us and Hawk, we might just make it to the Confederate lines before they can catch up."

"What are the odds of that happening, Johnny?" Charlie asked.

"I'd say they're 50/50, assuming all goes well, I don't miss, and you and Bill set some great fires."

"You won't miss, Johnny, but I've never set any fires before," Charlie said. "I'm scared."

"I know," Johnny said. "Mama, would you say a prayer for us?"

Diana recited the Lord's Prayer. Then Johnny led them and their horses toward the woods near the depot. Johnny and Bill tied the horses to some trees. There was plenty of grass for the animals. Diana and Naomi stayed with the horses.

Bill and Charlie dug a fire pit in the muddy side of a knoll. They gathered kindling and larger pieces of wood before constructing a pyramid in the pit. Bill had a flint. He sparked it against his knife and blew gently against the kindling. Fledgling flames curled from the pyramid. Bill took his time and added larger sticks. The fire still wasn't very strong.

Bill opened his saddlebags and returned with a flask of his father's whiskey.

"Bill, what are you doing with that whiskey?" Naomi asked.

"Not now, Mama," Bill said. "I'm not going to drink it, anyway."

He poured a small stream of the contents onto the fire, and the flames grew stronger and began to crackle. Bill took out his knife and approached his mother.

"Mama, I need part of your dress. Aunt Diana, yours too."

"Why?" they asked.

"We're going to make some torches. When we ride through town, we'll hold the reins in our teeth and throw the torches with both hands."

"That's a great idea, Bill," Johnny said.

Bill cut the hems of the dresses into several foot-long strips. He wound them around a dozen tree branches gathered by Johnny and Charlie – all about three feet long and pretty straight.

"We'll douse these with the whiskey just before we ride in," he said.

Bill tied ropes around the bodies of the horses and fashioned loops on each side of the saddle horns. He test-fitted a torch into one of the loops and pulled the lead rope. It tightened and held the torch in place. When he loosened the rope, the torch dropped to the ground.

"Charlie," he said. "Grab a torch. Light it with a match, toss it. Be careful. We don't have many matches." Charlie nodded. He was unusually quiet.

"Time to go," Bill said. "Johnny, go over the plan one more time."

"Sure, listen up," Johnny said. "Bill, you'll be in the woods behind the hotel. Charlie, you'll be in the woods behind the depot. When you hear the first shot, ride like the devil was behind you and start throwing your torches. Yelling "fire" at the top of your lungs. Charlie, burn the depot. Bill, you've got the hotel. The soldiers won't leave the hotel until they put out the fire. That's the key to our head start. Questions?"

"I've got one," Bill said.

"What's that?"

"How am I going to ride past a heavily guarded officers' quarters, start a fire, and get away without getting shot?"

"Ride fast," Johnny said.

No one laughed.

"Okay," Johnny said. "We might all get killed but it's the chance we take. Use this. At least you can make a few people duck before they start blasting."

He handed Bill the Navy Colt.

"It's loaded," Johnny said.

"You ain't exactly inspiring," Bill said.

"There's also a rifle in the scabbard of your horse,"

Johnny said.

Johnny leaned in and whispered in Bill's ear. "You won't panic," Johnny said. "Charlie will. That's why you're at the hotel – it's more important. And it's riskier. You've got to delay the soldiers. You got salt, Bill. Everybody knows it."

"What are you two talking about?" Charlie asked.

"Final details about the officers' quarters," Bill said. He turned to Johnny. "Thanks, I needed that."

"Okay, Charlie, say a quick prayer for us," Johnny said.

"Johnny, why don't you say it, you've always been Mr. Bible, you know," Charlie said.

"Blood on my hands, Charlie. I've got blood on my hands."

Charlie prayed. "Lord, please save our fathers, mothers, and us from the Yankees. Amen."

"Is that it?" Bill asked.

"That's it," Charlie said.

Johnny smiled. "You ought to give some lessons to preachers. Let's go."

§§

As soon as Bill and Charlie were in position, Johnny shimmied up the drainpipe to the roof of the dry goods store. He picked up the Sharps he'd left in the corner, settled in, and drew a bead on the first guard.

He fired. The first guard fell. Every head within

earshot turned towards the depot. Within seconds Bill and Charlie thundered down the main street, torches blazing. They threw the torches near the depot and hotel, while Johnny fired again. The second guard who'd been fumbling to load his rifle dropped like a stone.

"Fire!" Charlie yelled at the top of his lungs.

"Fire!" Bill shouted just outside the hotel windows.

The boys were performing to perfection. A guard raced out of the depot and was dead by his second step outside. Bill and Charlie, having flung all six of their torches, were already out of town and headed for the woods.

Then – disaster.

The wind shifted – it blew crosswise. The depot sprouted orange and yellow flames.

Johnny was already on the street with the Sharp slung across his back. He sprinted to the depot, grabbed a pistol from the body of the first soldier killed, and ran inside. There was another guard, one who'd been asleep. He was putting on his pants. He reached for a pistol and fired, but the shot missed Johnny and splintered the doorframe. Johnny dropped him with a shot to the forehead.

Johnny found the jail key in the guard's pocket. Fighting flames and smoke, Johnny turned the key. A half dozen prisoners stampeded for the exit. They knocked Johnny onto the wall in their haste to escape the inferno.

"Pa! Uncle Jake! Where are you?"

Johnny felt a hand on his arm.

"Right here, son, let's get out of here," Miles said.

They were barely outside when the roof collapsed behind them.

"This way," Johnny said. They turned the corner. Lieutenant Edwards stood in their way. Johnny cocked the Colt and aimed. Miles pushed his gun arm down.

"No, Johnny! He's all right."

Scanning his surroundings, ensuring the absence of other soldiers, the lieutenant said, "Mr. Collins, I need a favor."

"What?"

"Hit me. Make it look like I put up a good fight."

Miles hesitated. "I hate to do it, son, but here goes," said Miles, whipping a right cross against his upper cheek and eye. Jake hit him on the other side of his face.

Then Miles, Johnny, and Jake sprinted for the woods, where Diana and Naomi were already mounted. Jake, Miles, and Johnny swung into their saddles.

"Where's Bill?" Johnny asked.

"I don't know," Charlie said.

"I'm going to look," Johnny said. "He may need help."

"I'm coming with you," Jake said.

"Me too," Miles said.

Jake turned to Charlie. "Take the women and ride west."

"No, I'm coming, too," Charlie said.

Jake looked at his son. "We don't have time for this. Do as you're told."

Charlie led the way. Naomi and Diana, accomplished riders, galloped in pursuit. Miles, Jake, and Johnny took off in search of Bill. They found him a mile back behind his fallen horse and facing a fusillade of withering fire.

Bill yelled over his shoulder. "Get down! These guys ain't happy about losing their comfy beds! Shot my horse out from under me!"

Jake called to his son. "We'll cover. Break this way. We've got to scoot before they mount up."

Bill sprinted towards his father's horse. Bullets sprayed dirt and splintered trees at him, but he was not hit. He vaulted onto the horse behind his father. Jake applied the spurs and they raced away. Johnny followed – then stopped. He whirled around.

Miles had taken Bill's position behind the dead horse. Johnny stared in disbelief as his father fired down at the officers' quarters. He was delivering a different sermon this time, one of fire and brimstone. Every time he fired a blue belly fell.

"That ought to buy us a little time," Miles said.

Johnny looked at the soldiers and saw a familiar face – Hawk. The colonel was in his long johns and holding a

Sharps. He raised the buffalo gun and fired. A bullet whizzed past Miles' ear.

"Time to go," Miles said. Miles jumped onto Midnight behind Johnny, and they galloped away.

"Pa, I didn't know you could shoot like that."

"Johnny, you've never seen me that angry."

They rode through the night. Johnny was thankful they were alive. It had been an interesting chess match. Surprised by the attack, Hawk had lost a few pawns, but his recovery had been swift and sure. The colonel's queen was still intact along with his other major pieces. As Johnny analyzed the board in his mind, he saw mostly black pieces – those belonging to the Yankees and their diabolical commander. The white pieces were in full retreat.

Johnny realized he hadn't spent enough time analyzing Hawk's options. Hawk had survived, pieces intact, and his counterstrike might prove devastating. The game could be over soon unless Hawk blundered, or Johnny could devise and execute a series of maneuvers ingenious enough to avoid capture.

"Pa, I'm scared," Johnny said. "I don't see any way out. They've got the numbers, the horses, and the firepower. They're going to capture and kill us."

"Johnny, I can do all things through Christ who strengthens me, Philippians 4:13. Remember that verse? It's your Mama's favorite."

"Yes, Pa."

"You see, Johnny, to man things often *seem* impossible, but with God all things *are* possible."

"Pa, would you say a prayer?"

"I already have."

"Would you say it so I can hear it?"

"Sure. Lord, please deliver us from the hands of our enemies and bless us with safety."

"Thanks, Pa."

§§

Miles and Johnny found Jake and Bill after a short while.

"Any sign of the others, Jake?" Miles asked.

Jake was an expert on horsemanship and tracking. As a scout in the Mexican War, he had learned how to track most anything, animal or human.

"Yeah, Miles, we're on their trail. We should catch up with them soon."

"Okay. How do we shake the ones behind us? You know they're coming."

"Yes, I do. We'll use the Tennessee River. We'll disguise our tracks. I know an old Injun trick might come in handy. As long as these horses can swim, we'll be fine. But it sure would be nice to find them some grain. They'll need their strength."

In an hour they caught up to Charlie and the women. They were asleep. Bill tapped Charlie on the shoulder.

Charlie jumped nearly out of his boots.

"Good thing we weren't soldiers," Bill said.

Diana and Naomi woke up and ran to their husbands. There were tears, kisses, and hugs.

"You know, in all the excitement, I never got to hear what happened at the depot," Bill said.

The boys discussed the night's adventures, each relating his own experience.

Miles said, "Okay, off to the river. No time to stop. If you get sleepy, let one of us know. We'll double up and let you lean on the rider. It'll help rest the horses. But we can't stop. I guarantee you he won't."

Everyone knew, without explanation, who "he" was. He had destroyed their homes, farms, and families. He rode a white horse but dressed in black. He preached the gospel but killed his enemies in the name of that gospel. His name was Hawk. While he fancied himself an avenging crusader, an anointed abolitionist, the rest of the world saw through the veneer. They saw him for what he really was. A bad man.

On and on they rode, without sleep. They sang to stay awake, mostly gospel songs with a few ballads thrown in. Johnny wondered what had happened after they left town. How long had it taken for Hawk to form up and bring pursuit? The fires had provided a head start, but was it good enough?

§§

Johnny would have been relieved to know that Hawk had his hands full with the fire. The blaze delayed his pursuit.

The hotel did not have a rear exit. The only fire escapes were through the windows. Most of the residents jumped to escape the flames. Hawk's room was on the second floor. He opened the window and climbed onto the roof. When a captain heard Hawk's calls for help, he pulled a hay wagon from across the street and placed it under Hawk's window. Hawk jumped, landing in the wagon. His ankle bent under him. It turned out to be a bad sprain that further delayed his departure.

The colonel was irate.

"Who set these fires, Captain?"

"We don't know, Colonel. Someone saw a rider throw torches toward the front of the hotel. One of our sharpshooters shot the rider's horse out from under him up there on that bluff, but the rider's still alive and shooting."

"Show me!"

The captain led Hawk toward the back of the hotel and pointed to a wooded slope. Rifle fire rained from the slope. The captain, standing only a few feet away from the colonel, dropped dead. Hawk pulled a Sharps rifle from a saddle scabbard and returned fire. The shots from the slope ceased, but the enemy escaped.

More bad news. Soldiers from the other end of town

reported an escape. All the prisoners were gone including the two scheduled for execution in the morning. Hawk ran to the depot. Two dead guards lay outside a heap of smoldering ruins.

Two soldiers came around the corner of the smoking disaster. They supported a semi-conscious lieutenant.

"Throw some water on his face," Hawk said. "Maybe he saw something."

A sergeant opened his canteen and splashed water in the lieutenant's face. Edwards, not as coldcocked as he acted, opened his eyes, then threw his left arm in front of his face in a defensive position. He lashed out with his right and yelled.

"Get back, Reb. I'll make you sorry you were born."

"Easy, son," Hawk said. "It's the good guys. What happened here?"

"Sir, I was coming to check on the prisoners when I saw a rider. He tossed a flaming torch onto the porch. Place caught fire like it was made of matchsticks. I ran over to put it out, but before I could get there gunshots took out the guards. I got to the door and the prisoners were swarming out like mad hornets. A couple of them jumped me – that's the last I remember."

"What did the rider look like?"

"I don't know exactly. I never got close enough to see his face. He might have been a Reb, but he wasn't wearing a uniform. Had on a butternut shirt, like a civilian."

"Age?"

"No idea, sir."

"Who unlocked the cells?"

"Didn't see. I don't know. I just saw them come out. Sergeant Johnson should have been inside the jail, he would know, if he made it out of there."

"You're the only one left to tell the tale, son," Hawk said. Edwards couldn't tell if the voice carried sympathy or suspicion.

Hawk's eyes narrowed. "Corporal Edwards, find me some horses. We're going after them."

The lieutenant glared at Hawk.

"That's right, Edwards. You've earned yourself one of the rarest of all military accomplishments – a battlefield demotion. These prisoners were your responsibility and they're gone. Not sure you didn't help them. Well, don't just sit there nursing your shiners, get up and get me some horses and some men who know how to ride them. Now!"

Lieutenant – now Corporal - Edwards rushed to the barracks housing the cavalry unit. They were awake, alarmed by the fire and the fracas outside.

"Up men. The colonel has ordered us to pursue the escaping prisoners."

"The ones related to that sniper at Paint Rock?" a private asked.

"Yes."

"Weren't there some more men that just got shot out there?" the private asked.

"Right again," Edwards said.

The men grumbled. Their leader, Sergeant Thomas, voiced a complaint.

"Lieutenant, our measly army pay ain't enough to get us too excited about that job. That sniper is dangerous. It ain't like we're fighting a regular battle. You don't even see it coming and then it gets you."

"I understand, but the colonel is upset to say the least."

"Yeah?" Thomas said, "well, the colonel ain't here, and I don't feel like going."

Hawk burst into the barracks, quirt in hand. He struck Thomas with a sideways lash across the buttocks.

"Get up, men, right now, we can't let them get away!" Hawk said.

Thomas and the other soldiers sprang to their feet and rushed out of the barracks to saddle up.

"Corporal, you can stay here. I don't trust you for this mission," Hawk said.

Just then a soldier presumed dead or deserted walked into the barracks, clad only in strange strips of cloth, girding only his loins. Hawk, too stunned to speak, stared.

"Sir, I saw who done the shooting," the soldier said.

"He's a boy in his late teens, I would say. He captured me at a cave back in Paint Rock and stole my horse and pistol. He tied me up. I finally got loose. I took a horse from Bailey and got here just in time to hear the shots. I saw the boy shoot the jailer, set the prisoners free, and leave with two other prisoners into the woods there."

"Good work, son. Which two?"

"The sniper's father. The one you tackled by the tree. I didn't recognize the other man, but it seemed like he was at the hanging, too."

"Well done, soldier. Find some clothes and get ready to ride."

"Yes, sir."

"By the way, soldier," he asked. "What's the boy wearing?"

"My uniform, sir. He took that, too."

§§

Enraged, Hawk addressed his troops:

"Men, I am going to lead this unit. We are facing a formidable adversary who has killed your fellow soldiers and humiliated your officers, including your colonel. Who is this formidable adversary? The teenage son of a preacher man! Who will ride with me to rid the Earth of this young Rebel?"

The men hurrahed, left their barracks, and mounted their horses.

Hawk counted seventeen soldiers in the barracks, not

including the erstwhile lieutenant – now a corporal. Incompetence could not be tolerated. The corporal had failed to provide adequate security for the jail. Plus, was there not something suspicious about his survival? Why had he been allowed to live when the other guards had been killed? And why hadn't Edwards told him that the sniper was wearing a federal uniform? Had Edwards assisted the escape?

Hawk's mind turned to the task at hand. How could he catch up and capture them? They knew the terrain better than he did. They presumably knew people in the countryside who would provide them with food and shelter. They also enjoyed a significant head start.

The odds favored a successful escape, and Hawk knew it, but his ego was colossal. He could not accept defeat, much less at the hands of an adversary he deemed inferior. How could he improve his odds?

He needed a scout, one who knew the land as well as the fugitives.

Who is qualified? he wondered. *Why, Indians, of course. They have been here much longer and have an uncanny ability to track humans or animals. With the right Indian scout, we can find them. And I will march the men double time until I do.*

"Men, what kind of Indians they got around here?" Hawk asked.

"I'm not sure," Thomas answered. "I think maybe

Cherokee."

"Do you know where we might find an Indian scout?" Hawk asked.

"Not sure, Colonel."

"It's time to pay a visit to my barber," Hawk said. "He'll know."

Hawk walked to the barber shop. Bo worked up front during the day and slept in a single-room apartment with nothing but a bed, a small stove, and a window in the back. The back door to the barber shop was Bo's front door when he wasn't cutting hair.

Hawk rapped at the door until a groggy Bo answered. He was wearing long johns.

"Barber, I need to speak with you."

"What's the matter? You don't like your cut?"

"Haircut is fine. I need your help."

"With what?"

"Let me in, and I'll explain."

Bo opened the door.

"Do you have any idea what went on tonight?" Hawk asked.

"I was asleep until you woke me up, sir."

"We've had some prisoners escape from the depot. They headed west out of town."

"How does that involve me?"

"It doesn't, or at least I hope it doesn't."

"So why are you here?"

"I need the name of an Indian scout to help me track them."

Bo knew resistance was futile. Hawk would kill him or throw him in jail if he didn't cooperate. But just because he had to furnish a name didn't mean he had to hand over the best. Joe Waters was better than anyone. Still, Bo couldn't suggest the worst either. Word would get around, and Hawk would discover he'd been duped. Aside from Waters, there was only one other skilled Cherokee scout who would work for the Yankees: Lee Moon.

"Out with it, barber."

"Lee Moon. It took me a minute to think of him."

"Take me to him, and fast. They've got a head start."

Bo threw on some clothes and saddled his horse.

"Don't know if he'll be home, Colonel," Bo said.

"Let's hope for your sake he is."

§§

Johnny remembered the look on Hawk's face, and it frightened him. He was glad Pa was pushing them so hard. They had not stopped riding since they left Huntsville. They were exhausted and hungry, but Miles kept them going.

"How much farther to the river?" Miles asked.

"An hour at most," Jake said.

Behind them they heard the sound of hooves beating the ground. Cavalry.

"They're tracking us, Miles," Jake said. "Looks like they have our trail."

Miles did not hesitate. "Breakneck speed, everybody! We've got to make it to the Confederate lines."

"Where are they, Pa?" Johnny asked.

Jake answered. "They're all up and down the Mississippi, from Memphis to Vicksburg. If we can make it to the Tennessee River, I think we can shake them."

They arrived at the river thirty minutes before sunset. Jake explained the plan.

"Okay, everybody, listen up. I learned this trick from an Injun years ago. If we do this right, we just might lose 'em. Johnny, that big black stallion of yours will go first, and I'm going to lead him. We'll tie the bridle of the next horse to that black horse's tail. We'll do the same thing with the other horses. The horses will swim the river together. I'll lead 'em. The rest of you will swim behind the horses."

"What's so tricky about that?" Johnny asked. "Just cross the river with the horses – sounds simple enough."

"Not finished yet," Jake said. "We're not going to cross. We're going to swim with those horses upriver. They won't be able to track us in the water, and they won't be able to see us in the darkness. We've got some clouds, and it's not a full moon. Any questions?"

"Jake, have you ever actually done this before?" Miles asked.

"Once."

"Did it work?"

"No."

"Why not?"

"They had a pretty good Injun scout – he figured it out. They caught us, and would have killed us, if it weren't for the Texas Rangers in our unit. They fought like the devil, and the hunted became the hunters soon enough."

Miles turned to Jake and whispered.

"Do you think they've got an Injun scout?"

"Yes, I do. They've had some help from somebody who knows this country as well as I do."

"Okay, everybody do exactly what Jake tells you," Miles said.

Miles and Jake lined up the horses and tied them together.

Miles looked at Jake.

"You look a little worried. Something wrong?"

"Well," Jake said. "The current isn't too strong, but the river's filled with logs and rocks – and snakes. We ain't got a raft. Only fools would swim this river after dark."

"Fools – or desperate people," Miles said. "That's us."

Miles and Diana would swim together. Naomi and Charlie would swim together. Johnny and Bill would wade through the shallow part of the river near the bank and hold the guns and ammo above the water. Fortunately, the water level was a bit down, making this an easier task. Uncle Jake had stored the ammunition in a saddlebag smeared with lard or tar to keep it dry. He would guide the horses and watch for obstacles – and other things.

"Here goes nothing," Jake said.

He stepped into the river. He guided the stallion – Midnight – behind him. The other horses followed. Miles and the others waded into the river just before sundown.

§§

Hawk was elated.

"We're getting closer," he said. "I can feel it."

Moon had put them on the right path, but their quarry kept up a fast pace. The pursuers hadn't quite caught up.

Moon counted seven different sets of tracks; two were smaller – women.

Moon knew they were headed to the river. He guessed they were aiming for the Confederate lines, probably Corinth or Memphis. Many members of Moon's tribe wore the gray coats and fought with the South against the nation that had forcibly removed them

89

from their homelands.

Though he'd been shunned by his people for helping the blue coats, Moon was pragmatic. He had seen the Union Army move his people. He knew their medicine was strong, and he valued his own skin more than sentiment.

Keeping his life didn't mean keeping his land, though. His former home now belonged to a Huntsville banker – a vile, bloated sort who "allowed" Moon to live on the land as long as he did as he was told. Moon had an unsavory reputation in Huntsville and was equally disrespected by what few Cherokee remained in North Alabama.

Three things he was pretty good at, though: horse trading, tobacco farming, and tracking. With these three skills, Moon survived. If Moon was anything, he was a survivor, and surviving the Civil War meant choosing the right side. Moon had chosen wisely. He did not like the blue coats, but he figured they were going to win.

He had been praying when Hawk came into his cave with Bo the barber.

"Are you Moon?" Hawk asked.

"That's me. Would you care for a smoke?"

"Don't have time. I need you to track some fugitives. I hear you're good."

"No one better. What will you pay?"

"Fifty Yankee dollars if you find them."

"I'll do it for fifty dollars and a horse."

Hawk laughed.

"Fifty dollars and one of their horses if we capture them."

"It's a deal," Moon said. "But I will need to borrow a horse, and you will do what I tell you."

"Deal," Hawk said. He offered his hand.

Moon acted like he did not see the proffered palm. He might work for the blue demons, but he would not act like they were his friends.

Hawk recovered. "Let's go," he said. "They're several hours ahead of us."

Moon had done his job. Even the white horse soldiers could see the tracks. They passed a few creeks; Moon stopped each time. They zigzagged through the brush.

"They have a smart man leading them," Moon said. "An Indian or someone who lived with us."

"Figures," Hawk said. "Can't trust any of them."

Moon heard the insult but focused on what he would do with the fifty dollars.

§§

"How far off are they, Jake?" Miles asked.

"At least an hour."

"I hope it's longer," Miles said.

"If we're lucky, it'll be dark when they get to the river," Jake said. "That way they'll have to make camp, 'cause they won't know where we might have crossed. I hope we've slipped them for good."

"Something tells me we haven't," Miles said.

"I figure they'll head northwest to Memphis. They'll think we're heading for Confederate lines and try to cut us off," Jake said.

"Where else would we go?" Miles asked.

"I don't know. I heard the Yankees won a battle at Shiloh last month. Our boys fought hard and were winning the field, but Sherman was reinforced just in time. Rebs had to retreat."

"Where's the Rebel army now?"

"Last I heard, Corinth, Mississippi. Only a matter of time before the Union Army takes the town. It's not very far from Shiloh, and they could be there any day now. Corinth is a rail hub, and if the Yankees take it, they can seize the railroad. They'll keep cotton, beef, and other supplies from reaching Lee in Virginia."

"So, what you're saying is we could be running right into the Union Army," Miles said.

"Could be," Jake said. "But we might also find our guys."

And what happens if we do? Miles thought. *Will we be conscripted into the Rebel army?*

Miles no longer wanted any part of army life. He had served the Stars and Stripes in the Mexican War. He'd seen enough war – and he wouldn't fight to save slavery.

Miles didn't want Johnny in a gray uniform, either. Johnny had already done enough killing for two lifetimes. He needed to put it behind him and start over. Further fighting would only harden him more. Already Miles had noticed a change in his demeanor. There was a certain roughness now. Johnny's eyes were a little darker, and he smiled less. He'd barely laughed since Huntsville, which was out of character for his carefree, good-natured son.

"I'm not sure it's a great idea to find the Rebel army," Miles said.

"Why not?" Jake asked.

"They might make us fight."

"So?"

"Our boys will end up getting killed before their time. I want to see them grow up and have families of their own."

Jake remained silent for a few minutes.

"I hear you, Miles, but I'm not sure what choice we've got. What's ahead is unknown, but behind us is a madman for sure."

"Yeah," Miles said. "If we can get to Arkansas, to my brother's place, maybe we could hole up there awhile and wait this war out. See who wins."

"Not a bad idea," Jake said. "But between us and Arkansas is something called the Mississippi River, and it's probably crawling with soldiers, blue and gray."

"I guess we'll cross that river when we get to it," Miles said.

§§

It was dark when Hawk and his men made it to the river.

The colonel glared at his scout. "Moon, where are they? Where'd they go?"

Moon said nothing but knelt on the ground next to the river's edge.

"Answer me, Moon."

"I cannot say. I must see the tracks in the morning sun. We should have made camp before we reached the river like I told you. Our horses might have covered their tracks."

Scowling, Hawk ordered his men to dismount but to be ready at dawn. In his career as a guerrilla fighter, he had burned towns all over Missouri, Georgia, South Carolina, Arkansas, and Alabama, and he had never tasted defeat. Why was this situation different?

The sniper. Hawk had tried to suppress his admiration for the shooter's courage and skill, but he had to acknowledge the brilliance of the rescue. It was planned by an expert – someone who had coordinated the actions of a small but effective team. They had slipped into Huntsville, achieved total and complete surprise over a much larger force, and rescued the prisoners from a guarded fortification without suffering any casualties.

Amazing.

He'd trade his best soldier for that sniper, the boy who had ridden to his father's rescue. He was quite a shot, and was ruthless enough, even as a young man, to do the dirty work.

If only I could turn him, Hawk thought. *Together, they could rid the countryside of these stinking Secesh.*

Maybe he would give the young sniper a choice: switch sides or die, he and all of his family, including his parson father. If he converted to the federal gospel, they would all be spared. It was unlikely. After all, the Union army had killed the sniper's brother, burned his home, and captured his father. It was only natural for him to want vengeance.

Hawk was familiar with the emotion. He had been born and raised in Ohio. Like others, he felt the western call. He moved to Missouri, then to Kansas. A minister, he was opposed to slavery, and was not the sort to keep his views to himself. He'd found the perfect homestead in an area of Kansas settled mainly by slave owners.

Abolitionist friends warned him not to settle there. They knew Hawk's outspoken nature might provoke a harsh response from locals. Refusing to kowtow to the heathen, Hawk built his house there anyway as an exercise of his Christian faith. With respect to the issue of slavery, Hawk would not and could not remain silent.

He preached the gospel of Jesus and abolitionism to every person he encountered.

One day he was riding his horse near a local plantation when he saw an overseer thrashing a slave with a black quirt. Hawk shot the overseer on the spot, then hid the body in the woods. He hoped the buzzards and coyotes would disfigure it beyond recognition. He spat on the corpse and kept the quirt. He vowed to use the whip on any slave owner or overseer he encountered in the future.

The body was discovered by a boy hunting in the woods, and people soon suspected Hawk of the murder.

One cold winter's night, pro-slavery zealots burned him out. Hawk stared at the ashes of his home. Rage sparked in his heart and called for – no, demanded – revenge, a reckoning that would surpass the original crime.

Hawk rebuilt his house on the same spot, a veritable fortress of thick, solid logs. There was only one small window near the ceiling. Bullets could not penetrate the structure. He dug a long tunnel underneath the house that extended for several hundred yards into the woods, an escape route should he need one. Folks in the area called it "Fort Hawk."

After building his log castle, Hawk organized a militia of abolitionists, many of them recent immigrants who had moved to Kansas. In response to the Kansas-

Nebraska Act, both slavers and abolitionists poured into the territory to sway the vote on slavery. The abolitionists grew in numbers, and the election declared Kansas a free state, but that decision was hotly contested by slave owners, who felt the state had been stolen.

Feeling compelled by a higher law, abolitionists grew restive and moved to expel slavers from their midst. John Brown and his sons attacked several slave owners in Osawatomie, Kansas, dragged them from their homes in the middle of the night, stabbed them to death, and dismembered their bodies.

Hawk shared a common bond with Brown. They were from the same part of Ohio, and both considered themselves Christians who were willing to put legs on their faith while others stood still. Hawk even entertained Brown and his sons at Fort Hawk.

It wasn't long before Hawk was leading his own band of radicals with the intention of evicting the slavers from Kansas, and even Missouri for that matter. His men became known as "jayhawkers" for the aggressive way they attacked their victims, much like a warlike bird of prey would assault a peaceable jay. Hawk never made any apologies for his behavior or his men's. When asked for an explanation, Hawk claimed he was a modern-day Moses sent to liberate the slaves from the heathen, and that the evil Secesh had to be swept away as by the Jews of old.

Despite the higher purpose implied by this explanation, Hawk had another strong motivation for his conduct: revenge, plain and simple. He took a profound satisfaction when he settled the score by burning the homes of his enemies.

The difference between him and the sniper, he reasoned, was that Hawk's vengeance was righteous. With these thoughts swirling through his mind, Hawk rested his head upon a stone like Jacob. But unlike the Hebrew patriarch, when dreams descended, Hawk wrestled not with angels...but with demons.

§§

Thirty minutes before daybreak, Moon was up making coffee and saying his morning prayers. Hawk joined him. They sat in silence and waited for the dawn. Moon's custom was to speak only when spoken to, so it shocked Hawk when the scout asked a question.

"Why do you want them so bad?"

"They're dirty Secesh. They took up arms against their nation, and they dishonor God by owning their fellow man."

"No. Collins is a preacher. He goes for the blue."

"He owns slaves, I know that. I saw one at his farm."

"Jim's a freeman, not a slave."

"If Collins were truly a Union man, he would have enlisted."

"No. He's too old, and he thinks he can do more for

his country by preaching peace to his neighbors."

Hawk sipped his coffee.

"Not so with his sons," he said. "I hanged the older one for shooting at our men; the younger one is a vicious killer."

"Johnny? Can't be."

"Why not?"

"He adores his father. He wants to be a preacher like him."

"Really?" Hawk asked. He poured more coffee. "Well, he seems to have lost his religion."

"So why do you want him so bad?" Moon asked again.

"He reminds me...of *me*, I guess, and I know how dangerous that is."

Moon finished his coffee. He walked to the river to find the crossing. Hawk's second in command roused the men and watched the scout. Moon was across the river. He inspected the opposite bank. He came back.

"They have disappeared," Moon said.

"What are you talking about?"

"Come here."

Hawk walked to the riverbank.

"Five horses entered the river here. There are no tracks on the other side."

"Well, it's obvious, Moon, they never crossed the river. They stayed in the water and crossed somewhere else."

"Yes, but which way did they go? That we do not know."

Hawk's face turned red. "Blast it! How did they do that? Who would have thought to do that?"

"Their leader knows Injun. He tied the horses together, tail to bridle. They swam together."

"Well, they either went up or down river," Hawk said. He called for his second. "Jones, take seven men and head downriver, two horses on each bank. Search for tracks. They were in the water last night, but that doesn't mean they're in it now."

Jones saluted and gathered his men. Hawk looked at the rest.

"We'll head upriver. Moon and I will walk near the river. You will be up on the banks on either side. I want to take these prisoners alive, if possible, but if they start shooting, kill them all, even the women."

§§

Few things tire a body – human or animal – more than swimming. They had been in the water for three hours, when Charlie spoke up.

"I can't take this anymore, Pa. I need a break."

"Me too," Naomi said.

Diana gurgled agreement.

Johnny and Bill also longed for some rest, though neither had said anything. They were especially tired from lugging the guns and ammo.

Jake headed for the shoreline. "Okay, we'll take a little nap, let the horses eat some grass, and gain a little strength."

Jake led the way out of the river. He found an expanse of grass near a stand of trees and tied Midnight to a large oak. They sat in the darkness.

"Wish we had something to eat," Jake said.

"I've got something," Johnny said.

He opened his saddlebag and took out some jerky.

"May be a might soggy, but it's been pretty cold in the river. Doubt it'll make us sick."

They tore into the jerky, without conversation, tired and ravenous from the strenuous exercise.

"We'll sleep for a while, then go back in," Jake said.

Everyone stretched out and tried to get comfortable. Most of them were asleep within minutes despite the hard ground. But Johnny was restless. He rolled over on his side; Jake and Miles stepped away from the group. They spoke in hushed tones, but Johnny could hear them.

"How many men you think they have?" Miles asked.

"Fifteen, maybe twenty, but they won't all come this way," Jake said. "Okay, call it."

The distinctive sound of a fingernail flipping a coin pinged through the night.

"Heads," Miles said.

"It's tails," Jake said. "I win."

Johnny sat up. "What's going on?"

Miles and Jake jumped at the sudden interruption. Jake looked at Miles.

"Might as well tell him now."

Johnny walked over to the two men.

"We can't outrun the Yanks," Miles said. "They'll catch us tomorrow."

"We gonna fight?" Johnny asked.

"Nope," Jake said. "Those are battle-hardened veterans. They'll destroy us in a pitched battle. We're planning an ambush."

Miles moved closer to his son. "When they see our tracks tomorrow, we figure Hawk will get all lathered up. They'll charge along the riverbank and hope they can catch us."

"And they will," Jake said.

Johnny opened his mouth, but realized he was about to yell. He waited, then spoke with as little passion as he could muster.

"They'll pick us off one at a time. We'll be sitting ducks out there."

"True," Miles said. "Only we won't all be out there. It'll be your uncle."

Jake puffed out his chest. "I won the toss," he said. "Those Yanks'll start firing the second they see a head in the water. Once they figure out it's only me, it'll be too late."

Johnny was confused. "Because?"

"We won't be there," Miles said. "As soon as we are all up, Jake's headed into the middle of the river with the horses. The rest of us will wade in about knee deep. We'll walk three or four hundred yards then cut back into the brush to set up an ambush."

"Yep," Jake said. "You, your dad, and Bill will open up. Probably won't be the whole troop. We are guessing half of them are checking downstream. So, there might be ten or so. You boys will cut that number in half before they know what's going on. It'll be a turkey shoot."

Johnny understood. "You're going to wait until you can hear them coming – maybe half a mile. You figure they won't keep checking for signs once they see Uncle Jake out in the river. They'll run right in front of us."

Jake and Miles answered at the same time. "Yep."

Miles threw an arm around his son. "Now, get a little sleep. We need you to be your best tomorrow."

"Yes, Pa."

Miles walked back to the others and stretched out.

Johnny looked at Jake. "You're a brave man, Uncle Jake," he said. "You won the coin toss. You could have sent Pa out there."

"Well now," Jake said. "That wouldn't have been right."

"Why's that?"

"Well... on 'count of a couple of things." He grinned. "First, I didn't really win. It was dark and your Pa was a little ways off. He called 'heads' – it was heads."

Johnny's mouth dropped open.

"You cheated?"

"Yes, I did."

"Why would you do that?"

Jake burst into a full smile. "Cause, next to you, boy, your Pa is the best rifle shot in this state. I'm a fair hand with a pistol and a shotgun, but that's not what we need here."

§§

Just after dawn, they heard the jangling of sidearms and the thump of hooves. Colonel Hawk was on the wing. They didn't have much time. They gasped when they entered the cold water. Five feet from the shoreline, everyone but Jake turned and began to wade upstream. Jake clicked his tongue and coaxed the string of horses out into the river. As soon as they started swimming, he turned them upstream as well.

After ten minutes of walking, Miles motioned his group to shore. They knew what to do. The women headed inland about half a mile. Johnny, Miles, and Bill found cover, checked their weapons, and waited. Miles stood and waved to Jake, who was still downstream, making slow but steady progress.

Miles turned to Johnny and Bill. "Okay, boys, listen up. We don't know how many soldiers they'll have. They may be mounted or on foot. My guess is both. When they see Jake, they'll probably shoot at him and charge. When they do, they'll run into our line of fire. When we see 'em coming, we'll count to three and fire. Before we count, we'll call our shots. Our initial fire should thin their ranks, but we probably won't get 'em all, so we'll have to keep firing until we do. Boys, one thing I've learned in wartime is you never know what will happen once bullets start flying. You got to be smart; keep your eyes open and watch each other's backs. Any questions?"

"No sir," Bill said.

"I'm ready," Johnny said.

§§

Hawk had chosen to walk with Moon. He knew intelligence won battles. He wanted firsthand information as quickly as he could get it.

Hawk carried a Sharps and drummed his fingers on the barrel. Moon carried a tomahawk and a six-shot, 1851 Colt Navy revolver. He'd taken it from a dead Rebel officer after the Battle of Fort Henry. They had been traveling for two and a half hours without knowing whether they were headed in the right direction.

Finally, Moon spotted an unnatural object attached to the limb of a lightning-stricken oak that had plunged into the water the previous spring. He waded over, plucked a piece of cloth caught on a branch, touched it, smelled it, and took it to Hawk. It was a piece of Diana's dress.

"They're up ahead," Moon said. He held up the cloth.

"Good work, Moon."

Hawk raised a silver British Army officer's whistle to his lips and released a piercing signal. His men turned their mounts down to the water's edge. "We're going the right way, boys. They're up ahead of us somewhere. Be on your guard. They could be anywhere."

Hawk's horsemen were positioned in a line running perpendicular to the river on opposite banks and even with Hawk and Moon. Keeping a line reduced the likelihood of death from friendly fire. Miles, Johnny, and Bill spotted the soldiers at the same time when they rounded a bend in the river.

Moon pointed to the ground.

"Tracks," he said. "They came out of the water here – reentered there. Not long ago."

Hawk's eyes widened. His nostrils flared – a Bengal tiger smelling blood. He mounted his horse and laid on the spurs.

"Forward!"

The small squad accelerated along the shoreline. Each man strained his eyes in the early morning haze in hopes of spotting their prey.

They were a little over a hundred yards away when one of the soldiers stood in his stirrups, raised his pistol, and fired at Jake. He missed. Miles, Johnny, and Bill were set up in a line on the top of a bank and covered by heavy brush. They were ready. They had sighted nine horse soldiers. From their vantage they had not yet seen Hawk or Moon who were on foot near the river.

"Okay, Johnny, Bill, on the count of three. Johnny, you shoot the soldier who just fired, then shoot the others on the opposite bank. Bill, you and I will shoot the ones on this side of the river. I'll take the two close to the river, and you take the ones on the bank. One...two...three!"

Three rifles sounded nearly in unison, and several soldiers dropped, including the one who made the first shot. Johnny shot the three on the opposite side of the bank. Miles killed two nearer the river. Bill shot two that were higher on the bank, but he missed the third and hit his horse instead. The soldier scrambled behind the dead horse and began firing on Bill's position.

Rifle in hand, Hawk ran into a dense grove of trees near the riverbank, beginning a barrage on Bill's position. Johnny saw the crossfire and wondered how long it would be before Bill was shot; without a doctor, getting wounded might mean getting killed.

Johnny made his way downriver, staying on the

bank, searching for one of the guns responsible for the crossfire. The gunshots grew louder. Johnny was on the ground now, crawling toward the sound of the guns, using trees and thickets to cover his advance. He heard gunfire and realized that Miles was shooting at the soldier behind the horse, trying to buy Bill some time. Just then Johnny heard a familiar voice. His heart raced. It was Hawk.

"Moon, we've got a pest up there on that bank. I want you to circle around and sneak up on him. Use this pistol if you need it."

"This tomahawk will do," said Moon.

§§

In a flash Moon was crawling up the bank. Johnny wanted to kill Hawk, but he had to go after Moon, to keep him from killing his Pa. Moon scrambled on all fours up the bank, tomahawk in hand, which he used to propel himself forward. Miles was giving Bill some cover, oblivious to the danger approaching from behind.

Moon had raised his tomahawk, about to strike a death blow, when Johnny drew his pistol and fired, the bullet tearing through Moon's brain. Blood and gray matter flew through the air, spraying Miles' back. Miles wheeled around, staring at the dead face of Lee Moon. It was twisted in a crazed grin.

Miles and Johnny stayed on the ground, to minimize the size of their targets, and crawled toward the edge of the trees lining the riverbank, to see what was happening. They refrained from shots, not wanting to expose their position to fire.

Best they could tell, Hawk had one soldier left, the one shooting at Bill. He was still behind the horse. Johnny felt he could circle around and take him out.

"Pa, cover me. I'm going to circle around and see if I can't get a clean shot."

"Okay," Miles said. "Be careful, Johnny.".

Miles kept firing at the soldier who, in turn, continued shooting at Bill. Montgomery took turns firing at Bill and Miles. On all fours Johnny worked his way downriver and up the bank until he was about halfway between Hawk and the other soldier. Looking to his right, Johnny glimpsed the horse. He was close. He kept moving. The soldier didn't see Johnny who stayed low to the ground, in a copse of trees. Johnny waited for his chance. Miles poured some serious lead into the dead horse's head. The horse's blood sprayed the soldier.

He snorted and put down his gun for a moment. Johnny made a run for it. He circled the soldier and yelled. The soldier whirled around and was going to fire. He never got the chance. A slug from the Sharps smashed through his chest.

Only one soldier was left now — Hawk. Miles looked at Johnny. There was something different about the boy's eyes.

"Time to go, son."

"No, it's time to finish this, Pa," Johnny said.

Miles shook his head. "Killing the colonel won't end anything, Johnny. Won't change a thing. The war will still be here – people on both sides will keep dying. Best we can do is try to find a place where we can live in peace."

"But we can get him, Pa. We can kill Hawk. He's got nobody left."

"And he is long gone by now," Miles said. "I've seen men like him my whole life – sadistic – cruel. He's tough when he's got someone backing his play. Now he's alone; he'll run."

Miles pointed his rifle into the air and fired. He waited ten seconds and fired again. He waited another ten seconds and fired a third shot. Three shots. The all clear.

Jake and Miles stepped to the shoreline. Johnny and Bill waited in the brush and covered them just in case.

"There they are," Jake said.

He pointed. Miles saw movement in the cover about a hundred feet away. Diana stepped out first followed by Naomi and Charlie...

...and Hawk.

The colonel had a Sharps leveled at the trio. Even from a distance, Miles and Jake could see his malevolent leer. Hawk's voice bounced over the water.

"Collins, I've got your women – and this boy. I'm going to shoot them while you watch unless you do what I tell you."

"What do you want, Colonel?"

The evil smile widened. "Why, the boy, of course, Parson – your murderous, sniper son."

"What are you going to do with him, Hawk?" Miles asked.

"Never took you for a stupid man, Parson," Hawk said. "What do you think? I'm going to put him on trial, then hang him for murder, multiple counts."

"Not going to happen."

Hawk pressed the muzzle of his Sharps against Diana's ear. "He comes out now, or she dies on the count of three. One...two..."

Johnny stepped onto the riverbank.

"I'm here!"

Miles opened his mouth to protest, but Johnny held up his palm. "I've got this, Pa. I can handle him."

Hawk had cut the distance between the groups in half, but his rifle was still menacing Diana.

"Down with the rifle, boy – and the pistol – and everything else you might use to kill a man. You're pretty good at that, you know."

"So are you," Johnny said.

Johnny handed his Sharps to Miles and his pistol to Jake.

"That's it, Colonel," he said.

"Over here, boy," Hawk said. "Hands in the air."

Johnny did as instructed. Hawk pulled a pair of handcuffs from his pocket and handed them to Diana. "Put them on, Mama," he said. "Nice and tight. If they're loose, I'll shoot him where he stands."

Diana fastened the cuffs. Charlie had to help her a little.

"Okay, Hawk," Johnny said. "I've surrendered. Now let them go."

Hawk's laugh carried no mirth. "Boy, why would I give up three perfectly good hostages? You fine people show me where the horses are. We'll be riding back to Huntsville."

"Hawk, you hurt one hair on their heads, and I'll kill you," Miles said.

"Preacher, I thought you were a man of peace – well, until you bushwhacked my men. But I'm willing to let bygones be bygones. You can come fetch these women and the little boy tomorrow. But Young Collins is going to stand trial – and hang."

There was a sudden movement in the brush. Jake, Miles, and Hawk all aimed their guns at the sound. A soldier on horseback emerged. He had a rifle pointed at Hawk. The colonel glared.

"Corporal Edwards, what are you doing here?"

"That's Captain Edwards to you, sir," the soldier

said. "General Buell saw fit to promote me. My first assignment was to find you and arrest you."

"Can you tell me one reason why I would ever come with you?"

An Indian slid out of the brush next to Hawk and held a cocked pistol against the colonel's temple.

Edwards gestured with his rifle.

"Is that answer enough? Colonel Hawk, meet Joe Waters, Cherokee scout. I assure you he will have no issue with pulling that trigger."

Hawk dropped his rifle. Charlie scrambled to pick it up. Diana fished a key from Hawk's pocket and released Johnny, who took charge of the rifle.

Hawk had not yet lost his swagger. "You said you are here to arrest me...ah...Captain. On what charge."

"Conduct unbecoming...cruelty to prisoners...illegally detaining civilians...and anything else General Buell can think up by the time we get back."

While Johnny kept an eye on Hawk, Waters retrieved the colonel's horse. Hawk, hands bound behind him, mounted (with some reluctantly accepted help from Charlie). Waters took the reins.

Hawk looked at Johnny. "I'm coming for you, boy. No matter where you go or what you do, I'm coming for you. And when I find you – whenever I find you – you will answer for your crimes. You will answer to me."

Johnny patted his Sharps. "I'll be waiting for you.

And I'll be ready. You might not like my answer."

Waters led Hawk away. Edwards put his arm over Johnny's shoulder.

"You okay, young man?"

"I am, Captain," Johnny said. "Thanks. I owe you my life."

"You've been given a second chance. Don't waste it on men like Hawk. He's not worth it." He swung onto his horse. "And if you decide to enlist, I hope you'll choose our side. We're not all like him, you know."

"Thanks for the invitation, Captain, but I don't want any part of this uncivil war."

Johnny watched Hawk ride off on the back of Waters' horse with his hands tied behind him. The horse disappeared into the distance. They spent the rest of the morning finding corpses of Hawk's men. They retrieved all the ammunition, weapons, and supplies they could – and stripped off the uniforms. They ate what little food they had been able to find and by mid-afternoon were moving westward – five men wearing ill-fitting Union uniforms and two women.

"Where are we going, Pa?" Johnny asked. The others were listening for Miles' answer.

"We're heading west to Arkansas. The prisoners in the depot told me enough to know we can't stay in Alabama. You're going to meet your namesake. John Collins. Uncle Johnny, to you. I'm hoping we might could seek refuge there and avoid this war. We'll camp here tonight and leave at daybreak."

They made camp before dark. Johnny stared at the last amber rays of golden sun, with its promise of tomorrow gilded against the western sky.

§§

At daylight they broke camp. Jake and Miles had plotted a southwesterly course that would take them to Tupelo, Mississippi, south of Corinth. From there they would cut across the state and hope to find a good place to cross the Mississippi into Arkansas. Fort Smith was still in Rebel hands. Once they made it to Fort Smith, it was a short ride to Uncle John's plantation.

When the war with Mexico ended, Jake, Miles, and his brother John had returned home. Jake stopped in Tupelo. Miles and John continued on to Paint Rock.

It wasn't long, however, before John grew restless. He left the farm for trails west. He got as far as Fort Smith, Arkansas, where he fell in love with a beautiful actress performing in a play at a local theater. Her father was a planter with many acres and slaves. His was the largest plantation in Arkansas, Cross Hollows.

A year or two after John left, Jake visited Miles in Paint Rock. He had planned to stay a week but once he met Miles' sister Naomi, he never left. They married and homesteaded next to Miles and Diana.

The last time Miles had seen John was John's

wedding, a society affair, which made Miles somewhat uncomfortable. But when they were alone, John was just like he used to be. Miles and John were close growing up; Miles had named his son after his brother. Despite the years of separation, Miles knew John would help.

§§

Captain Edwards ushered his prisoner into General Buell's headquarters. Buell glared at Hawk from behind his desk.

"Colonel Hawk, I have received numerous complaints from civilians about your conduct."

"General, I'm not ashamed of anything I've done," Hawk said. "Sometimes you must baptize with fire, you know."

Buell shook his head. "That's not what we learned or taught at West Point," he said. "There is a line between war and murder. You crossed it, and for that you are being court martialed."

Hawk struggled to maintain his composure. "Weren't you at Shiloh, General? I was. These Rebels aren't going to roll over. The only thing they'll listen to is brute force – the hard hand of war. That's what they need. A little discipline. The Good Book tells us what happens when you spare the rod. We have spoiled these Secesh too long. They've lived like royalty down here with slaves doing their bidding."

"Doesn't the Bible also tell fathers not to provoke

their children to wrath, Hawk?" Buell asked. "There used to be a lot of Unionists in this part of Alabama and in East Tennessee. What happened? You have provoked our own good citizens to wrath. Thanks to you, the Confederate Army has hundreds of new recruits."

"So where will I be transferred, General?"

"Transferred? Maybe you didn't hear me. Next week I'll be presiding over your court-martial. If you are lucky, I will recommend your complete dismissal from the Army. You are unfit to command. You might even go to prison."

Hawk turned purple. His words came out with spitting fury.

"Mark my words, Buell. Before this war is over, the Army will thank me for showing it how to fight this war. This is a war of conquest, and to conquer a people, you must bring them to their knees. They must beg for mercy."

"Hawk, you're insane." Buell looked at Edwards. "Captain, confine this man to his quarters until the court martial has been concluded."

Hawk shouted over his shoulder on his way out. "You will regret this, Buell. I have friends in high places."

He was still ranting when an aide closed the door to the general's office. Buell put his head in his hands. "Hawk, you'll be lucky if we don't hang you."

Edwards escorted Hawk to his quarters. Hawk's body trembled with rage.

§§

Johnny and the others rode through the Great Forest in Mississippi. Maples, pines, and chestnuts presided over lush grasses. What made this forest special, though, was the water. For thousands of years large streams and tributaries carved deep ravines and gorges into the terrain and hollowed out spacious caves. There were too many waterfalls to count. The soothing sound of falling water was constant.

"It's at least two days' ride through the forest," Jake said.

"Maybe we ought to slow it down a little," Miles said. "Nobody's after us. We all could use some rest."

"I agree," Jake said. "Let's find the biggest waterfall we can and have a little swim."

§§

The boys and Jake went in search of a suitable place to swim. Naomi sat and propped her back against a tree. She was asleep within minutes. Diana and Miles found a place a little ways off and sat. Diana put her head on her husband's shoulder and began to weep.

Diana and Miles sat on the ground.

"Gene...Gene's gone," Diana said.

The preacher, father of a dead son and the husband of a grieving mother, could not think of anything to say.

118

"We should have done something. Why didn't we do something?" Diana asked.

"What could we have done, Diana? Gene was headstrong."

"I don't know. I just can't forget the way he died--his face. And how he was buried--cremated, I should say."

"Yeah, I know, dear. I've had nightmares."

Diana sniffled and sat up straight.

"And now, Johnny. We've lost him, too," she said.

"No, darling. He's just looking for a swimming hole."

"I know that," she said. Now she was angry. "Aren't you paying attention to anything? He's changed. He won't pray. He's a killer. Have you looked at his eyes? They don't sparkle anymore. They are flat – dull. My boy has the dark eyes of a killer." Miles winced, then tried to recover. "It's the war, Diana. It's temporary. Wait and see. After it's over he'll come back. He's still a good boy, in his heart, and in his soul."

"You think so, Miles? How many has he killed? How many in just the last few days?"

Miles turned away.

"He'll be all right, Diana. He hasn't killed anybody who didn't deserve it, I'll tell you that."

"I wish you'd talk to him," said Diana.

"When the time is right, dear, I will. He's got to sort some things out on his own."

"I guess you're right." She sat without speaking for a moment. When she resumed, her voice had no emotion. "When's it going to end, Miles? When will this war be over? And how?"

"Who knows? The North's got more men and better weapons. The South's got better marksmen and a lot of pride. They're both Americans, and Americans aren't known for quitting anything, especially war. It will get uglier – two dogs snarling over the same piece of meat. They'll stay at it until the bitter end."

"And then what?"

"Then one dog will eat the other. One will grow fat, and the other will lick his wounds, and growl with bitterness. That's how I see it. And that's why I want to head west and get away. Pretty soon, there will be a shortage of soldiers – no one will want to volunteer. They'll start conscripting young men to fight, and we need to be clear of these parts when they do."

"So why are we going to Cross Hollows? Isn't that still in the South?"

"My brother is a man of influence there, and I think he can keep us out of harm's way. Let not your heart be troubled, Diana. The Lord is with us, and He will protect us," Miles said.

Diana thought about Gene again but didn't want to talk anymore. She stretched out on the ground and fell into a troubled sleep. Miles bowed his head and prayed for the souls of his sons.

§§

The next morning, the families left the forest, a little rested but hardly renewed. A mile outside the forest, they came upon a young Indian woman and her companion, a white man sporting a long beard. She was several years younger than he, and very pretty, with long, black locks falling past her hips. They were riding toward the forest on a beleaguered-looking mule. Since the Trail of Tears, stories were told of Cherokees who remained in the forest and used their superior knowledge of the landscape to avoid capture.

Jake greeted them in both English and Cherokee. The man studied the blue uniforms with undisguised contempt.

"You Yanks is mighty far from t'others," he said. "You come on any of Braxton Bragg's boys, you could be in fer a rough day."

Miles stepped forward.

"Mister, we've had our two sons hanged by an evil man calling himself a Union colonel. He burned our farms and our town back in Alabama. We took these uniforms off a few of his men after we sent them to the afterlife."

The bearded man narrowed his eyes.

"Well, you don't sound like any Yankee I ever heard." His face softened. "Name's Samuel Merck. This here's my wife, Alabama Crow. She's a Cherokee. Me, I'm just a mountain man. Want to stay out of this mess. They ain't found my hideout yet, and I'd just as soon keep it that way."

"We're on our way to Arkansas," Miles said. "Have you seen any troops?"

"The blue coats are marching south from Shiloh toward Corinth," Samuel said. "The Rebels are holed up in Corinth. Shiloh was a slaughterhouse. Thousands died there – both sides."

"How is it in Tupelo?" Jake asked.

"No fightin' if that's what you mean."

Miles touched the bill of his cap. "Thanks."

"So long," Jake said.

"By the way, mister," Sam said. "You might want to change your clothes. Them Rebs ain't happy. Best guess is they'll shoot first and ask questions later."

The couple disappeared into the woods.

Jake, Miles, and the others disrobed and put on their original clothes. Then everyone mounted up and rode towards Tupelo and the house of Mary Thompson, Jake's aged mother.

§§

Mary Thompson lived in a small frame house in downtown Tupelo not far from the church where she practically lived. After her husband died, unable to meet the farm's rigorous demands, she had sold it. Jake had asked her to move to Paint Rock and live with his family, but she didn't want to leave her home.

It was a bright Saturday afternoon when Mary received her unexpected visitors. She opened the door, and her sparkling blue eyes misted over.

"Jake, it's so good to see you, son. Diana, you too. Two of my babies come home."

Jake and Diana hugged their mother. They sat together in the front parlor and told her about the recent events, including the death of her grandsons at the hands of Hawk. She cried and embraced her children, comforting them with a mother's love while they comforted her.

"Oh, you have to stay with me. There's room."

"Thanks, Mama," Diana said, "but we're heading west to Arkansas to stay with Miles' brother. He's a wealthy planter. He knows a lot of people. He might be able to keep our boys out of this war."

Johnny shook his head. Mary looked at Johnny with sharp, probing eyes.

"Good luck with that, Diana." She pointed to Johnny. "This boy's a fighter. I can see that. I saw that same look in Jake's eyes years ago before the Mexican War."

Johnny felt a fierce pride surge within him. He smiled.

"Mama, where's the best place to cross the Mississippi?" Jake asked. "I can't remember where we crossed last time. Thought you might remember it from a letter or something."

Mary's memory was legendary.

"Friar's Point, that's where you crossed. You sent me a letter from Cross Hollows. I've still got it somewhere."

"Friar's Point. That's right. Thanks, Mama."

"I'm not sure about it now, though," she said. "Everyone says the Yankees are coming. They want the Mississippi. You better keep your eyes and ears open."

After dinner they stayed up late and reminisced about years gone by. Mary found bedding for her guests, and they were soon fast asleep.

They woke to a hearty breakfast. Afterward, Mary sent them on their journey with plenty of food including biscuits, smoked jerky, and bacon. When her children weren't watching, she slipped a leather pouch with twenty-five twenty-dollar gold pieces into Jake's saddlebags. Through cloudy eyes, Mary stood at her front porch and watched them go. She wondered whether she would ever see them again.

§§

Friar's Point was two days west of Tupelo. Refreshed and supplied, they rode for the Mississippi. Everywhere they went, they heard rumors of the Union occupation of Memphis and other port towns. Several ferryboats and horse boats were still operating out of Friar's Point, but they would likely be shut down by the Union Army after occupation.

Hearing the news, Jake and Miles forced everyone to ride through the night. They arrived a half day ahead of schedule and were relieved by the absence of Federal troops as they approached the riverbank.

Near the port Jake spied a grizzled captain of a horse boat, a raft of sturdy logs strong enough to carry horses and riders across the river.

"What's your fare?" Miles asked.

"Well, normally it's a hundred dollars, but for good Southern folks like you, I'll make it seventy-five."

The man was not from Mississippi. His accent was thick. Johnny didn't know what it was exactly, but assumed it was French.

"Seventy-five dollars?!" Jake was incensed. "You've got to be kidding me, you crook."

"Well, you see, the price gets higher the closer them blue coats gets to Friar's Point, if you know what I mean. When they get here, my business might disappear. I've got to lay up for winter, you know, like the squirrel in the old fable. It's just business. Don't take it personal. But I tell you true, them Yanks won't like your Southern accents very much – and you don't seem real interested in running into 'em."

"We don't have that kind of money, mister," Jake said. Bill tapped him on the arm and whispered in his ear.

"Yes, we do, Pa. Look in your saddle bags."

Jake found the gold. Jake blinked in surprise but could not speak.

"Grandma slipped that in your bag before we left," Bill said. "Told me to keep it a secret, that you'd be too proud to accept it."

Jake took two coins out of the saddle bag.

"Here's forty dollars, mister. That's a fair price," he said.

The ferryman was unmoved. "You must be hard of hearin'. I said the toll is seventy-five."

Johnny grew impatient. He didn't like the little man.

"Hey mister," Johnny said.

"What is it, boy?"

"I want to show you something."

"What's that?"

"You see that tree across the river?"

"Yeah, what about it?"

"I'm going to shoot that top branch."

"You can't do it."

"I'll bet you I can."

"How much?"

"Your fee."

"You're on, boy."

Johnny was surprised no one scolded him for wagering, which went against everything Pa preached. Johnny pulled the Sharps from its scabbard, aimed, then fired. The branch fell.

The ferryman was astonished, then angry, then apoplectic. He cursed in a stream of broken English and French. He began walking away. Johnny watched him. The ferryman reached for something in his pocket, screamed, and whirled.

Johnny flung himself to the ground. A knife whizzed over his head. Johnny reloaded and aimed his rifle.

"Mister, I've killed seventeen men by my count. You'd already be eighteen, but I don't want your blood to upset my Ma. Just the same, this rifle's going to stay trained on you until you get us to the other side. It was a fair bet. You lost. Now get us across that river before I change my mind and blow your head clean off."

Frenchie's complexion took on a pale yellow cast. They all boarded the horse boat. Frenchie's hands trembled. Diana noticed that Johnny's did not.

No one said a word as they crossed the Mississippi, but everyone understood. Johnny was different. He was more than hardened. He was dangerous. He was someone willing to use the force of arms to get what he wanted, regardless of the consequences.

They had all been upset by Frenchie's extortionate pricing, but they would have paid the fee and accepted it as the cost of doing business in wartime. They would not have been willing to kill the man over his fee. Nor would they have wagered such an outlandish sum on one rifle shot.

Diana probed Johnny's darkened expression for any remaining sign of humanity. She realized the family was crossing the Mighty Mississippi, but that her son had made a crossing of his own. He'd traveled from the river of life to what the Mexicans called the "Perdido," the lost river, the river of death.

When they disembarked, Johnny warned the ferryman of dire consequences should he tell anyone anything about them or where they crossed.

"You've seen me shoot," Johnny said. "Hitting you across this river won't be hard and you'll never know where I am. So, keep your mouth shut."

He reached into his pocket.

"By the way, here's your fee."

Johnny handed over two double eagles. The ferryman took the money with a puzzled expression.

"What about the bet?" Frenchie asked.

"We were always willing to pay a fair price," Johnny said. "But we won't be cheated."

"Thank you," Frenchie said. "Just who are you, boy?"

"Do you really want to know that?"

Frenchie paused for a second. "No, mister, I don't think I do. I never want to see any of you again."

Frenchie scurried to the horse boat, looking back at Johnny every few seconds, as if to reassure himself that

Johnny's rifle remained in the scabbard.

§§

So, Johnny and his band began their trek across Arkansas. They passed through the badlands of the Ozark Mountains where, unknown to them, marauders posing as Confederate soldiers had been terrorizing the countryside, pillaging, plundering, burning, raping, and murdering the innocent.

With wartime came spoils, and not just for victorious armies. War presented lucrative business opportunities for outlaws who knew the armies and authorities could not be everywhere at once. They also understood that citizens in remote, outlying areas had no way of knowing where the genuine armies were located or who the true soldiers were.

Unsuspecting citizens were as sheep before these wolves, men who made pretenses of authority, then unleashed chaos. Such a scene was about to play out to an unsuspecting family in a remote village in the Ozarks. Their lives would forever be altered.

Wilson was the gang's leader. He remembered all the settlers in the mountains from his former job delivering mail. He knew where the nicer places were, those with the fancier silver – the places with the most livestock – the homes with the prettiest girls and women. Wilson's taste in women went to the younger side. He liked them in their later teen years, and he knew every house where one resided.

Wilson received his wicked epiphany in April of 1862 after the Battle of Pea Ridge, won by Union forces. He knew civilians would be worried about Union occupation and would want protection. Many would be excited to see Confederate soldiers. Thinking these men were there to protect them, the civilians would invite them inside their homes. Once inside, the "soldiers" would do the unthinkable.

Wilson was the chief, and he got first pick of the women. They divided the money and valuables equally. There were ten men in the gang, and they had grown wealthy by way of their treachery.

Given the lack of telegraph lines, the only means of communication was word of mouth. Wilson never left any witnesses to attest to his atrocities. After his men murdered the victims, they threw their bodies into pyres and burned them beyond recognition. After he was whiskeyed up, Wilson always presided over a mock funeral where the drunken thugs had a riotous time.

Wilson had been saving the best for last. He remembered the farm for having the most beautiful teenage girl he had ever seen. Her hair was the color of coal. Her complexion was olive; she might have had some Cherokee blood. Her eyes were dark. Her parents called her Christine. Wilson called her Pocahontas.

Wilson ordered his men to call him John Smith that

day; he was about to capture his Indian princess. One of the men laughed at the remark. Wilson put a bullet just past the man's ear – the laughter stopped.

"This one's going to be my wife," Wilson said. No one challenged his authority.

"What about the others?" Benson asked. He was twenty-one.

"Do whatever you want," Wilson said. "I never much wanted in-laws."

§§

Since crossing the Mississippi, Johnny and his family had made good time through Arkansas. The countryside offered abundant game – deer, rabbit, and wild turkeys were everywhere it seemed. Every night Diana and Naomi grilled whatever the men brought back from hunting.

They had seen a few settlers, but no one spoke or approached. They stayed in their houses. Johnny thought their behavior odd, given the hospitable nature of most Southerners, but he was unaware of the chilling effect Wilson's crimes had imposed on the Ozarks. People didn't know who was responsible. Many blamed the murders on Federal soldiers or Indians. They were jumpy. Miles and Jake sensed their anxiety.

"What's wrong, Miles? Why is everyone so skittish?"

"I don't know, Jake. We'd better be careful. They act

like they're scared of something or somebody. There may be men like Hawk in these parts, too."

Johnny heard the conversation.

"That's right, Pa. And one thing I've learned. A man's uniform doesn't mean a thing in this war. That's how Hawk caught Gene. He fooled him by wearing a Confederate uniform."

Miles turned to Johnny.

"You're right, son. We'll have to use some discernment here. Test the spirits, so to say, to see whether someone's good or evil."

They crested a hill and looked down into a beautiful valley. Johnny spied a deer next to a grove of oaks at the valley's edge about three hundred yards away. Johnny aimed and was about to shoot when the deer bolted. Instead of running toward the cover of the trees, the deer ran the opposite direction through the valley.

"Did you see that?" Johnny asked.

"What, son?" Miles said.

"Something down there spooked that deer."

"We'd better be careful," Jake said.

They rode into the valley. They heard noises coming from the trees – human voices – voices in distress. Some were female.

"Pa, someone's in trouble. We've got to help!"

Johnny spurred his horse and ignored Miles' shouts.

Miles and Jake had no choice but to follow. By the

time they caught up, Johnny had dismounted and tied Midnight to a tree branch. He had his rifle in his hand.

"There's a house up there somewhere," Johnny said. He pointed. "See the chimney? It's just above the trees yonder."

"I see it," Miles said. "What's your plan?"

"I'm going to climb that big tree and see what's going on. What happens after that depends on what I see."

"Well, be careful, son," Miles said. "A lot of lives at stake. Think about your Mama, aunt, and cousins back there."

"I hear you, Pa."

Johnny climbed a tall tree with his rifle slung across his back. He surveyed the scene. He could see the house. Men dressed as Confederate soldiers were abusing its occupants. One of the men had seized a teenage girl and was trying to force himself on her. Another soldier wrestled with an older man, probably the girl's father, who was trying to prevent her violation. Another had captured an older woman. Some were plundering the house, while others were slaughtering hogs in a pen behind the barn.

Johnny studied their weapons. He saw knives and pistols. He felt sure they had rifles, too, but they were probably in scabbards on their horses. For the purpose of any fight between him and them, Johnny reckoned, they were unarmed. He was beyond the range of their pistols, and it would take them some time to double back to the horses, find their rifles, and return fire.

In just seconds Johnny decided whom to kill first. The worst of the bunch was the one trying to rape the girl. He brought the rifle up, aimed, and shot. Wilson's head exploded. His blood sprayed the shocked men behind him.

Next Johnny killed the man who was after her mother, and then the man fighting the father. The girl's father rushed to his daughter, grabbed Wilson's pistol, and shot the two soldiers returning from the hog pen. Johnny shot two other soldiers who were on their way to their horses.

By Johnny's calculation, he had killed five. The girl's father had killed two. He had originally counted ten. Where were the other three?

The answer came soon enough in the form of triangulated gunfire pouring into the tree near his position. Johnny had not seen the shooters when they slipped out of the house and into the woods.

They kept a steady fire on his location. The family had retreated to the safety of the house. The father knocked out the front window and began shooting. He distracted one of the men firing at Johnny.

Southern boys could shoot, something the Union forces had learned the hard way. Rebel sharpshooters had earned a reputation for lethal accuracy. One of Wilson's men had qualified as a sharpshooter before deserting the Confederate army.

Johnny was hiding behind the thickest branch of the tree. In his zest to reload, he was momentarily careless. He let his left arm dangle slightly away from the branch. Almost immediately he felt a deep, coursing pain from a bullet striking his left arm. He lost his balance and fell to the ground. He clutched his arm but refused to scream. Miles and Jake rushed over, ripped makeshift bandages from Johnny's shirttail, and bandaged the wound.

"They're up ahead, Pa. Three of them. And one can really shoot. Be careful."

Bill and Charlie ran over to Johnny.

"Charlie, whatever you do, don't shoot," Johnny said. He smiled just before he passed out.

"Is he dead, Bill? Is Johnny dead?"

"No, Charlie. Not yet, but we'll need to do something about that wound, or he will be."

Miles and Jake inched forward. They heard voices.

"Bob got him. That was some shot. I think there was just one, but man, that sucker could shoot. Let's go finish him."

"Be careful," Bob said. He was holding a Whitworth rifle. "There could be others. Keep your pistols drawn."

Miles studied the gang from behind a tree. He searched for the leader. He would have been the one who shot Johnny, and Miles knew he was the most dangerous.

Miles assumed it was Bob – the one with the Whitworth.

Bob dies first, Miles thought.

Miles had never seen a fancier rifle, but at close range nothing was better than the ten-gauge Miles was holding. Jake was more than accomplished with his Navy Colt revolver.

"At the count of three, Jake, shoot like your life depends on it."

"Just like Mexico," Jake said. "You got it, Captain."

"One...two...three!"

The shotgun roared. Bob fell over still clutching his pretty gun. Jake poured lead into the other two. As soon as they knew the men were dead, Miles and Jake raced back to Johnny and carried him toward the little house.

Miles waved a white handkerchief.

"Mister, we're friends. My boy's been shot. He was the one shooting from the tree. Help."

The door opened, and a man about Miles' age walked outside. The man was still shaking.

"Come inside, mister. Your boy saved our lives. I've never seen such shooting."

They took Johnny to a bedroom and laid him on a bed.

"We need a doctor," Miles said. "Do you know

where we might find one?"

"Doc Simpson in Fort Smith, but that's a day's ride from here."

The man's wife stepped forward. She'd been examining Johnny's wound. She was Cherokee but spoke passable English.

"My name is Ayoka," she said. "I can keep him alive until the doctor gets here. I learned healing from my people. Our medicine is strong. It will keep his wound from getting worse."

"I'll ride with you to get Doc Simpson," the man said. "He saved many a soldier's life at the Battle of Pea Ridge, and he is a friend of mine from the war."

"Which war?" Miles asked.

"The Mexican War," the man said.

"I don't believe we caught your name," Miles said.

"Nelson. Joseph Nelson."

Introductions were then made.

"We'd better get moving," Miles said.

§§

They rode through the night.

"I hope he's here," Nelson said.

They knocked on the door. A tall, white-haired man answered. Nelson related the events from the day before. Simpson didn't say anything. He walked to the back part of his house, spoke to his wife, and came back.

"Half a minute, gentlemen. I need my equipment."

He returned with a saddlebag. Nelson was already saddling the doctor's horse.

"Much obliged, Joseph," Simpson said. "Let's go. Speed is essential. It may mean the difference between life and death, between saving the arm and amputation."

Frightened, Miles rode like the wind; the others struggling to keep up. When they arrived at the Nelson farm, they found the teenage girl applying a poultice of medicinal herbs to Johnny's wound. She was staring at Johnny with soft, warm eyes.

"He's been sleeping since you left," she said.

Miles was struck by the innocent beauty of the girl.

"And what's your name?"

"Christine. Christine Nelson. What's his name?"

"Johnny. Johnny Collins. He's my son."

"He sure was brave to fight all those men for us," Christine said.

"Brave or foolhardy, I guess a little bit of both," Miles said.

Simpson arranged his instruments, then studied the wound.

"Whatever you've been doing, girl, keep it up. I thought that wound would have turned a little green by now. I don't think it's infected. That bullet's got to come out though, and it's going to hurt. I don't believe in cutting a patient without him knowing it. It's worse when he's asleep and comes out of it that way. I've got some smelling salts. That'll rouse our young hero."

Doc placed the smelling salts under Johnny's nose, then splashed some water on his face. Johnny woke with a start and reached for an imaginary gun.

"I've got 'em, Pa! Bill, Charlie, watch out, Hawk's on the way!"

Diana was sitting by the bed holding Johnny's uninjured arm. She saw Christine place a gentle hand on her son's chest.

"Son, it's all right," Diana said. "Doc is here to help. He's got to take out that bullet."

"No. No. No. I'll heal on my own. He's not going to cut me."

"Son," Doc said, "I won't lie to you. It's going to hurt. But I can save your arm if you'll let me. I hear you're quite a shot. If we don't get that bullet out right now, you'll go through life with one arm. You'll never be able to shoot that rifle again."

Doc knew just what to say. This was his second war. Removing bullets was as natural to him as breathing.

"Joseph, do you have any whiskey in the house?"

"Yes, Doc."

"Get me some."

"Johnny here's going to have his first taste of whiskey. That's the only good side of this, son. That whiskey will take some of the pain away."

"Mrs. Nelson?" asked Doc. "Can you bring me a

towel?"

"Sure, Doc."

Doc poured Johnny a whiskey.

"Pa, I thought you said that was firewater, the devil's brew."

"It is, son, but right now it's for medicinal purposes, and that's all right."

"Drink it slowly, Johnny," warned Jake, but it was too late. Whiskey sprayed from his mouth, as he coughed and gagged.

"That stuff tastes awful," Johnny said.

"Let's try that again," Doc said. "Now drink it real slow. And when you finish, we'll give you another. I've added a little laudanum. The soldiers love it."

Johnny started to feel a lot better, but kind of loopy at the same time.

"Am I drunk, Doc?" Johnny asked.

"I think you're getting there, son. Don't make it a habit, okay?"

"Right," Johnny said.

"Okay, now let's take that little bullet out, shall we?"

Simpson picked up a scalpel with his right hand.

"Even with the whiskey, this won't feel good, Johnny, and when it hurts, I want you to chew on that towel. Okay?"

"Okay, Doc."

Doc probed the wound with his finger first, then

began to cut through the dermis. The nerves shouted *"pain"* and Johnny ground his teeth into the towel. Tears poured from his eyes. Johnny's right arm broke free. He punched Simpson in the face.

"Hold him!"

Miles and Jake pinned Johnny to the bed.

After what seemed an eternity – especially to Johnny – Simpson held up the bullet for everyone to see.

"This boy will live, and with two arms, not one," he said with conviction.

Everyone was thrilled. A weak smile flashed across Johnny's face.

"I think I need another whiskey, Doc," Johnny said.

His eyes snapped shut.

Diana was frantic.

"Is he dead?"

"No," Simpson said. "Just exhausted. Let him sleep. And let this girl here keep doing what she's been doing with those plants she's got. He'll need to heal up here for a few months. He doesn't need to rush it."

Christine flashed a big smile. She looked up to see Diana grinning at her and blushed. She excused herself from the room.

"He's welcome to stay here as long as he likes," Nelson said. "All of you."

Although he was ready to see his brother, Miles decided to follow Simpson's orders. The Cherokee medicine seemed to be healing the wound, and he didn't want to jeopardize Johnny's recovery. Anyway, he was close enough to Cross Hollows to visit his brother sometime soon.

"Doc, do you happen to know John Collins? Owns a plantation called Cross Hollows?"

"Why, yes sir, I knew John," Simpson said. "He was a great man."

Immediately Miles caught the use of the past tense.

"What happened to him, Doc?"

"He's with many other brave soldiers buried near the Pea Ridge battlefield. He was one of the finest officers in Arkansas. He led his men into that battle with dignity, honor, and courage. Why do you ask?"

"He was my brother."

"I'm sorry."

"How did he die?" Miles asked.

"I think it was a regiment out of Kansas that killed him. They say the leader is a real bad man. He's been known to burn towns to the ground. Wipes 'em off the face of the Earth. After Pea Ridge I heard he took some soldiers and headed east."

"Do you know his name, Doc?"

"Yeah, it's easy to remember...Hawk, like the bird."

Miles grimaced.

"How is John's family?"

"His wife Victoria is running the plantation, but she's

having a hard time. There aren't many able-bodied men left. She sure could use some help," Doc said. He eyed Miles and Jake.

"Doc, thanks for everything you've done for my boy. What's your fee?"

"Ten dollars."

"That's fair," Miles said. "More than fair really."

Miles paid the doctor.

"Doc, would you mind taking me to the battlefield sometime? I'd like to see where my brother is buried."

"I'd be honored, sir. Your brother was a friend. Now that I know who you are, I sure can see the resemblance. Sure can."

Doc swung his roan toward Ft. Smith, and rode away.

"That's a fine fella there," Miles said.

§§

The Collins and Thompson families stayed the summer. The Nelsons treated them like kin. They shared their home, their food, and their lives. Miles, Diana, and all the rest pitched in with all the chores. Mr. Nelson became fast friends with Miles and Jake. They regaled each other with war stories about the Mexican Campaign.

For the most part, Johnny remained in his bedroom. He grew a little stronger every day. Christine visited and applied the poultice every afternoon for several weeks.

Diana always watched from the next room – just to be proper.

She knew Christine was in love with her son and she suspected the feeling was mutual. Johnny never said much with Christine in the room. Christine talked enough for both of them. She peppered him with questions about guns and growing up in Paint Rock. Johnny responded in monosyllabic fashion or with short, pithy remarks that never really meant much.

One day, Diana walked into Johnny's room.

"Johnny, can I talk to you?"

"Yes, Mama."

"I notice Christine has been tending to your wound."

"Yes, Mama."

"I think she's been doing a good job, don't you?"

"Yes, Mama."

"I think she cares for you, son."

Johnny's cheeks colored. "Mama...I don't want to talk about that."

"You know, Johnny. There's nothing wrong with that. You're nearly eighteen. Your Pa wasn't much older when he married me, and I was about Christine's age."

"Mama, can we talk about something else?"

"Why don't you say anything when she's in here?"

"I don't know. It's not like talking to Bill or Charlie. We didn't have any girls my age back in Paint Rock. Just Lucy Ann, and she's nothing like Christine. Christine is

144

so pretty. I get nervous. My hands get shaky when she's in here. They never shake when I fire a rifle but if she's anywhere near me, I feel clumsy as an ox. Dropped my fork and my glass the other day. She just picked them up, smiled real big, and went back to the kitchen."

"I think she loves you, Johnny. When you get better, I think you ought to take her fishing. I hear she's pretty good at that."

"Really? I didn't think she'd like boy things like that."

"Boy things? Johnny, your Pa and I used to go fishing all the time. I always caught more fish, and they were always bigger."

"Well, I just don't see Christine catching more fish than me."

Christine stood down the hallway concealed from view. A smile spread across her face.

"Johnny, I'll check in on you later," Diana said. "It's my night to cook dinner."

Christine rushed back to the kitchen and acted like she had been there the whole time. But Diana could tell nothing had been done since she left. She smiled in the ways of a knowing mother and began prepping for supper.

§§

Johnny made steady progress until one day he felt strong enough to use the arm. When Diana wasn't around, he told Charlie to bring him his rifle. Johnny held the Sharps, sighted an imaginary target, and put it down again. Pain throbbed through his arm and shoulder – the muscles had atrophied from disuse.

Charlie returned the gun before anyone knew it was missing. The boys repeated the routine every day. After about two weeks, when Johnny lowered the rifle, his arm did not ache.

Johnny had always been active, especially in the summer. He loved being outdoors – working, fishing, and hunting. Miles had insisted that Johnny follow the doctor's orders and rest the arm. For the most part, Johnny complied.

Finally – enough was enough. Johnny resolved to sneak out of his room and shoot at something. When Charlie brought the rifle, he was surprised to see his cousin fully dressed.

"Let's go, Charlie," Johnny said. "We're heading out that window and going hunting."

"Johnny, you know you're not supposed to do that."

"I don't care. I'm doing it today. I'm pronouncing myself healed."

"It's your fault if we get caught," Charlie said.

Johnny grinned for the first time in a long while.

"So what? We're too old for a whuppin'."

Johnny and Charlie slipped out the window and walked into the woods.

"Take me for a tour, Charlie," Johnny said.

"You're going to love it, Johnny. I've seen some huge deer, and there's a great trout stream only a half-mile away."

Just over a hill Johnny spotted a large whitetail buck about 150 yards away. He crouched down, braced the gun, and fired. The deer's ears arched, he paused for a second, then scampered off, unharmed. Johnny could not believe his eyes, and neither could Charlie. He had never seen Johnny miss – anything.

"What happened?" Charlie asked.

"Buck fever and rust," Johnny said. "I've been in that bed too long."

Johnny switched to trees for some target practice. After a dozen or so shots, he had returned to form.

"Where's that trout stream, Charlie?"

"Just the other side of that hill yonder."

"Let's go."

§§

The boys were surprised to find Christine in the stream with a fishing pole in her hands. A string of beautiful trout hung from a nearby tree. There were a few bass as well. Johnny recalled the conversation with his mother.

"How are the great hunters?"

Her eyes never left Johnny. Charlie wasn't sure if she knew he was there.

"I heard a shot, then this little deer pranced over the hill. Now I see why."

Johnny bowed up a little. "He was a ten-pointer if I've ever seen one," he said. "Wasn't a baby at all. Huge."

"Well then," Christine said (she made no attempt to stop giggling), "how'd you miss him?"

Johnny looked down. "I'm rusty."

Christine got very serious. "Johnny Collins, what are you doing out of bed?"

"Bored."

"Do you want to fish with me awhile?"

"Yes. I mean no." Johnny didn't really know what to say. His temples were pounding – his heart was racing – his throat was suddenly dry as hot sand. "I mean, I like to fish, but they're probably going to be looking for me pretty soon."

"Oh, I see. You're scared a girl can catch more fish than you? Huh? Is that it?"

Johnny's bravado returned. "You think I'm scared? Of you? You're on. Charlie, pay attention. I'm going to have to teach this little girl how to fish."

There was an extra pole shoved into the sandy bank. Johnny grabbed it and baited the hook with one of the earthworms Christine had brought. He dropped his line in the water and waited... and waited...and waited some more.

"Fish aren't biting," he said.

Christine began to say something, but he put a finger to his lips. There was silence for about ten minutes until Christine couldn't take it anymore. She burst out laughing.

"Let me show you how to fish," she said.

She put her own rod aside, snatched the one from Johnny's hand, and baited the hook. Then she tied something that looked like a small insect to the worm and tossed the line into the stream. She tugged on the line a little to keep it shallow. Twenty seconds later, a large trout attacked the line and plunged to the bottom of the creek.

Excited, Christine began working the line. Her smallish fingers were a picture of dexterity and grace. Johnny watched, dumbfounded. Christine began to struggle.

"This is a monster," she said. "Help me!" And though Christine had caught bigger fish unaided, she said "Help me, Johnny! This fish is huge!"

Johnny splashed over and stood behind her. He placed his right arm around her right shoulder and his right hand in front of hers on the pole. He repeated the move with his left arm. They pulled.

Johnny and Christine backed up to the bank, pulling in unison. Their legs tangled. They lost their balance and fell. They slid off the muddy bank into the water. The rod, presumably still attached to the whopper, bobbed its way downstream.

Charlie was on his knees laughing. Johnny would never live this one down. Charlie's laugh was notorious – loud – from the belly. Johnny had been known to cuff Charlie's head to make him stop. Not this time.

Charlie wiped tears from his eyes and looked up. When Charlie looked up, he saw Christine had somehow ended up in Johnny's arms. Neither made any effort to move. Oblivious to the laughter, the escaping fish, the cold water, and the rest of the universe, they stared into each other's eyes.

Johnny Collins and Christine Nelson had fallen in love, and the world was right.

"Hey, Johnny," Charlie said. "We'd better get back. Your Pa's gonna be awful sore."

Johnny snapped out of his trance. He looked at the position of the sun.

"You're right, Charlie. We'd best be getting back. Christine, are you coming?"

§§

Johnny helped Christine out of the stream. They walked back to the house in saturated clothes. To their surprise, no one seemed upset by their tardiness or alarmed by their wet clothes. Diana and Miles simply grinned and exchanged a knowing glance.

"Johnny, who caught all those fish?" Diana asked.

"Christine." Johnny mumbled.

"I didn't hear you, son."

"Christine caught the fish."

Miles began laughing.

"Your Mama did the same thing to me years ago," Miles said.

Christine blushed and walked into the house. She looked at herself in the mirror. She could not stop smiling. Her mother joined her at the mirror looking almost as happy.

"You love him, don't you?"

"Yes, Mama, I do. He makes me feel..."

"Warm and tingly inside?"

"Yes Mama, how did you know?"

"That's the way I felt about your Daddy years ago – and I still do."

"What do I do, Mama, what do I do?"

"Wait for him. He feels the same way. I can see it in his eyes."

"Oh, Mama, how can I wait? I'm so excited."

"Just relax. What's meant to be will happen. It might not be next week, and it might not be next year, even, but true love is worth waiting for. Don't ever settle for anything less or anyone else. Be patient and wait for him."

Mr. Nelson walked into the room. He had been eavesdropping from the hallway.

"Christine, I hear you taught Johnny how to fish today, is that right?"

"Yes, Daddy."

"Do you love that boy?"

"Yes, sir."

"I'm kind of partial to him myself," Mr. Nelson said. "I just hope he doesn't take you away from us. I don't know what I would do without you."

Christine was a daddy's girl. The Nelsons' other child, a boy named Sam, had died of the influenza when he was seven. Sam was two years older than Christine. After Sam died, Ayoka suffered several miscarriages. She had finally given birth to Christine, but nearly died in the process. After the traumatic delivery, Doc Simpson warned them not to have any more children.

Nelson was devastated. He had lost his son; he would never have another. There would be no one to carry the Nelson name on to the next generation.

One look at Christine had been enough, though, to change his point of view. With her dark brown eyes and olive complexion, Christine had captured his heart. He had resolved to love her with all he had. He would teach her everything he would have taught a son. She spent most days with her daddy working on the farm, fishing in the stream, or hunting in the woods. She was his pal.

He was a little hurt she had chosen to confide in her mother about Johnny, and not him. He supposed that was only natural given the nature of the conversation. Still, as nice as Johnny was, it was hard to think of anyone being worthy of Christine.

Now the inevitable had come. He had seen it when they walked into camp and watched it develop with each passing day. He had thought about ending it and had almost broached the subject with his wife.

In the end, though, he let love take its course. He didn't want her to grow up a spinster and never experience the joy of true love. He had studied Johnny carefully, looking for any character flaw. He couldn't find any.

Johnny came from a fine family. Johnny's father was a Mexican War veteran, a farmer, and a preacher, and his mother was a virtuous woman who worked hard. She had been relentless about helping Ayoka and Christine with whatever needed to be done.

Johnny had displayed great courage and bravery; he'd sacrificed himself for the survival of people he didn't know. Joseph admired Johnny's gritty determination to recover from the wound. This quality was what the old timers called "pluck," an essential ingredient to survival on the frontier.

While Joseph wasn't excited by the prospect of losing a daughter, he knew Johnny would make a fine son, someone who would protect his daughter long after her Daddy was gone. If asked, Nelson decided he would give his blessing.

§§

In many ways Johnny's relationship with Christine resembled his recovery. Over the summer it grew stronger and stronger; it felt better and better. They spent many hours fishing and hunting. Christine tutored Johnny on the art of fishing while Johnny gave her some shooting lessons. They loved being together, and it showed.

One day they went hiking. Ignoring Johnny's warning, Christine sprinted ahead up a steep incline. She began clawing her way up the side of a mountain. A rock under her right foot gave way.

She shrieked and fell.

Johnny caught her just before she hit the ground. Looking up, she saw terror in Johnny's eyes.

"Christine, watch what you're doing! You could have been killed!"

"I knew you'd catch me."

"But what if I hadn't been there?"

"If you weren't here, Johnny Collins, I wouldn't want to live," she said. She began to cry.

Johnny stroked her hair. "I'm not going anywhere. I love you...I mean...uh...I like you...I mean...you know what I mean."

He hadn't meant to say it. But his heart's desire could not be silenced. The words just slipped out – from heart to mind to mouth and out.

"You can't take it back, Johnny Collins," she said. "I heard it."

"Oh yeah? Well, what are you going to do about it?"

Neither had ever kissed anyone. Neither had seen their parents kiss. Affection was a private matter. But their lips knew what to do.

They would never forget the magic moment of their first kiss. Johnny sank to the earth with Christine in his arms.

"I guess I should have asked your Mama for permission to court," Johnny said.

"You still can. She'll be so excited."

"What about this? Will she be upset with me?" Johnny asked. The bravado of the adolescent sniper had melted in the fierce, blazing uncertainty of love.

"She'll be happy for us," Christine said.

"Just the same, I'll get her permission before I kiss you again."

"You want to bet on that?" Christine said.

She pushed Johnny on his back and kissed him, again and again...

Johnny came up gasping for air. "Why did you do that?"

"It's easier to get forgiveness after than permission before. I couldn't help it," Christine said.

Just then they realized the sun was nearly over the

horizon. They had to make it back to camp. They scrambled down the mountain, smiling, love songs singing in their hearts.

§§

Johnny's recovery had been the reason for their summer sojourn, but the arm had healed, and yet they remained. Johnny had begun his courtship of Christine, and Johnny's parents couldn't bear the thought of leaving without some sense of closure.

In the last week of August, however, circumstances changed, when an expensive carriage rolled to a stop at the Nelson home. Two black footmen jumped off the back and held the door. Doc Simpson stepped out and offered his hand to an elegant woman.

One of the slaves walked up to the farmhouse, knocked on the front door, and stepped back. Ayoka, Diana, and Christine had been preparing lunch in the kitchen. Ayoka answered the door. She was initially alarmed by the sight of an unfamiliar stranger, but any reservations she might have felt were relieved by the slave's slow, sweeping bow. He smiled and doffed his hat. He then addressed Ayoka in a polite, nonthreatening manner.

"Please accept the arrival of Mrs. Victoria Collins and Doctor Nicholas Simpson," he said.

Diana and Christine peeked from the doorway. After one look, Diana raced down the steps.

Victoria opened her arms.

"Diana, is that really you?"

"Yes," Diana said. "Victoria, you look so beautiful."

"It's been too long," Victoria said. "On the way over, Doc told me of your tragic experience with those dreadful Yankees back in Alabama, and how your brave son rescued a family in distress. I came to see why you haven't already paid me the honor of a visit."

"It's a long story," said Diana. She looked at Ayoka.

"This is my sister-in-law, Victoria," Diana said. She gestured to the Nelson family. "This is Ayoka Nelson and her daughter Christine."

Ayoka motioned to the door. "Would you honor us with your presence at lunch?"

Victoria smiled. "Absolutely," she said. "But the honor will be all mine."

Victoria was one step over the threshold when Ayoka pointed towards the carriage.

"Would your attendants like to come inside for lunch?"

Victoria almost giggled, but she saw the look in Ayoka's eyes. The invitation was genuine.

Victoria took a moment. "My...ah...attendants...well, they will be fine where they are."

She breezed into the house and took a seat in the parlor.

While Ayoka and Christine finished getting ready,

Diana and Victoria caught up. They hadn't seen each other since Victoria's wedding. Miles and Diana could not afford to travel to Cross Hollows. And there were always duties at the farm and the church.

John Collins had been active in commercial and political affairs in Arkansas. While both brothers longed for a reunion, they had never been able to make it happen. Now, after Pea Ridge, they would have to save their meeting for the other side.

In the parlor Diana told Victoria about the budding romance between Johnny and Christine.

"That's why we haven't come to see you," Christine said. "We've been watching them fall in love. She's a wonderful girl. She's special, and Johnny knows it. He's a little shy, so it's taken him a little while to figure things out."

Victoria waved her fan. "I must say, Diana, that girl is beautiful. I don't think I've seen another girl in Arkansas to rival her."

"It's just a matter of time before we'll be having a wedding."

Victoria bounced on the edge of her seat. "Oh, you must let me host it at Cross Hollows."

"I don't know about that, Victoria. With Miles being a preacher, he'll probably insist on a church wedding."

"Let me talk to him about that. I thought church was where two or more were gathered together. Read that somewhere in my New Testament, it seems."

They heard the sound of horses outside. Victoria looked out the front window and gasped. She had forgotten the striking resemblance Miles had to his younger brother. A tear rolled down her cheek.

"Miles still looks the same," Victoria said. "So handsome – so much like my John."

"You haven't seen young Johnny yet," Diana said. "He looks a lot like his father. He and Christine make the most beautiful couple you've ever seen."

Miles was with Jake and Joseph. They hurried to the porch where Doc Simpson was leaning back in a chair and smoking a cigar.

"Hello, Doc," Miles said. "Why do I think that isn't your carriage?"

Simpson knocked some ash from his cigar. "Because you know your sister-in-law. Once she discovered you were here, your days of peace and solitude were numbered. I also thought I might look in on my patient."

The men heard shouts coming from the woods – loud, hearty cheers of victory. Johnny, Bill, and Charlie burst from the trees. Each held a wild turkey.

"How about that for a progress report, Doc?" Miles asked.

"Doc!" Johnny dropped his turkey and sprinted to the porch.

Doc extended his hand for a handshake, but Johnny

grabbed him in a bear hug.

When he let go, they shook hands. Doc stepped back and appraised Johnny.

"If the lad were any healthier, he'd have killed me," Doc said. "I pronounce him fully healed and released from my care."

"Thanks to you," Johnny said. "And Mrs. Nelson."

"Johnny," said Miles. "Let's go inside. There's someone important I want you to meet. Your Aunt Victoria. She was married to your Uncle John."

On the way inside, Miles once again felt how strange it was to refer to his brother in the past tense. Every day since hearing the news, Miles had regretted not making time to see his brother.

Victoria stood to greet them. Other than Christine, Johnny reckoned Victoria was the prettiest woman in the world. She was certainly the fanciest. Her dress was satin, fringed with elegant lace. He'd seen her servants standing by the coach. And when she spoke, she sounded like someone from one of the Charles Dickens novels he loved to read.

Victoria remained seated and offered her hand. "Hello, Miles," she said.

Miles pulled her from the chair – gently – and embraced her. "Victoria," he said, "you're as beautiful as ever."

"And you're still as handsome," she said. "Those

Collins boys were always the dream of every young woman I knew."

She looked at Christine and smiled. Christine blushed and returned to the kitchen.

"And you must be Johnny," Victoria said. The boy was the spitting image of his father and uncle, only younger and with more hair.

"Next to your father and my late husband, you may be the handsomest boy I've ever seen."

In the kitchen Christine met jealousy for the first time. Her mouth twisted, and her lips compressed. Why should that bother her, she wondered? His aunt's just complimenting Johnny for his good looks, and that in turn was a compliment to Christine, wasn't it? And yet, she didn't feel that way. Growing up was hard, she decided. She returned to the conversation unfolding between Johnny and Victoria.

"Thank you, Aunt Victoria. You're so pretty – and fancy."

Christine stomped her right foot down against the hardwood floor of the kitchen, and the noise echoed through the small dwelling. Everyone turned; Christine's face went crimson.

"Aunt Victoria, that's Christine," Johnny said. "And I think she's the prettiest girl in the whole world."

The wisdom of these words was profound, and the timing impeccable. Miles, Jake, and Doc turned to

Johnny and smiled.

"I see you've also learned some male survival skills, Johnny," said Doc, and the room erupted with laughter. Even Christine smiled.

§§

Ayoka announced lunch was ready, and the crowd divided– one group of younger folks – one group of adults. The Collins, Thompsons, and Nelsons dined with Doc and Victoria in the kitchen around a long table. After everyone was served, and grace pronounced, the mealtime conversation took on a more serious tone.

"I guess you probably know why I'm here, Miles," Victoria said.

"Tell me anyway."

"I need your help. I want you and Jake and your families to come live with me at Cross Hollows. Since John died it just hasn't been the same. I need a strong man to manage the plantation, someone who's strong but compassionate. My current foreman is, shall we say, a little unpleasant, harsh even."

"You know how I feel about slavery, Victoria. It's not right."

"I understand, Miles, and I respect your opinion. But couldn't you look the other way for a while for the sake of a sister-in-law in need? I'll lose the farm if I don't get help."

"On one condition."

"What's that?"

"Free your slaves. The ones who want to stay will become paid laborers and share in what you earn. I freed my father's slave, and he stayed with me. He prospered when we did – and he has suffered right along with us. Now that we've been burned out, he's gone to Illinois to be with his family and to look for work. He went with my blessing and as much money as we could spare."

"Sharing profits with Negro slaves? That's outrageous. Unheard of."

"Those are my terms," Miles said. There was not an inch of give in his voice. "You'll find that people support what they help create. If you give folks a reason to work with you, they'll work harder and better than if they were whipped. You'll make more money than you ever did. And Jake here will have to consent to be co-foreman. I can't do it without him."

"What will be your fee?" Victoria asked, now a little cool on her original idea.

"I want you to build me a church where I can preach. I want three meals a day for me, my family, and all the workers, the right to hunt on your property, and some land to call my own. Jake will need a parcel as well. In exchange, everyone in the family will help you. We'll make Cross Hollows the most profitable plantation in Arkansas."

"Is that it?"

"There's just one more thing."

"What's that?"

"The old foreman goes."

"Agreed," Victoria said. "But you will handle his dismissal. He's a vile and vicious person, I assure you. Most unpleasant."

"Jake and I can handle him," Miles said.

"It might take both of you," Doc said. "Burt Maxwell's a pretty rough boy."

"Who hired him?" Miles asked.

"Your brother," Doc said. "Never could understand that seeing as your brother was such a gentleman. I've heard that Maxwell wore two different faces: one for when your brother was in town, and another for when he was away."

Miles sat in silence and remembered his brother.

"I was hoping you could head back to Cross Hollows with me this afternoon," Victoria said.

Miles and Diana thought about Johnny, and how a sudden departure would break his heart.

"What about tomorrow morning?" Miles asked. "That'll give our lovebirds one more night together. It'll be hard for them to say goodbye."

"Who said anything about goodbye?" Victoria asked. "I would love to have that stunning creature at Cross Hollows. I will teach her how to be a lady. A girl with her beauty deserves a life of culture."

Victoria could not explain her feelings, but she somehow imagined Christine as the daughter she never had. She and John had been unable to have children. Christine would be her adopted daughter, and Johnny would be more like a son than a nephew.

Christine had the dark eyes of her Cherokee mother, but an olive complexion more resembling her father. No one would suspect she was part Cherokee. There would be no social stigma. Victoria drifted into her own thoughts and began to imagine the parties she would throw – the wedding she would host. It would be a fabulous affair for—

Joseph Nelson's deep voice snapped Victoria back to reality.

"Whoa there, Mrs. Collins, ma'am! You're talking about my one and only child – my baby. I didn't raise her up in my ways to see her take on somebody else's. She's already a lady in my eyes."

"In my eyes, too," Ayoka said.

"Oh, I didn't mean to say she wasn't a lady." Victoria scrambled to extricate herself from the mess she was making. "She is lovely – stunning. I would love to assist her in getting an education. That's what I meant."

Joseph and Ayoka exchanged knowing looks.

"Well," Joseph said after a long and uncomfortable pause, "there are some things to ponder here. What you offer is wonderful – a real opportunity – one my

165

Christine will probably never have again. Ayoka and I will be crushed for our darlin' girl to go away, but if she's with Johnny and these other fine Christian folks, we know she'll be okay. They won't let nothin' untoward happen."

Victoria needed her proposition to work. She was desperate. Miles could see the tension in his sister-in-law's shoulders.

Mr. Nelson sat for a moment in silence, pondering Victoria's invitation. "So, I will give permission, but like Miles here, I have a few conditions of my own."

Victoria sagged in her seat. "Of course you do," she said. "And what are they?"

"First off, Christine has to agree. No one's draggin' her away kickin' and screamin'."

"I would never—"

"Second," Joseph said, "we can come and visit whenever we want – and for as long as we choose."

"Most assured—"

"Last," Miles could tell Joseph was enjoying Victoria's discomfort, "we get treated like honored guests – I mean *both* of us. No one treats us like those boys out there standin' in the heat next to your carriage."

Victoria gathered herself. "Of course, Mr. Nelson. Whenever you come – and you are *always* welcome – you and your wife will be treated as part of the family."

Joseph wasn't going to let it go.

"Maybe you didn't notice. My wife is Cherokee. We're proud of it even if the rest of society ain't. I don't want her insulted or mistreated or shunned or nothin'."

Victoria's cheeks glowed beet-red partly from anger and partly from shame. She realized she had already been thinking of ways to hide Christine's Cherokee lineage.

"Why, I never have been talked to this way before," she said.

"No offense intended, ma'am, I meant no offense," Joseph said. "Just speakin' my mind. I ain't one to beat around the bush."

Victoria began to cry.

"I agree – I agree to all of it," Victoria said. She looked up, eyes red rimmed and blurry. "Maybe it won't work. I'm not even sure if Christine likes me." She looked around the table for a friendly face. "Could one of you ask her for me?"

All eyes shifted to Joseph. He and Ayoka had their heads together and were whispering. Ayoka pushed back and nodded. Joseph looked at Victoria.

"Ain't wild about none of this," he said. "But as much as I hate to... I guess I will."

§§

Mr. Nelson did the only thing he could do under the circumstances, what all fathers of beautiful daughters are forced to do: let them go. He couldn't bear to see her with a broken heart, so he accepted one instead. There was only one person in the world who would be able to persuade Christine to leave the home she loved: him. As much as he hated to do it, he accepted his lot with a quiet dignity and resigned himself to a future without his darling girl.

Christine cried at first. "I will not go. This is my home."

Joseph wrapped both arms around his daughter.

"Christine, you know I love you and have never lied to you. I see a future for you with that boy. Johnny loves you and can take care of you long after I'm gone. Your future here is to grow old without romance – without the love every woman and man needs, the love of a spouse. How can you refuse to drink from love's fountain once you've tasted its sweet water?"

"Oh, Daddy, don't go waxing poetic on me again," Christine said. Joseph Nelson was a simple man who spoke with the easy drawl of dropped consonants and colloquialisms. He used "ain't" and other grammatically incorrect constructions. But he was smart and well read. Christine loved the way her father could quote line after line of Alexander Pope, William Wordsworth, and Shakespeare.

"There's truth in those poems, baby girl," he said. "There's reasons why they were written. I've never written a poem, but if I did it would be about how precious love is. When you find it, it's worth more than all the gold in the world. I don't want you to lose your chance at that is all."

She sniffled. He continued.

"I ain't seen any boys I'd trust you with 'til Johnny, and now I can't see any other boy for you but him. I see those stars in your eyes. You need to follow your heart and find your future. It's out there waiting for you."

"Daddy, I'm going to miss you and Mama."

"Relax," he said. "We won't be far away, and you're going to come back here every once in a while. Just think of all those fancy dresses you're going to wear. I want to see my daughter dressed up like a princess. That's what she deserves because that's what she is."

"Who said you never wrote poems, Daddy? You can charm anybody with that tongue of yours. When you started speaking, I was scared and wanted no part of that lady and her ways. Now that you've finished, I can't wait to get there. Johnny will be there, too. Oh, Daddy, you've made me so happy."

Tears of joy replaced the torrents of sorrow.

Joseph walked out of the room, with misty eyes. Christine followed – beaming. He remembered her first steps, her first hunt, and all those times on the stream, fishing together. He remembered her endless questions about God, life, and people. A montage of memories unfurled in his mind – a baby becoming a toddler, a daring child, and finally an older teen that had blossomed with nature's full beauty. His baby girl had grown up.

And life would never be the same.

§§

When Johnny heard they would be leaving for Cross Hollows, he was more excited than Miles had expected. Johnny had never forgotten his vow of vengeance. Cross Hollows was one town closer to Lawrence.

At night, Johnny often dreamed of Gene's death, the grisly hanging replayed time and again in recurring nightmares. Sometimes the dream would end with Johnny killing Hawk. Other times, Hawk taunted Johnny, gloating and bragging about Gene's death.

The only cure for Johnny's bitterness, he knew, was to kill Hawk. Anything less would dishonor Gene's memory and his own integrity. Johnny kept the feelings about Hawk to himself. He built a wall between himself and the outside world where this was concerned. It was the one thing he kept hidden from Christine, her parents, and even his own family – his burning desire for revenge. Rage stirred deep within his darkened heart. It was a simmering fire, which could be easily stoked into an uncontrollable inferno with the right catalyst.

§§

Johnny's thoughts returned to Christine. He was faced with a dilemma. He knew Christine was his true love and that he was destined to marry her. If they left the Nelson farm, how could he ask Mr. Nelson for her hand in marriage? Johnny wanted to do things the right way. He tossed and turned during his last night at the Nelson place, mulling it all over in his mind.

When he woke up, he had made his decision. He would ask before they left and hope for the best. In the excitement of the preparations for departure, most people had forgotten it was Johnny's birthday. Johnny hadn't.

How could Mr. Nelson say "no" on his birthday? But no one had mentioned the special occasion. His gnawing suspicion was confirmed by the absence of any special greetings from Mama at breakfast. They ate mainly in silence with some scattered conversation regarding the impending move. Johnny couldn't take it anymore.

"Ain't nobody going to wish me happy birthday?" he asked.

"Oh Johnny, I'm so sorry," Diana said. "It slipped my mind what with the move and all."

"Sorry, son," Miles said.

"That's okay. I just wanted to let everyone know that I have turned eighteen," he said. He hoped Mr. Nelson would understand the significance of the age.

"I guess we can call you a young man now," Miles said. "Hate to make you work on your birthday, but we've got a lot to do to get ready to go."

"I know, Pa. May I be excused?"

"Sure, son, go tend to the horses. Make sure they're grained and watered."

Johnny left the table.

Coward, he thought. *Should have asked at the table.*

But it had to be more personal. He wanted to talk to Mr. Nelson alone.

A little later Joseph came out of the house and began walking toward the barn. Johnny joined him. He was nervous. It took a while, but he summoned the courage to speak.

"Mr. Nelson, could I have a word, sir?"

"Sure, Johnny, what would you like to talk about, son?"

Joseph noticed Johnny's hands were trembling, and his voice was faltering. He looked Johnny in the eye and saw a boy struggling to become a man, trying to find the right words to say. Suddenly, he knew why.

"Johnny, is there something you would like to ask me? It's all right. Just slow down and say it."

"Mr. Nelson, I love your daughter, and I'd like to marry her – with your permission."

"Yes. I give it, but I think you ought to court a few months. If you feel the same come December, we'll have a wedding."

Johnny jumped in the air and threw his arms around Joseph.

"Thank you, sir, oh, thank you."

"You're taking my princess, Johnny. You better treat her right."

"I will, sir. I promise."

Mr. Nelson felt tears welling up in his eyes, and he didn't want Johnny to see.

"You'd better go back and help your folks. They're probably wondering where you are. Have you told them yet?"

"No, sir."

"Well, you'd better get to it."

Johnny raced back to the house. He found his parents loading food and other supplies into saddlebags.

"Ma, Pa, I've got something to tell you."

"What's that, Johnny?" Diana asked.

"Mr. Nelson just gave me his permission to marry Christine."

"Oh, Johnny, I'm so happy for you," she said. She hugged her son.

"I can't think of a better wife for you," Miles said.

Victoria had been talking with Christine about the latest fashions, telling her about dresses she was wanting her to wear. They were walking out of the house toward her carriage when they overheard Miles' remark.

"What's this about a wife, Johnny Collins?" Christine asked.

"Christine? I didn't know you were there, or I

wouldn't have—"

"You wouldn't have what? Out with it. Are you saying we're going to be married?"

"I was going to tell you. I just got through talking to your Pa."

"*Tell* me? Talking to my Pa? When were you going to get around to telling me I was getting married?"

"I was on my way. I just figured..."

"A girl wants to be asked, Johnny Collins, not told. I suppose I'll have to wait until I'm asked and asked proper."

Christine stared at Johnny with a coquettish grin.

"And after we've had a good and proper courtship."

Oblivious to the conversation, Joseph walked up from the barn. He smiled and clapped Miles on the back.

"I guess you heard the great news. I'm getting a son, and you're gaining a daughter."

Nelson was surprised by the stony silence. He looked at Miles, then at Johnny, whose mouths were open in disbelief, and then finally at Christine, whose chin and nose were upturned toward the sky.

"In due time, Mr. Nelson, in due time," Victoria said. She smiled and escorted Christine to her carriage. Diana joined them.

After several hours of packing, they were ready to go. Christine hugged her parents, who promised to visit soon. She stepped into the carriage with Victoria, Diana, and Naomi. Miles, Jake, and Doc Simpson rode in front of the carriage.

Johnny, Bill, and Charlie rode behind. Christine stared at her parents and her home place. She lifted her hand and waved goodbye to her parents and the only way of life she had ever known.

§§

Cross Hollows Plantation was in the northwest corner of Arkansas. They passed through Fort Smith on the way. The fort was still in Confederate hands though the Union command had cast a covetous eye in its direction. No one knew how or when, but most felt it would eventually fall to the Yankees.

They arrived mid-evening. The women accompanied Doc to his house, where they had been invited to spend the night. Johnny, Bill, and Charlie spent the night in Doc's hay barn. Miles and Jake ventured into Fort Smith to get the latest updates on the war at a local tavern.

§§

Miles and Jake walked into the saloon and sidled up to the bar. Jake placed a gold piece on the bar and ordered two whiskeys. He gave one to Miles. The bartender eyed them with suspicion.

"Where you from?" he asked.

"Alabama," Jake said.

"Why you in Arkansas?"

"Federal soldiers burned us out."

"Where you headed?"

Jake was about to answer when Miles cut him off.

"Not too sure. We were hoping to get the lay of the land, if you know what I mean, see where Billy Yank might be hanging out. We'd like to avoid him."

"If you want to avoid the war, you'd better clear out of Arkansas. Hindman's the new commander for this district. I hear tell he's going to force men to fight."

"When?" Miles asked.

"I'm not sure. Could be any day now. Action's gettin' kind of hot up north of here near the Missouri border. They need men. Conscription's comin' any day now."

"What's the age?"

"Any able bodied male eighteen to thirty-five, least that's what I hear. We don't have as many men as they do up North. They got lots of Irish and Germans. Soon as they get off the boat, they hand 'em a gun. We can't import soldiers, so we make men out of boys."

"Thanks for the heads up, mister," Jake said.

The door swung open, and a Confederate officer stalked towards the bar. He ordered a drink, then looked at Miles and Jake.

"Why ain't you men fighting this war? We could use some help."

"I'm a preacher," Miles said. "I don't believe in fighting except in self-defense."

The officer turned to Jake. "And what's your

176

excuse?"

"He's with me," Miles said. "He's helping me on my missionary journey, like Barnabas helped Paul."

"Who?"

"Paul and Barnabas. Son, you need to read your Bible. Have you ever obeyed the gospel's call?"

"Ain't got time for religion, preacher," the officer said. He left the bar and sat down at a poker table.

"Works every time," Miles said. "Now let's skedaddle before he starts wondering what a preacher is doing at a bar."

§§

They rode back to Doc's house. Miles knocked on the door. A sleepy Simpson opened the door. Miles and Jake related the information they had garnered. They rousted the others from their slumber, resolved to travel by night to Cross Hollows – away from the watchful eyes of Rebel soldiers.

The ladies slept in the carriage. The men and boys rode, half asleep.

The next afternoon, they reached their destination. An enormous white mansion rose from the ground at the end of a road grooved by wagon tracks. Massive oaks bracketed the road with welcoming arms. Beyond the trees lay the cotton planted in countless and seemingly endless rows.

Miles admired the house but spent more time

surveying the rich fields. He was astonished by his brother's wealth. Then Miles recalled how it had been obtained and was less impressed.

Slavery.

Slavery was nothing new. It had been practiced for thousands of years before America was born. From the perspective of history, it had only recently fallen into disfavor – at least in the North. The Romans and Egyptians had perfected the practice. They used slave labor to build colossal monuments to themselves.

Miles stared at the mansion and realized nothing had changed over the millennia. The mansion was a palatial monument to the plantation owner and built on the backs of slaves.

They approached the house. Several slaves came out to greet them and to carry everything inside.

Victoria swept out of the carriage like a queen. She addressed a tall, black woman. "Liza, this is my family. Please see to their things. They have full authority in all matters. Is that understood?"

Liza curtsied. "Yes, ma'am."

Miles raised a finger.

"Liza," he said, "I am Victoria's guest, but I am not your master. I'll take my own things, as will the rest of us."

"But Massa, I's been tol' what to do. I's got to do it."

Miles' eyes were dark. "Victoria, remember our

deal," he said.

"Liza, he's a little stubborn," Victoria said. "If he doesn't want your help, I won't force him."

"Yes, ma'am," Liza said. She pointed to Victoria's luggage. Several slaves toted it inside.

"Liza, where are the men?"

"They just finished their breakfast, and 'bout to go to work. Mr. Maxwell been crackin' his whip hard since you left. Wants that cotton ready for harvest."

"Where is Mr. Maxwell?"

"Out to the barn. Said he's teachin' one of the young'uns the meaning of hard work. I don't think you wants to go out there, ma'am."

"Why not?"

"Beggin' your pardon – ain't no place for a lady. Like I say, it's been kinda rough while you been gone."

Victoria turned to Miles.

"Now it's your turn to remember our deal. Please go visit with Mr. Maxwell."

"Be glad to," Miles said. "Jake, let's go."

"Sure, partner."

"Where's the barn?" Miles asked.

"Liza will take you," Victoria said.

"And then she'll leave," Miles said. "Like she said, no place for a lady. Things might get a little unpleasant."

Victoria raised her eyebrows. "I thought you were a preacher."

"I am. But I figure there's room for some righteous anger, and I bet my brother might have told you something about my fighting spirit."

"He told me a few stories, but I always thought they were tall tales told by a younger brother with a bad case of hero worship."

"Well, miss, my brother always told the truth. He just laced it up a bit sometimes."

"If I don't hear back from you and Jake in twenty minutes, I'll send Johnny with his rifle. From what I hear, he's quite a shot."

§§

When the men rounded the corner of the mansion, they saw a large red barn surrounded by a maze of stalls and stables. It was spacious enough to hold dozens of horses. Miles gasped at the size of the corrals. Not far from the barn, they heard the pop of a bullwhip – and screams.

"Please, Boss, no more. I'll work hard. I'll do what you say. Please."

"Isaiah, you got three more coming. When we're done, you can go to the house. They'll get you ready for the day's work."

Miles and Jake hurried around the edge of the barn and through the large door. They saw a mountain of a man holding a bullwhip. The lash had to be over fifteen feet long. Jake looked at the man's bulging forearms and thick, corded neck.

"You remember all that tough talk you were making back there with Victoria?" he asked.

"Yeah."

"You feel like taking it back now? Look at the size of that guy."

"I came prepared."

Miles pulled a rope out of his pocket. He fashioned a honda knot. He had the reputation of being able to lasso almost anything, but to Jake's knowledge Miles had never roped a human being, let alone an elephant like Maxwell.

"You serious? What's your plan if you miss? Better yet, what's your plan if you *don't*? You think you can drag him anywhere? He'll drag you and use that rope as a noose. You'll be swinging from those barn rafters up there."

"That's where you come in," Miles said. "I won't miss anything as big as that head. When he feels the cinch tighten around his neck, he'll drop the whip. And when he does, you pick it up. "

"And what happens if that just makes him mad?"

"I'm going to say a quick prayer it doesn't. And anyway, it might not be necessary. He might be willing to visit with us, and he might accept his termination gracefully and leave without giving us any problems."

"Do you really believe what you just said?"

"No. Not a bit of it. That's why I brought this rope. And this," Miles said, handing Jake a pistol.

Maxwell raised the whip. Miles shouted.

"Maxwell!"

The brute wheeled, whip at the ready.

"What?"

"Can we visit with you a minute?"

"Can't you see I'm busy, mister?" he said.

"Miz Collins sent me here to tell you something," Miles said.

"Go ahead."

"You're fired. Jake and I are the new foremen. You won't be needing that whip anymore."

"Good luck making me leave," Maxwell said.

Maxwell raked the whip across Miles' midsection. Miles dropped the rope. Jake pointed the Colt and cocked it.

"Put down that whip, Maxwell, or I'll shoot."

Maxwell feigned as though he were withdrawing the whip, then flicked his wrist quickly, strafing Jake across the right arm. The pistol skidded across the hardened clay floor, and the overseer kicked the pistol out of Jake's reach. He began to laugh.

"You two? Going to manage Cross Hollows? You ain't men enough. Besides, you're not gonna live to try." Maxwell picked up the pistol and fired it out the gaping front door.

"I mean, seeing as how you shot at me first, no one would question that I killed you in self-defense."

He reached under his barn jacket and withdrew a pistol.

"Oh...I guess you didn't think I had one of my own, did you?"

Johnny's voice came from behind Maxwell. "Drop the gun, mister." Maxwell pivoted his head with deliberate caution. Johnny had come in the barn's back entrance and was aiming his Sharps.

"And just suppose I won't, runt? What are you gonna do about it?"

Johnny's dark eyes narrowed, the same cold expression Miles had seen several times.

Johnny's voice dropped to a low growl. His hands were relaxed and steady.

"That's the only warning you get, mister," he said. "Throw that pistol down now or die with it in your hand. I've killed tougher men than you."

Maxwell lost his swagger. He looked at Jake. "Really?"

"Yeah," Jake said. "I've seen him do it."

Maxwell dropped the gun...and the whip. Miles breathed a sigh of relief.

Johnny kept the rifle trained on Maxwell's chest and knelt down beside the slave.

"What's your name?" Johnny asked.

183

"Isaiah."

"This man beat you a lot, Isaiah?"

"Right regular, sir," Isaiah said.

Johnny stood. He kept his right hand on the trigger. He pointed to Maxwell with his left.

"Take your shirt off, fat man." Maxwell did as he was told. "Isaiah, pick up that whip. Time he learned what the business end feels like."

Miles took a step forward. "No, Johnny." Johnny kept talking to Maxwell. "Grab hold of that railing yonder with both hands."

Isaiah picked up the bullwhip. Johnny nodded. The slave slapped the leather across Maxwell's bare back. Maxwell didn't flinch. "Draw it back farther and lay into it. Again."

The second stroke drew blood from the top of Maxwell's right shoulder. The big man grunted.

Johnny nodded. "Not bad, but this is your last chance. This one is for every scar he's ever put on your body."

Isaiah drew back the whip. When he brought it forward, he released the whip with all of the strength he could muster. A crimson chasm opened between Maxwell's shoulder blades. The erstwhile overseer shrieked and fell to his knees.

"No more," he begged. "No more."

Johnny walked over to the fallen man and kicked

him in the ribs.

"That's for whipping my Pa."

His boot struck Maxwell's gut.

"That's for whipping my Uncle Jake."

He raised his foot and launched a vicious kick to Maxwell's jaw. The man's body lifted slightly, then collapsed in the dirt. Maxwell's voice was weak and trembling.

"What was that for?" he asked.

"That was for me. I don't like to be insulted. Won't tolerate it. Especially from the likes of you."

He bent over and helped Maxwell to his feet. The big man wobbled like he was standing on the deck of a ship at sea.

"Justice has been served," Johnny said. "Now, Maxwell, you've been fired. Get your things and get. Never come back. If you talk about what happened here today, I'll find out about it. Then I'll track you down and kill you. Do you understand me?"

Maxwell staggered to his hat, dusted it off, and put it on.

"A man needs his gun," he said.

Jake unloaded the pistol and handed it to Maxwell, who began to walk away. He turned around for a moment.

"I'll tell you one thing, boy," he said. "You're the one should be runnin' this place. You remind me of me when

I was your age."

Johnny's rage disappeared, replaced by a sickening, scorching knot in his stomach.

Miles and Jake walked behind Maxwell until he was off the property. Johnny stayed behind in the barn. As soon as they were out of sight, Isaiah stood in front of Johnny.

"Thank you, sir," Isaiah said. "Thank you. I'll never forget what you done for me today. Never."

Johnny couldn't speak. He just nodded then watched the slave walk out of the barn, his head high, his back a bloody mess.

The first tears were misty droplets. They grew steadier, until they came fast and full. His chest heaved. He saw nothing through the tears, not even Christine.

She'd followed him to the barn at a distance. She was troubled by the rifle in his hand. When he went around to the back, she slipped into one of the outside stall doors and climbed into the loft.

She'd watched everything and now knew the other side of Johnny Collins. The dark side. She stared at him with a look of love and pity.

§§

After Maxwell rode away, Miles summoned the slaves. Over Victoria's vociferous objections, he insisted on holding the meeting in the grand ballroom, which only the house servants had ever seen.

Though Miles Collins had a knack for farming, everyone agreed his greatest talent was public speaking. He had a way with words. His speeches and sermons weren't drab lectures. They were filled with stories and life experience. Though he lacked formal education and did not know the difference between a metaphor and a simile, he was a storyteller par excellence.

Today, though, Miles didn't intend to deliver a long sermon. He just wanted an introduction. He wanted to explain the new rules and relationships at Cross Hollows.

"Folks, I've called you here today to tell you about some changes here at Cross Hollows. My name is Miles Collins, brother of your late master, and this here's my brother-in-law, Jake Thompson. We're the new foremen. As you probably know, Mr. Maxwell is gone – dismissed by Mrs. Collins."

A slow murmur rose through the crowd. Miles motioned for quiet.

"So, with a new boss come some changes. As of this moment, you are free men and women. Isn't that right, Victoria?"

Victoria nodded.

Silence swallowed the room. Miles squinted in confusion and looked at Jake, who shrugged. Miles turned to the assembled.

"I think I spoke clearly but let me try again. You are no longer slaves. If you wish, you can leave. If you want to stay and work, you will be paid."

A long arm rose up from the back.

"Beggin' your pardon, sir, but ain't kind to play no joke like this."

"It's no joke, my friend, I can assure you," Miles said. "If you wish, you can head out right after the meeting. We'll supply you with food and clothing and manumission papers."

A tidal wave of cheers echoed from every wall. Women wept – men embraced – children danced. When the celebration slowed, another hand went up.

"What if we stay?"

"We want to build something special at Cross Hollows. Those who leave will be given their back wages. Those who stay will earn a daily wage and share in the profits. I'm sorry I cannot give you exact numbers, but I haven't had time to review the farm's finances. You each have earned a piece of the profits, with your sweat."

"Do we have to move out?"

"No," Miles said, "at least not until we build you something better. Now, to be above board, I must tell you that Mrs. Collins will make more than anyone. She owns the place – she must pay upkeep and taxes."

A voice interrupted.

"But you sayin' she ain't owning us no more?"

"That's right. You are free."

The room swelled with jubilant bedlam. After a few minutes, Miles held up both hands.

"One more thing," he said. "I hope you will help me build a church. I am a preacher and I want us to worship God together."

The air left the room.

"We ain't had no church before," a woman said.

The man next to her said, "And we ain't never been to church with a white man, let alone a white preacher, that's all."

"We're all equal in the eyes of God," Miles said. He motioned to Isaiah. "Isaiah, can you come here, please?"

Isaiah stepped forward.

"Would you show these people what Maxwell did to you this morning?"

Isaiah peeled off his shirt and turned around. The crowd murmured; many of them had similar scars – all from the same whip. But there was a collective, audible gasp when Miles opened his shirt to reveal the crooked wound across his belly. It was still weeping blood.

"We bleed the same blood because we are made by the same God," Miles said. "And we will work side by side as brothers and sisters in Christ if you so desire. Who wants to stay?"

"We will!"

Miles beamed at the new congregation – the most unique in the entire country. It was one of the happiest days of his life because he loved people regardless of color, and he had been able to set them free. At the far side of the room, Johnny wiped tears from his eyes and wished he might one day be half the man his father was.

§§

The next few months were joyous times at Cross Hollows. The emancipated employees celebrated their newfound freedom with hard work. Incentivized, they worked with more enthusiasm and efficiency than ever before. Miles created work teams and allowed the members to select their own supervisors.

The groups met at the start of each day and reviewed the impending work. When they finished, they discussed the work in progress and went over any problems they had encountered that day. Then they devised solutions for the next day.

Work began at dawn and ended at sunset. Fifteen-hour days under the hot Arkansas sun often weakened the heartiest soul. To avoid exhaustion, team leaders used rotating schedules. Fresh legs got the more demanding jobs. Johnny, Bill, and Charlie worked, sweated, and sang alongside their new compatriots. At first, the arrangement was uncomfortable for everyone but in less than a week, they settled into an easy rhythmic unity. The boys worked under the leadership of Ezekiel, an older man who knew more about cotton than most people could ever hope to learn. They obeyed his instructions and were the better for it.

When told of the experiment, most of Victoria's friends and neighbors ridiculed Cross Hollows. They predicted imminent bankruptcy. Some felt threatened by emancipation, fearing it might prove contagious.

Despite the criticism, Cross Hollows' cotton crop looked abundant. Harvest grew closer and speculation spread, as people tried to predict the size of the bumper crop. Gamblers placed bets. Those who wagered on disaster suffered agonizing losses when the crop exceeded the highest estimate by three hundred bales.

Victoria was astounded and generous. She retained one-third of the profits for upkeep and taxes and divided the remaining two-thirds among her new employees. Miles took up a collection to build a church. Against all odds, and defying all expectations, harmony reigned at Cross Hollows.

§§

During the first week of November, Johnny spoke with Bill and Charlie about sneaking off to the Fort Smith Fair. Johnny had heard Aunt Victoria talking about the fair. There would be horse races, livestock judging, and cooking contests. There would also be shooting competitions, for both pistols and rifles.

"There's good prize money," he said. "I can use it to buy a wedding ring."

"If you win," Bill said.

Johnny laughed.

"Ain't no if about it," Johnny said.

Johnny knew Miles and Jake wouldn't let them go. He remembered why they left Fort Smith the last time. The young people had been disappointed. They'd never had a chance to be in such a big place. Johnny didn't count the time in Huntsville – it had hardly been a pleasure trip.

They had wanted to see the fort and the town. This was their chance to have some fun. Johnny decided they would do it, whether their parents approved or not.

It wouldn't be the same without Christine, though, and Johnny wanted her to join them on their expedition. The problem with this idea, he thought, would be Aunt Victoria. Since arriving at Cross Hollows, Victoria had stolen his fiancée, introducing her to society friends and dressing her up like a doll. Johnny had been reduced to a spectator. He wanted to be a player again.

"Christine, we're going to Fort Smith," Johnny said.

"Who's we?" she asked.

"Me, Bill, Charlie, and you, I hope."

"Do your parents know?"

"No, and we're not about to tell them. We'll leave them a note."

"Johnny Collins, what are you going to do in Fort Smith?"

"I heard Aunt Victoria talking about some fair up

192

there."

"Yes. As a matter of fact, she's supposed to take me. We're going shopping."

"Well then, there we are. We'll leave a note for our folks that we've gone hunting, and then we'll catch up with you. Aunt Victoria will play along. You watch. She knows how hard we've been working."

"Do you want me to talk her into it, Johnny?" Christine asked.

"If anybody could, it would be you. She loves you like a daughter."

"Okay. I'll do it."

"When are you leaving?" Johnny asked.

"Day after tomorrow."

"Good. No word of this to anybody, though, okay? And tell Aunt Victoria not to say anything. Let me know tomorrow." He kissed her goodbye.

"Oh, why not?" Victoria said when Christine asked her the next day. "The boys have been working so hard, and we need to show off your dresses there in Fort Smith. I've got some friends I'd like you to meet."

"Victoria?"

"Yes?"

"While we're there, would you chaperone me and Johnny? Let us court some? We've been missing each other."

"Why certainly, dear. But do you think Miles and

Jake will let them go?"

"No. Johnny wanted you to keep it from them. They'll join us sometime after we leave, and they'll leave a note behind saying they went hunting."

"Oh, I see. I get to take the blame."

"I guess so."

"That's fine with me. I think I'm up to it. You kids need to have a little fun. It's been so hot lately, and everybody's been working so hard. I'll take a little extra money, and we'll have a marvelous time."

"Oh, I'm so excited," Christine said.

"Me too, dear. Me too."

§§

The next morning Christine found Johnny.

"We're on," she said. "We'll leave after breakfast tomorrow. After we leave, wait for at least an hour, then slip away. We'll wait for you somewhere down the trail."

Johnny's eyes were glowing.

"I can't wait," he said.

Victoria told the rest of the family about her trip to Fort Smith for the fair, and how she was taking Christine with her. Miles looked up from his ham and eggs and glanced over at Johnny.

"Be careful," he said. "Whatever you do, don't let anybody know about the boys. I've been hearing more talk about conscription."

"I know most everybody in the regular army,"

Victoria said. "They're not going to be conscripting my family. They enjoy my parties too much. They wouldn't want to risk missing the fanciest balls in the South. The Cross Hollows Christmas party is the most popular event of the winter social season."

"I wouldn't be so sure of that, Victoria," Miles said. "The more men they lose, the more desperate for soldiers they'll become. While you're there, I'd appreciate it if you'd keep your eyes and ears open for any news."

"I'll do it, Miles. We'll leave early tomorrow."

The next morning, Diana got up before dawn and made breakfast. Miles, Jake, and the boys loaded the carriage. After the meal, they said goodbye. When Christine got in the carriage, Johnny winked at her.

When they had been gone about an hour, Johnny found Miles and Jake.

"We're going hunting – me, Bill, and Charlie – if that's all right with you," Johnny said.

"No more than one night," Miles said. By Johnny's calculation, they could make it to Fort Smith, have some fun, spend the night, and return before they were missed.

The boys had stayed up late the night before, making their preparations. They were ready. Johnny packed every gun he owned, including the pistols taken from the soldiers and his trusted rifle. Soon they were on their way. Bill, who had learned the tracker's art from Jake, quickly found their trail. They caught up in a few hours.

"Hello boys," Victoria said. "Are you ready to have some fun?"

"Yeah," they replied with big smiles.

Christine walked over to Johnny.

"Can I ride double with you?" she asked brazenly. Johnny noticed she never acted that way when his mother was around.

"Sure. Climb up here, darlin'."

Victoria smiled and walked back to her carriage dreaming of the wedding.

Christine jumped up on the horse and threw both arms around Johnny. He leaned back and she planted a sideways kiss on his lips.

"Yeehaw!" Johnny cried. He spurred Midnight forward to the front of their newly formed caravan. "Fort Smith, here we come. I'm ready to shoot my guns!"

They arrived at Fort Smith just after noon. The place was crawling with Confederate soldiers. The little group from Cross Hollows rode to the town square. Johnny found a schedule of the day's events posted on a notice board in the middle of town.

Pistols were at 2:00 p.m.; rifles at 3:00 p.m. His guns were cleaned and oiled. Johnny had taken extra care with the pistols. The rounds were measured and meticulously loaded. He didn't want a misfire.

Since the harvest, Johnny had practiced shooting every day. The hard farm work had dulled his skills a little, but he felt good about his progress. He had spent considerable time with his pistols. Now, he shot equally well with either hand. He was eager to see how he ranked against the competition.

"Well, I know what I'm doing," Johnny said. "You can find me at the shooting contest. Christine, are you going to watch me?"

"Victoria and I are going to attend the cake baking contest," she said.

When Johnny's face fell, she laughed. "Of course, I'm coming. I wouldn't miss it for anything."

"Neither would I," Victoria said.

§§

A group of men set up standard targets in a large clearing – concentric circles with a red bullseye in the center. The other rings were white.

Johnny signed up and paid the entry fee. Officially, the prize money had been posted by a wealthy planter who loved firearms and wagering. Without publicizing its involvement, the Confederate government was using the event to scout for talent. First prize was $300, second $200, and third $100 – all in twenty-dollar gold pieces.

Once the targets were arranged, the sponsor announced the rules. There would be three rounds of five shots each. Each round would feature a target at a different distance with the targets placed progressively farther each round. For the third and final round, contestants would fire five shots as fast as possible. Scores would be averaged, and the top three scorers after three rounds would have one last round, shooting as fast as possible at the farthest target.

Johnny figured he would have to be very accurate in the early round because even an amateur could be accurate at twenty-five feet. He was right. Many people had fine scores, but Johnny rode the bull on every shot. He fared only slightly worse in the next two rounds. After the scores were averaged, Johnny had made the final cut. He squared off against two much older men.

Johnny admired the control they had over their weapons. They flashed their guns and fired in a whirling motion with amazing accuracy.

First up was the tall man on his left. Johnny heard someone call him captain. The captain stepped calmly to the line. At the count of three, the captain fired his shots as fast as he could. Every shot hit the target; and one was a bullseye.

Next came the shootist on Johnny's right. He seemed to know the captain. They exchanged remarks and knowing glances. With poise, he raised his pistol and fired rapidly, quicker than the captain, and the results exceeded all expectations. He hit three bullseyes; the other two were in the second and third rings just outside.

All eyes turned to Johnny. He had not watched the others. He spent the time loading his pistols.

"It's your turn, kid," the host said.

Johnny stepped forward. By this point he had his fair share of admirers. To Christine's irritation, more than a few were young ladies.

Johnny drew his revolver, whirled, and fired. His shots came faster than those of the other two. His gun was "quiet" – there was no wobble or wiggle. He squeezed the trigger; he didn't pull it. To the crowd's delight, Johnny also hit three bullseyes, but one errant shot in the outer rim of the target cost him the title.

The host announced the winners. The largest hurrah didn't go to the champion but to the unlikely second-place finisher, the teenage shooting sensation. A bevy of attractive young women surrounded their new knight errant. Christine pushed through the crowd, turned Johnny around, and kissed him flush on the lips.

"Congratulations, Johnny," she said.

Johnny basked in the glow of her kiss. What a day. He was still in a fog when he was unexpectedly joined by the other two finalists.

"That was some fine shooting, kid," the champ said. "The captain and I agree. You may be the best young shootist we've ever seen, and we've seen quite a few, doing what we do."

"Thank you, sir. What is it you do? Are you in the army?"

"Yes and no," the captain said. Both men were charismatic in their own way. When the captain spoke, he did so with authority, and it was clear the champion deferred to the captain as his leader.

"Who are you?" Johnny asked. "Why does he call you captain?"

"It's my present rank. I will soon be promoted to colonel, but for now you can call me Captain William Quantrill. Most of my men just call me Captain."

The champion held out his hand. "I'm Lieutenant Coleman Younger," he said. "Most folks call me Cole."

"Quantrill..." Johnny's mouth dropped open. He knew the name – had seen it in the newspapers. Quantrill was a famous guerrilla leader, a legend. He struck fear into the hearts of every Yankee in Missouri and Kansas. His men were the fiercest fighters in the Confederacy. They were rumored to fly "the black flag" like pirates, meaning they gave no quarter to their prisoners and expected none in return.

"Your reaction tells me you've heard of me somehow," Quantrill said. "But who are you? Who is this magnificent young shootist?"

"My name's Johnny, Johnny Collins. And this here is my girl, Christine. Over there's my cousins and best friends Bill and Charlie Thompson."

Victoria stepped forward. "Aren't you forgetting someone?" she asked.

"Oh yeah, this is my aunt, Victoria Collins."

Aunt Victoria's legendary beauty momentarily transfixed Quantrill and Younger. When they recovered, they bowed. Quantrill kissed her hand. Younger followed suit.

"Is there a Mr. Collins?" Younger asked.

"He died at Pea Ridge," Victoria said.

"Sorry to hear that, ma'am," Younger said.

But Johnny didn't think he looked sorry.

"He was a great man," Victoria said.

"He would have to be," Quantrill said, "to marry a beautiful Southern lady such as yourself."

Victoria blushed. It had been a long time.

§§

All three pistol contest finalists excused themselves to rush to the rifle contest. Johnny was more confident with his rifle, and he soon demonstrated his proficiency to a stunned crowd, striking a bullseye from four hundred yards to win. Younger and Quantrill finished second and third.

Johnny was now a celebrity. Even the planter staking the contests walked over to greet the unlikely champion. Quantrill and Younger found Johnny after the prize presentation.

"Where'd you learn to shoot a rifle like that?" Younger

asked.

"From my Pa back in Alabama."

"He must be some kind of shot. What does he do?" Quantrill asked.

"He's a preacher."

"Why are you in Arkansas now?"

Johnny told them the whole story, how Hawk had interrupted his baptism, hanged his brother, captured his father, and burned their farm, which forced them to seek refuge with his Aunt Victoria at Cross Hollows. He related how he had rescued his father and uncle from the Huntsville jail, and their long, arduous escape from Hawk.

Quantrill and Younger listened in rapt attention. Johnny noticed the name "Hawk" meant something to them. Every time he said the name, their expressions grew hard, their eyes narrowed, their lips tightened.

"Johnny, we have something in common, believe it or not," Quantrill said. "Hawk killed my brother, years ago. I was a young man filled with wanderlust once, and I left my home in Kentucky to head west to the gold mines. I was going to stake a claim and strike it rich. My older brother was with me, along with a slave. Hawk killed my brother in the middle of the night and stole my slave. He shot me and left me for dead, but I survived. I woke up every day thinking of the same thing – revenge."

"What happened next?" Johnny asked.

"I returned to Kansas and infiltrated his band of Red Legs. I pretended to be one of them, so I could learn the name of the man who murdered my brother. Hawk had left the area by then. He was riding with another regiment, so I wasn't able to kill him, but I killed his henchman, the one who actually pulled the trigger. Hawk prefers to have others do his dirty work. But make no mistake, Johnny, Hawk was the man who ordered the killing."

Johnny felt the color drain from his face while Quantrill continued.

"Johnny, you and I are brothers of the soul. We have the same rage in our hearts. Cole and I have talked this over, and we would like you to join up with us in the pursuit of Southern honor."

Johnny was speechless. In a flash, he thought of the wedding and his obligations to his family, to Christine. Then his mind returned to Hawk.

"Is there any chance we'll go to Lawrence, Kansas? I'll join if you tell me we'll go to Lawrence, and that I'll get a chance to avenge my brother's death. I want to be the one to kill Hawk. Oh, and Bill and Charlie come with us, if they want to. They've got the same score to settle. Hawk hanged their brother, too."

Quantrill agreed.

Johnny told them he would need to say goodbye to

his parents at Cross Hollows. The two men nodded.

"It is possible, Johnny, that they might try to change your mind," Quantrill said. "Many people have the wrong impression of me. I'm a Southern gentleman. I'd like to meet your parents and let them know I'm not the ogre I've been made out to be."

"That would be fine with me," Johnny said, "but you'll need to persuade my Aunt Victoria."

"That sounds like a rough job, but someone has to do it," Cole said. He smiled.

A colonel in the regular army walked over to the group. He extended his hand.

"Congratulations to this fine young Southern boy. Best marksman I've ever seen. Who are you, son, and where are you staying?"

"I'm Johnny Collins. I'm from Alabama. The Yankees burned us out, so I'm staying with my folks at Cross Hollows plantation, with my Aunt Victoria. She's here somewhere."

"Victoria Collins? The wife of Colonel John Collins?"

"Yes sir. He's my namesake, though I never got to meet him."

"I'm honored to meet you, son. Your Uncle John was a brave man. He died with honor at Pea Ridge leading a charge that sent many a blue coat to their Maker."

The colonel straightened his jacket and drew upright

as if delivering an official communique.

"Son, I won't lie to you. General Hindman just heard about your shooting skills and sent me here to recruit you into the army. We'd like to test your rifle skills and see if you would like to become a sharpshooter. We'll swap out that Sharps of yours fir a fancy Whitworth rifle – the finest in the world."

Quantrill intervened.

"This boy has made other plans, sir. He will be joining us in our epic quest for Southern justice and our continuing defense of Southern honor. He will be my personal bodyguard on my diplomatic mission to Richmond next week where I'll be discussing battle tactics and war strategies with the Secretary of War."

The colonel frowned.

"Son, if honor's important to you, you'd better ride with me. Do you know who these men are, and what they've done? What has he told you? A pack of lies, I'll wager. These men ride under the black flag. They don't fight with honor like your uncle fought. Remember, a good name is worth more than rubies."

"Sir, I would respectfully request that you not challenge my honor," Cole said. "My father was a good man, a statesman. He was killed by a vicious band of Kansas Red Legs who cared nothing for the laws of war. My father was a Unionist. That didn't keep them from killing him and leaving my mother alone in winter to feed a family."

The colonel bobbed his head in half-apology and looked at Johnny.

"Think it over, son. Either way, you've got to use your talents to fight this war. You can't stay on the farm, not with your shooting skills. We need your help."

Quantrill stepped up next to Johnny. "And he can serve the cause best by staying alive, Colonel, living to fight next spring in Kansas and not dying on some forgotten ridgetop in Arkansas."

Quantrill emphasized "Kansas."

Johnny thought about his options. Go with Quantrill to Lawrence and avenge his brother's death, or fight with the regular army, and possibly die without securing the vengeance he craved.

After the colonel left, Johnny turned to Quantrill and Younger.

"My mind is made up. I'm going with you. My Pa warned me the army might force me to fight. Told me to stay away from them. He was right."

"I'm looking forward to meeting your father," Quantrill said.

"Yeah," Cole said. "From the sound of it, he kind of reminds me of my own daddy."

Johnny noticed Cole flick away a tear with his right hand. Cole knew Johnny had seen and appreciated how he'd refrained from comment. He liked the kid, and he would take care of him. He would protect him from Quantrill and the others if it came down to it.

§§

Johnny looked for Christine. He knew it would be unpleasant to postpone their wedding. They had enjoyed only a few outings together since coming to the plantation and those had been closely chaperoned by Johnny's parents. The trip to Fort Smith was supposed to be special, their first chance to break away from prying adult eyes. Though it was generally understood that Johnny and Christine were to be married on Christmas Day, Johnny had never formally proposed. He had planned to do it before they returned to the farm.

Now, the wedding would have to wait until he returned from Lawrence. Once he killed Hawk, Johnny could start a new life with Christine. He would lay down his guns forever and reclaim a life of peace. Johnny didn't feel right about getting married before he took care of his unfinished business with the man he hated.

Johnny walked around the fair in search of a ring. He finally found a vendor who recognized Johnny on sight.

"You looking to spend some of that prize money, young man?" he asked.

"Yeah. I want to buy my girl a ring."

"I don't have any rings, but I do have this fancy gold necklace and locket in the shape of an angel. You see, under the wings here there's a heart-shaped locket. You can place a picture inside. You could get your picture made and then put it in the locket once the picture is ready. That way you would always be close to her heart."

"How much do you want for it?" Johnny asked.

"Twenty dollars."

"That's a lot of money."

"Is she worth it?"

"Oh yeah." Johnny handed a gold piece to the smiling salesman.

"By the way, mister, will you wrap it for me?"

"Sure, son. I'll even put the picture in there for you if you want me to."

"That'd be great."

Johnny found a photographer and had his picture made. He then returned to the vendor, who carefully placed the picture inside the locket. He wrapped the necklace with a pink cloth and returned it to Johnny.

§§

Christine and Victoria were wandering about – doing wedding things. Victoria had every expectation of being both the hostess at the wedding and the matron of honor. Christine would be attended by some society girls she had met that summer. Bill and Charlie were to be Johnny's groomsmen, and Miles would serve as preacher and best man. Miles, Isaiah, Jake, and some others had been building the church. The Collins-Nelson wedding would be the first performed there.

It was hard to tell who wanted the wedding more, Christine or Victoria. While Johnny and the boys worked in the fields, Christine and Victoria had devoted themselves to the wedding plans. They covered every detail.

Johnny was not eager to encounter the wrath of women deprived of a wedding. He went to the only available older men for advice.

"You are in a pickle, son," Cole said. "That girl is beautiful, and I know you don't want to lose her or break her heart."

"Here's what you do, Johnny," Quantrill said. "Make us the bad guys. It was either go with us or go with the army. Either way, you weren't going to make that wedding. That colonel back there was going to conscript you. Tell her you'll be safer traveling with us on a diplomatic mission to Richmond than getting shot at and perhaps killed in Arkansas. Didn't Victoria's husband die at Pea Ridge?"

"Yes sir."

"She'll understand, and she'll make your fiancée understand, too."

"That's a good idea," said Johnny. "But one thing. After Lawrence, I'm coming back for the wedding."

"Maybe we can come with you," Cole said. "I'd like to see it."

"Me too," Quantrill said. "But Johnny, I think it might be best if you tell her tomorrow. You ought to spend one more night together before you dash her dreams."

"Yeah, I agree," Cole said. "Besides, I'd rather stay in your aunt's good graces. I might get to dance with her tonight."

"I hope I can keep it a secret," Johnny said. "But she has a way of figuring things out."

"They have their ways, kid. They sure do," Quantrill said.

"Do your best, Johnny. Good luck. And if she gets it out of you, I'm sure we'll know about it real soon," Cole said.

"I bet you're right," said Johnny, laughing.

§§

They found Christine and Victoria admiring fancy stationery.

"There you are," Johnny said. "We've been looking all over for you."

Christine and Victoria turned around.

"Do you remember my friends from the shooting contest? They'd like to join us for the evening if that's all right."

"Don't mind if they do. Not at all," Victoria said.

"I hear there's going to be a dance later, ma'am," Cole said. "Could I escort you? I was hoping I could dance with the prettiest woman I've ever seen."

Victoria flushed.

"I'd like that, Mr. Younger," she said. "I'd like that very much."

Not to be outdone, Quantrill executed an extravagant bow. "I hope your dance card leaves a spot open for me," he said. "It would be an honor to dance with the loveliest lady in Arkansas. Or Missouri, for that matter."

"You are a pair of smooth talkers, aren't you," said Victoria. "Beware those flattering lips. That's what my Mama always told me."

"Oh, but these lips speak truth, not flattery," Quantrill said.

Victoria's cheeks were glowing red. She fought to regain control of the situation.

"If my ears don't deceive me, I believe I hear a fiddle, guitar, and banjo. I love music. Come on, boys, let's dance. Christine, you and Johnny have a good time. Meet me back at the carriage at midnight. Have fun but behave."

"I believe these two gentlemen will now escort me to the dance."

§§

The two warriors squired Victoria towards the music. Johnny held out his hand. "Christine, how long has it been since you've been to a dance?" he asked.

"Why, I don't reckon I've ever been, but I've been

taking some lessons from Victoria."

"Well, you can teach me, then," Johnny said. "I always thought dancing was for sissies, but I used to feel the same about girls until I met you."

"Let's go."

Johnny pointed in the direction of the music, "Charlie, Bill, I think I saw several pretty girls earlier. Go get 'em."

They followed the sound of the music. Victoria was waltzing with Cole and having a great time.

Christine practiced with Johnny outside the dance floor, behind some hay bales that were being used as makeshift chairs. She took Johnny's right hand and placed it behind her waist. She placed his left hand in her right.

"Now you just move in time with the music. You lead," she said.

Johnny tried, but he kept stepping on her toes. When he did, Christine burst out laughing. Johnny was embarrassed. Everybody else was doing it. Why couldn't he?

He counted and thought, thought and counted. His legs tangled with Christine's, and he fell. Christine landed in his arms.

"We've got to stop doing this," she said.

"I like how it ends up, though," Johnny said. His lips pressed against hers, and soon they were lost in their own world.

Johnny made Christine stand. He got down on one knee. He stared deep into Christine's eyes, retrieved the package from his pocket, and held it out. She unwrapped the gift, removed the necklace, opened the locket, and stared at Johnny's picture inside. She grew faint from emotion.

Johnny's voice took on a confidence he had never known. "Christine, I love you, and I want to get married and live with you for the rest of my life. What do you say?"

"Yes! Yes! Yes, Johnny Collins! Yes! Yes! Yes!"

"There is something I need to tell you though, Christine, something very important."

"Save it, Johnny," Christine said. "I want to treasure this moment forever." They kissed again. Johnny could scarcely feel the ground beneath his feet. They seemed to be floating outside of the world and its constraints.

§§

Victoria sounded agitated. "There they are," Victoria said.

She was accompanied by Bill, Charlie, Quantrill, and Younger. Quantrill spoke in a forced falsetto.

"Oh Romeo, Romeo, wherefore art thou, Romeo?" he said.

Johnny took his lips from Christine's and winced.

"I'm sorry, Aunt Victoria."

"Do you realize what time it is?" she asked. Her façade softened. "Of course not. And I don't blame you, but we've got to get back to the carriage. Christine, sweep the hay from your dress before you step into the light, please." Victoria bent down next to Johnny and whispered in his ear, so softly that Christine could not hear.

"Your friends have told me everything. It's all my fault for bringing you here. Your Pa's going to be frightfully angry, but I will handle him. Whatever you do, Johnny, don't tell her tonight. Let her float on love's clouds tonight. Heartbreak is always easier in the morning."

Johnny walked over to Quantrill and Younger.

"I thought you guys were going to keep things a secret," he said.

"Johnny, women have a way of getting things out of you," said Cole.

"We tried," said Quantrill. "But your auntie is very persistent."

§§

Christine stepped into the carriage to spend the night. She wondered why Quantrill and Younger were still there camping with Johnny, Bill, and Charlie, but she soon slipped into a deep sleep. She basked in the warmth and afterglow of love and dreamed of the wedding.

Victoria hid her tears from Christine. It was hard to sleep. She tossed and turned, dreading what was to come – the wrath of her brother-in-law and the heartbreak of the girl she considered her adopted daughter. And all because she had helped them sneak away to the fair. It was all her fault, and she knew it.

They rose early the next morning. Victoria thought it best to tell Christine the bad news after breakfast. But not every plan works to perfection.

Christine rose before Victoria the next morning and found Quantrill and Younger drinking coffee with Johnny, Bill, and Charlie. She had heard about Quantrill and his raiders. They were infamous for their guerrilla raids in Kansas.

Kansas!

Intuitively, Christine knew. Johnny hated Hawk, and Hawk was from Kansas. Her fiancée's sudden friendship with the bushwhackers made perfect sense. Quantrill and Younger were still here because Johnny wanted them here – and he would be leaving with them, headed to Kansas to get his revenge. That was what he was going to tell her last night.

Christine walked up to Johnny and slapped him hard across the face.

"So, all those kisses, all those sweet 'I love yous' last night, were all lies. You knew all along you'd be leaving with them. There's not going to be a wedding, is

215

there, Johnny Collins? You're leaving me."

She began to sob. Johnny tried to comfort her, and she slapped him again just as Victoria emerged from the coach. She rushed to Christine.

"Child," Victoria said, "this is all my fault. I shouldn't have brought Johnny with us."

"It's nobody's fault, ma'am," Cole said.

"He's right, ma'am," Quantrill said. "A boy like Johnny was meant for war, not for the farm. His country needs him. General Hindman would have conscripted him, anyway. Yesterday, a colonel spelled everything out to Johnny – gave the boy two choices: go with us or fight with the army. Trust me. He'll be safer with us. I mean, would you rather him ride with us or those other soldiers who were shooting yesterday? You have to admit we were a little more accurate."

"Yes," Victoria said, "but if I hadn't let Johnny come, they wouldn't know about him."

"I'm not sure about that," Quantrill said. "I saw that colonel again at the dance last night, and we got to talking. He told me a brute named Maxwell joined the army a few months ago and told them about a boy who killed some men with a rifle. Said the boy was living at Cross Hollows. General Hindman was planning to conscript these boys the last part of November to fight some battles up north of here. You might have saved their lives, by introducing them to us."

216

Quantrill turned to Christine.

"Dry your eyes, pretty girl. He'll be safe with us. We'll take good care of him. I plan to attend your wedding after next spring's campaigns. I need Johnny's help. Going to raid Lawrence, Kansas, the home of our hated foes. We can get more revenge there than anywhere else."

"Revenge!" Christine stomped her foot. "That's all this war is to men like you – and to you, Johnny Collins."

"I've got a promise to keep...to my brother," Johnny said. "It's a promise I made before I met you."

Quantrill's voice was soft and smooth. "Christine, this man Hawk killed my brother, too. We need to kill him before he kills anyone else. Sometimes revenge can serve a higher purpose – justice."

"He'll get what's coming to him," Johnny said. "That's for sure."

"There's no use talking, is there, Johnny?" Christine asked. "While you're riding around the country with the likes of these killers, I'll be home alone for Christmas. There won't be any wedding, will there?"

Johnny couldn't think of anything to say.

"Well, don't expect me to wait forever," she said.

Johnny hated the tears – the pain – on Christine's face. But as long as Hawk drew breath, Johnny knew there would never be any peace in his heart.

§§

The ride home was quiet. All pretense was gone. Johnny, Bill, and Charlie would ride in with the others. Victoria would tell Miles and the others what happened and accept full responsibility. Miles and Jake wouldn't like it, but she hoped they would understand.

Miles was sitting on the front porch when he spotted the carriage flanked by the boys and two strangers. Miles felt his heart beat faster. Something was wrong. He sensed it. He called for Jake to join him on the porch.

"I don't like it, Jake."

"Me either. Something's wrong."

The carriage stopped in front of the porch, and Victoria stepped out. Lines of concern crossed her face in jagged edges revealing her lack of sleep and worried mind.

"Hello, Miles. I guess you see we've got company."

"Who are they?" Miles asked.

Quantrill and Younger dismounted and walked up behind Victoria.

"Let me introduce our new companions," Victoria said. "Miles Collins, Jake Thompson, meet Captain William Quantrill and Lieutenant Cole Younger."

The men shook hands. Diana and Naomi came outside and were introduced as well.

"Well, gentlemen, welcome to Cross Hollows. We'll share some coffee and some conversation," Victoria said.

Quantrill and Younger cast approving glances at the mansion and its decorous interior. They joined their hostess, Miles, and the others at the great table in the dining room. After exchanging small talk regarding the mansion and its origins, Victoria stared at Miles.

"Miles, Jake, I will just say it. These men have recruited your sons into their brigade."

"How did they do that?" Miles asked. "I thought the boys were hunting."

"They lied, and I helped them, and I'm sorry. It was partly my idea. I wanted to reward them for their hard labor in the fields this fall. They needed to have some fun. They're still boys, you know."

"Victoria, how could you do that?" Miles asked. "This is exactly what I wanted to avoid. We could have kept them out of this war."

"With all due respect, sir, you could not have," Quantrill said. "General Hindman had heard about your son's prowess with firearms and his deadly reputation and issued orders for his conscription. A man named Maxwell reported your son's whereabouts. An officer approached Johnny in Fort Smith. I intervened on your boy's behalf and said that Johnny had joined my regiment instead. Johnny and the boys will be my personal bodyguards on an important diplomatic mission. We'll leave tomorrow morning for Richmond, where I will confer with the Secretary of War."

"Quantrill. Of Quantrill's Raiders?" Jake asked.

"Yes, sir."

"I've heard that name before," Miles said. "Yes, it's all coming back to me. From Missouri, right?"

"Yes, sir."

Miles' voice was challenging. "The one who's been terrorizing Kansas?"

"The way you speak, sir, it doesn't sound as though you're very proud of our contributions to the Confederate cause," Quantrill said with a hint of agitation.

"I've already lost one son to guerrilla warfare," Miles said.

"Yes, I understand that, Mr. Collins. Many fathers have lost sons in this horrible crucible of the soul. To win this war, the South must fight just like your honorable son fought – with vicious determination, willing to make the ultimate sacrifice for the cause of freedom."

"Needless and pointless sacrifice," Miles said. "Don't you think that shooting from behind bushes isn't quite right somehow?"

"There's only one thing that's right, Mr. Collins, the Confederate cause. All other concerns fall prostrate before it."

"So, how would you fight this war?" Miles asked.

"I would change tactics. I'd lie in wait, then strike when they least expect it with small guerrilla fighters armed to the hilt, six revolvers to the man. And I would take this style of fighting to the North, to their own backyards. The Northern people will not support a bloodbath fought house to house, one day at a time, for decades. Eventually, they will give up and recognize the Confederate States of America as an independent, sovereign nation."

"And what will happen to our sense of decency? Our sense of honor? What kind of people will such a war produce, Captain?" Miles asked.

"It will produce heroes, Mr. Collins. I will tell you this, as I will tell the Secretary of War next week: if we refuse to fight like the devil, the devil will come to Dixie in the form of the Union Army."

Quantrill spoke with evangelical fervor.

"You mark my words," he said. "Those Yankee scoundrels will lead a war of conquest throughout the South. They will loot our stores, burn our homes, molest our ladies, seize our political offices, and humiliate our men. Clinging to some notion of honor will not keep the dishonorable from your doorstep. They will come. Johnny has told me what Hawk did to your church. This same man murdered my brother. What he did to your son, your church, and your farm is simply a harbinger of a dark harvest to come. Surely you can see that."

"I see a lot of things. Hawk came in response to the guerrilla war waged by my son and his friends. I had warned my boy not to fight that way, but he ignored my counsel. It looks like my other son will do the same. He is free to fight with you, Captain, but he'll do so without my blessing. If he must fight, I'd prefer he do his fighting on the field of battle, not the field of ambush."

Cole had been silent.

"Mr. Collins, if I may," he said.

"Sure, son, speak your mind," Miles said.

"You remind me so much of my late father. He was a Unionist as you appear to be. He stood by the American flag. But he was shot and killed by a band of Kansas Red Legs for his money. He didn't want me to get involved in the war either, but we couldn't avoid it. After he died, the Red Legs returned to our family's farm looking for the rest of my father's money. They grabbed our personal servant, slung a noose around her neck, and hoisted her up on a tree four or five times. They tried to get her to tell them where it was. She wouldn't do it, so they left her for dead. A friend happened by and cut her down. She had the $2,200 hidden in her undergarments the whole time."

Miles had gone pale.

"Then they came after me," Cole said. "I joined Captain Quantrill to avenge my father's death, just as Johnny has to avenge his brother. He seeks vengeance for the death of his brother and your son, and vengeance, in my opinion, is justice, sir."

"Vengeance is mine, sayeth the Lord," Miles said.

He turned to his son. "Johnny, we've heard from your new friends. What do you have to say? What about the wedding we were going to hold?"

"The wedding will have to wait, Pa. I made a promise to Gene, and I've got to keep it. We will raid Lawrence next summer. I hope to kill Hawk then. The captain has assured me I can come home after that raid. Then I'll marry Christine and be the best farmer I can be."

Diana spoke up.

"Johnny, sounds like you're not fighting this war for freedom, but vengeance."

"Vengeance, honor, and justice, Mama," Johnny said. "Hawk has murdered my brother and insulted our family."

"Johnny, I've learned Hawk might also have played a role in my brother's death," Miles said. "Doc told me. But the Lord will repay him for that and his other crimes in the age to come."

"With all due respect, Pa, I'd like him to pay in the age that is," Johnny said. His eyes narrowed. "Why can't he pay for his sins here, too?"

Miles was watching Quantrill, who was grinning.

"Well, do what you're going to do. Gene wouldn't listen, either. You'll probably get yourself killed somewhere, or, even worse, you might become a ruthless killer yourself. As this might be our last conversation we ever have, I will give it to you straight. Always live your life by the Good Book. In your quest for vengeance, do not kill the innocent. If you do, you'll bear the mark of Cain, son, and it won't wash off."

Miles stood and began to pace.

"If your life is in danger in wartime, and you have to shoot, shoot in self-defense, to protect yourself. Don't ever forget where you came from. Whatever you do, wherever you go, never ever lose your faith in God and the Lord Jesus Christ. I hope one day you will accept Jesus as your personal savior and be baptized for the remission of your sins. What shall it profit a man to gain the whole world and yet forfeit his own soul? You know my feelings on this matter, and you know I love you. I will speak no more to you until I see you again – hopefully on this side of the river."

Miles excused himself. On the way out, he glared at Quantrill and Younger.

"Men, my son better come through this alive. If he doesn't, I might just forget I'm a preacher for a while."

Miles had the look in his eyes that came to the Collins men when they were angry. It bespoke danger; even hardened characters paid attention to it. After Miles left the room, Quantrill and Younger exchanged curious glances.

"Now I know where you get it," Quantrill said to Johnny. "I'd hate to make that man angry. I'll bet he could work himself up into a righteous fury."

"Yeah, I agree," Younger said.

§§

They left at dawn the next morning for their journey to Richmond, Virginia, the Confederate capitol. Johnny kissed his mother goodbye. Miles was purposefully absent, as was Jake, who likewise frowned on their decision.

At last, Johnny came to Christine. He held her and kissed her, wishing they had more time. When he pulled away, he noticed she was still wearing the necklace.

"Keep that necklace and locket close to your heart, as you will always be close to mine. After Lawrence, I will come back for you. We will be married."

"When, Johnny? When?" Christine asked.

"I don't know, but please wait for me. Christine, promise me you'll wait. No matter how long it takes. I'll come back for you someday. And when I do, we'll be married that same day. No more waiting, because then I'll be home to stay."

"Johnny, I promise. I'll wait for you. I will love you always, Johnny Collins."

"I love you too, Christine, like I've never loved a woman, and like I never will again." They kissed, lost in the heartbreak of the moment. Diana, Naomi, and Victoria were all crying. Johnny swung into the saddle and rode away, Midnight prancing into a steady canter.

"So long, Johnny Collins." Christine sobbed and

stared at his fading figure. Diana and Victoria held her, and they all released a cascade of tears. Johnny turned and looked one last time at Christine. He wondered if he would live to see her again.

§§

Over the course of their journey to Richmond, Quantrill explained the reasons for their mission. He was planning to meet with the Secretary of War to seek a commission as a colonel of partisan rangers that would grant him the authority to recruit additional soldiers to his command. He was also hoping to exert some influence over the future conduct of the war. He sought to replace the Napoleonic style of warfare practiced by General Lee with his own guerrilla tactics.

The day after his arrival, Quantrill attended a meeting with Secretary of War Seddon. It was attended by Mr. Wigfall, a member of the Congress of the Confederate States of America, Johnny, and the others.

Quantrill walked into the room with his usual bravado.

"Good to meet you, Mister Secretary," Quantrill said.

"Captain Quantrill, to what do I owe the pleasure of your company?"

"Sir, I appreciate your meeting with me. I have come for two reasons. First, I seek a colonel commission in the partisan rangers. Such a rank would allow me to recruit more men, and the legitimacy of recognition would afford me greater protection from my enemies."

"What is your second reason?" Seddon asked.

"To propose a change in our military strategy. We are losing this war. To win, sir, we'll need to adopt different tactics. I have come as a missionary preaching a new style of warfare. I have come to convert you, and by converting you to save the South before it's too late. If my gospel falls on deaf ears, the South will fall, one state at a time, and the Union will have won its war of conquest."

He took a moment to let his brash introduction take root.

"The South must break the shackles of Northern oppression, as our forefathers broke the chains of English despotism. Their revolution succeeded, however improbably, because they were willing to fight 'til the death using guerrilla tactics. Our revolution can succeed, but only through the same methods."

"Quantrill, you preach barbarism," Seddon said. "Barbarism is dishonorable."

Quantrill fumed.

"So, tell me, Quantrill, for curiosity's sake, how would you fight this war, had you the power, which you most certainly do not?"

"I would field an army of barbarians. The hunters would become the hunted. I would wage a vicious guerrilla campaign in the North, taking the fight to the

Yankees in their own backyards, until they and their families experienced the true cost and pain of conquest – the blood of their sons, the burning of their buildings, the robbing of their banks, the derailment of their trains. I would strike them in their storefronts, in their halls of government, and in the supposed comfort of their homes. I would strike on city streets and country lanes, from town to town and house to house, until their will to fight was broken, and their desire for peace was strong."

"Quantrill, you're insane. Honorable men would not wage such a war. To do so would be wrong, criminal even."

"Mr. Secretary, you err in judgment when you assume there is honor in war, and that your enemy shares your sense of honor and moral restraint. What you will not do, what Lee will not do, the North most certainly will. They will conquer and pillage, burn and loot, as they have in Kansas first and now Alabama. And when they do, it will be too late for you and the South to react and respond. Our glorious cause will have been forever lost. And we will have been conquered."

His face crimson with rage, Quantrill stormed out of the room, unsuccessful on both fronts. He would remain a captain, and it appeared the Confederacy would continue to fight like Napoleon. From the moment he left the war room, Quantrill knew the war was lost. The Confederacy was doomed.

If the high command would not heed his counsel, maybe it would listen to action. He would show them how to win this war. He would execute a devastating guerrilla raid that would strike fear and terror into the heart and soul of his enemy. In his mind Quantrill could think of only one place for such a raid.

Lawrence, Kansas, he thought, *the home of the Kansas Jayhawkers.*

They were known as the "Red Legs" for the red goiters attached to their pants. The Red Legs had looted, pillaged, and murdered their way through Missouri. Many valuables and horses plundered from Missouri had been transported to Lawrence. Sacking Lawrence would serve two purposes: plunder and revenge. They could recapture what was stolen from Missouri. They could also exact a terrible vengeance on the Red Legs and destroy their headquarters.

As they left Richmond, Quantrill gave the city one last look. He took off his boot and shook it as he pointed towards the capitol.

"That's for rejecting my plan of salvation," he said. "If only you had listened."

Johnny thought he saw a small tear in the corner of Quantrill's eye. Quantrill was a complex character. Johnny could never quite gain a fix on who he really was. He always seemed to be hiding something.

§§

On the trip to Richmond, Quantrill had forced them to stop along the way for what he called marksmanship training, during which they practiced shooting pistols from a variety of different positions. Quantrill and Younger taught Johnny how to carry as many as six loaded pistols at one time. They showed him how to draw and fire with accuracy while mounted. With just a little training, Johnny was just as accurate as they were.

Riding away from Richmond, Quantrill seemed detached, lost in thought. His mind was preoccupied with planning the Lawrence raid. He was imagining the countryside, debating where to cross into Kansas. He was thinking of who would participate in the raid, pondering the qualities of his different guerrilla captains.

The raid would be very risky. Deep in the Kansas interior, they would be cut off from lines of supply and support. Getting caught meant certain death. For any major raid requiring the coordination of different guerrilla companies, Quantrill always put it to a vote. The majority ruled. He didn't think he could get the votes.

He would have to deliver a powerful speech to persuade the reluctant, to sway the swing voters. He began to rehearse the presentation, flossing his mind for anything he might use to inflame and incite his men into voting for the venture.

§§

In January of 1863, Quantrill swung back through Arkansas, picked up some of his men who had chosen to stay, and headed west to winter in Texas. He and Johnny agreed it would not be wise for them to return to Cross Hollows. Goodbyes the second time around are often more painful. He allowed Johnny to write a letter to Christine. In the letter, Johnny let her know they would be returning to Missouri sometime in March.

Due to unexpected flooding, the letter did not arrive at Cross Hollows until March. Every time she read the letter, Christine missed Johnny more. She longed to see him; over the next few months her longing evolved into determination and expectation.

One morning, in the first week of May, she confided in Victoria, telling her she had to see Johnny. If she were near him, she could make his food, mend his clothes, bring him ammunition, and spy on the enemy. In short, she was willing to do anything to be close to him and help him survive the war. She could do nothing for him at Cross Hollows.

"You can live," Victoria said. "What good will you be to Johnny if you get yourself killed? Those Yankees aren't like our Southern men. They're not above molesting a woman, especially if she's pretty. And what happens if they find out you've been helping one of Quantrill's Raiders?"

"I know, I know, but it's a chance I've got to take. I

love him too much not to see him and help him."

"There's nothing I can say to talk you out of it, is there?"

"No, ma'am."

"Well, I'll tell you what, then. I'll give you everything you need to make that journey safely. I will assign two of our employees as your personal bodyguards. I'll give you enough money to rent a nice room, and a carriage to take you there."

"Oh, Victoria, I couldn't let you do that," Christine said.

"Well, you can't stop me, either. We'll see you off tomorrow."

The next morning, Christine headed north to Missouri, unsure of Johnny's whereabouts, but excited by the thrill of the hunt.

§§

In Texas in the winter of 1863, Quantrill introduced Johnny as Quantrill's newest raider. He began by relating Johnny's back story with the hated Hawk. Next, he discussed Johnny's prowess with firearms. At Quantrill's urging, Johnny provided a demonstration, shooting a target from 350 yards away with his Sharps.

"Wow!" It was Bill Anderson, the battle-hardened guerrilla captain. "But what about pistols?"

Johnny picked out a tree twenty-five yards away and placed six shots in a close pattern in less than five blinks of an eye. Several raiders applauded.

"But what about human targets? Has he shot anybody?" Anderson asked.

"A few," Johnny said.

"He's also modest," Cole said. "He's killed at least fifteen Yanks."

"Sounds like my kind of guy," Anderson said. "Glad to have you on board, Johnny."

"Thank you, sir."

§§

Every new guerrilla had to be trained, and training was a mixture of education and experience. Quantrill knew how to teach, having been a schoolteacher. He taught them how to skirmish in small companies ranging from ten to twenty men. Each guerrilla carried between four to six revolvers, usually lightweight .36 Navy Colts, loaded and positioned on their bodies for easy access and rapid fire.

Each raider was required to practice daily with his pistols until he had achieved mastery. He had to demonstrate proficiency from prone, standing, and mounted positions. It was this level of training that produced shootists like Cole Younger, who once killed a militiaman with a pistol from seventy-one yards away.

The best teacher in life was experience, though, and Johnny learned volumes on his first raid with Cole in late March after they had returned to Missouri. The raiders were camped in the woods below the Snibar River when they received word that a band of Red Legs had torched a house and killed an innocent boy. The boy's mother found the guerrillas and requested justice for her son. She related the Red Legs' last known location and their direction of travel.

Based on her report, Cole led his men toward what he called the "Big Cut," a steep bank offset by ravines on both sides. Cole told his men to remain in the brush and wait until the soldiers were halfway across. Then they would charge, pistols blazing. Excited, Johnny waited, his heart racing.

"Easy boys, let 'em go by first. Hold your horses. Don't let them give us away. Watch my hand for the signal. When I bring it down, scream the Rebel yell and kill those cowards."

They waited for what seemed a lifetime. When the last Yankee made it onto the narrow trail, Cole's hand went down. Screaming, he led his men into the fray, his pistols firing rapidly. Johnny was beside him. There were fifteen Red Legs in all. With the first Rebel yell, the bluecoats turned to fire, but they were no match for Quantrill's Raiders. Cole shot four, Johnny three, and the other guerrillas killed the rest.

They came back to camp, one of the raiders proudly displaying a few scalps. Quantrill smiled.

"How did young Johnny do?" he asked.

"Captain, Johnny was everything we thought he'd be, and more. He killed him three Red Legs, he did," Cole said.

"Congratulations, Johnny. Well done, my young protégé. You will be leading your own company before too long. No doubt in my mind you will."

Johnny beamed with pride. These men were his new family. They were his brothers. This was where he belonged, and fighting was what he was meant to do. He did it so well.

He recoiled in shame. What was it he did so well? He killed people. That's what he did best.

He remembered his conversation with Gene only a few days before the hanging, how he wanted to be like Pa when he grew up, how he wanted to be a preacher, and how he didn't want to kill. Now killing was just something he did to win a war, avenge his brother's death, it didn't really matter. What a difference a year had made. What changes would next year bring? Would he be scalping his victims like Little Arch Clement had done that day? Would he be tying knots in a silk cord, to keep a running count of his victims, as had Bill Anderson?

§§

Johnny was fighting in Cole Younger's unit under the command of John Jarrette, Cole's brother-in-law. Jarrette took full advantage of Johnny's shooting skills.

Johnny had distinguished himself from the other Raiders. He was the fastest, deadliest shootist anyone had ever seen. In one battle alone, he fired three pistols in a whirling motion and killed eleven soldiers after which the Yankees placed a cash bounty of $2,000 on his head.

Every raider had a nickname, and most came from Quantrill, but Johnny's came from the Yankees instead. A Yankee survivor who had witnessed Johnny's blazing pistol work called Johnny, "that Badman." The nickname stuck.

Soon friends and foes alike were calling him "the Badman." Late at night, tormented by the dying faces of the men he'd slain, Johnny would think of his nickname...and shudder. It certainly fit.

§§

Christine arrived in Kansas City in early May of 1863. She rented a room from Mrs. Elizabeth Andrews, a widow in her mid-forties who was raising two daughters. Her husband had died in battle the year before. Mrs. Andrews decided to rent the extra bedroom in her house, and Christine responded to the ad. Christine liked Mrs. Andrews and the feeling was mutual.

Christine hoped Mrs. Andrews might have some information about Quantrill's location, given her Southern sympathies. Christine sought to gain her confidence in hopes of finding Quantrill's Raiders.

"So do you have a beau, Christine?" Mrs. Andrews asked while they were washing dishes together.

"Yes, ma'am."

"Tell me about him."

"His name is Johnny, and he's the reason I'm here. He's fighting with a man named Quantrill, and I came to find him, so that I could see him and help him."

"I know some of his men, and a few of the girls who take clothes, food, and ammunition to them out in the field."

"Really? Could you take me to them?"

"I can't afford to, Christine. General Ewing has told everyone he's going to go after the guerrillas' women. He's going to put them in jail. I can't risk that. My daughters need me."

"I understand," Christine said, her face downcast.

"But I can tell you where to go. And I can point the girls out to you. They come into town every two weeks or so. Haven't seen them lately, so they're probably due for a visit."

"Oh, thank you, Mrs. Andrews. Thank you."

The next week Christine was shopping at the marketplace when Mrs. Andrews pointed to three girls across the way. One was around eighteen, another looked fifteen, and the youngest had to be either 9 or 10.

"Do you see those girls?"

"Yes."

"They're the sisters of Bill Anderson, a guerrilla captain and one of Quantrill's officers. They're always buying stuff and taking it out to their brother."

"Thank you, Mrs. Andrews."

Christine walked over to the girls.

"Excuse me," Christine said. "Are you the sisters of Bill Anderson?"

They shrank back.

"I'm a Southern girl myself, from Arkansas. I think my fiancée is riding with your brother. I came from Arkansas to see him and help him. Can you take me to him?"

"I'm Josephine Anderson. What is your name?" the oldest asked.

"Christine Nelson."

"And what is his name?"

"Johnny Collins," Christine said.

"I will ask around and see if he is there. If he is, I will ask him to confirm your relationship. He'll have to know who you are and describe you well enough for us to know you're not a spy. We'll be back in two weeks. Be ready to go with us if you speak the truth."

The next two weeks dragged by. Christine went to the marketplace daily and stared at the patrons. She had almost given up on seeing them again when they sidled up beside her.

"We found your boyfriend. He told you to go back to Cross Hollows, that you'd be safer there," Josephine said.

"No, I won't."

"He also said you would probably say that, and that if you insisted on staying, he'd like to see you."

"I'm ready when you are." Christine said.

They finished buying their supplies and headed south out of Kansas City toward the deep woods. The sunset came and went, and they were still riding. Christine glimpsed small red tongues of fire wavering in the darkening distance.

"We're almost there," Josephine said. "I see their campfires."

A hundred yards from camp, a voice cut through the gloom.

"Stop! Who goes there?"

"Josephine Anderson, her sisters, and the fiancée of Johnny Collins."

"Come on in. Did you bring food?"

"Yes," Josephine said, "and we're going to cook for you."

"Thank you, girls. I'll be in camp as soon as my watch is over."

The news flashed through the camp. Johnny leapt to his feet, eager with anticipation. He sneaked up on Christine from behind and put his arms around her.

239

"Hello, sweetheart," he said.

She turned, dropped her gift baskets, hugged and kissed her man, releasing herself to her passion. Months of separation had stoked their desire. Other soldiers lived vicariously through the young sweethearts. They saw their own girls in Christine's face and form. When the kiss ended, Christine reached for her baskets.

"Johnny, I've been busy. I've sewn you a fancy new shirt, and we brought some food."

Several soldiers hurrahed.

"Wow, Johnny, you said she was purty, but don't she just beat all. I do believe she's the purtiest gal I've ever seen," Little Arch Clement said.

"Yeah, son. She's beautiful," Bill Anderson said.

Christine's face flushed in the darkness.

"Thank you," she said.

"Well, let's get busy, girls," Josephine said. "We've got some food to make."

Two hours later they were eating goose, potatoes, corn, and beans, topped off with sweet potato pie.

"Well, we'd better get going. Need to get back to Kansas City. Don't want to give our boys away," Josephine said.

Johnny and Christine held each other. Then it was time to go. Johnny leaned forward and whispered in her ear.

"We've been planning the Lawrence raid. It'll be later

this summer. After that, you and I are leaving for good and heading west. We'll build a place of our own. Is that a deal?" Johnny asked.

"Wherever you go, I will go."

Molly was the youngest of the Anderson sisters. She had been waiting patiently with her other sisters, but she just couldn't wait any longer. She walked over and tapped Christine on the shoulder.

"Christine, no more kissing. We've got to get back."

"You're right, Molly. Goodbye, Johnny, I'll see you next visit."

"Until then," Johnny said.

The soldiers cheered the goodbye kiss. Johnny watched Christine disappear, then he walked back to camp ready to face his fellow soldiers who would tease him for his romantic interlude. He didn't care. It was worth it. He slept better that night than he had in months, dreaming of a western homestead where they would raise a family together.

§§

Throughout the summer, Christine and the Andersons would visit, usually at biweekly intervals. Their visits fueled Johnny and gave him the drive he needed to survive the raids, which were becoming more frequent.

It was July when everything changed for Johnny and Christine. Christine and the Anderson sisters were almost to the guerrilla camp when they were captured by Federal soldiers who had been trailing them since Kansas City. The commanding lieutenant ordered his men to use the girls as bait to lure the guerrillas, then as leverage to force the bushwhackers' surrender.

Bill Anderson went searching for his sisters, and Johnny for Christine. They took a small company of guerrillas with them, including Cole, Frank James, and Little Arch Clement.

They heard screams in the distance and spurred their horses into a gallop. They arrived to find the girls being taken away by the soldiers who were yelling insults at the guerrillas.

"We've got your women now, Quantrill. Any more raids, and we'll kill them. All of them. We'll keep these girls in protective custody. We won't be able to keep them safe if you don't put down your guns and stop the killing."

Anderson let out a stream of profanities.

"I am Bill Anderson, and those are my sisters! If they are harmed, I will kill each and every one of you, and it won't be an easy death, either. I'll burn you alive, and I'll scalp your hides. Do you hear me, you cowards? You cowards who hide behind the skirts of women?"

"Call us what you will, Mr. Anderson. It doesn't change the game. The cards are still in our favor."

Quantrill appeared.

"What's the matter, boys?"

"They've taken Christine and several other girls, Captain," Johnny said. "What are we going to do about it?"

"There's nothing we can do for them, son. If we charge, they'll kill them for sure. But that's not what they're up to. They don't care about the girls. It's a trap. Men, disband and retreat. Every man for himself. We'll rendezvous later at the Big Cut."

Quantrill and his men galloped back to camp just as a separate company of Federal soldiers was preparing to charge. Johnny looked back over his shoulder. He shouted, "I love you," one last time to his girl.

Christine heard and smiled. "I love you," she yelled in reply.

Johnny never heard her; he was galloping away with Bill and Charlie by his side. They were joined by Cole. They followed old guerrilla trails and escaped.

They spent that night digging out a cave in the side of a riverbank, which would be their home until they were given the signal to rendezvous. They built a fire inside the cave. They were thankful to be alive, but Johnny was in anguish about Christine.

"Where will they take her?"

"Kansas City would be my guess," Cole said. "That's where Ewing's command is."

"I'd like to kill him," Johnny said.

"Wouldn't we all?" Cole said. "But someone would recognize us, and they'd kill the girls for sure then."

"So, what do we do?" Johnny asked.

"We wait. Not even Ewing would be stupid enough to kill defenseless women. Wartime or not, that would unleash a firestorm at his doorstep. More than likely, he'll just exile them, whether north or south I don't know."

§§

The only thing protecting Christine from the soldiers was the watchful eye of Julius Hawk, who had been leading the militia that evening. After his inglorious dismissal from the regular army, he had come home to Kansas. After speaking with a good friend, a former senator who still had Lincoln's ear, he was reinstated. In fact, he had been given a floating commission, granting him the authority to do as he wished, however he wished. He led bands of marauding soldiers and Red Legs across Kansas and western Missouri. They slashed and burned – Hawk's *modus operandi*.

He had lobbied Ewing to get tough with the guerrillas. Realizing the guerrillas lived off the goodwill of the people and the countryside, he wanted to destroy their support network, and banish disloyal populations, to cut off the guerrillas' lines of supply. He persuaded Ewing to issue General Order No. 10 authorizing the capture and incarceration of any person caught aiding or abetting the guerrillas. The prison population swelled daily as new girls were captured.

In Kansas City to discuss strategy with Ewing, Hawk had happened by a local marketplace and overheard an interesting conversation among four girls. There had been something in one of those voices that had intrigued him, the sound of a young woman getting ready to see her beau.

On a hunch, Hawk borrowed some soldiers from Ewing and followed them. He'd never been able to find the guerilla's camp. He figured he could capture the girls and use them as leverage to bargain with Quantrill for his surrender.

All had gone as planned until Quantrill sniffed out the trap and executed a masterful retreat. His plot foiled, Hawk had to settle for a few captives.

Hawk was not above using girls as pawns on his martial chessboard, but there were lines even he refused to cross. He had always protected women. He refused to allow the ruffians in his ranks to mistreat or violate them in any way.

Prison was enough – exile sufficient. One prisoner at a time, they would win this war by depriving the guerrillas of the ones they loved most. Maybe, just maybe, his tactics would cause some of these savages to lay down their guns out of concern for their lost loves.

§§

Prisoners required a prison. General Ewing requisitioned a three-story building and the one next to it. The three-story structure was known as the Thomas Building after its former owner. It was seven years old. The first floor housed The Longhorn Tavern. The second floor was vacant and was hastily converted into makeshift quarters for the female prisoners. The adjoining building became the new guardhouse. The makeshift prison and guardhouse opened in late July.

The Thomas Building and guardhouse shared an outer foundational wall. Each of the buildings was braced by internal wooden pillars located in their basements with common floor joists running the length of both buildings. They were interconnected and interdependent. If one fell, they would both topple.

Christine and the Anderson girls were taken to the makeshift prison during the second week of August. They joined other female prisoners, some of whom the Andersons recognized, including Nanny McCorkle and Charity Kerr, who were both related to John McCorkle, one of Quantrill's scouts. Charity spotted Josephine right away and threw her arms around her.

"Oh Josephine, we've been here for weeks now. How'd they catch you? How is your brother? Did you see my John?"

Josephine described their capture. Then she introduced Christine.

"I notice the floor seems kind of wobbly here," Christine said.

"Yeah. One of the guards here is a nice guy. He's ashamed of what they've done to us. He says the building isn't safe, that it will collapse any day. He told us to stay by the windows and be ready to jump out if it does."

They stared at each other, their faces white with fear. Just the day before, the tavern owner on the first floor had moved out.

Several prominent citizens had reported the hazard to General Ewing including a provost marshal and an army surgeon. A building inspector deemed the building unsafe and delivered a report with that conclusion to Ewing. Instead of trusting a professional's opinion, Ewing relied instead on a second opinion from his adjutant, a man who bore no fondness for guerrillas or their women. The adjutant assured Ewing the building was safe, and Ewing took his word for it.

The most disturbing report came from Mrs. B.F. Duke, a Kansas City landlord who had rented some rooms to Federal soldiers. She had overheard them bragging about how they were going to kill the guerrillas' women by undermining the foundations of the Thomas Building to cause its collapse. After uncovering the plot, she had evicted the tenants and reported her allegations to the general. Ewing did nothing.

On the morning of August 13, 1863, the room swayed, and the walls shook. The room was full of young women and girls ranging in age from nine to twenty-five. They were lined up next to the windows, afraid to walk or place any weight upon the floor.

Two guards were assigned to the prisoners, one nice, the other mean. The nice one they knew as Joe. The mean one they called Brutus. They worked in twelve-hour shifts. Brutus worked from 2:00 a.m. to 2:00 p.m. Joe would sometimes arrive a little early to relieve Brutus, who didn't mind leaving early.

Earlier that morning, Molly Anderson, only nine years old, had been "sassy," according to Brutus. As punishment he affixed a twelve-pound ball to her ankle. Joe disliked Brutus and had reported the mistreatment of prisoners to his superior officer, but Brutus was never disciplined.

After Brutus fastened the iron ball to Molly's ankle and locked it, he kept the key in his pocket. While he was locking the chain, plaster from the ceiling began falling like sleet. He looked up, panicked, and ran from the room. He took the stairs three at a time while leaving his prisoners to fend for themselves.

Joe had been worried about the building. He raced up the stairs. The building was about to fall. The women were at the windows preparing to jump. Joe knew he might not make it back down the stairs, but he accepted this fate with courage. His concern for the prisoners outweighed any concern for his own safety. He opened the door and tried to reassure the prisoners. He gathered them together for a prayer.

"Ladies, this building will collapse in the next few minutes. Our best chance for survival is out those windows. If we don't jump, the third floor above and the guardhouse next door will fall on us, and we'll be buried under the rubble. We could break some bones when we land, but that's better than dying."

The floor began to creak, and the falling plaster became a blizzard. They could barely see. The walls shook and groaned. Splintering timbers screeched; dust choked their lungs. Several of the girls were seized by fear and could not move.

"At the count of three, ladies," Joe said, "Jump farther and higher than you ever have before!"

"One...two...threeeeee!"

Those who could leaped from the windows to the ground below. A microsecond later, the building chased them. Some were struck by falling bricks.

Fate was random. Of those who jumped, some still died. Of those who did not jump, some survived. Little Molly tried to jump, but she couldn't lift the ball around her ankle. Oddly enough, she didn't die, though her injuries were significant: two broken ankles, a broken back, and a severe laceration across the face. She was disfigured for life.

Josephine jumped before the building collapsed, but her body aligned perfectly with the bricks forming the cornice of the third-story window above and her head was pulverized. Had she landed three feet over, the bricks would have missed her.

Someone heard Josephine utter several muted cries, from somewhere beneath the debris, asking for someone to lift the bricks off her head, but by the time they were removed her spirit had already flown.

§§

One by one the girls were dragged from the rubble. General Ewing, Hawk, and a detachment of soldiers stared at the wreckage.

"General, you've just made my job more difficult," Hawk said. "We can expect some furious guerrillas, and I can't say that I blame them in this instance. You shouldn't have treated those girls this way."

"Get off your high horse, Hawk," Ewing said. "I seem to recall that capturing the girls was your idea."

Mrs. B.F. Duke was among those searching through the rubble for survivors. She reached down and picked up a blood-soaked necklace lying on the ground, one with an angel in the center, and a locket underneath the angel's wings. She showed it to the two officers.

"You men have no conscience," she said. "One day,

you will face God's judgment."

"Madam, my conscience is clear," Hawk said. "The prison was not my responsibility. I was commissioned to catch them, not to incarcerate them. In many respects, these women alone were responsible for their fates. Instead of remaining loyal to their nation, they chose to aid and abet the enemy. They committed actionable treason for which they were lawfully arrested. Even an uneducated woman like yourself should realize that."

Duke shook her head in disbelief. She clutched the necklace and decided to find Quantrill and tell him the grim news. Unbeknownst to any of the Yankees, she was Bill Anderson's cousin. She had visited the girls every night, during Joe's shift. She had been trying to determine where the girls would be sent. She figured it would be somewhere up north.

She stared in disbelief at the blood-stained necklace. It belonged to the pretty girl who was going to be married – Christine, yes that was her name. Mrs. Duke wondered if Christine's body had been recovered.

So far, rescuers had retrieved four corpses from the rubble. They lay under a cloth tarp in the middle of the street. Trembling, Duke lifted it long enough to see a girl with raven hair. The face was unrecognizable, reduced to a bloody pulp. There was no necklace.

Mrs. Duke did not look forward to telling the dead girl's fiancée. How could she tell him Christine's face resembled a fractured tomato? And how would she break the news to Bill about the death of Josephine and Molly's injuries?

Mrs. Duke checked behind her to make sure she was not being followed. She went to her house, gathered some food and supplies, and headed south toward the guerrillas' camp. She had a sad story to tell, and as much as she didn't want to tell it, she was never one to shirk responsibility. She had to report what happened.

§§

"General, you need to clean up your mess," Hawk said. "I'm heading back to Lawrence. I've had enough of this city for a while. It reeks of incompetence."

"Hawk, you're partially to blame here, and you know it. I'll make sure the record reflects that."

"You'll keep my name out of that report if you know what's good for you. I have certain information. I suspect I know how that prison really collapsed. You'd be wise to refrain from any investigation. You might not like what you find. Your best course is to pretend this never happened. Besides, who's going to complain? The victims are either dead or seriously injured, and their families have been or will soon be banished from the state."

Ewing was speechless.

"It's only a crime if it's reported," Hawk said, "and neither one of us will. I'm going to forget this whole unfortunate incident ever happened and ride back to Lawrence. I suggest you forget it and bury it. No complaint, no investigation, and no report. After we have won the war, this incident shall be an insignificant, albeit tragic, footnote in a larger epic struggle – a righteous conflict that shall not lose its righteous character because of one isolated episode. The writing of history is one of war's most valuable spoils. We need not fear the historian. Our reputations will survive this war intact, of that you may be sure. We'll be rightfully seen as the crusaders we are."

Hawk surveyed the landscape like an explorer discovering a new world.

"The only problem you and I have, General, is out there somewhere, in those woods – Quantrill and his raiders. If I were you, I'd dig those girls out, give them a good Christian burial, and I'd spend the rest of my time getting ready for Quantrill. When he and his men learn of what happened here today, and they will, they will be as the fiends, demanding a profound vengeance. We'd best be ready. Good day."

Hawk mounted his horse and rode away towards Lawrence. Ewing stared at the departing figure with an open mouth. He understood the wisdom of the counsel he'd just received but was dumbfounded by the lecture just delivered by a subordinate. Hawk reminded him of someone else. From his stern countenance to his self-righteous fortitude, Hawk was the spitting image of Ewing's brother-in-law, William Tecumseh Sherman. The only difference was their hair color. Bill's was red. Hawk's was black.

§§

Mrs. Duke rode all night to the Snibar River. A friendly farmer told her the guerrillas had regrouped in the Blackwater River area. She rode that way.

"Captain Quantrill?"

"Is that you, Mrs. Duke?"

"Yes sir. I am the bearer of dread news."

"What's the matter, ma'am?"

"Captain, may I speak with you somewhere a little less public?"

"Certainly. Should I summon anyone else?"

"Bill Anderson, and the one called Johnny Collins. I don't know him yet."

Quantrill called for the other two and they went inside the dugout cave. A fire flickered in one corner. Mrs. Duke was trembling by the time they sat. "This is the hardest thing I've ever had to do, so please bear with me," she said.

"What is it?" Anderson asked. "You can tell me, cousin."

"Bill, this involves your sister Josephine." She looked at Johnny. "Mr. Collins, this also concerns Miss Christine."

Johnny's face drained of color. "Tell us!" he said.

"They have died."

Anderson and Johnny stared in disbelief. "What? No!" Johnny's agonized voice was a screech.

"No!" cried Anderson.

"Yes, it is true."

Quantrill, ever the commander, remained in control of his emotions. "How did they die?"

"After their capture they were placed in the Thomas Building in Kansas City. Some of my renters – soldiers who don't know about my kinship with Bill – were talking about undermining the foundation one piece at a time until it faltered. I reported the plan, but no one believed me. The building collapsed today. Many of the girls were killed by falling debris."

"I brought you this," she said, extending a hand to Johnny.

Johnny, nearly catatonic, nodded and closed his hand around the locket. He made no effort to hide his tears, which were streaming down his cheek.

"What was the Yankee reaction?" Quantrill asked.

"General Ewing spent a lot of time talking to another officer – a colonel named Hawk."

Johnny's knuckles went white around the locket.

Quantrill kept pressing. "And?"

"Hawk blamed Ewing for the location of the confinement. Ewing blamed Hawk for capturing the girls."

Johnny's voice barely registered. "It... was...Hawk?"

"Yes," Mrs. Duke said. "The colonel didn't deny that. Said it was legal – cited some order Ewing had signed. Said he had the authority to pursue and arrest anyone who assisted the guerrillas."

The only sound in the cave was the hiss and pop of the fire. Quantrill stared at Anderson and Johnny. They were lost in their grief. Quantrill buried his head in his hands as if in prayer. His compatriots could not see his broad smile.

Now he knew Lawrence would be a bloodbath.

§§

The captains knew about the plans for Lawrence but had not yet taken any action. The raid was not popular among the rank and file. Without their support, it would not happen. Now Quantrill had what he needed – a cause – a lightning rod.

He gathered the raiders in the largest of the caves where he knew his voice would carry – and resonate with authority.

"Men, we have just received tragic news from Mrs. Duke. She traveled all night in heroic fashion to deliver her report. We have learned it was Hawk who captured the Anderson girls and Johnny's fiancée, Christine. He took them to Kansas City where they were incarcerated in a makeshift prison. Renegade Federal soldiers began removing the foundational planks from the building in hopes of causing a collapse. Their nefarious plans came to fruition this morning. Five of our precious girls were killed. Bill Anderson lost his sister Josephine. Her skull was crushed. His other sister, Molly, is alive but has suffered debilitating injuries. Johnny Collins, our newest comrade-in-arms, lost his beautiful fiancée, Christine. He now carries her blood-stained necklace in his hand. Hold it up for all to see, Johnny."

Johnny brandished the necklace high above his head.

"We have always done our best to fight as Southern men of honor, have we not?" Quantrill said. "We have never made war on women or girls. Our enemy has burned our houses, killed our aged fathers, turned our mothers out in the cold dead of winter, captured our sisters, banished our lovers, and has now stooped so low as to murder innocent girls in the most savage and inhumane manner. What shall we do about this, men? Do what you will. I'm going to Lawrence, the home of the Red Legs, the home of Hawk, and I'm going to burn it to the ground. I'm going to kill any man or boy big enough to hold a rifle."

To the man, everyone cheered.

"Who'll go with me to Lawrence and get justice for our girls?"

Every man stood and hurrahed.

"Lawrence!" yelled Quantrill, and the crowd began

chanting it back to him, their voices echoing through the cavern.

§§

Mrs. Duke stayed with the guerrillas for several days. She comforted her cousin and Johnny as best she could. She cooked meals for the men and mended tattered clothes. She left on the eighteenth, the day before Quantrill was to head west for Lawrence.

She slipped back into Kansas City on the morning of the nineteenth and went straight to the hospital to check on Molly. When she walked in, her face turned ashen. She was looking at a ghost.

Christine sat up in her bed. "Hello, Mrs. Duke."

"Ah...hello, Christine. You look...you look—"

"I know, I look pretty good for someone who should have died. I would have, but Joe kept digging through the bricks and timbers until he found me."

"But I found your necklace on the ground. It was covered with blood, and I saw a girl with your hair color lying dead under the tarp."

"My necklace broke off during the fall," Christine said. "You probably saw poor Loralei. She has...uh, had the same hair color as me."

Mrs. Duke's breath started coming in great heaving gasps.

"Oh... I... I have made a terrible mistake."

"What is it?" Christine asked. "What's wrong?"

"I thought you were dead. I took your necklace to Johnny. I told him you had died."

Christine stared in disbelief. "He will do something terrible," she said. "He has a fearsome temper. I have to get to him."

She started to get out of bed, screamed in pain, and sank back on the thin mattress. She looked at Mrs. Duke with desperation. "Do you know where they are?"

Mrs. Duke leaned close. "They are going to Lawrence. They're gonna burn it to the ground."

§§

Johnny normally rode in Captain Jarrette's unit with Cole Younger, Bill, and Charlie, but for this raid Johnny reminded Quantrill of their deal in Arkansas and requested permission to lead his own band consisting of himself, Bill, and Charlie. Quantrill agreed but issued a caveat.

"You know you might have to wrestle Anderson to see who gets to kill Hawk."

The raid began on August 19, 1863. They headed west from the Blackwater River. The next day they picked up over a hundred soldiers from the regular Confederate army near the Grand River. Another fifty men, mainly farmers with scores to settle, joined them along the way. Altogether, they were four hundred fifty men strong when they crossed the Kansas border about ten miles south of the town of Little Santa Fe.

Johnny, Bill, and Charlie rode in silence. Bill and Charlie had lived through the same saga. Hawk had ruined their lives, too. None of them were the way they used to be. They all had a hard edge to them. Like Johnny, they had lost their brother, their home, their hometown, and their father's blessing. They were truly rebels now and they were on their own.

Bill and Charlie had seen Johnny angry before, but they had never seen his rage last this long. His eyes remained slits; he never smiled. They knew what he was thinking about: vengeance on Hawk. They wanted it, too. They needed it, somehow, to make the killings make sense.

Quantrill had received scouting reports revealing the troop locations of the federal patrols along the Kansas-Missouri border. Anticipating guerrilla raids, General Ewing had scattered patrols everywhere. They were spread out fifteen miles apart. Armed with this vital intelligence, Quantrill maneuvered his way past the pickets almost without detection.

Only one of these federal patrols, near Aubrey, Kansas, ever saw the raiders. Captain Pike and a command of about a hundred men spotted Quantrill's force and sent a warning telegraph to Ewing's headquarters in Kansas City. Ewing was out of the office in Leavenworth, however, and did not receive the message in time. Lawrence was not warned.

Quantrill did not know how many fighting men they might face in Lawrence. One newspaper reported as many as 1,200 troops there. He received another estimate of 500. He and his men might be sorely outnumbered.

Quantrill knew that surprise was critical, so he favored a dawn attack. They arrived around forty-five minutes after sunrise. On Mount Oread, a small hill overlooking Lawrence, Quantrill turned to his men and spoke.

"Men, this is the home of Hawk and the Red Legs. You might remember how they have burned your homes and hunted you like dogs, offering you no quarter. No quarter will be given them today. Do not touch a girl or woman, but kill every man you see, and every boy big enough to hold a rifle."

Some men in the rear were grumbling. Someone said it would be sure suicide to attack and that he was thinking about going back to Missouri.

"Do as you please, men," Quantrill said. "As for me, I'm going to ride into Lawrence. When we're finished, there will be nothing left."

§§

The men following Quantrill into Lawrence unleashed a blood-curdling Rebel yell and galloped forward. To their amazement, they had achieved complete surprise. No one was ready for the attack. The town had not been warned. Nor was it adequately protected. Only a few squads of soldiers were stationed there. They lived in small camps on the outskirts of town.

Quantrill's men galloped to the tents. They shot every soldier they saw. A few of the Yankees made a run for the river, but they were killed before they reached the other side.

Two of Quantrill's finest had scouted the town several weeks before the raid and provided valuable reconnaissance. From this information a "death list" had been compiled. It targeted those most wanted for execution. Tops on Johnny's list was Julius Hawk.

The scouts had prepared a map, one Johnny studied until he had it memorized. He leaned over Midnight's neck. His only thoughts were of Gene swinging from a tree and Christine's broken body. A half dozen Union soldiers fell to his guns.

Hawk had built a new house and furnished it with items pilfered from homes in Missouri before they were burned. Three pianos graced his parlor, spoils from one of his infamous Jayhawker raids. At his order, his men had set an entire town to the torch. Only three buildings survived the conflagration.

Johnny, Bill, and Charlie rode up to the house with lighted torches in their hands. They beat on the door, but no one answered. Johnny smashed in the door with his boot. He found Mrs. Hawk sobbing in the back bedroom.

"Where is that husband of yours?"

"He heard Quantrill was coming and left. It's just me."

"I don't believe you, ma'am," Johnny said. "Who else do you have in this house? Who are you hiding?"

He stood upright and screamed into the echoing house.

"Hawk, you hanged my brother, burned my hometown, you destroyed my family's farm, you kidnapped my father, you captured and murdered my fiancée! Come out and take your medicine!"

The woman quit crying and cocked her head to one side. "Young man," she said, "he is gone. He left in his nightshirt."

Johnny, Bill, and Charlie pushed in every door in the house. They combed the barn. They found no one. Johnny was on his way out of the cellar when he sensed movement to his left. Three children were quaking in the crawl space: a teenage boy, a teenage girl, and a younger lad.

He herded them up the stairs.

"Look what I found," Johnny said. "How old are you?" Johnny asked the older boy.

"Seventeen."

"What's your name?"

"Julius Hawk, Jr., sir."

"Where's your Pa?"

"He left, sir. He told me to come with him, but I didn't make it out in time."

"No, you didn't. Well, I'll tell you what. Your no-good Pa murdered my fiancée and my brother, and that blood's got to be paid for, you understand me?"

"Yes, sir."

"Take me to your Pa."

"I don't know where he went."

"Well then, show me where you last saw him."

Johnny addressed Mrs. Hawk.

"Ma'am, you and your two younger ones must leave the house. We're about to burn it down."

The woman, suddenly calm and stately, ushered her children into the yard. The oldest child led Johnny to the edge of a cornfield behind the house.

"He heard someone yell Quantrill was coming, and he ran in there. He told me to come too, but I was worried about my brother and sister and Mama. I didn't want to leave them behind."

Johnny yelled into the corn. "You hear that, Hawk? Your boy has more courage than you. You kill innocent girls; he protects them. He's more of a man than you'll ever be."

He looked at Bill and Charlie.

"Fetch a rope."

When they came back, they gave the rope to Johnny. Johnny fashioned a noose and tossed it over the limb of a large oak. Johnny told Bill and Charlie to put the boy on Bill's horse and the rope around his neck, but to keep the noose loose. He had no intention of hanging young Hawk. He was merely going to use him as bait to lure the senior Hawk from his hiding place. Johnny waited and waited, but Hawk, Sr. refused to show himself. Johnny decided to try a different tactic. He called out into the field.

"Look familiar, Colonel?" No answer from the corn. "This is Johnny Collins speaking. Do you remember how you hanged my brother back in Alabama? Do you remember what you did to my family, how you burned us out? Unless you come out right now, your son is going to hang for the sins of his father. And we'll burn your house and barns to the ground."

The dam of Mrs. Hawk's resolve ruptured. "You cannot do this," she said between sobs. "He's just a boy!"

The girl, about fourteen Johnny guessed, stood next to him. Her lips trembled, but she refused to cry.

"Ain't you got no heart, mister?"

"My heart was broken by your father," Johnny said.

Mrs. Hawk slapped him full in the face – twice. Johnny stood, expressionless. The boy kept screaming for his father.

"Pa – help! Pa – save me! They're gonna hang me! Pa!" No answer from the cornfield.

Mrs. Hawk fell prostrate to the ground, begging and pleading for the life of her son. The scene reminded Johnny of how his mother had begged Hawk for mercy. Johnny was cut to the heart. He had intended to hang Colonel Hawk, not his son, and he realized he was about to recreate the heinous act the colonel had committed, the one that caused so much pain to so many.

Johnny stared into the cornfield.

"That's your son, Hawk! Do you love him enough to fight for him, or are you a yellow coward?"

The noose had been left loose. The boy flipped his head around and freed his neck. Bill and Charlie put his head back in the noose and cinched it up a bit tighter this time.

"One last chance, Hawk. We'll duel. Better man walks away, and the score will be settled. If you kill me, my men won't harm you."

The boy on the horse got control of his panic. Tears still stained his face, but the sobbing and shouting had ceased. His lips were moving as if in prayer. Then a look of serenity spread over his face, and he fixed his eyes on Johnny with a triumphant, challenging glare, which Johnny would remember the rest of his days.

Mrs. Hawk erupted. "Julius, be a man. Come out here and save our boy!"

Then the boy spoke in an even, serene voice.

"I don't deserve this, mister," he said. "I've never killed anyone. I'm not guilty of my father's sins, whatever they are. If you kill me, it won't be justice. It will be murder."

The boy was right, and Johnny knew it. When he looked at him, Johnny saw Gene.

"Bill, Charlie, cut him down, I can't do this," Johnny said.

With relief on their faces, Bill and Charlie drew their knives and reached for the rope. They were about to cut the boy loose and take him off the horse when Quantrill appeared.

"We don't have time for this, boys," Quantrill said. "We've got to get back to Missouri. They'll be coming after us soon enough."

Quantrill turned his horse, rode past the animal under the oak, and raked his spurs across its flank. The startled horse bolted. Johnny winced when he heard the neck snap.

"No!"

Johnny ran to the tree and severed the rope with his knife – too late. The boy was dead. Johnny fell to his knees and buried his face in his hands. He could not hold back the tears. He barely felt Mrs. Hawk and her daughter pummeling him with repeated blows to his back. He was completely broken. The younger boy said something under his breath as he glared at Johnny, Bill, and Charlie. After a few minutes, Johnny staggered to his feet. Frightened, Mrs. Hawk and her daughter withdrew. Johnny turned to face them.

"I came here for vengeance," he said, "not to kill the innocent. I beg your forgiveness, though I will never forgive myself. Your son – your brother – now rests with the angels, just like my brother. And now, like your husband and father – I bear the mark of Cain."

§§

From his hiding place in the corn rows, Hawk swore an oath of vengeance. He would kill Johnny Collins and the three other men responsible for his boy's death. Still, he made no move as Johnny approached the house with a torch.

Johnny looked at Mrs. Hawk. "You have ten minutes to save what you want. Bill and Charlie will remove what you want to keep. Then I'm going to burn this place to the ground."

One of the items removed was a bureau and chest of drawers. Johnny rifled through its contents. He pulled out a black shirt and pants, the uniform Hawk had worn in Paint Rock. He also took Hawk's infamous black flag.

"You might turn your heads," Johnny said, "what with you being ladies and all." He stripped and put on the black outfit. He cut off a portion of the flag and fashioned a bandanna, which he pulled over his nose.

When Mrs. Hawk faced him, she flinched.

"Mrs. Hawk, do you have everything out of the house that you want?"

"Haven't you taken enough?" she asked.

"Not hardly. The score's not quite settled," he said. "Okay, boys. Light it up!"

Bill and Charlie tossed their torches into the house. Before long, smoke billowed from almost every window. Hawk watched seven years of hard work go up in smoke.

"Now the barn!" Johnny said. The flames spread quickly, torturing Mrs. Hawk, and taunting her cowering husband, who watched in silence.

Johnny mounted Midnight and rode to the edge of the cornfield. "Hawk, today I have exacted my revenge. A home for a home – a barn for a barn – a boy for a boy – an eye for an eye! We are even. I am through with you and your kin. I am through with this war."

§§

Hawk smelled the death streaming from his blazing house and barn. His hands trembled with rage. Collins had called him a sinner and a coward, but Hawk knew he would do everything exactly the same if given the opportunity. He wasn't about to apologize for living his life the right way and fighting for his beliefs. He was not a coward. He simply knew his country needed him to keep living. It would not win the war without him. His

269

self-preservation assured the survival of the Union.

He knew his beliefs and code separated him from lesser men. How dare the kid question his values? He was an American hero.

He repeated his self-delusion over and over, but his eyes could not leave his son's lifeless body.

I will kill those men, he thought. *Quantrill...the ones called Charlie and Bill. And I will make Johnny Collins suffer before he dies.* If it was the last thing he ever did, he would kill those four men. He knew their faces. He knew Johnny's name. The other two he had called Bill and Charlie. The one who kicked the horse was Quantrill himself.

The secret of his cowardice died with his son. Hawk would manufacture a credible story. He was fighting the invaders on the other side of Lawrence when the brigands attacked his home and killed his son. No one would believe the bushwhackers.

He was still fashioning the false narrative in his mind when a foot smashed against his cheek and drove him to the ground. He rose up, knife in hand.

Mrs. Hawk's laugh was caustic and mirthless.

"Now you want to fight? I have always known you had faults, but I never figured you for a coward. Julius Hawk, fearless leader of the Reg Legs – the man who hid in the cornfield and watched his son die."

"Shut up, woman!" Hawk leveled his wife with a

slap across the mouth. "The Bible requires a wife to be submissive to her husband."

His wife let the blood flow from the side of her mouth. "It also commands a man to love his wife as Christ loves the church. That means you would sacrifice your life for mine if need be. Well, now I know you won't do that – you didn't try to save our son."

He hit her again, this time with a closed fist.

"I told you to shut up!"

"The house is gone," she said. "And so are we. The children and I are going to my mother's in Ohio."

She walked on unsteady legs out of the field. She stuffed a few things in a carpetbag and headed towards the burning streets of Lawrence, with her arms around her stunned children.

Hawk crept from the field and sat down by his son's lifeless body. He cradled the oddly angled head in his lap and stroked the hair. In the morning he would bury his boy. Then he would begin his quest — to kill Johnny Collins and the others.

§§

Johnny, Bill, and Charlie reached the top of Mount Oread and looked back toward Lawrence. Billowing smoke cut irregular columns through the August sky.

"Boys, I'll get you back to Missouri," Johnny said. "I'll do that much. Then I'm heading west and getting out of this war."

Bill shook his head. "Wherever you're going, that's where we'll be," he said.

Charlie nodded in agreement.

"Well, why don't we just go right now, then?" Johnny said. "Quantrill's heading southeast and they're all following him. Let's head west somewhere, maybe California, who knows, who cares. Let's just get out of here."

"Amen, brother," Bill said.

"Let's go," Charlie said.

"One thing, boys," Johnny said.

"What's that?"

"You are never to call me by my given name again. I am no longer worthy to be called a Collins. I'm not worthy of a name. From now on, I wear a label. From now on, you will call me 'The Badman.'"

§§

Johnny flashed back to the burning streets of Lawrence – women holding their dead husbands, the little boys and girls crying for the fathers that would never return. A grieving mother staring at her dead son. And the face of young Hawk as he died.

He tightened the black bandanna around his face and rode on. In his former life, he had been Johnny Collins, a young man with the highest and noblest of ideals – a boy with every intention of seeking and saving the lost, someone who would grow up to be a man of God like his father. Baptized not with water but with the fires of war, immersed in the blood of his many victims, Johnny was now a man riding a black horse on the road to perdition, a grim reaper who carried death in his right hand. He had died to the life for which he had been intended and been born again as The Badman. He was ashamed of who he'd become. There was blood on his hands, and Johnny didn't see how it could ever come off. His soul had been stamped with the dark brand of cruelty and singed by the sin of murder.

He knew he could never face his parents again, especially not his mother. It saddened him to think of their growing old and dying without his saying goodbye. But it grieved him far more to think of their seeing the monster he'd become. He resolved to have someone send a letter to them, a missive saying he and his friends had died on the way back from Lawrence. Though not true in a physical sense, the message would be spiritually correct. And his parents would be spared the pain of discovering their son's fall from grace.

The friends rode west. They made camp on the eastern edge of Colorado Territory. They were glad to be out of Bleeding Kansas. In the morning, Johnny would begin his quest for a new life, one without war, without violence. He was just eighteen years old, but he felt like he'd survived two lifetimes.

And so it was that a new persona was conceived by

Colonel Julius Hawk on May 2, 1862, in Paint Rock, Alabama, and delivered to the world by Captain William Quantrill on August 21, 1863, in Lawrence, Kansas. While Hawk was the father, having planted the seeds of hatred and violence, Quantrill had cultivated the lad and taught him how to kill, and kill, and kill again, until death had become his specialty and violence his second nature. Together, Hawk and Quantrill, and the hard brand of war they espoused, had brought forth the fastest shootist the Civil War had ever produced –and the deadliest the Wild West would ever know.

The Badman.

Book II: The Death Of The Badman

The trembling journalist handed the letter to The Badman who read it aloud to Bill and Charlie:

Mr. & Mrs. Miles Collins
Mr. & Mrs. Jake Thompson
Cross Hollows Plantation, Arkansas

Dear Collins and Thompson Families:

It is with deep sympathy and profound regret that I write to inform you that your sons, Johnny Collins, Bill Thompson, and Charlie Thompson, were killed on August 21, 1863, by Federal soldiers in a skirmish following our greatest victory at Lawrence. They served their country honorably and died bravely. Knowing they were sorely outnumbered, without hope of success, they boldly led a counter-charge. They killed forty of the enemy before finally succumbing to superior numbers.

Their selfless heroism saved the lives of many of their fellow soldiers, as their spirited maneuver bought our men valuable time for a successful retreat. I regret to say that your sons' bodies were left to the enemies' disposal, and we will likely never locate their unmarked graves. They were probably thrown in a trench pit somewhere near the Kansas-Missouri border. While we mourn their untimely deaths, we shall never forget their lives. They were and shall remain Southern heroes, fighting and dying for a glorious cause.

Please give my regards to Lady Victoria and my condolences to the Nelsons on the tragic loss of their beautiful daughter, Christine. Like Johnny, she, too, died for the cause, an innocent victim of the cruel fiend Hawk, whose villainous deeds are too lengthy to recount here. One day he will pay for his crimes against humanity.

Unfortunately, he hid in a cornfield while your sons burned his house. Johnny and the boys had placed Hawk's son on a horse and put his head in a noose with no intention of hanging him, but solely to lure Hawk out of hiding. Instead, the heartless coward hid in the cornfield behind his house, refusing to fight for his son. The horse was kicked by another soldier, against your sons' wishes, and when the horse galloped off young

Hawk's neck snapped, a regrettable end to his life. Should anyone report that Johnny, Bill, and Charlie murdered young Hawk, consider that a lie. Young Hawk's death was an unfortunate and unwanted accident. If Hawk had been man enough to face his enemies, he could have saved his son. Not long before they were killed, I overheard Johnny and his friends tell Cole Younger they regretted the boy's death.

Mr. Collins, Johnny rode up to me before he led the charge. He knew he would likely perish, and urged me to write this letter to you, and to give you these his last words. "Pa, I love you. You are not to feel guilty or responsible for our last conversation, or the loss of your sons. You have been and will always be a great father."

To his Mama he told me to write the following: "Mama, I love you. I will see you on the other side, where we can sing gospel songs together."

I encourage all of you to be proud of your sons. They were and shall remain true to the cause. They were and shall remain Southern heroes.

Your humble servant,
Captain William Clarke Quantrill

"That looks really good, mister," Johnny said. He still had his pistol pointed at the journalist's head. "You did a real nice job."

Johnny walked over to Bill and Charlie.

"I say kill him," Bill said. "He knows who we are, because of the contents of the letter."

"We've done enough killing, Bill," Charlie said. "I'll never forget young Hawk's face. I've been dreaming about it."

"My head agrees with you, Bill, but my heart agrees with Charlie. Maybe there's another way. We cut him in for a share on some of our exploits. Make him one of us. In exchange, he writes up stuff in his newspaper to throw people off our trail. You know, false descriptions. Maybe he even makes things up, makes us look like Robin Hood or something."

"Yeah, Badman," Charlie said. "You'll be Robin Hood, I'll be Friar Tuck, and Bill can be Little John. Hawk will be the evil sheriff if he ever comes looking for us."

"I still think we ought to shoot him," Bill said. "But I'll go along with it."

Johnny walked over to the frightened writer.

"We've been talking things over, specifically whether to kill you or not. We thought long and hard about killing you, and we still will, if you don't do exactly what we say."

278

"Anything, mister, anything," the writer said.

"You are now part of our gang. We'll cut you in on some jobs now and then, but most importantly we're going to let you keep living. In exchange, you will be our writer. After a robbery, you'll write us up, make us heroes and legends, say we rob from the rich and give to the poor. Stuff like that. You'll also arrange for someone trustworthy to deliver this letter. Deal?"

"It's a deal," the journalist said. "My name's Rogers, by the way, Tom Rogers. I take it you're Johnny, Bill, and Charlie, right?"

"Wrong," Johnny said. "They were friends of ours who died in the war. We've left the fighting, but we told them we would do this for them, seeing as they saved our skins once. And by the way, Rogers, never ask another personal question, or it will be your last."

"Yes sir," Rogers said.

"Now tell me who we can trust to send this letter for us."

"Archibald Rasmussen. He's a scrapping young lad about twenty-five, handy with a gun, Indian fighter, not partial to either side of the War. Pretty savvy. Won't ask any questions as long as you pay him."

"Sounds like my kind of guy," Bill said.

"Rogers?" Johnny asked.

"Yes, sir?"

"That letter better get there. I'll have a way of

knowing if it doesn't."

"Yes, sir. How will I know when you'll be in town, sir?"

"You won't," Johnny said. "Don't worry. I know where to find you. One of us will keep an eye on you."

He stepped towards the door, then tossed the quivering man a twenty-dollar gold piece.

"Here's the first payment."

Thanksgiving 1863, Cross Hollows Plantation

Miles, Diana, Jake, Naomi, Joseph Nelson, Isaiah, and Isaiah's wife Ruth sat down at the great table to enjoy Thanksgiving together. Victoria was not there. She had left with Mrs. Nelson to Kansas City to take care of Christine who had sent a letter regarding the prison collapse, her injuries, and her survival. Even though Miles and Jake had offered to help, Joseph stayed behind to tend to his farm and livestock. Miles and Diana planned to join Victoria, Mrs. Nelson, and Christine in Kansas City for Christmas.

Miles had just finished the blessing when they heard a loud knock on the front door. Miles and Jake went to the door, concerned it might be Federal soldiers.

Miles opened the door to find a young man.

"I'm here to deliver a letter to Miles Collins and Jake Thompson," he said.

"I'm Miles Collins. Who's the letter from?"

"Captain William Clarke Quantrill."

Miles' heart sank as did Jake's.

"Come on in, son," Miles said. He ushered the young man into the dining room. "You can join us for Thanksgiving. I never caught your name?"

"Archibald Rasmussen," he said. Miles introduced him to the others.

"Mr. Rasmussen has come to deliver a letter from Quantrill."

"Quantrill?" Diana and Naomi blanched at the same time.

"Read it, Miles," Diana said.

Rasmussen sat down. He was unaware of the letter's contents, but he knew he was hungry. The meal looked delicious.

With shaking hands, Miles broke the seal.

Miles began to read aloud. He was soon interrupted by the baleful wails of Diana and Naomi. Jake remained quiet in the crushing awareness he was now childless.

Miles had finally had enough. Surprisingly, the man he blamed most was not Hawk but Quantrill. Miles was blessed with the gift of discernment. He had seen through Quantrill's façade and recognized the vainglory driving his behavior.

But something bothered him about this letter. It would have been out of character for Johnny to give any last words before charging. His son would have rushed to the sound of the guns. Miles had witnessed that in Arkansas when Johnny impulsively rode to Christine's rescue.

And Quantrill didn't seem like the type who would take the time to listen to Johnny's last words closely enough to write them later, especially not in the middle of a retreat.

Another thing seemed odd. Parts of the letter referred to Johnny and his cousins in the present tense: "They *are* brave young men." If Johnny and the boys had died, how could they "remain" heroes, how could they "remain" true to the cause?

The description of young Hawk's death was odd as well. Quantrill had gone out of his way to emphasize its accidental nature, as if to defend Johnny, Bill, and Charlie (who were reported to be dead) against charges of murder. Why would a man who had ordered the execution of that many in Lawrence be so concerned about the death of one teenaged boy, especially Hawk's son, the son of the man who had supposedly murdered Quantrill's brother? No, Quantrill would have laid his cloak to the execution instead. He would have cheered the boys on to new depths of violence.

The more Miles contemplated the letter and its

contents, the more certain he was that the words were not Quantrill's. Instead, the letter was written by someone with a conscience, someone who knew a lot of personal information about the Collins family. The author thought Christine was beautiful, assumed she was dead, and knew Diana loved to sing gospel songs.

Miles knew who wrote the letter – Johnny. It was not in his hand, but there were too many clues. It was as though he wanted them to know he was still alive – only lost.

A man who had lost his way, who was now so overcome with grief, anger, and guilt that he could never come home again. He felt ashamed and unworthy. And the many words devoted to young Hawk's death served only to underscore his guilt feelings. But if Johnny were lost, Miles felt sure he could still be found – and restored.

§§

"Jake, I'd like to meet with you in the parlor a moment," Miles said.

They sat opposite one another.

"Jake, Quantrill didn't write that letter, Johnny did."

"Interesting," Jake said. "I was thinking the same thing. But why?"

"I think the boys feel they're too far from home to come back again. Quantrill turned them mean."

"So, what do we do? What do we tell the ladies?"

"Let's tell them what we believe," Miles said.

"But all we've got is our gut. We don't have any proof."

"Then maybe we ought to find Quantrill and confront him with this letter," Miles said.

Jake shook his head hard. "Miles, I'm not sure that's such a great idea. I see that look in your eyes. Saw it in the war right before we climbed the walls of that fort and killed twenty Mexican soldiers. I know you're tough, but I'm not sure you're a match for Quantrill at your age. We ain't young and strong like we used to be."

"Maybe not. But I can still shoot a rifle, and you ain't bad with that Colt of yours. Besides, you'll be there to keep me in line if I get a bit angry and out of sorts. And if there's one person who might get me that way it's Quantrill," Miles said.

"All right," Jake said. "But you might have to keep a tight rein on me, too. I didn't care too much for that jackleg, either."

They walked back to the dining room. Diana was missing.

"She fainted, Miles," Isaiah said. "She's up in her room."

"Thanks, Isaiah."

Miles walked into their room and found Diana sobbing.

"Diana," he said, "Jake and I don't think the boys

are dead."

Miles explained his reasons.

Diana looked skeptical, but she wanted to believe. "Then, what can we do? Who knows where he is?"

"It won't be easy, but we know three men who were at Lawrence with Johnny: Bill, Charlie, and Quantrill. Bill and Charlie are probably still with Johnny. Quantrill's not with them, but he might know where they went."

"So, you're going to find Quantrill?"

"Yes."

"And you're going to get yourself killed, Miles Collins. Those men are monsters. I read the papers. I read about what they did in Law—"

Diana stopped. When she realized what she had just said, the tears began again.

"I just called our son a monster."

"And he might have been that day, Diana," Miles said. "I've seen what war does to people. But we don't know the circumstances. I think Johnny went into Lawrence thinking Christine had been murdered. Such a thought could change any man."

"When will you leave?"

"Tomorrow morning," Miles said. "But first I'm going to cross-examine our young mail man. Someone gave him that letter. I want to know where...when...and who."

§§

Miles and Diana walked downstairs. They found everyone at the table - waiting.

Miles prayed. "Dig in, folks," he said.

"I'm sorry to be the bearer of such horrible news," Rasmussen said.

"That's all right, son, but I'd like to ask you some questions about that letter after the meal," Miles said.

"Sure," Rasmussen said. He sounded confident but inside he was squirming. Rogers had told him not to read the letter and not to say who had paid for its delivery. Rasmussen had a bad feeling about what would happen if he said too much. He had been warned not to reveal the letter's point of origin, as doing so would place his life in grave danger. But future danger was miles away; two sets of bereaved parents were right across the table. What would he do?

After the meal they adjourned to the parlor.

"Son, I'd like to ask you a few questions about that letter," Miles said.

"I'll do my best to answer," Rasmussen said.

"Who hired you to deliver it?"

"I can't say."

"Where were you when you were hired to deliver this letter? Where was it sent from?"

"I can't tell you that, either."

"You can't or you won't?" Jake asked. His face

smiled; his voice growled.

"I was told not to disclose any of that information. If I did, my life would be in grave danger."

"Your life might be in grave danger if you don't," Jake said.

Rasmussen began to maneuver. "Mr. Thompson, I know you're upset by the loss of your sons. But I gave my word, and I don't break it for anyone."

"Not even a mother who has lost all three of her sons?" Naomi asked, just before sobbing.

Miles gave Jake a warning look, meant to rein him in. He then turned to Rasmussen. "Mr. Rasmussen, we have reason to believe that our boys are still alive. In fact, I think my son Johnny wrote the letter. Johnny likely hired someone to hire you to deliver it. He wants everything secret because he doesn't want to be found."

"Why should I violate my client's wishes?" Rasmussen asked.

"Because my son's soul is at stake. He's lost – not in a physical sense, but spiritually. I need to find him before it's everlastingly too late. It's Hell without Jesus, son. I haven't told you this, but I'm a preacher, and I was about to baptize Johnny when a wicked Union colonel named Hawk stopped the ceremony to hang two young Southern boys. One was my other son Gene. The other was Jake's son Luke. Since that day Johnny's heart has grown dark and mean. It's gotten worse because he thinks the Yankees killed his fiancée. But she didn't really die. I think if I could tell him that and visit with him about grace and redemption, I could bring him back. Restore his soul."

Rasmussen tried to wipe a tear from his eye without notice. Everyone saw it. His resistance was slipping. He was facing a kindhearted preacher and a mother who had lost three sons.

Rasmussen cleared his throat. "I'll tell you this much, Mr. Collins. The guy who hired me said there were three young men who gave him the letter. He said one of them did all the talking. Said the fella had scary eyes."

"Where did the letter come from? Where'd you get it?" asked Miles.

Rasmussen paused. He thought about his parents and siblings back home. What might happen to them if he told? Right now, he hadn't said anything that would lead the outlaws to his family's doorstep.

"Who gave it to you?" Jake asked.

"I can't say, Mr. Thompson. I just can't. If I tell you, someone might hurt *my* family."

"You're gonna be hurt if you don't tell us what we need to know," Jake said. He reached for his pistol.

Rasmussen's gun was out, cocked, and aimed before Jake cleared leather.

"Don't, Mr. Thompson. I'm pretty good with this

pistol. As good as I am, though, at least one of those men might be faster and better. From what I read about Lawrence, I can't afford to have them angry with me or my family. I heard Mr. Collins read the letter. I heard about how that boy died, how his neck was broken. I don't want anything to happen to my family. I got nothing against any of you – and I hope you find peace, but I'm going to leave now, and it would be best if no one followed me."

"Thanks, son," Miles said. He had crossed the room and was standing in front of Jake. "You've given us some hope."

Rasmussen holstered his gun and nodded to Diana. "Sorry for the gunplay, ma'am," he said. "Bad form. I guess I'm a little jumpy."

Diana waved the bad manners away. Rasmussen addressed the room.

"Good luck to all of you. I like you people. If you find your boys, please don't ever let them know I said anything."

"Your secret's safe with us," Miles said. "Thanks again."

Rasmussen walked out, mounted, and rode away. He could not get out of Arkansas fast enough.

Jake moved towards the door. "Let's go, Miles!" he said. "We can still follow him."

"No," Miles said. "I think he's done all for us that he

can. We'd be better off finding Quantrill."

"Well, you do that," Bill said. "I'm going to follow that kid. I think he knows where our boys are."

"Okay, Jake, I'll go with you, but if we lose his trail or he loses us, we'll find Quantrill instead. Agreed?"

"Agreed," Jake said.

§§

Miles and Jake packed several months' worth of supplies.

Miles turned to Diana. "I love you, darling. It could take a while to find them. The boys rode with Quantrill, you know, and the Yankees ain't found him yet. They've been trained how to disappear."

"Do whatever it takes," Diana said. "Just bring them back home."

Jake and Miles kissed their wives goodbye. They saddled up and rode west. They followed Rasmussen's tracks and hoped he would lead them to their lost boys.

§§

After several months of rest and recuperation, Christine felt ready to walk. Christmas was only four days away. She'd been hurt but was lucky when compared to the ones who had perished. She had landed on her left side and broken her left arm, collarbone, and tibia. At Victoria's insistence, Doc Simpson had traveled to Kansas City to tend to Christine. He treated her daily, followed her progress, and made sure she obeyed his orders. She was making a remarkable recovery.

"Doc, I'm ready to walk," she said one day.

"Let me take a look at you," Doc said.

He lifted the arm, then the leg, to test her range of motion. No limitations. She seemed as limber as the teenager she was.

Oh, to be that young and healthy again, he thought.

"Christine, I pronounce you healed."

"Did you hear that, Christine?" Victoria said. "You're healed. Now we can start planning that wedding. Didn't Johnny tell you he'd be coming back home after Lawrence?"

Christine's face brightened.

"Yes, he did. I wonder where he is. It's been months now."

"Probably biding his time and waiting for the right chance to leave," Victoria said.

"Yes, but I'm worried," Christine said. "On the night the building collapsed, someone told the guerrillas the Yankees murdered me. Johnny might think I'm dead and never return."

"Nonsense," Victoria said. "Don't you think he'd look for you?"

"Well, the person who told Johnny saw a dead body and thought it was mine. She told him I had been killed."

Christine related her conversation with Mrs. Duke at

the hospital, how Mrs. Duke had told Johnny that Christine had been murdered, and how Mrs. Duke had given Johnny the blood-soaked necklace. Victoria's face betrayed deep concern.

"Christine, do you know where the guerrillas might be? Surely someone knows their hideouts. Why don't we find out firsthand? Maybe we could find Cole or Quantrill. They should know where Johnny is."

"The Missouri brush ain't no place for two ladies."

The familiar voice from the doorway was tinctured with melancholy.

"Daddy!"

Christine ran into Joseph's arms.

"Easy there, missy," Doc said. "Maybe we oughtn't to run before we walk."

Christine covered her father's face with kisses.

"Daddy, who's taking care of our place?"

"Isaiah from up at Victoria's. He said he'd watch after things while I came up here." Suspicion creased Christine's brow.

"You never leave the farm. What's going on?"

"There's some news about Johnny, and I thought I should be the one to tell you."

"What?"

"His folks got a letter from Quantrill, and before I say anything more, you need to know that Miles doesn't believe it," Joseph said.

"Go on."

"The letter said Johnny, Bill, and Charlie were killed coming back from Lawrence. Again, Miles thinks Johnny wrote it, and that Johnny, Bill, and Charlie are still alive."

Christine, Victoria, and Mrs. Nelson began crying after the word "killed" and didn't hear anything else. After the wailing subsided, Mr. Nelson tried again.

"You didn't hear me," he said. "I told you Miles doesn't think the letter is true. Neither do Diana or Jake or Naomi. And neither do I. We all think Johnny, Bill, and Charlie are still alive. We also think Johnny wrote that letter, not Quantrill."

"But why?" Christine asked. "Why would he do such a thing?"

"Probably because he doesn't want to be found," Joseph said.

"Where could he be?" Victoria asked.

"Nobody knows," Nelson said. "He's either still with Quantrill or he has left the war. Miles and Jake have followed the man who delivered the letter. He wouldn't say where it came from, but he did say that three young men matching the boys' description paid for its delivery."

Christine looked up at her father and searched his eyes to gauge his true feelings.

"What do you think, Daddy?"

"Johnny's still alive, but he's not the same boy we knew. He's dangerous. I read about the Lawrence Massacre. If he had a hand in that, I don't want him anywhere near my daughter. I don't want to see you get your heart broken. Johnny's on a dark path. Anyone walking it with him could wind up hurt or killed. I don't want that way of life for my little princess. I've come to take you back to the farm."

"No, Daddy! No!" Joseph jumped back a little. In all her life, Christine had never yelled at him. "I love Johnny, and I'll never love anyone else. I can't go home knowing I didn't try to find him."

"You will come home with us. You don't have a choice."

Christine turned to her mother, who had been sitting quietly in a chair.

"Mama, talk to Daddy for me, please."

Mrs. Nelson shook her head. She agreed with her husband. Johnny had become a violent man. Christine would be happier and safer with a man of peace, whether she realized that now or not.

"No, dear, your Daddy's right. We need to go home. We'll leave tomorrow. There will be other boys, and life will go on, better than it was before."

Christine would not listen. "Leave me alone! I love Johnny and you'll never take him away – at least not from my heart. I will die an old maid before I marry someone I don't love."

Mrs. Nelson and Victoria tried to console her, but Christine pushed them away.

"Why don't you get some rest, dear?" Ayoka said. "We'll be leaving bright and early in the morning."

"Your mother is going with me tonight," Joseph said. "I've got a room at the hotel."

"I'll see you in the morning," Christine said. She was suddenly very calm. She hugged her parents.

"Goodbye, Mama, Daddy," she said. "I mean, good night."

§§

Following Rasmussen was a bad idea, but Miles had gone along with Jake until it became obvious they were on a wild goose chase. They went from Cross Hollows to Fort Smith, then on to Houston and finally Galveston. They arrived in time to see Rasmussen waving at them from the deck of a ship sailing out to sea.

"I guess that's that," Miles said.

"We could find a boat and follow him," Jake said. At least he laughed.

"No thanks. I doubt we'll ever see that boy again."

"Never is a long time," Jake said.

"Well, I wish we could say the same about Quantrill, but right now he's the only man we know who might know where our boys are."

"I agree, but do you think he'll talk to us or shoot

us?"

"That depends."

"On what?"

"On whether he's still friendly with Johnny."

"Where do you think Quantrill is right now?" Jake asked.

"Who knows? It's wintertime, so he won't be campaigning. Last winter, he went to Arkansas, then to Texas. I remember we got that one letter from the boys, mailed about this time of year, from somewhere in Texas. What was the name of that town they mailed it from? It's on the tip of my tongue."

"Hold on a minute, and I'll tell you," Jake said.

He dug through his saddlebag and withdrew the worn letter. "Looks like it came from the Confederate Military Headquarters, Western District in Bonham."

"Off to Bonham, then," Miles said.

§§

Around ten o'clock, after everyone had left her room, Christine packed her possessions into two large trunks. She loved Johnny more than anyone in the world, and she was determined to find him if it took her the remainder of her days. She opened the window and eased out. Once outside, she reached back and pulled out her trunks. She had almost retrieved the second one when the door to her room burst open. Victoria and Doc. Why were they there? Christine looked for an escape route.

"Christine, it's all right," Victoria said. "See, I'm coming with you!"

She slid two trunks through the door.

"We'll find him together. Your parents are asleep in the hotel. Wait for us. We'll bring the carriage around."

"Victoria, thank you. I love you," Christine said.

"I couldn't bear to see your heart broken, dear. We'll be right there."

Doc and Victoria walked outside. Doc brought the carriage to the door and loaded it. Doc stepped down from the carriage and handed the reins to Victoria.

"Well, ladies, I hope Mr. Nelson never finds out about this," he said. "Good luck. Where will you go?"

"Wherever Johnny is, that's where we'll go," Christine said.

"Well, how will you find him?" Doc asked.

"I'm sure we'll find a way," Victoria said. "Never underestimate the power of female intuition. Or Victoria Collins. I'm pretty good at getting what I want."

Victoria stepped up to the carriage and grabbed the reins.

"It's been a long time since I've had to drive my own carriage, but I've always been good with horses," she said. "Hang on, Christine, this could get interesting."

She clicked her tongue and flicked the reins.

They headed north and west from Kansas City. They

were on their way to the home of Zerelda "Zee" James, the mother of two of Johnny's guerrilla friends – Frank and Jesse.

§§

Zee James stood six feet tall. She was not afraid to speak her mind, which she did to anyone who would listen. She was proud of her sons. She believed strongly in the Confederacy and the right of citizens to govern their own affairs. Her first husband, a Baptist preacher, had left Missouri for the California gold fields to preach the Gospel, get rich, or get away from Zee, nobody knew for sure. He never came back and succumbed to illness at an early age.

Zee married again, but she divorced her second husband after he was abusive to Frank and Jesse. Finally, she found Dr. Samuel who was content to work hard, keep his mouth shut, and be a good father to her boys. Their marriage worked because he let her wear the pants.

Christine had been to the James farm several times during her stay in Kansas City. Zee gave her food, clothing, and ammunition to take to Frank and Jesse. Zee had grown to adore Christine. Frank soon viewed her as their little sister; and Jesse was infatuated, though he knew she belonged to Johnny.

Zee had tears in her eyes after finding Christine at the hospital but was relieved she had not died and would recover. Zee hadn't spoken to Christine since that visit though, and Christine wondered why. Maybe Zee was scared to come to town for some reason. Where were Frank and Jesse? Had they seen Johnny?

It was information Christine needed. Zee was always the best source because she knew everything and would usually tell you everything she knew as long as you weren't wearing Yankee blue. The only thing Zee liked better than talking was cooking and eating. She loved to cook a huge meal, then talk and talk and talk. The food was so good that everyone listened and said not a word, which pleased Zee to no end. For all her foibles, Zee was a sweet lady and Christine loved her.

§§

Hawk had watched Johnny Collins steal his clothes and the black flag sewn for him by the ladies of Leavenworth. He had seen Johnny burn down his house and barn, put on his black suit, and ride out of town. Hawk recognized the man who kicked the horse and killed his son as Charley Hart, who had lived in Lawrence before the war. He was surprised to hear Johnny call him "Captain Quantrill."

So, Charley Hart was the notorious Quantrill? Hawk laughed. Charley Hart had joined the Red Legs for a few months. Then he had disappeared, and no one knew why, not that anyone cared. Hart was never popular in Lawrence. He sure wouldn't be now.

Hawk had to hand it to Hart. The Lawrence raid had been brilliantly planned and executed. Hart's retreat from Lawrence had worked to perfection. With his performance at Lawrence, Charley Hart had become, in Hawk's estimation, the finest cavalry officer of the War. Hawk didn't think of him as Charley Hart anymore. The loathsome Hart had been replaced by the formidable Quantrill.

While Hawk hated Quantrill for his son's murder, Hawk respected him as a ruthless warrior who was willing to use any means necessary to win. Hawk wondered what would happen if the South were to alter its tactics and unleash a guerrilla war on the North. What if gentleman Lee were replaced by a savage like Quantrill? Hawk shuddered at the thought.

After their successful retreat to Missouri, Quantrill had ordered his men to disband. They disappeared into the friendly countryside. Throughout the fall, Hawk searched for Quantrill and his men, leading daily campaigns into the Missouri woods. Hawk searched farm by farm without success.

Then winter set in and the military campaigns ceased. Battles were fought in the other seasons of the year, especially spring and summer. Quantrill and his men wintered in northern Texas, which was still in Confederate hands. So was the Indian Territory. It was protected by Cherokee chief Stand Watie.

It would be suicide for Hawk to ride south through the Indian Territory. He was too well known. He would have to wait for spring campaigns to catch Quantrill. Once found, Quantrill would be tortured until he revealed the location of Johnny Collins, and the two other young men present at the hanging.

Once he had the information, Hawk would slit Quantrill's throat and lift his scalp. His scalp would decorate the pommel of Hawk's saddle, a grisly trophy for the world to see. Quantrill would be first. Then Johnny. Then the other two. The corners of Hawk's mouth twisted into a diabolical grin.

§§

Quantrill had no intention of being captured. After Lawrence, he surprised Union General Blount near Baxter Springs, Kansas, where he inflicted astounding damage. Blount barely escaped with his life.

In the winter of 1864, in Texas, Quantrill lost control of his men. He had been warned by a Confederate officer that guerrilla chieftains were often killed by their own. He was advised to seek an officer's commission in the regular army. Quantrill declined the invitation. He preferred his independence.

Quantrill's raiders, hardened by war, were unable to adjust to civil society in their winter quarters in Texas. They soon made trouble, too much trouble. They kept the saloons and brothels busy. They picked fights with

Texas boys, over Texas women, which too often ended in gunfire. Several prominent citizens made vociferous complaints about the raiders to the regular Confederate army.

In response, Confederate General Ben McCulloch had Quantrill arrested. After Quantrill escaped, he rode back to the guerrilla camp in an effort to restrain his men's behavior.

"What have we here?" he asked. "We're soldiers, not ruffians. What is this I hear of your getting drunk, picking fights, and plundering farmers?"

Bloody Bill scowled.

"We don't fit in down here, Captain. McCulloch don't like us, neither do his men. They ain't been fighting like we have. They don't know what it's like. They look at us like we're the devil or something."

"And some people just might agree," Quantrill said. "It's one thing to plunder and loot the enemy; it's another to harass the home front. From now on, boys, you'll do only as you're told, and I'm the one telling you by order of General Hindman, who originally commissioned us as partisan rangers."

"Since when did you become a saint, Captain?" Anderson asked. His tone was demeaning, and he nearly spit out the word, "captain."

Anderson wasn't finished. "What did you tell us about Lawrence? We could get more revenge and money there than anywhere else."

Another guerrilla chimed in.

"I guess we've had about enough of your telling us what to do, Captain. I guess it's time for you to go."

"Men, have I not led you all this time to victory upon victory. Think about what you're doing."

"We've thought about it," Anderson said. "You're out. You've got thirty minutes to get your things together and clear out."

"Who'll join me?" Quantrill asked. "Who'll join their only true leader?"

Frank James and several others stepped forward. They packed their belongings and gathered outside the camp. Anderson and several others covered them with their Colts. Several guerrillas were sad to see Quantrill go. It was the end of an era, the end of something special.

"We'll see you boys back in Missouri," Anderson said. "Save some for us."

"I hear there's plenty to go around," Quantrill said.

He rode north toward Indian Territory. He was joined by Frank James, Cole Younger, Jim Younger, and others. Jesse James stayed with Anderson.

§§

Quantrill was halfway to Indian Territory by the time Miles and Jake rode into McCulloch's headquarters. Miles requested a meeting with McCulloch. He claimed he had come to report the location of a band of hostile Comanches, which was not totally untrue given several skirmishes they had fought on their journey from Galveston. They were ushered into the general's office.

"Welcome, gentlemen," McCulloch said. "What can you tell me?"

Miles and Jake told about their scrapes with the Comanches.

"But that's not what we're really here for, General," Miles said.

McCulloch looked up; his eyes narrowed.

"Yes? How can I help you?"

"We're here to find our boys. They once fought with Quantrill's Raiders, and we think they might be stationed nearby."

"Let me tell you, gentlemen. I am not a fan of Mr. Quantrill. He and his men have been guilty of dishonoring the Confederacy, and honor is something I take seriously."

"I agree with you, General," Miles said. "I'm a preacher. We warned our boys not to go with him, but they were young, only teenagers, and they wouldn't listen. Quantrill took them away without our consent, because my son Johnny is one of the best rifle shots in the world, the sharpshooter of all sharpshooters you might say."

McCulloch sat up. He was very interested.

"Just two days ago, I arrested Quantrill for certain crimes committed by his men on our local citizens, but he escaped," the general said. "I understand there has been a rift in the raiders, and he's lost his command. Most men are now fighting under Bloody Bill Anderson. A few left with Quantrill. I was told they were headed north to Indian Territory."

"Thank you, General. By the way, didn't you fight in the Mexican War?" Jake asked.

"Sure did. And you?"

"Yes sir. Both of us did," Jake said.

"Well then, gentlemen, let's have ourselves a little drink and reminisce a bit, shall we?" McCulloch said. "Orderly, set up three whiskeys, and bring us some cigars. I'm going to drink with some old soldiers tonight. They can start their journey in the morning."

They told stories well into the night, then McCulloch found them some bed rolls and a warm place to sleep. It was a welcome change after several months of cold winter nights and sleeping on rocks with one eye open. The next morning, after breakfast, McCulloch sent them on their way with fresh supplies.

"One last thing," he said. "The guerrillas are camped by a creek near Sherman, Texas. If it's your intention to go there, take this Rebel flag with you and wave it. Otherwise, they'll shoot you on sight. And whatever you do, don't go in the morning. They'll shoot you anyway 'cause they'll be sleeping it off, and they'll be angry with you for waking them up. Good luck, men."

"Thank you, General," Miles said.

Miles and Jake rode toward Sherman.

"What's your plan, Miles?" Jake asked.

"Well, we've got to go there. Somebody there might know where the boys are."

"I mean, what's your plan for us not getting killed? I don't like the sound of anyone named 'Bloody Bill.' I figure he must have earned that name."

"Well, like the general said, Jake, we'll wave the flag, tell them we've been sent by General McCulloch with important news, and then we'll pray for the best. What else can we do?"

"I don't know."

"Once we're in there, we'll tell them who we really are and why we're there," Miles said.

"You know I used to hear this Indian say a word: *Hokahey*, and it sounds really appropriate to me for some reason," Jake said.

"Yeah? What does it mean?"

"It's a good day to die."

"Jake, the eternal optimist. I prefer a different saying, found in Philippians 4:13."

"What is it?" Jake asked.

"I can do all things through Christ who strengthens me."

§§

Bloody Bill Anderson stared at the two men approaching the camp. Who would be crazy enough to enter his camp uninvited? Surely the Raiders' reputation was well known. He stood at the edge of the camp with a rifle in his hands.

"Stop right there! Not one step more. Throw your guns down, and, while I'm thinking about it, empty your pockets, too."

Miles and Jake complied.

Bloody Bill and Jesse James, his young protégé, walked over to the visitors.

"Which one of you is Captain Anderson?" Miles asked.

"That would be me," Bloody Bill said. "Who are you, old man, and why do you offend me with your presence? I don't recall inviting you to our fine camp. That makes you a trespasser in my book. Jesse, tell these old men what happens to trespassers around here."

"They don't last long," Jesse said. He was grinning.

"My name is Miles Collins. This here's Jake Thompson. We've come to find our boys: Johnny Collins – Bill and Charlie Thompson."

Bloody Bill and Jesse heard the names, put away their guns, and extended their hands.

"Welcome, gentlemen," Bloody Bill said. "Your sons were fine soldiers. Johnny is a legend here – the best man with a gun I ever seen. Have a seat. We'll share some whiskey and tell you what we've heard and what we know."

They sat around a fire. Jesse stared at Miles.

"You sure can see the resemblance," Jesse said. "It's like I'm staring at an older Johnny."

"What can you tell us about our boys?" Jake asked.

"There's only one man knows," Anderson said. "Quantrill was the last person to see them or speak to them. He hasn't told us everything. I think he's holding something back. But he did say he was rounding up the men to leave Lawrence when he saw Johnny about to hang a teenage boy. This boy was the son of Julius Hawk, our biggest enemy, the murdering fiend who captured our girls. Quantrill said he didn't feel right about it and tried to stop the hanging, but Johnny pushed him out of the way. He said Johnny kicked the horse out from under the kid, the noose cinched tight, and the boy's neck broke."

Miles grimaced but said nothing as Anderson continued.

"According to Quantrill, Johnny snapped out of his rage, realized what he'd done, and starting praying to God for forgiveness. He turned to Quantrill and asked that Bill, Charlie, and him be discharged from further service. Quantrill granted the request. They were last seen riding west. Knowing Quantrill as we do, we've wondered how much of this story is true. Quantrill himself ordered us to kill any boy big enough to hold a rifle, so we don't understand why he would have tried to stop the hanging. We think he would have ordered it, but we really don't know what happened."

"Where is Quantrill?"

"Probably with Stand Watie somewhere," Bloody Bill said. "They're blood brothers. The chief supposedly taught Quantrill all he knows, which Quantrill passed on to us."

"Who is Stand Watie?" Miles asked.

Bloody Bill and Jesse both stared and laughed.

"The chief of the Cherokee Nation," Bloody Bill said. "He fights for the South because a Cherokee never forgets. They remember Old Hickory and the Trail of Tears. This war's been payback for them."

"How would we go about finding Chief Watie?" Miles asked.

"You don't," Bloody Bill said, "not if you want to stay alive."

"Are you friends with Chief Watie?" Jake asked.

"Was," Bloody Bill said, "until I kicked Quantrill out of here."

"Could you send something with us to show him we're not Yanks?" Miles was beginning to feel desperate.

"How about someone instead?" Bloody Bill said.

"That would be great," Miles said. "Who?"

"Me," Jesse said. "I'll go."

"I can't spare you," Bloody Bill said. "You're too good with that gun."

"I have to, Captain. Johnny was one of my best friends. Bill and Charlie, too. It'll take someone with a fast gun and a mean streak to keep these old men alive, and you know it. We owe it to Johnny. Think of all the times he saved our skins. Besides, Quantrill won't kill them if I'm there. Frank won't let him."

Bloody Bill's handlebar mustache twitched back and forth.

"I'll want a full report. Meet us at the Blue Cut come spring. I'll need you when the fighting starts."

"Yes sir," Jesse said. His eyes flashed with excitement. For the first time, Miles realized how much Jesse reminded him of Johnny.

"All right, men," Jesse said. "They've got a week on us, but I know all his old hideouts, and he ain't had time to find new ones yet."

§§

The chase was on. Winter was morphing into spring, so Jesse, Miles, and Jake traveled light, but were unable to catch up with Quantrill who had indeed joined up with Watie. A small band of Cherokees reported that Watie and Quantrill were on their way to Fort Smith to raid the fort, which had recently fallen into Union hands.

Jesse, Miles, and Jake rode east to Arkansas only to learn from Confederate sympathizers that Quantrill's Fort Smith raid had been canceled, and that Quantrill had returned to Missouri.

"Well, what do we do now?" Jake asked.

"I don't know about you two," Jesse said. "But I've got to get back to Missouri. Captain Anderson needs me there. Spring campaigns will be starting soon."

"Thanks, son," Miles said. "I'll never forget your help."

"Me either," Jake said. "Thanks."

"The least I could do for Johnny, Bill, and Charlie. Here's hoping you find them. I miss them too. Goodbye and good luck."

"Until we meet again," Miles said.

§§

Christine and Victoria finally made it to the James Farm. A friendly dog announced their arrival, and soon the James clan came outside to greet their visitors. Zee stared at Christine in disbelief.

"Is that you, child?" she asked.

"Yes, ma'am."

"Oh, come here," Zee said. She threw her arms around Christine. "And who is this with you?"

"Victoria Collins. She's like my aunt. She came to nurse me back to health."

"Well, she's done a great job, I'd say," Zee said. She

ushered them into her home. "You look as lovely as ever. You will both stay with us through Christmas, I insist on it. It will be wonderful to have you around. But tell me, what brings you to see me?"

Christine and Victoria related the events of the last few days, and how they were intending to search for Johnny. At the mention of Johnny's name, Zee's eyes betrayed deep concern.

"I will tell you everything I have heard at lunch tomorrow, dear," Zee said. "But for now, let's get your things inside and show you to your rooms. You must be exhausted. Catch up on your sleep, then we'll talk. I do have some news that might interest you."

Christine and Victoria slept soundly, wearied by travel. They rose around noon to the sounds and smells of the kitchen. Christine and Victoria rounded the corner into the kitchen where they found a bustling Zee cooking a feast.

"I thought you girls never would get out of bed," she said. "I've been banging these pots for an hour. Thought the noise might stir you from slumber. Should have known it would be the smell that roused you."

"Christine told me you're a wonderful cook," Victoria said.

"I do my best." Zee stuck her head out of the kitchen. "Reuben, get down here! It's time for lunch. These ladies are starving, and I could use something myself."

Dr. Samuel descended the staircase. He smiled at the ladies.

"I see she got you up," he said.

"Yes, sir," Christine said.

"Well, it'll be worth it, dear, that's for sure," he said.

They were soon enjoying a fine Southern meal: fried chicken, potatoes, homemade bread, and a variety of vegetables. Apple pie for dessert.

Zee dominated the conversation but kept it mainly on the surface until Christine just couldn't stand it any longer.

"Zee, I just have to know the news about Johnny."

Zee stared at her plate for a few seconds before speaking.

"Christine, my boys came by to see me one last time before heading to Texas for the winter. I asked them about Lawrence and Johnny."

"What did they say?"

"Seems Johnny and the Thompson brothers deserted after Lawrence. The boys haven't seen them since. Quantrill was the last person to talk to them. Cole Younger happened to see them as they were riding away. He said it looked like they were heading west. Jesse thought they might be going to California. Johnny used to talk a lot about seeing the ocean. Frank had a different opinion. He thought they would go to a big city with a nice theater 'cause Johnny has a real passion for plays and music. Frank and Johnny used to read Shakespeare together. They traded lines they had memorized."

"So, Johnny's still alive?"

"Yes, dear," Zee said. "But there's something I have to tell you, something everyone seems to agree on, something you need to know. They say Johnny was practically foaming at the mouth as he rode through the streets of Lawrence that day, pistols blazing, shooting soldiers left and right. He kept yelling 'Remember Kansas City!' 'Remember Christine!' Quantrill told Frank that Johnny snapped out of it only after he hanged young Hawk, the son of his arch enemy. Quantrill said he tried to stop Johnny from hanging the boy, but Johnny kicked the horse out from under the kid, and the boy died instantly. Quantrill said that afterward Johnny grew a conscience, fell prostrate to the ground, and began mumbling what might have been a prayer. Quantrill said there was something about the hanging that snapped Johnny back to reality. When he came to and realized all he'd done, he wasn't good as a soldier anymore. Quantrill discharged Johnny and the Thompsons from further service on the condition they would remain loyal to the Confederacy."

Christine's voice was a whisper. "Gene."

"What?"

"It was Gene, Johnny's brother. He was put on a

horse and hanged by Hawk the same way. Johnny must have seen the boy and thought of his brother."

"Oh," Zee said. "And now he feels guilty because he did the same thing Hawk did?"

"I think so," Christine said. "Zee, do you think Johnny's a lost cause?"

"Christine, you'll never know if you don't find him. War brings out the worst in men. He might need you to show him a different way of life. Maybe you could help him find the path to peace. And bear this in mind. Frank and Jesse said they've known Quantrill to lie. They don't believe he's telling the truth about what happened with the hanging. They think it more likely that Quantrill hanged the boy and let Johnny and his cousins bear the blame."

"How can I ever hope to find him, to ask him what happened?" Christine asked. "The West is so big."

She began to cry. Victoria had been listening intently to the dialogue and its revelations. She leaned over and placed a comforting arm around Christine's shoulders.

"Trust me," she whispered into Christine's left ear. "I have a plan."

§§

"So, what about us? What are we going to do, Miles?" Jake asked.

"I don't know about you, Jake, but I sure could use a home-cooked meal, and something tells me they need us back home for a little while."

"Yeah, I feel the same way. Cross Hollows is just a day's ride from here. Maybe we'll be there for breakfast."

"I hear you. Let's ride all night. I'm homesick."

They were greeted at Cross Hollows by the crowing of a bantam rooster strutting near the barn.

"Wow, this place is so beautiful. Pretty soon it'll be planting season," Miles said.

"Yeah," Jake said. "I wonder if we'll be here to see it."

"Who knows? I just wish we could find the boys and bring them back before harvest."

"Do you think we'll ever find them?"

"I don't know, Jake. Maybe Quantrill knows something he's not telling. If it's God's will, we'll find them. Now let's go have us some breakfast and see our wives. We can worry about chasing Quantrill tomorrow."

As they approached the plantation, Isaiah and Naomi ran out to greet them.

Naomi was breathless. "Oh Miles! Diana's really sick. The last couple of days especially."

Miles rushed into the house and ran up the stairs to their bedroom. He found Diana asleep. He felt her face. It was hot. He swept her hair back and found a small pock growing near her left temple, and two more near the center of her forehead.

Diana opened her eyes.

"Miles, is that you?"

"Yes, dear. I'm here. Can you turn over? I want to look at your back."

She removed her shirt. There was a pustule on the back of her left shoulder.

"Miles, what is it?"

"Diana, sugar, I'm not a doctor, but I think I had what you had once. Now I don't want you to worry, 'cause I survived. I think you have the beginnings of smallpox."

"No!"

"Yes, dear, I believe you do. I'm going to have Jake ride to Fort Smith to get Doc. I'm okay. Since I had it, I can't get it again. I'll stay here and tend to you. Oh, I forgot, Jake's had it too, and he survived. You will, too."

Miles kissed her crestfallen face and went downstairs to convey the news. Jake left at once for Fort Smith.

Overnight Diana took a turn for the worse. By morning, pustules covered her body. By the time Doc arrived, the pocks had turned colors; infection was coursing through her pale body. Doc met with Miles in the parlor.

"I don't know how to say this, Miles."

"Just say it."

317

"She's dying. She won't see tomorrow. You need to make every moment count."

Miles collapsed onto his knees and wept. When he gathered himself, he climbed the stairs one more time, this time to say goodbye.

"I'm dying, Miles. I know it. I'll be with Gene soon."

"I love you, Diana. You've been such a wonderful wife. I will love you forever."

"I love you too, Miles Collins," she said. Speaking was a struggle. Miles kissed her and held her close.

Suddenly Diana felt strong enough to run her fingers through his hair. Then she probed his eyes deeply with hers and took both of his hands.

"Miles Collins, you promise me something."

"What's that, darling? Anything. You name it."

"Find our lost son and preach the Gospel. Find Johnny, wherever he is, however long it takes, and do whatever it is you have to do to save him. Don't stop until he's been baptized. Will you do that for me? Will you do that for me, please?"

"I will. The Lord willing, our lost son will be found. And baptized."

"Promise me, Miles."

"I promise."

"I love you, Miles Collins. I always have..."

Her words faded into whispers, and her hands, so warm only seconds before, turned cool. Sweet Diana was forever gone.

Miles cried, his lips still touching hers. He slowly backed away. Then he sang her favorite gospel song in hopes her departing spirit might be listening.

§§

Christine hugged Zee James goodbye.

"Zee, this was a Christmas I'll always treasure."

"I will miss you, sweet girl. And I hope you find him... and help him heal. You'll be in my prayers."

"Thanks, Zee. If I find him, I'll never lose him again."

Victoria walked up to them with Jeremiah, Zee's servant, who was carrying the luggage.

"We'd better get moving, Christine. We've got quite a few miles ahead of us."

"Where will you go?" Zee asked.

"Wherever the wind blows us," Victoria said.

After they left the James Farm, Christine turned to Victoria.

"Where are we going?" she asked.

"First, Kansas City for supplies, then St. Louis, San Francisco, Denver, and all across the West," Victoria said. She smiled and tossed her head.

"Sounds fun, but kind of dangerous, two women alone in the West," Christine said.

"Oh, we won't be alone. We'll be joined by some interesting company. It will be *some* company, all right.

You'll see."

As was her custom, Christine sang as they traveled, drawing from her repertory of gospel and folk songs she had learned from her parents and Johnny. Victoria didn't mind. Christine had the most beautiful voice, a smooth contralto that was sweet to the ears.

Victoria loved opera and theater and was known to quote lines from poems and plays. As a young woman, she had traveled in an acting troupe, until she fell in love with one of her fans and settled down. She loved the stage, and the bond that developed between actors.

During her years as an entertainer, Victoria had heard some amazing singers, but Christine's voice was special. She was not the piercing, overpowering soprano so often found in the stuffy operas. Christine had a smooth, honeyed tone that connected with her audience. Johnny loved to hear her sing.

Victoria recalled how Johnny would throw his arms around Christine and say, "How's my ravin' beauty?" as a play off his nickname for her, the Raven. Every time she heard her nickname, Christine would flash a smile as big as Texas. Victoria simply had to see that smile again.

Victoria grinned, a twinkle in her sparkling eyes. This was going to be fun. Her plan was brilliant. If Johnny Collins was out there, he didn't stand a chance. They would find him, and wedding bells would ring.

§§

After presiding over Diana's funeral, Miles gathered all the supplies he might need for a long journey. All of his money and gold pieces. Every gun he owned.

A man makes his plans, but the Lord chooses his steps, he thought.

He had dreamed of living out his days at Cross Hollows, preaching in the church and enjoying the life of a farmer, growing old with his wife and family. All those dreams had died with Diana. All joy was gone. His only reason for living was Johnny. Diana had given him a great quest, but it was one he would have accepted anyway. Johnny was his boy, his only son left in a world turned cruel. But he was lost, and it was up to Miles to find him.

"Looks like you're going to be gone awhile," Jake said. He pointed to the bulging saddlebags and the extra rifles.

"I reckon so," Miles said. "But I don't see your horse packed and saddled."

"No, Miles, I won't be going with you this time. Diana's dyin' got me to thinkin'. I love Naomi too much. Got to stay with her, protect her. Without Diana, Naomi would be alone. I'd take her with us, but I don't think she could take our type of hard travelin'."

"I understand. Jake, you've been a brother and my best friend. Just wanted to tell you that. Never know what will happen out there where I'm going."

"Miles, I don't have the words, but you know I feel the same way. Now find our boys and bring them back home."

Miles mounted up and began his long journey to Missouri. He didn't know how or if he would ever find Johnny, but he would pray every day that he would. He would start with the man he blamed most for Johnny's fall from grace.

He would start with Captain William Quantrill.

§§

Unknown to Miles, Julius Hawk was also searching for the great guerrilla leader, and was closing in. During the last months of the war, in the spring of 1865, Quantrill had organized a guerrilla band and traveled east from Missouri to Kentucky.

Quantrill still longed for a prolonged, house-to-house guerrilla war to be waged in the North. He felt the North would surrender once her citizens had felt the horrors of war.

He was in Kentucky, on the way to Washington, when he heard the news of Lincoln's assassination. Quantrill was devastated. All hopes of lasting glory disappeared. His undisclosed wish had been to assassinate Lincoln and rekindle the war – to be remembered as the war hero of a reborn South. He secretly desired to succeed Jefferson Davis as the next president of the Confederate States of America.

Grandiose dreams in his head collided with contradicting facts on the ground. In reality, the South was a lost cause. Booth had beaten him to Lincoln. The assassin had been killed – his co-conspirators hanged. The murder had not changed the course of the war.

Lee had surrendered along with most Southern boys. Only the unrepentant, hard-core purists remained. They lived on the run, a reality in which Quantrill took great satisfaction. He had not surrendered and never would. He still believed.

§§

Hawk found tremendous joy in bringing the recalcitrant to justice, which was swift and permanent. He hired mercenaries to track and kill the roving guerrilla bands still at large. One of his men was named Edwin Terrill. His job was to locate and capture Quantrill.

Terrill was handsomely paid by Hawk, and he hired the best available Indian scouts to help him track his quarry. Acting on a tip from a blacksmith, Terrill found Quantrill and his men hiding in a barn in Kentucky owned by a man named Wakefield.

Quantrill and his men had spent the night in the barn and were still there when Terrill and his men arrived. They surrounded the barn. Quantrill was shot in the back while trying to escape. Falling from his horse, Quantrill told his captors he was a Union soldier with the

Missouri home guard. Later that day, he confessed his true identity.

The bullet severed several vertebrae in his spine. Quantrill was paralyzed from the waist down. The soldiers placed him on a cart and carried him to a military hospital in Louisville.

Quantrill lived for another three weeks in that hospital, and it was an interesting three weeks indeed. A variety of visitors came to visit the famed guerrilla before his death. First, Katie King, his mistress and rumored bride. Quantrill kissed her goodbye and gave her all of his money, which she later used to fund a brothel in St. Louis.

Next came a Catholic priest, excited to preach to a captive audience. Quantrill's legs were paralyzed, but not his heart, and his tear ducts worked perfectly. Whether the tears were sincere or feigned, no one knew, but after several visits from the priest, Quantrill confessed his sins and accepted rites from the Catholic Church.

His next visitor was an ex-preacher named Julius Hawk, and his conduct in Quantrill's room was not nearly so benevolent.

"Captain William Quantrill, or should I say, Charley Hart," Hawk said.

"Hawk!"

"That's right, vermin, your old nemesis. You made

me look like a fool at Lawrence, I'll give you that. But wasn't it old Ben Franklin who said he who laughs last, laughs loudest?"

Hawk took in the dilapidated surroundings.

"The wheels of justice spin slowly, son, but you finally got what was coming to you. You are paying for your sins," he said. He sat on the bed. "I remember that morning very clearly. I saw Johnny Collins place my son's head in a noose. Two other young raiders helped him. That noose was swinging from the oak tree behind my house. Then, if memory serves, I saw you kick my son's horse out from under him. I watched my son's neck break. I saw him die."

Quantrill's eyes widened with fear.

"I swore an oath then and there that I would kill everyone who took part in my son's hanging. I hired Terrill to find you, but he was told not to shoot you or in any way harm you. I wanted a clean slate to work with, wanted to stain it with your blood. I wanted a healthy victim to disable, then kill, slowly, and painfully. Instead, he shoots you and gives me a paralyzed invalid who can't feel any pain...at least from the waist down, I understand."

"What do you want from me, Hawk? What more can you do to me? I'm not afraid of dying. I've only got a few days left, anyway."

"I want several things. Right now, I control how you

die. If you give me what I want, I'll have the doctor make it quick and painless. If you refuse, death will be a long, torturous process, I assure you. Through the years I've perfected certain techniques in securing information, as you probably already know."

"What do you want?"

"First, I want the names of the two men who helped Johnny Collins kill my boy. I want you to tell me the last known whereabouts of Johnny Collins and his friends. And I want you to tell me the names of Johnny Collins' closest associates in the guerrillas. I figure I'll find him if I find his friends."

Quantrill spat at Hawk and laughed as he watched his spittle drip from Hawk's nose.

"Never," Quantrill said. "I'll die first."

Purpling with fury, Hawk said, "You'll wish you were dead. Slow and painful. That's how it will be, but just remember, the moment you tell me what I want, I'll call the doctor. He'll give you some laudanum, and I'll put you out of your misery."

Hawk pulled a knife from a sheath on his belt and a small whet stone from his pocket. He sharpened the blade as he talked.

"I think the doctor said from the waist down. Let's test that out, first," Hawk said. He drew back and punched Quantrill in the right thigh. Quantrill displayed no emotion.

"Okay, how about here?" Hawk pinched Quantrill in the gut. The Rebel leader winced.

"Ah, that's more like it."

Hawk took the knife and drew it across the upper dermis of Quantrill's left arm. Quantrill held out for a few moments, then howled.

"Are you ready to talk?"

"No. Never!"

Hawk looked to the door. "Terrill!"

Terrill stepped into the room.

"Bring me some coals and my fire poker. It's time to get serious with Mr. Quantrill here."

Several minutes later Terrill reentered with a scuttle of smoldering coals. A twelve-inch fire prod with a leather grip protruded from the glowing pile. When Hawk removed the small poker, the tip blushed red. He held it about a foot above Quantrill's left eye.

"Do you want to leave this world blind, Captain?"

Quantrill remained silent until the poker was within an inch of his eye. When he felt the heat, he slammed his lids shut.

"All right! I'll tell you everything I know!"

"I knew you'd listen to reason. First, who were the two men with Johnny Collins who helped put my son's head in that noose?"

"Bill and Charlie Thompson, Johnny's cousins. They're from Paint Rock, Alabama. You hanged their older brother."

"Who were Johnny's closest friends in the raiders?"

"Bill and Charlie, of course, but also Jesse and Frank James."

"Where is Johnny today?"

"I don't know."

"Don't lie to me!"

The poker had not moved. Quantrill was not ready to test Hawk's resolve.

"The last time I saw him was in Lawrence, and that's the truth. He told me they were leaving the war and heading west. I haven't heard from Johnny or the Thompson brothers since."

"West. Interesting." Hawk lay the poker back in the scuttle. "What are Johnny's hobbies and habits?"

"He loves music and the theater. You might find him at an opera house or some such – when he ain't killing someone. That's what he does best. And that's what he'll do to you if you chase him."

"I wouldn't be so sure of that," Hawk said. "I know how to handle myself."

Despite the fear etched across his face, Quantrill laughed.

"Hawk, Johnny Collins is the fastest, deadliest gunman I have ever seen. If you were half as smart as you believe yourself to be, you would leave him alone, and pray that he never finds you. Best guess is that he'll probably come looking for you some day."

"I hope he does. It would save me a lot of trouble."

"You find him, or he finds you – either way, you're a dead man," Quantrill said, with a faint grin, the pain robbing him of the strength to laugh.

Hawk stood.

"Well, I am a man of my word, so when your death comes, it will be quick. But I think you need to learn one more lesson before you leave this world."

He picked up the poker.

"I'm not a surgeon, but how hard could it possibly be to remove a tongue?" Hawk spit on the tip of the poker. It sizzled. Quantrill flinched. Hawk enjoyed the moment of fear.

"Seems to me," he said, "that it should come out readily enough. A few seconds with this poker should cauterize it nicely, one would think." Of course, Terrill would have to hold him down. He looked at the door again. "Terrill, get back in here!"

No response.

"Terrill!"

Hawk growled and stalked out of the room. The second he passed through the door he saw Terrill to his left. The man was sprawled on the floor – unconscious or dead. Hawk heard a noise behind him. He turned.

The last thing he saw was a rifle butt closing in on his face. The owner of the rifle began tying Hawk's hands and feet. He then walked into Quantrill's room. He wore a black bandanna on his face, which he removed as he began to speak.

§§

"As much as I dislike you, Captain, I couldn't let him burn off your tongue. I need you to tell me about my son and my nephews."

The man lowered the bandanna.

"Miles Collins, as I live and breathe," Quantrill said. "You'll pardon me if I don't stand."

Miles did not smile. He sat next to the bed on a small chair. He had overheard the conversation between Quantrill and Hawk, but he still had some unanswered questions.

"Those two are tied up outside, but someone will find them soon. Talk – and do not even think about lying to me."

Quantrill took a moment.

"Mr. Collins," he said, "I will tell you anything you want to know. You don't have to believe this, but a priest converted me to the Gospel several days ago. I only have a short time left, but I want to live it as best as I can."

A broad smile cracked Miles' stern visage. "I never deny the healing power of the Gospel," Miles said.

"Mr. Collins, first I want to apologize for everything I have done to your family. I turned Johnny into a killer.

330

I taught him everything I knew about guerrilla warfare, and he was a model student. He is the deadliest man I've ever seen with a gun."

"I accept your apology, but take little pride in my son's aptitude," Miles said.

Quantrill nodded. "I understand. I'm not proud of my life either. But there's more. I have a confession to make. I slandered Johnny to the other guerrillas. I told them Johnny kicked the horse out from under young Hawk, when, in fact, I did. When Johnny saw the kid in that noose, and heard the boy's mother crying, he had second thoughts. I heard him tell Bill and Charlie to cut the boy down. I spurred the horse before they could do it because I wanted to hurt Hawk."

Quantrill swallowed – or tried to. Miles handed him a glass of water. Quantrill sipped, coughed, and continued.

"Johnny was devastated. He told me he was leaving with Bill and Charlie – going west. Mr. Collins, I beg your forgiveness, and if you ever find Johnny, please tell him I'm sorry for everything."

"Anything else?"

"Yes, sir," Quantrill said. "Tell him it's not too late. He can still be forgiven, regardless of his past, that vengeance leads only to death – and not just Hawk's – his own as well. Tell him even 'The Badman' can be forgiven."

Something in Quantrill's eyes changed. They glazed over and lost focus. "Badman...Badman...Badman..."

Miles touched his shoulder.

"What is it, what are you trying to tell me?"

"Badman...Badman..."

"Tell me, Quantrill." Miles could feel his temper rising. He gripped the captain's shoulder, but Quantrill was already stepping across the threshold of eternity.

"The Badman," he said. "Johnny Collins...the Badman."

The light in his eyes dimmed, then vanished.

From his spot on the floor outside the room, Hawk heard Quantrill's voice but had a hard time making out the words. He thought he heard the word "Badman," but he wasn't sure. It didn't make sense.

There was someone else in the room. Hawk reasoned it was the person who was responsible for his splitting headache. Hawk heard a chair scrape against the floor and saw a man walk to the window of Quantrill's room. Hawk closed his eyes to feign unconsciousness, but when the man came closer, Hawk snuck a peek. It was Miles Collins.

Collins walked out of the room. He looked at Terrill and Hawk. For a moment, the preacher's hand rested on the butt of the pistol on his hip. He removed his hand from the weapon and pulled the bandanna up across his mouth and nose. Before he covered his face, he spit in

Hawk's direction, then walked down the hall.

The visit with Quantrill had been productive for both Hawk and Miles, for the same reason. They had learned the names of Johnny's best friends in the Raiders (other than Bill and Charlie): Jesse and Frank James. They might just know how to find him.

It was June 6, 1865, when Quantrill died. Little did Hawk or Miles realize how difficult finding the James Brothers would prove to be.

THE LOST YEARS, LEGENDS, AND THE SEARCH FOR JOHNNY COLLINS
(August 21, 1863-July 4, 1875)

This period might best be referred to as "the lost years," when Johnny was living in the Land of Nod...

...separated from his family...

...pulled from his roots...

...removed from his love...

...lost in his confusion...

...lost to himself...

...lost in his sin...

...versed in the ways of violence...

...accomplished in mayhem...

...acquainted with the pleasures of sin...

...alone in the halls of darkness...

...a shootist extraordinaire...

...a pistoleer with no peer...

...an outlaw on the lam...

...a desperado on the run...

...a man without a country...

...the nomad who roamed...

...a friend to the wind...

...a harbinger of death...

...a stranger to steeples...

...forgetful of the kindness he'd been shown...

...a prodigal pilgrim who wandered alone...

...in a wild western country with sins unatoned...

...but never out of the sight of God.

He was drowning in deep sorrow, from the sins he had to own. Would there be a brighter tomorrow? Would he find the lights of home? Was there a path back home? Was it forever lost...or merely overgrown?

The Legend of the Hellhound

Hawk continued his quest for Johnny. He became a Pinkerton detective, nicknamed the "Hellhound" for the relentless, brutal methods he used to track and kill various criminals. He rose through the ranks of the Pinkerton organization until he occupied a spot just below Allan Pinkerton's son, William. Despite his high station, Hawk preferred to remain in the field, which some found odd. But Hawk wanted to supervise the investigation of the James-Younger gang - personally.

The Legend of the Preacher Man

Miles Collins lived as a drifting, subsistence farmer. He searched for Jesse James. He finally found him by settling on a small farm in rural Missouri not too far from Kearney, and a short ride from Hawk's office in Kansas City.

Miles kept a low profile. He grew his own food and led a very private life. He quit shaving and cutting his hair. He spoke rarely. When he did, it was mostly in monosyllables. At random times, though, he stood outside and practiced flowery sermons, Bible in hand, to the astonishment of passersby, who thought him insane.

Miles promoted this perception – it allowed him to see without being seen. He could watch others without receiving the same scrutiny. His appearance and eccentric behavior discouraged folks from getting too close. Folks in Clay County called Miles "The Preacher Man," only never to his face. Mostly, they avoided him.

Miles had a distinct advantage over Hawk and the Pinkertons when it came to finding Jesse James. He had seen Jesse and heard his voice. Miles had spent part of a winter with Jesse while searching for Quantrill. They had connected; Miles felt he had gained Jesse's trust and respect. If Jesse knew where Johnny was, Miles was sure he would share the information.

Miles kept a close eye on Hawk and his band of detectives. They had significant resources at their disposal to aid in their pursuit of the outlaw: money, undercover operatives, politicians, and the railroads.

The Legend of The Raven

Christine and Victoria scoured the opera houses of the West. Christine became an actress and singer. Everyone called her "The Raven." Her beauty and vocal quality were the stuff of legend, and she performed to packed houses wherever she went. Many thought it strange that she remained single. She rebuffed overtures from politicians, railroad magnates, cattle barons, and even a European prince, who had sailed the ocean to see her and hear her sing.

Every night, she scanned the audience and hoped she would spot Johnny. She dreamed of the moment when she would again see his face. In that instant, he would know she still lived, that she had never stopped loving him, and would never love anyone else. She would tell him everything with her eyes.

For several years, Hellhound, The Preacher Man, and The Raven all searched for Johnny Collins. They used different tactics for different reasons, but all without the slightest success. Each began to wonder whether Johnny was still alive, or if he had already died, a victim of the ever-growing violence of the Wild West.

The Legend of The Badman

They were unaware that Johnny Collins had become a legend all his own. He was "The Badman," the fastest, deadliest gunslinger in all the West. He wore a black hat and a sable coat under which he concealed five pistols worn guerrilla style: twin Schofields holstered at the hips, two Navy Colts hidden in his vest, positioned for cross-draws, and another in a concealed, leather shoulder holster. This was business as usual for a trained guerrilla.

Yellow journalists and dime store novelists recounted his exploits, exaggerating the number of notches on his guns, but only slightly. He had killed many but only after due warning. Those who challenged The Badman were cautioned to walk away and advised they faced certain death if they drew. The ones who heeded the warning lived. The blindly arrogant who didn't, died, usually from two shots, one to the forehead, the other through the heart.

Stories, ballads, and songs described The Badman's prowess with his pistols in grandiose style. A particular favorite rang out from many a saloon piano player.

He shoots his pistols faster than
the lightning strikes the canyon.
He's killed him 37 men, his last

was Tommy O'Banion.
Over hill and over dale,
He can't be caught; he won't be jailed.
Sailors sing and poets tell
The Ballad of the Badman.
Right or wrong, you're singing his song,
The Ballad of the Badman.

Every time Johnny heard the ballad, he smiled. He even composed a second verse, which he sang only when alone:

They say he rides across the West
upon a mighty stallion,
that somewhere tied across his chest
is a blood-stained medallion,
the locket worn by sweet Christine
they say she was his everything.
Lift your glasses high and sing
The Ballad of the Badman.
Right or wrong, you're singing his song,
The Ballad of the Badman.

Before the stories and the songs, and the dime store novels, Tom Rogers (the journalist who'd transcribed the letter no one believed) burnished the legend by glorifying the exploits of The Badman in his newspaper columns. According to Rogers, The Badman robbed from the rich to give to the poor, like a Colt-wielding

Robin Hood. The Gilded Age was one of corruption and scandal in public and private sectors alike. Sam Grant's cronies and kinfolk abused the public's trust. Railroads fleeced homesteaders. The banks gouged everybody.

In a climate of large-scale graft, it was hard to fault a brigand like The Badman for stealing from much bigger thieves like the bankers and robber barons. The Badman became a champion of the people, a folk hero who used his Navy Colts to strike a blow for the working man, the man who earned his money by sweat, not speculation. When The Badman robbed a train or bank, it was a risky proposition requiring tremendous planning and precise effort. By contrast, the robber barons were masters of the soft fleece that cost the public much more.

Soon the myth outstripped reality. No one knew who the real Badman was. It was a mystery, an issue of intrigue to both the small and the great. Lawmen, journalists, and politicians advanced different theories, and several outlaws made false confessions in search of infamy. Others donned black outfits in imitation. Some shadowed Rogers believing him to have a special relationship with the famed shootist.

During these years The Badman, with Bill and Charlie, robbed banks and trains in Tennessee, Texas, Kansas, Kentucky, Missouri, Colorado, and California. They grew wealthy. Sometimes they rode with former guerrillas. On other occasions, it was just the three of them.

Badman, Bill, and Charlie went by many different aliases depending on where they were. It was sometimes hard to recall which name was used where, a common problem after the war where many were running from a scarred past in search of a brighter future. Bill and Charlie honored Johnny's request. They addressed him only as Badman unless they were in public, in which case he was usually either "Nathaniel Smith" or "Alexander Jones."

§§

Badman, Bill, and Charlie had never planned to ride with Jesse James. They were in Dallas to visit their old guerrilla buddies, Cole and Jim Younger, and Jesse happened to be there. After smokes and a few whiskeys, Jesse made some jokes about "The Badman," doubting he was real and suggesting he was just a figment of a dime store novelist's ridiculous imagination. Only Bill and Charlie knew the truth, and Johnny had sworn them to absolute secrecy, but the temptation proved too much. Johnny confessed on the spot. The James and Younger brothers hooted their approval.

"I always kind of thought it was you," Jesse said. He conveniently forgot his earlier skepticism. "There was only one man in the world who could do that kind of shooting – Johnny Collins."

"I don't answer to that name anymore, not even to

Bill and Charlie," Johnny said. His face was a stone. "Call me the Badman in private, or Nathaniel Smith or Alexander Jones in public."

"All right, Badman, well I've got an idea," Jesse said. "What do you think about teaming up for some jobs now and then. What would folks say about that? Jesse James and the Badman together. That would really upset Hawk and the rest of those Pinkertons."

"Hawk?" Johnny's voice was the hiss of an angry rattler. "He's still alive?"

"Oh yes, and meaner than ever," Jesse said. "They call him The Hellhound. He always gets his man. I'd like to kill him, but he's too smart. Never gives me the chance."

The Badman recovered his composure. "I don't know," he said. "We're used to doing our own jobs, and I don't answer to anybody."

"Understood," Jesse said. "But I could sure use your gun. I'll even give you an extra share. How about that?"

"On one condition."

"What's that?"

"If the stars line up and we get a chance at Hawk, I'm the one to kill him, and I get to do it how I want."

"As long as I get to watch," Jesse said.

"I wish Bloody Bill could be there," the Badman said. "When I think about his sisters...and Christine..."

The outlaws looked at the Badman, who was

suddenly silent. The dark moods were often an uneasy calm before a violent storm. Jesse remembered that from the guerrilla days, as did Cole. Bill and Charlie had seen the behavior many times since then.

"Let's do it," the Badman said. "Let's rob us some banks and trains."

And the partnership was formed.

Rogers relished writing about how the two paladins had joined together to fight the banks, trains, and robber barons. He quoted at least five anonymous widows whose mortgages had been paid in full by the new partners in crime.

§§

It had taken many years, but Hawk had assembled a vast network of contacts and associates willing to assist his apprehension of the James brothers including attorneys, informants, neighbors, church members, undercover operatives, and others he had threatened or bribed.

Old Man Askew lived on a farm less than a quarter-mile from the James farm, which was visible from his front porch. He was getting on in years and had never had sons. He needed help. One day a young Pinkerton named Jack Ladd showed up at Askew's door disguised as a farmhand seeking work. Askew asked him a few questions, but more or less hired him on the spot.

Ladd was a hard worker who mainly kept to himself.

He got to know the Askews pretty well, befriending them and attending church with them every Sunday at the Baptist Church. It was in the church choir where Ladd first encountered Jesse James.

Jesse had a nice tenor voice and loved to sing. One Sunday, he surprised the locals by attending church and singing in the choir. After church, he rode off with Frank, who had been waiting outside.

Ladd sang with Jesse that day and became the first Pinkerton to see the outlaw's face. Jesse and Frank returned to the James farm for Sunday lunch. They left before Ladd could inform Hawk. The drop-ins became a pattern.

Ladd was frustrated by these whirlwind visits, but he gained Jesse's trust – from a distance. Jesse would often nod at him as he and Frank rode past the Askew place. One day, Ladd noticed Jesse talking to Askew. Ladd walked over and shook his hand.

"Sorry to interrupt," Ladd said. "But I don't want to seem standoffish."

"Askew here says you've made a pretty good hand. Says you work sunup to sundown without gripin'."

"I like it here."

"What's your name?"

"Jack Ladd."

"Where you from?" Jesse asked.

"Here and there."

343

"I see," Jesse said. "Did you fight in the War?"

"Yes, sir."

"For which side?"

"South, of course. I didn't catch your name," Ladd said.

"'Cause I didn't say," Jesse said. He turned his horse and rode to his mother's.

"Strange boy, that one," Askew said. "His brother, too. I wouldn't get too close to them if I were you, Jack."

"Why is that, Mr. Askew?"

"He's got a temper, and his brother's been known to kill a man or two. He didn't tell you, but I will. That there was Jesse James."

"The Jesse James?"

"That's right, son. That's why you'd better hang back. He was sizing you up, seeing if you might know how to use a gun. He's probably looking for new recruits for his gang. They rob trains, banks, and what all."

"Really? Riding with Jesse James. I bet that'd be something."

"Maybe, but a lot of people who ride with Jesse go missing. I've heard he and Frank will be staying at their mom's farm next week enjoying a few meals and recruiting for their next robbery. They'll understand if you turn them down."

"Thanks, Mr. Askew. I'm kind of like you. I'd rather earn my money, not steal it, and I'm not too keen on getting shot at or killed."

"Good thinking. I'll see you back at the house for dinner."

Askew smiled. It was nice to have good help.

§§

Miles was the consummate spy. He watched everyone and everything. He attended the Baptist Church. He sat on the back pew and read his Bible. The first time he went, people tried to talk to him, but he just grunted and kept reading. He didn't even look up. After that, everyone left him alone, and Miles was free to observe. The only ones who looked at him were the children, who loved to stare at his beard.

Miles remembered Jesse saying he belonged to the Baptist Church. Jesse was a religious man, as odd as that might seem. Miles thought he just might catch the robber at church someday. Miles was there the day Jesse sang in the choir. He made eye contact with Jesse from a distance. Jesse looked him over before tilting his head and walking away.

Miles noticed that Jack Ladd, Askew's farm hand, was always watching Jesse. One Sunday Miles studied Ladd as he walked outside the church building after services. He followed Ladd's eyes. They were staring at the departing figures of Jesse and another man riding with him. Ladd had no idea he was being watched. Who would suspect a crazy preacher man of espionage?

After that day at the church, Miles began to follow Ladd. Ladd rose at sunup, worked until sundown, ate dinner with the Askews, and retired to his place in the barn. Twice a week, though, he slipped out of his room, saddled a horse, and rode toward Kansas City. He always returned early the next morning in time for the chores.

After a few weeks, Ladd altered his routine. He slipped out every other night. Miles had begun to suspect Ladd might be a Pinkerton, someone trying to catch the James brothers. If they were captured, Miles would lose any information Jesse might have regarding Johnny's whereabouts.

Then Ladd's routine had changed yet again. One day he skipped his morning assignments, saddled his horse, and filled his saddlebags. It looked like he was leaving for a long journey. Miles saddled up and followed him to Kansas City.

In Kansas City Ladd hitched his horse and walked into the Wayside Tavern. He sauntered over to the bar with a smile on his face. The Wayside was a long, narrow dive with just enough room for a long oak bar and stools. He ordered a whiskey. Miles glanced inside from the street, to make sure Ladd didn't leave through a back door. Miles had just turned his head back toward the street when someone pushed him. Miles landed on his buttocks.

"Get out of the way, drunk."

The voice was familiar.

Miles looked up to see Julius Hawk scowling down at him. The former colonel walked into the bar and sat next to Ladd. Miles edged into the joint and sat where he could eavesdrop.

"They're coming in tonight," Ladd said. "They're staying with their mother for a few days. I've heard it from several reliable sources."

"Yeah? Who?"

"Askew, and one of Jesse's cousins I've gotten to know at church."

"Good work," Hawk said. "If we pull this off, you're due a big promotion. Tomorrow night, we strike Castle James."

Miles had long ago mastered the art of invisibility. He wandered out of the bar, and no one noticed. He mounted and rode back to Clay County. He had to warn Jesse.

Miles knew he had to risk a visit to the James Farm. He hoped he wouldn't get shot – always a possibility for anyone approaching uninvited. The beard and long hair had served their purpose. Hopefully, Jesse would remember a clean-shaven, well-groomed Miles Collins.

§§

Hawk was excited. His preparations were about to pay off with the capture of the most notorious outlaws in the land. Hawk would be famous as the Pinkerton who brought them to justice. More importantly, they might lead him to Johnny Collins, Bill Thompson, and Charlie Thompson. Tomorrow night, justice would be served.

Hawk had arranged with the railroad for a special boxcar to deliver ten mounted mercenaries to Kansas City. They would ride through the woods to Clay County and surround the James Farm. Hawk would lead the operation.

They would do their best to capture the outlaws alive. Hawk would handle the negotiations with the James family. If the James brothers surrendered, they would be shackled and taken back to Kansas City. On the way, Hawk planned to torture them into disclosing the whereabouts of young Collins. If they refused, he would kill them. Hawk was sure he could get his prisoners to talk.

They always did.

§§

Miles rose at dawn. He shaved his beard and trimmed his hair. After a while, he looked like the man Jesse might recognize. Miles ate a biscuit and swung into the saddle.

It was a cold winter's morning, and his breath fogged as he rode. He dismounted at the James farm and tied his horse to an oak tree. He knew he was being watched. He hoped it was by Jesse, not Frank. The front door swung open, and Zee walked outside.

"Mister, what do you want?"

"I'm here to speak with Jesse, ma'am."

"He's not here."

"I think he is, ma'am, and I really need to speak with him."

"You must not have heard me, mister."

The front door swung open. Frank James walked outside. His pistol was cocked and pointed at Miles.

"Did you hear what she said, mister?" he asked. "You best get back on that horse and ride off, or you might just disappear."

"You must be Frank," Miles said. "Please don't shoot; I'm a friend of your brother's. I've come to warn him about a Pinkerton raid planned for tonight. I've also come in search of my lost son, Johnny Collins. I'm Miles Collins."

The door opened once more. Jesse stared in disbelief at their visitor.

"Frank, Ma, it's okay, I know this man. He's Johnny's father. Hello, Mr. Collins, it's good to see you again. Come on in. Ma here will fix you something to eat."

"Sorry, mister," Frank said.

"My apologies, sir," Zee said. "There's a lot of people who want to kill my boys. Can't be too careful."

"I understand," Miles said.

While they were eating, Miles told them about his career as a crazy preacher spy.

"I shaved my thick beard this morning."

Jesse, Frank, and Zee all laughed.

"That time at the church, you looked so familiar to me," Jesse said. "I knew I'd seen those eyes somewhere before."

"Now let me tell you about the raid," Miles said. "I followed Mr. Askew's farmhand to Kansas City last night. He met with Julius Hawk, the Pinkerton. You boys know who he is."

Jesse grimaced.

Frank frowned.

"They know you're in town. They intend to take you back to Kansas City, dead or alive."

"I'm going to kill that farmhand," Jesse said. "And Old Man Askew, too."

"Right now, I think you boys had better leave before it's too late," Miles said. "I've done some checking around. Hear tell Hawk has a well-armed posse on the way. They'll probably get here around sunset and surround this place. You know Hawk likes to burn people out. He burned my home years ago in Alabama. It might be wise to leave Clay County for a while."

"Thanks for the warning, Mr. Collins," Frank said. "We'll leave." He looked at his mother. "Ma, no use losing the homestead. Let them inside if you have to –

prove we're not here."

"Mr. Collins," Jesse said, "how can we ever repay you?"

"Help me find my boy."

Jesse thought of the talk he'd had with Johnny – the one about "Johnny Collins" being dead and how he never wanted to be called by that name ever again. If anyone came around asking about him, Jesse was supposed to say he'd been killed in battle after the Lawrence Massacre.

It had been hard for Jesse not to tell Johnny about Christine's visit to Zee's, but Johnny had made it clear. People from his past were not welcome. Johnny had threatened to kill Jesse or anyone else who dared to reveal the truth. Jesse James did not fear other men, but he had a healthy respect for Johnny's skills as a shootist.

Jesse studied Miles' face. He saw the mist in the old man's eyes. His resolve weakened.

"Johnny's mother died of smallpox a while back," Miles said. "On her death bed she made me promise to search for our lost son and never stop until I found him. I think he's still alive, and I can't bear the thought of going to my grave without seeing him again."

The last brick in Jesse's wall of resistance cracked.

"Mr. Collins, come outside a minute," he said. Jesse did not look at his mother.

When they were clear of earshot, Jesse put his arm

on Miles' shoulder. "What I'm about to tell you, I've told no one, other than Frank. And I'm taking a chance in telling you. Truth is, Mr. Collins...best I know, Johnny is alive."

"Why are you whispering?" Miles asked.

"I told Ma he was dead 'cause Ma's friends with Johnny's girl – you know, Christine. Your son told me the man known as Johnny Collins had died and made me swear I'd never reveal his survival to anyone. He said if I did, he'd kill me. He goes by a different name now."

"What name is that?"

"You wouldn't believe me if I told you, and if I did, he'd kill me for sure."

"He wouldn't if I were around," Miles said.

Frank stepped from the shadows where he'd been listening. "I wouldn't be so sure about that," Frank said. He looked at his brother. "Jesse, let's not do anything to get ourselves shot."

Jesse nodded.

"Mr. Collins, I'm afraid I agree with Frank on this one. I'll tell you this much, though. Johnny Collins was alive and well last time I saw him. He still shoots as fast and straight as he ever did, and he has done some amazing things since the War."

"What about his cousins, Bill and Charlie Thompson? How are they?" Miles asked.

"Alive and well," Jesse said. "They're with Johnny."

"Can you lead me to them?"

"That wouldn't be smart, Jesse," Frank said.

Jesse looked at Miles. The man seemed to be aging by the minute.

"I'll tell you what I'll do, Mr. Collins," he said. "Every year we have a reunion of Quantrill's Raiders. We get together, reminisce, and stage a raid, usually on a Yankee-owned bank or train. The raid is always on August twenty-first, the anniversary of the attack on Lawrence. We change the location and host every year. Last year we were in Dallas with Cole Younger. This year, it will be in Denver, and the host is supposed to be your son. We always need about a month to scout our target, but this year's raid is the biggest to date, so we've agreed to meet on the Fourth of July to give us extra time for planning."

Frank picked up on his brother's idea.

"If you just so happen to be in Denver at that time, you might go to the Lost Cause Saloon. It's Johnny's favorite place. Ask for a bartender named Red. Tell him Dingus wants to see you. Then shake his hand like this, with the thumb out and the pinkie turned inward, and tell him, 'Never Surrender, Raiders Forever.'"

"Like this," Jesse said. He demonstrated the secret grip.

"Red will show you to the back room," Jesse said. "If we're lucky Johnny will be there. Sometimes he doesn't arrive until the second or third day though. Even though he's hosting, that might not change. He marches to his own drum, that's for sure."

"Where are you going now?" Miles asked.

"The best place to hide is always a big city," Frank said. "You can blend in with a lot of people. Get lost in a crowd."

"I agree," Jesse said. "Where do you want to go, Frank? Chicago? New York? San Francisco? New Orleans?"

"Somewhere warm," Frank said. "I'm too old for the cold."

"Where will you go, Mr. Collins?" Jesse asked.

"I'm going back to Arkansas," Miles said. "I guess I'm a bit homesick. Been gone too long. But I'll be in Denver for the Fourth."

"Not growing that beard back, are you?" Jesse asked. "Tell you the truth, it didn't suit."

They all laughed.

"No," Miles said, "I reckon I won't need one there." He walked towards his horse. "You boys be careful and stay alive."

"We'll do our best, Mr. Collins," Jesse said.

"See you in Denver," Frank said.

Zee opened the door to fuss at her boys about supper getting cold. She was just in time to see Miles doff his hat and wave goodbye.

§§

Hawk was on the train with the rest of the posse. The railroad had donated the use of a special boxcar. It was spacious enough for ten men and horses. Heavy shutters kept the curious from seeing inside. Hawk had learned that his vast network was matched, if not surpassed, by that of the James gang.

They were loyal to Frank and Jesse. They refused to turn them in and warned them of any danger.

But there would be no warning tonight. Hawk had seen to that. Tonight, the James boys were in for the surprise of their lives. The train slowed and creaked to a halt, the screeching sound of metal against metal announcing their arrival. Before they opened the boxcar, Hawk gave the posse last-minute instructions.

"Okay, men, we're going to ride to the James Farm. I'll lead the way. We will surround the place. I'll do the talking. We might have to encourage them to come outside. Perkins, did you bring the flare?"

"Yes, sir."

"Taylor, did you bring our housewarming present?" Hawk asked. He was referring to a newly invented incendiary device specially ordered by Allan Pinkerton from an arms merchant in New York.

"Yes, sir."

"And all of you, remember this: I want the James boys alive if at all possible. Do not fire your weapons without my command. I will shoot any man who fires without my permission. Is that understood?"

"Yes sir."

"Ladd, open that boxcar," Hawk said.

The door rattled on its tracks. Hawk spurred his horse. "Hyahh!" The posse followed.

§§

Everyone was in bed and asleep at the James Farm – except Zee. She was listening for the sound of horses. An hour crawled by; all quiet. She was wondering whether the raid had been canceled, when she heard the low, steady drumming of hoof beats pounding on the Missouri sod. They grew louder with every second then stopped.

A resonant baritone cut through the night air.

"Hello to the residents of Castle James! I am Julius Hawk of the Pinkerton Detective Agency. I have a warrant for the arrest of Frank James and Jesse James. We have reason to believe they are staying inside this farmhouse. They have one minute to come outside. If they do, we will arrest them peaceably. They will be given a fair trial for the offenses of robbery and murder for which they are being charged. If they do not come out here, I will set this farmhouse on fire. Do I make myself clear?"

Dr. Samuel, Zee, and their children left their beds and huddled together in the living room near the fireplace. Zee opened the window and yelled.

"This is Zerelda James, the mother of Frank and Jesse James. They're not here! They heard you were coming, and they're a thousand miles away."

"You lie, woman! We know they're in there, and your lies won't save them. You have thirty seconds left. What will it be, Frank, Jesse? Are you going to come out here, or will we have to get nasty?"

"I'm telling you the truth, mister. They're not here. You've got to believe me. Come inside and see for yourself."

"Do you think I'm a fool, woman? If I were to walk inside, your sons would shoot me between the eyes. Fifteen seconds left. If you love your sons, you'd better tell them to walk out here right now with their pistols on the ground and their hands behind their heads."

"They're not here, I tell you!"

"Perkins, let's shed a little light on the situation," Hawk said. "Toss that flare inside the living room. If they're in there, that flare might light up the room, maybe give us a target. Taylor, get the weapon ready in case we need it."

Perkins approached the farmhouse, worried he was about to die. Jesse James was an excellent shot. He threw a rock through the living room window. He sparked the flare and heaved it.

Zee was standing near the window when the rock

357

broke the glass. She felt the flare whiz by. It landed on the floor near the fireplace. Dr. Samuel beat the flare with his cane and flipped the smoldering stick into the fireplace.

Chaos erupted.

The oil in the flare mixed with the embers in the fire. An explosion rocked the farmhouse.

Little Micah was lying on the floor in the middle of the living room a few feet from the fireplace. Blue flame shot forward and blew a hole in his stomach. The explosion mangled Zee's right arm. Still, she crouched over her dying son and tried to comfort him. Dr. Samuel took one look at the boy's wound and knew it was fatal. He also knew Zee's arm was lost. He screamed out the window.

"Stop! You've killed my little boy, and maybe my wife, too!"

Hawk ordered two men to kick in the front door. They charged inside. Hawk and two others followed. The rest ringed the house to prevent escape.

What Hawk's men saw when they entered the living room made them sick – even Hawk. A little boy, nearly blown in half, was being comforted by his mother, whose arm was a bloody mess. The boy was trying to speak but couldn't. Finally, he went limp. The woman looked up at Hawk and screamed.

"You'll pay for this! My boys will kill you for this!"

"Where are your sons, madam?" Hawk asked.

"I told you the truth. They're not here."

"Men, search the house and the barns. They're here somewhere. They've got to be."

Hawk secured the room. He looked behind the curtains and door. He looked at Zee.

"I regret any injury to your person or to anyone in your family, but those who harbor criminals are just as guilty. I suspect you've aided, abetted, and assisted your sons in all sorts of mischief. Tonight, you've paid the price."

One of his men entered.

"Sir, we've looked all over. No one here."

"Did you find any tracks?"

"Yes sir. Three horses – two in one direction, and the other going the opposite way."

"How fresh were they?"

"About a half-day old I'd say."

"Someone warned them," Hawk said. He turned to Dr. Samuel. "Sir, I want the name of whomever alerted you to our arrival."

"I don't know what you're talking about," Dr. Samuel said.

"I notice you have two more sons here," Hawk said. "Which one do you want to lose?"

Samuel burst into tears. "No! No! It was the preacher man...named Collins."

Hawk's eyes blazed. He snarled.

Zee tried to focus through her grief and pain.

"This will make the papers. You can't cover it up. Frank and Jesse'll read about it. There won't be anywhere on earth where you'll be safe." She pointed to Jack Ladd who had stepped into the room. "Or you either – Judas!"

The color drained from Ladd's face. He did not speak.

"Mount up, men," Hawk said. He assigned men to follow the tracks. "The rest of us are heading back to Kansas City. Let's leave these people to their grief. This will be good practice for them. Frank and Jesse will be next. Madam, when you see your sons, tell them they were the ones who killed this boy. They exposed their family to danger, then left like the cowards they are."

Frustrated and embarrassed, Hawk led his men back to Kansas City. January 26, 1875, a day of disappointment and death. The James brothers had escaped and soon the world would know.

He was no closer to finding Johnny Collins and the Thompson brothers. Frank and Jesse were gone, and they were his only link to the ones he was after. Quantrill could not help anymore. All Hawk could do was keep his field assets active, and hope for the best.

§§

Miles rode up to the plantation mansion and tied his

horse to a stately oak. Isaiah came out to greet him.

"Howdy Miles."

"Isaiah, it's good to see you! How have you been?"

"Very good, everybody's doin' fine. We've all wondered where you've been. Hadn't heard from you in a long time. Been years, it has."

"It's a long story," Miles said.

"Well. I do like a good story. Come on in and tell us all about it. Let me tell Jake and Naomi you're here."

Isaiah walked upstairs and returned with Jake and Naomi.

"Miles, I'm glad to see you didn't get yourself killed," Jake said.

"It's so good to see you, Miles," Naomi said. "We were worried about you, since your last letter was, oh, say, six years ago?"

"I'm sorry," said Miles. "But I've got quite a story to tell."

"Well, it's just about time for dinner. I think I smell some fried chicken. We'll eat and listen," Naomi said.

"Sounds good," Miles said.

As they ate, Miles told them everything.

"Jake, I came back to Cross Hollows because I wanted to preach a few sermons in that church, and because I want you to go to Denver with me and find our boys," Miles said.

Jake looked at Miles, then Naomi, then back at

Miles.

"Count me in," Jake said. "I've thought about them every day, hoping they were still alive, praying for them. Hearing they're still out there gives me hope. When do we leave?"

"The guerrilla reunion starts in July, so I figure we'll leave in April. That'll give us plenty of time to make it."

"I can't wait," Jake said.

§§

Hawk read a telegraph from the Chicago field office and smiled. An undercover agent had spotted Jesse James in the Chicago area. He appeared to be following Allan Pinkerton. The Pinkertons had been alerted to his presence and were taking all necessary precautions. The trail was hot again, and Hawk would follow Jesse James to the ends of the earth if he had to, because a Pinkerton never gave up. He always got his man.

Hawk had not realized how long his journey would be. Jesse had led him all over the country, first to Chicago, then to Nashville, New Orleans, St. Louis, Dallas, Santa Fe, and now he seemed to be heading to Denver. Hawk telegraphed the Denver office. He would put an end to the chase there. He would arrest the James brothers and bring them back to Kansas City for hanging.

Or maybe Frank and Jesse would die while trying to escape, after revealing the whereabouts of Johnny

Collins. Hawk believed justice should be swift. A jury was not needed. He was judge enough. His verdict and sentence should be quickly meted. Hawk smiled and thought.

Yes, I will hang those scoundrels and feed their bodies to the vultures.

§§

It had taken Miles and Jake several months, but the first part of June found them in New Mexico Territory camping in the valley below Raton Pass. They rode north all month amazed by the beauty of Pikes Peak and the waterfalls and springs below. Finally, on the night of July 3rd, Miles and Jake sighted the lights of Denver glimmering in the distance.

"We should be there sometime tomorrow, probably late afternoon," Jake said.

"Tomorrow can't come fast enough," Miles said.

§§

Bill and Charlie had been working hard to prepare for the Raiders reunion. They had seen to every detail by reserving rooms at several hotels and working a special deal for drinks with Red at the Lost Cause Saloon. Johnny had been scouting for the guerrilla raid that year, which was to be the most daring, outlandish heist in American history, but also the riskiest. They were planning to rob the United States Mint.

The Mint had opened in the 1860s. It was highly

guarded by a network of local, state, and federal law enforcement. The Mint had been robbed once before by a disgruntled employee who was quickly arrested. He had only stolen a few bars of gold.

Johnny's plans were more grandiose. Johnny had befriended an employee of the Mint, a young man named Tucker, who knew the delivery and shipment schedules. One night over a few whiskeys, Johnny broached the topic of the Badman. Tucker confessed to holding a certain fascination for the outlaw. He'd read all about his various gunfights and robberies. Johnny took a chance and revealed he was a part of The Badman's band. The Badman wanted Tucker to help him execute the most magnificent robbery in American history, one for which he would be handsomely compensated.

Johnny said the target was the Mint. Tucker's participation would be worth an even share of the stolen gold along with safe passage to Europe, South America, or wherever else he wanted to go. Tucker couldn't wait to join and promised to do everything in his power to help.

Armed with inside information and the assistance of the deadliest guerrilla fighters in history, Johnny was confident of success. They would plunder millions in Yankee gold and use it to help themselves and others.

Johnny let Bill and Charlie make the arrangements

for the reunion, such as hotel rooms, whiskey, and gambling tables. The Raiders were a good mix of bank robbers, farmers, politicians, ranchers, gamblers, gunfighters, train robbers, and sheriffs, but during the reunion they were all brothers. They always reminisced and enjoyed themselves.

Most of the Raiders were due in by July 1st, but Johnny planned to come in a few days later. He always liked to make a grand entrance. He had something very special planned for his host year.

Everyone in Denver had been talking about how The Raven would be performing at the Denver Opera House on July 4th, singing and acting in a musical adaptation of Shakespeare's *Antony and Cleopatra*. Johnny had heard about her exotic beauty and melodious contralto voice. He was intrigued about why she had never married. This was Johnny's first chance to hear her sing.

For this year's grand entrance, Johnny planned to attend the opera, meet The Raven, flirt with her, and bring her to the Lost Cause Saloon as his date. Every one of his colleagues would be envious. It never occurred to Johnny that she would say no – few women ever did. Johnny was especially handsome. His blue eyes, wavy brown hair, dimpled smile, and tall, muscled physique distinguished him from other suitors. He was irresistible to most women.

Johnny smiled and braced himself for a magical

evening.

Johnny wore a Mexican sombrero and concealed his guns under a brown duster. His black Badman suit was in a little house he had bought with cash not too far from where Rogers, the journalist, lived. Only Bill and Charlie knew where it was, but they didn't have a key.

On the way to his house, Johnny passed by the Denver Opera House. It was just a few hours until show time. He spotted Black Jack Foster and his ruffians on a three-day bender. The smell of whiskey leeched from their torsos.

Black Jack was his usual boisterous self. "Tonight, boys, we're going to have us a little fun with that Raven, yes we are," he said. "I hear she's real purty, and she thinks she's too good for any man. I think we're good enough for her, boys, don't you?"

A drunken chorus shouted its affirmation. Foster and his boys had a notorious reputation about town. Black Jack had roughed up several prostitutes at the Lost Cause Saloon. He was fast on the draw. Story was he'd killed at least twenty men in gunfights.

Johnny frowned. Foster was many things, but Johnny had never known him to lie. Whatever he said he was going to do, however despicable, he always did. Johnny had been planning to attend the play as a citizen. He had thought about wearing a New Orleans style gambler's suit. He changed his mind.

Tonight, he would wear black.

§§

Hawk followed Jesse and Frank to Denver but lost track of them in the city. He had undercover agents planted all over the city, however, so he felt confident they would soon be found. Jesse and Frank would then be in his custody, and the games would begin.

Hawk decided to celebrate the Fourth at the opera, listening to The Raven, the singing sensation he had read so much about. Two of his agents would be joining him, a reward for their hard work. The others knew where to reach him should there be any new developments.

§§

Johnny was opening the front door to his hacienda when Bill and Charlie walked up.

"Where have you been?" Bill asked.

"Scouting," Johnny said.

"Everyone's been asking about you," Charlie said. "Jesse and Frank are here; so are the Youngers."

"Sounds fun, boys, but I'm going to the opera, and you're going with me."

"What? Well, you'll probably see Frank James and Cole Younger. They're going to see The Raven," Bill said.

Johnny opened the door and ushered them inside. He walked to his bedroom and emerged a few minutes later carrying his Badman suit. He would change at the theater.

"Why are you bringing the suit?" Charlie asked.

Johnny described his encounter with Black Jack.

"That's why I need you boys there. Who knows what will happen? I'm not going to let them do anything to The Raven, that's for sure."

"Sounds like a wild night at the opera," Bill said.

Johnny and Charlie laughed, and they walked outside, mounted their horses, and rode to the opera house.

§§

In the dressing room of the opera house, Christine was getting ready for the show. Victoria was helping her with her makeup and wardrobe.

"Victoria, I'm getting tired," Christine said. "I think this might be my last show for a while, maybe even for good."

"You'll get your second wind," Victoria said. "You always do."

"How many times have we played Denver?" Christine asked. "Why should tonight be any different? I'll never find him. I'm just wasting my life waiting for someone who's probably already dead." She started to cry.

"Sweet girl, don't cry," Victoria said. "Your singing means so much, to so many. Find comfort in your music."

"It's all I have left," Christine said. "My music, and you."

"Go out there and sing like it was your final performance. Kill them with your devastating beauty and your songs. You are a perfect Cleopatra. The dark skin, the long eyelashes, the smile. If I were a man, I'd find you irresistible. Play like Johnny's out there tonight, and that he's your Antony. If he's really dead, die with him tonight. Make the audience feel what you feel."

"You always know just what to say," Christine said. "I can't wait to go out there now. Tonight, I am Cleopatra, and the whole world will feel my love for Johnny, and the pain in my heart."

"Well, child, you will be great," Victoria said, "but to tell you the truth, I feel a little queasy. I'll try to stay for the start of the first number, then I'm going back to the hotel."

"I hope you get to feeling better," Christine said. By now, she was used to Victoria's little spells, usually improved with a little "medicinal" brandy. "I'll see you after the show."

They could hear the announcer. In a matter of moments, the curtain would rise to reveal the exotic Egyptian queen. Christine felt the excitement stirring deep within. She was ready.

§§

It was around 5:00 p.m. on the Fourth when Miles

and Jake tied their horses to the hitching post outside of the Lost Cause Saloon. They found Red and gave him the special handshake and watchword. They were led to a room at the back of the saloon. Red opened the door, and Miles and Jake were staring at a roomful of dangerous men, including Jesse James.

Jesse looked up, smiled, and walked over. He shook hands with Miles and Jake, then turned to face the other guerrillas.

"Boys, this here's Miles Collins, the father of Johnny Collins, and this is Jake Thompson, the father of Bill and Charlie Thompson. Treat them like they were your own fathers."

"Jesse, where are our boys?" Miles asked.

"Haven't seen Johnny. I saw Bill and Charlie earlier today, but they stepped out a few hours back, and I haven't seen them since. Some people were talking about going to the opera, to hear The Raven sing. Johnny and the boys might be there. Johnny really loves music, you know."

"Thanks. I guess we'll walk over and buy us some tickets."

"No need. Your son bought a bunch for us. We've got at least ten extra. Here you go." Jesse handed two tickets to Miles.

"Do you know where we might find a room?"

"I arranged with Red here for two rooms upstairs,

rooms 7 and 8, I believe."

"Thanks, Jesse," Miles said.

"Thanks," Jake said.

"Where's Frank?" Miles asked.

"I don't know. I bet he went to the opera house for the play, as much as he likes Shakespeare. I'm going to stay here and play me some poker with the boys."

Miles and Jake found their rooms, unpacked their bags, and got ready for the play. They went downstairs, ate a steak, and rode over to the opera house. They presented their tickets to the usher who showed them to some excellent seats, ten rows from the front in the center section. They searched the opera house but did not see any sign of their sons.

"Hello, Mr. Collins."

Miles turned around to find Frank James sitting next to Cole Younger.

"Mr. Collins, that really you?" Cole asked.

"Yes sir. It's been a long time, hasn't it? Glad to see you're still alive and well. Have you seen my son?"

"No, sir."

"Cole, you remember Jake Thompson, Bill and Charlie's father? Frank, I don't think you've ever met."

"Good to meet you," Frank said. He shook Jake's hand.

"Nice to see you again, Mr. Thompson," Cole said.

"Have you seen my boys?" Jake asked.

371

"Earlier today. Don't worry, you'll see them."

"And not a moment too soon," Jake said.

§§

Hawk pulled the Pinkerton card to get three seats close to the front, ten rows back in the left section. Hawk would have had an excellent view of Miles had it not been for the ponderous form of Black Jack Foster sitting on Miles' left. Jake sat next to Miles on the right.

Hawk wasn't watching anybody or anyone that night. He had stepped out of his Pinkerton role for the evening – he needed vacation from the James brothers. The mice had exhausted the cat. He was there to enjoy a nice, relaxing night of music and Shakespeare, and he couldn't wait to see and hear The Raven.

§§

Johnny's generous donations to the theater had ingratiated him to Bigsby, the stage manager. Johnny had paid for various improvements; he was one of the theater's chief patrons. In return, Johnny was given the key to the back door of the theater and was allowed to come and go as he pleased. Bigsby knew Johnny as William Hawthorne.

It was Johnny's custom to arrive after the play started and watch the performance in a seat set up especially for him between the stage and the front row in the side stairwell area. He was to the left of the actors on stage, and to the right of the audience. The area was obscured by shadows cast by the stage lights, which made him virtually invisible to the audience and actors alike.

The theater was a hemisphere. The dressing room was in the center of the semicircle at the back of the theater, about five feet from the back exit. The dressing room had two doors, one leading to the backstage area, and the other leading to the stage itself. The backstage door opened to a walkway that arced around the stage with stairwells on each side leading down to the auditorium.

The stage lights cast shadows on the walkway area between the stairwells and the front row. A side exit was located in this area between the front row and the stairwell not far from Johnny's seat. The side exit opened only from the inside and locked once closed.

Tonight, he was a little earlier than usual. Johnny wanted to watch the opening scene. Johnny was dressed as William on his way to the theater, but after entering through the back door, he went to the dressing room and changed clothes. Emerging as The Badman, Johnny walked outside and faced Bill and Charlie, his black bandanna not yet over his nose.

"Boys, tie our horses to the tree nearest that side exit. Charlie, watch the horses. Bill, you can watch the play, but keep your gun handy. If anything funny happens slip out the side exit, the one by my seat, warn

Charlie, and get the horses ready for a fast ride."

He pulled the bandanna over his nose.

"Now, boys, I'm going to hear The Raven."

He walked down the curved path toward his seat. Bill exited the back door and went around to the front. After the usher took his ticket, Bill found his seat. He was a few rows in front of Hawk.

Bill scanned the crowd in search of Black Jack. As he did, Hawk saw him.

There's something familiar about that face, Hawk thought. *It's been a long time – it's aged, but I've seen it before.*

He rummaged through his memory, got nothing, and decided to enjoy the production.

§§

"Ladies and gentlemen, tonight we are privileged to present, for your listening pleasure, a true singing sensation. She has performed across the West, and across the ocean, for dignitaries, royalty, tycoons, barons, magnates, and ordinary folks like you and me. Just last year, she sang at the Royal Palace for Queen Victoria. We are fortunate to have her with us tonight."

Boisterous applause. Bigsby waited for the clamor to subside. "The Raven and her wonderful troupe of players will present *Antony and Cleopatra*, and there's no need to tell you who will play Cleopatra."

The crowd roared its approval.

374

"This show has been made possible by Mr. William Hawthorne, our gracious benefactor. Thank you, Mr. Hawthorne, wherever you are."

Black Jack wiped the red eye whiskey from his lips after a long pull on the bottle he'd bought from El Loco, a notorious bar and brothel three blocks over.

"Get on with the show!"

Miles caught the full blast of Black Jack's fetid breath and coughed.

"You got a problem, old man?" Black Jack said. "Don't be coughin' on me if you got the consumption, you hear?"

Miles had his hand on the Navy Colt in his pocket. He knew a dangerous man when he saw one. Miles meekly nodded, and Black Jack returned his gaze to the stage where a stagehand was in the process of drawing back the scarlet curtain.

It rose very slowly. By design. Bigsby loved the suspense.

§§

What the audience saw and heard next was extraordinary. Victoria had spared no expense on the production. She spent lavishly, for costumes elaborate, sets exquisite, and cosmetics exotic.

Scene one found "The Raven" in an Egyptian headdress, wearing a half-mask composed of various jewels with eyelets long and wide enough to see

Christine's beautiful brown eyes. She was sitting in a golden boat with silver oars rowed by slaves. Attendants waved fans made of fronds over her head.

The Raven began to sing. From the first phrase, the crowd fell silent, mesmerized by her dulcet melodies and the versatility and range of her voice. All were entranced, but especially the men, who were captivated by her legendary beauty.

With her olive complexion and brown eyes, The Raven was perfect for the role of the Queen of the Nile. She had become a beautiful woman.

Johnny was lost in another world. In all his life he had known only one other girl as beautiful who sang so well. He closed his eyes and listened. The Raven sounded just like Christine. He felt an irreparable hole in his heart.

At the end of the song, a handsome actor stepped forward, portraying Marc Antony. His muscular legs rippled below the hem of his toga. Johnny was anticipating a love scene. He watched Antony draw closer and closer to Cleopatra, until his lips were almost touching hers.

Before they could kiss, Black Jack jumped up from his seat. He fired both pistols into the ceiling, then rushed the stage by way of the stairwell. Four cronies joined the coordinated attack. Black Jack punched Antony in the mouth and tried to take his place.

Christine resisted. The crowd roared. A chorus of boos rose up from folks upset by the interrupted kiss and Black Jack's misconduct.

Johnny was in his usual place when he saw Black Jack climb onto the stage and run toward Cleopatra. Johnny knew he had to do something. He jumped up and climbed the stairwell to the stage. Having escaped the initial assault, Cleopatra raced toward the other side of the stage. She ran into Johnny. In a fluid flash, he pushed her to the side and drew two pistols.

"Black Jack, back up, and throw down your guns!" Johnny yelled.

Rogers was in attendance. Though he had not anticipated an appearance by the legend he had helped create, he knew a valuable chance at publicity when he saw one. He pointed at Johnny.

"It's The Badman!"

The crowd began to chant.

"Bad-man, Bad-man, Bad-man!"

Johnny heard the roar of the crowd, as did Black Jack. The crowd had come for a play but were in for a gunfight. The Badman motioned to Bill. Bill left his seat, walked down the aisle and out the side exit, to warn Charlie and ready the horses.

The Badman glared at Black Jack; Black Jack glared back. Christine, still wearing the half-mask, watched the two men, frightened but fascinated.

Was this man who had come to her rescue really the legendary gunfighter? Was this The Badman?

Black Jack didn't want any part of the famous shootist but did not want to show fear in front of his gang.

"So, this is the famous Badman, huh, boys? Doesn't look so tough to me, but I guess we see why he's killed so many men. He draws on them first. If I turned around, he'd probably shoot me in the back. He was about to shoot me, without giving me a fair chance. Kind of a coward if you ask me. Kind of yellow."

Johnny spun the pistols in his hands in a clockwise, then counterclockwise cycle. The pistols resembled two black wheels; they spun fast and gracefully. The spinning guns mesmerized the crowd. Then, he gradually decelerated their rotation before holstering the pistols with a slow, deliberate motion.

The other members of Black Jack's gang stepped up. Now it was four to one. They pulled back their dusters to display their sidearms. Unknown to Johnny, a fifth member of the gang was holding a rifle trained on Johnny's head. He was looking down at the action from the mezzanine level above.

"Your mouth is as fat as your head," Johnny said. "You've got one chance to leave here alive – walk away now. You draw...you die. All of you. I never miss."

"You're starting to believe the dime novels," Black

Jack said. "Ain't no one that good. You're just a legend in your own mind, a tall tale, that's all."

The rest of his gang laughed, but they sounded a little nervous. They had seen the spinning pistols.

"Remember, boys, behind every legend there's a kernel of truth," Johnny said.

Johnny watched their eyes. The one to Black Jack's immediate right was afraid. Johnny would shoot Black Jack first followed by the two on his left. Then he'd come back for the coward.

Black Jack's eyes widened, a sure sign. Before Black Jack's gun was halfway out of the holster, he was dead with a bullet in the temple. The men to his left each got a shot through the heart. The man on the right, hands trembling, had his gun half-cocked and had barely cleared leather when a slug from Johnny's Schofield ripped through his left eye.

Miles had seen the fifth man, as had Cole. Black Jack's henchman was raising his rifle when Cole and Miles shot him at the same time. He fell from the mezzanine above to the floor seating below. Thankfully, no one was hurt by his falling body.

The crowd cheered. This was the best show they'd ever seen. Johnny bowed with great flourish, then remembered a line from another Shakespearean play, one his father had read to him as a boy. Johnny raised both hands above his head.

"*Vini, vidi, vici!*"

Frank looked at Miles. "In case you haven't already guessed, that's your boy. He loves to make a grand entrance at these reunions, and this year's beat all I ever saw."

Miles had known the moment the crowd began chanting "Bad-man." He'd flashed back to Quantrill's death bed and remembered his dying words: "Johnny Collins...Badman." The words seemed like dissociated nonsense then.

Not anymore.

Everything now made perfect sense. The voice, the swagger, the gunplay, and the Latin phrase Miles taught him as a boy, an apt epilogue to what had transpired on stage.

§§

Hawk had figured it out, too, just slightly after Miles. He had also overheard portions of Quantrill's dying declarations. So, Collins was the Badman? Hawk smiled. The nickname certainly fit.

He also knew why that cowboy in front of him seemed so familiar. He was one of the Thompson brothers, one of the men who hanged his son. Hawk had seen the Badman motion Thompson toward the side exit just before the gunfight.

Hawk's brain saw Johnny's plan as clearly as a photograph. Two of his men had come with him.

"Follow me, men. We can't let them get away! There's a side exit to the actors' left. They'll be leaving that way. We'll circle around the theater and catch them."

Just before the gunfight started, Hawk and his Pinkertons ran up the aisle toward the back of the theater. They raced past the ushers, out the front entrance, and circled the theater in counterclockwise fashion.

"I'm guessing we are about to run into two well-armed men guarding three horses."

They stayed close to the wall and crept around the back of the theater. Hawk peered around the edge. He saw the Thompson brothers about twenty feet away. They were facing the opposite direction. They held the reins of three horses. One was a big black stallion. They were staring intently at the side exit.

"On the count of three," Hawk said.

He counted and they moved. Hawk cocked his pistol and aimed at Bill's head.

"Bill and Charlie Thompson, drop your guns. Move and you're both dead!"

Bill and Charlie dropped their Colts. Hawk ran to the side exit. He heard shots inside, then the roar of the crowd.

§§

Inside the theater, after the last man fell, Johnny

walked over to Christine. She was crying and trembling. He swooped her up in his arms and carried her through the side exit. He intended to mount Midnight and ride into the night. When the coast was clear, he figured they would head to the Lost Cause Saloon and revel in his grand entrance. Maybe he could persuade The Raven to sing a few songs for his old mates.

When he stepped through the door, Johnny felt the unmistakable presence of the business end of a Colt next to his temple.

"You're mine, Mr. Badman," Hawk said.

Miles, Jake, Frank, and Cole burst through the side exit. They didn't like what they saw on the other side. Bill and Charlie were handcuffed, some stranger was holding Christine, and Johnny's hands were above his head.

For all of his intelligence reports and resources, Hawk had never seen a picture of Frank James or Cole Younger. He had no idea who they were. He did, however, recognize Miles.

"You're too late, preacher man," he said.

Miles stopped in his tracks. Hawk pointed to the ground. Miles, Frank, and the others dropped their weapons.

Hawk reached for Johnny's bandanna. "Okay, ladies and gentlemen, let's unmask The Badman – although I am sure most of us already know who he is."

382

Hawk tugged on the bandanna to reveal the handsome and unhappy face of Johnny Collins. "Johnny Collins, do you remember me? It's been a few years, huh boy?"

Christine, still wearing the mask, screamed and fainted.

"Hawk!" Johnny snarled.

"I've got you, boy," Hawk said. "The wheels of justice grind slowly, but they do move. I'm going to take you back to Lawrence, you and the Thompsons, and then I'm going to hang all three of you from the same tree where my son died."

Hawk turned to Miles. "They killed my boy," he said. "I'm going to kill them. And I'm going to enjoy it."

"He wasn't supposed to die," Johnny said. "You know that as well as we do if you were watching from the corn. We weren't going to hang him. It was Quantrill who kicked the horse without our consent."

Hawk tsked like a scolding schoolmarm. "Johnny, you should have known. You don't put a man's head in a noose unless you mean for him to die. You did it. Now, you will pay."

Just then Hawk recognized Jake.

"Both fathers, how touching."

One of the Pinkertons splashed some water from a canteen on Christine's face. She shook her head and sat bolt upright on the ground where she'd been placed. She looked around, spied Johnny, and scrambled to her feet.

She took off the mask.

"Johnny!"

She rushed toward him with her arms open. The two Pinkertons stepped up to restrain her advance, holding her back, keeping her from reaching Johnny. Johnny turned around to see an older, even more beautiful version of the woman he loved.

"Christine?"

"Yes," she said. She stared into his eyes.

"But you died in Kansas City. Mrs. Duke saw your body." He lowered his hands very slowly, palms out, so Hawk could see he had no malintent, and reached inside his shirt. He pulled out the pendant. "This had your blood all over it."

"Mrs. Duke was wrong, Johnny. She mistook me for another girl who died. A girl named Loralei."

"How could she ever mistake you for another girl? No one else has your face," Johnny said.

"That's just it. Loralei's face was crushed...beyond recognition. Mrs. Duke had found my necklace lying on the ground. It had broken off my neck during the fall. When she looked at Loralei, without a necklace, she mistook her for me."

"Oh," Johnny said. That made sense.

Christine continued. "It took them a while to find me under the rubble. Mrs. Duke left Kansas City to break

384

the news to you and the others before I was rescued. When she saw me in the hospital after she got back from the guerrilla camp, she was very upset. It was too late to tell you the truth. You had already left for Lawrence. I've been searching for you ever since, to let you know I'm alive, and that I still love you."

Johnny couldn't think of anything to say – except one word.

"Christine...Christine...Christine."

Hawk's sardonic laugh shattered the magic.

"Now, isn't that touching?" he said. "I remember you now, Missy. You're the little half-breed princess I caught in the Missouri woods all those years ago. Sorry about the building. I warned Ewing, but he wouldn't listen. Glad you got to see your man one last time. We've got to leave you, though, ma'am. He's got a date with a rope."

Christine burst into tears. "Not...not again. I...I... I've looked so long..."

"That makes two of us," Hawk said. "Mr. Collins here is a very bad man, a notorious murderer. Killed more men – and boys, I might add – than anyone rightly knows. But I do know one thing. He murdered my son, and he's going to pay with his life. Justice must be served."

"Okay, men," Hawk said. "Let's take these prisoners to Kansas. They're wanted for murder, multiple counts."

Hawk and the other Pinkertons led Johnny, Bill, and Charlie towards the train station.

§§

After Hawk and his men took Johnny and the others away, Christine ran to Miles.

"Where is Victoria?" he asked.

"She's at the hotel. She wasn't feeling well tonight." She hugged Miles as tightly as she could. "It can't end this way," she said.

"It hasn't ended yet," Miles said. "Frank, Cole, do you think the Raiders might help me and Jake rescue our boys?"

"I can't speak for anyone else," Cole said, "but count me in."

"Me too," Frank said. "We need to go tell 'em what happened. See who wants to help."

"Okay," Miles said. "Meanwhile, Christine's going to take me to see another someone I haven't seen in a long time."

§§

Victoria was staying at the Imperial Grand Hotel on the second floor. Christine knocked on the door.

"Who is it?"

"It's me," Christine said.

"What's wrong? The show can't be over already."

"I'm not alone," Christine said. "Are you presentable?"

Victoria, always presentable, ignored the question and flung open the door. "My dear, what in the world happene—" When she saw Miles and Jake, she clutched the doorframe for support. It took a moment for her to recover her legendary poise.

"Miles Collins. Jake Thompson. My, you do know how to surprise a lady."

She flung her arms around their necks. Miles gave her a synopsis of the evening's events.

"What can we do?" Victoria asked.

"We're going to rescue Johnny," Miles said.

"From the Pinkertons? Is that even possible?"

"It will be with the men we're taking," Miles said.

"Where are they going?" Victoria asked.

"Lawrence, Kansas," Jake said. "Hawk intends to kill them for hanging his son."

"He's probably put them on the train to Topeka," Miles said. "From there it's only a day's ride to Lawrence. I don't know if we'll get there in time. It might depend on whether Hawk holds a trial first and schedules a formal execution later. They won't have to wait for a gallows if he hangs them like he hanged Gene years ago, and the trial might be nothing more than a hastily assembled kangaroo court."

"Whatever we do, we'd better do it quick," Jake said. "Time's wasting."

"Jake is right," Miles said. "We'd better get moving."

Christine and Victoria spoke in unison. "No!"

The men looked puzzled.

Victoria daubed her eyes once again with a handkerchief, then said. "We're going with you."

"This is no place for ladies," Jake said.

"I'll take my chances," Victoria said. "And you both know I ride better than either of you."

Christine and Victoria were ready to go in ten minutes. They left instructions about the remainder of their belongings at the front desk and were ready to swing into the saddle by the time Jake appeared with the horses. Victoria mounted Bill's horse. Christine took Midnight.

They rode to the Lost Cause Saloon. Frank and Cole had everyone assembled. As soon as Miles and the others entered, all activity stopped. The entire group stared at the two beautiful women.

Cole stepped forward to make the introductions. "This is Mrs. Victoria Collins and Miss Christine Nelson. Those at the show tonight might recognize Miss Nelson as The Raven."

The crowd erupted with applause.

Cole rapped the butt of his pistol on the doorjamb.

"Now," Cole said. "Miles has something to say."

"Gentlemen," Miles said. "Several things happened tonight. Black Jack Foster disrupted the show and tried to molest Miss Nelson. My son Johnny stopped it and killed him – along with three others from Foster's gang."

There was a swell of approval.

"Unfortunately, Johnny's old nemesis, Colonel Julius Hawk, who is now a Pinkerton, was in the audience. He's arrested Johnny and is taking him to Lawrence, Kansas, for execution."

A voice from the back. "How can we help?"

Cole took over.

"As you might have heard from Bill and Charlie, Johnny had been planning our biggest score ever. We were going to rob the United States Mint and divide the gold. Miles and Jake here are asking us to reconsider. Frank and I are going to ride with them to Lawrence to rescue Johnny, Bill, and Charlie. Anyone who wants to go is welcome. If you don't go, no one will hold it against you."

Jesse stood up.

"I'm going to Lawrence, men! Who'll ride with me?"

"Lawrence!" they screamed over and over, some still remembering Quantrill's speech from years before.

"To your horses!" Jesse yelled. "It's time to ride!"

§§

Miles silently wondered whether the train might have been faster, but there was no stopping old horse soldiers who smelled battle. Their hearts were racing with emotion and nostalgia. Quantrill's Raiders belonged on horses, not trains. They had been the best cavalry unit in the Civil War. Their lightning raids were the envy of almost every fighting force. Their tactics had been just as successful against banks and trains after the War, and Miles hoped they would be enough to rescue Johnny. It would take a good plan, and a delay in the execution on Hawk's part. Miles did what he always did when life grew murky and hope seemed dim. He prayed.

Miles, Jake, Christine, and Victoria soon discovered why the Yankees thought of Quantrill's Raiders as the devil's cavalry. Quantrill had learned horsemanship from Native Americans who themselves had mastered the horse after acquiring it from the Spaniards.

The Indians had shown the Raiders how to ride sidesaddle, so as not to present a target to the enemy. With much practice, the Raiders had also learned how to shoot their pistols with speed and lethal accuracy from any position on the horse. They were more than mounted soldiers. They were horse warriors.

Jesse was the leader of the operation by vote of the guerrillas. After a long ride, he finally signaled a stop near a small mountain stream. They watered their horses and let them graze while they caught a few hours of shut eye. Then they were off again.

This pattern repeated itself several times, but finally, after a week of hard riding, they crossed the border into

Kansas. Jesse was discussing battle plans with Miles, Jake, Frank, and Cole. They would send a spy into Lawrence, just as Quantrill had years ago, to see if Johnny, Bill, and Charlie were still alive, and if so, to ascertain the date of their execution. They would schedule the rescue based on this intelligence.

One of Quantrill's old scouts was chosen for this mission, and he rode off ahead of the guerrillas. He posed as a cattle buyer. The raiders remained outside of Lawrence in the dense underbrush and waited.

§§

As Miles suspected, Hawk had boarded the train for Topeka. Hawk ordered his men to keep a pistol trained on the prisoners at all times. If the train were attacked, they were to shoot the prisoners without hesitation.

Hawk didn't expect any resistance. The two aged fathers were no match for his Pinkerton agents. In truth, Hawk hoped they might try something. He loathed Miles Collins almost as much as Johnny. On the train, Hawk walked over to Johnny with a sneer on his face.

"Badman, you should have joined in with me years ago. You'd have made some kind of Pinkerton. Could have used that gun of yours. I would have made you a great man, a man of honor, a law-abiding citizen, a defender of the law, and a paragon of virtue. A true hero. It's too late though. Now, I've got to teach you a lesson – make an example of all three of you."

"You like having a captive audience, don't you, Hellhound?" Johnny said. "Why would anyone voluntarily listen to you?"

Hawk drew his quirt and lashed it hard across Johnny's face. Blood flicked across the boxcar.

"Son, you need to learn a few things. That's the problem with you, the James brothers, and the rest of your kind. You don't have any respect for the law," Hawk said.

"Whose law?" Johnny asked.

"My law," Hawk said. "Don't you know? I am the law. And I make the law."

"I don't respect you or your law," Johnny said. "You're a murderous coward who didn't even have the salt to fight for his boy."

Hawk cracked the whip across Johnny's chin one more time.

"I'll enjoy watching you hang," the Pinkerton said. "Did I tell you I'll be your hangman? You'll have to bear with me, though, I'm not a professional. I just might botch things up. Might take a while."

Snickering, Hawk walked over to the other end of the boxcar. Johnny winced at the pain in his face but refused to make a sound. The other Pinkertons smiled. They enjoyed his discomfort.

The train stopped, the doors swung open, and the prisoners were placed on horses for the ride into

Lawrence. Hawk planned to house them in the local jail there. The Denver office had telegraphed ahead to Judge Stone, and a jury would be selected and assembled soon after their arrival. Johnny, Bill, and Charlie would not be afforded legal counsel, and there would be no motions to transfer venue. Those decisions had already been made.

Their cases would be heard in Lawrence where many still remembered the brutality of the Massacre. Johnny, Bill, and Charlie would be tried, convicted, and hanged with all due haste. Judge Stone was not exactly impartial. He had lost two brothers and a son to Quantrill's Raiders. In flagrant violation of established and applicable rules of ethics, the judge had refused to recuse himself.

Stone greeted the train and shook Hawk's hand. "Welcome, and congratulations, Colonel."

"Do we have a trial date?" Hawk asked.

"We haven't even arraigned these prisoners yet," the judge said.

"I have," Hawk said. "That's good enough. They have all pled guilty. All we need is a sentence from you, which I will leave to your discretion." He winked. "And I humbly offer my services as the executioner."

"Offer accepted," the judge said. "When the time comes, don't feel the need to hurry. I think a slow, painful hanging is in order. The trial will be a week from now. That's as soon as we can do it."

"Fine," Hawk said. "And we'll hang these men the day after trial."

"How is that possible?" the judge asked. "It may take a while to find a carpenter to build the gallows."

"Forget the carpenter," Hawk said. "All I'll need are three horses, three nooses, and a tall oak tree. I'll supply the tree."

§§

Miles was amazed by the distance they had covered in a week. They were a half day's ride from Lawrence and awaiting news from the scout. They all wondered if the boys were still alive.

It was Frank James who first spotted the scout. Miles woke Jake from his nap to receive the news. Victoria and Christine came as soon as they heard. To their relief, the scout said the boys had not yet been hanged, but they had been found guilty at a trial held earlier in the day and sentenced to death. They were to be executed on the oak tree behind Hawk's house at high noon on the morrow.

"Okay, listen up, men, here's the plan," Jesse said. "At 11:30 tomorrow morning, Frank and I will rob the First National Bank of Lawrence. Cole, you and your brother Jim will start shouting at the top of your lungs, 'It's Jesse and Frank James! They're robbing the bank! They've already killed three men, and they're riding this way!' Everyone will scatter, which will leave Hawk without a lot of extra help."

"That's where we come in, Jake," Miles said. "We'll find Hawk and take him out if we can. Then we'll get our boys and ride out of town."

"Once we're done at the bank," Jesse said, "we'll circle around and help you with Hawk if need be. After we've rescued Johnny and the others, we'll rendezvous at Mt. Oread."

"What does rendezvous mean, Dingus?" Jim Younger asked. He always used Jesse's nickname.

"It means to meet, knucklehead," Jesse said. "After that, it's every man for himself. We'll split up and branch out in small groups. We'll ride in different directions like Quantrill taught us. Any questions, men?"

"Where are we staying tonight?"

"We'll camp on Mt. Oread tonight. No fires. No noise."

"What if someone sees us?"

"That's a chance we'll have to take," Jesse said. "If they do, the plan will change. We'll ride straight for the boys, kill Hawk, and ride out of town as fast as we can. Any other questions?"

"Yes," Christine said. "Where do Victoria and I come in? What do we do?"

"Stay at Mt. Oread and wait for us."

Both women answered, "No!"

Jesse thought about insisting but saw the flame in

Christine's eyes and changed his mind.

"You and Victoria can ride with me and Jake," Miles said. "But Christine, it won't do you and Johnny any good for you to get yourself killed. I'll want you both to ride behind Jake and me at all times. Is that clear?"

"Yes sir," she said. She was not happy.

§§

In the jail, Charlie read his Bible while Johnny and Bill shared stories. They talked about growing up in Paint Rock. They talked about their mothers, about how much they missed them, and how they had been so happy to see their fathers again. Charlie interrupted their nostalgia with a disturbing question.

"What's it gonna be like in Hell?"

"Shut up, Charlie," Bill said.

"We'll find out soon enough," Johnny said. "But don't worry, boys, there are degrees in Hell, and your workstations won't be as hot as mine. Murderers get the hottest fire, I'll bet."

He laughed but he felt something unusual in his heart.

Fear.

"Bill, Johnny, just the same, I'm going to pray tonight for forgiveness of our sins," Charlie said. "If the Lord somehow gets me out of this, I'll change my life and be a better man."

"Oh, that's just fear talking, Charlie," Bill said.

"You'll be back robbing trains and making money the easy way in no time at all. And we will too."

"Bill, you don't seem too worried," Charlie said.

"No, I'm not. It's all over when you die," Bill said. "You just fade to black. In some ways, it will be a relief. I won't have to worry about you anymore."

"Bill, you don't believe in God?" Johnny asked. "I know I've seen you praying in times past, before a raid or a robbery."

"I used to believe, Johnny, but somehow, somewhere, I just stopped. I think it was after I killed that railroad conductor in Missouri, you know, the one with the long side whiskers."

"But Bill, you didn't mean to do it. I saw it happen. It was an accident."

"I know," Bill said, "but somehow I felt just as bad. After that, I found it was easier not to believe in anything. That way you didn't have to feel any guilt."

"But you know in your heart you're wrong, don't you, Bill? You know there is a God, and you also know where we're going, you and me. Charlie, I'm not so sure about. I don't think I've ever seen him kill anybody or do anything mean to anyone, at least not on purpose. No, Bill, I think that noose is going to kill our bodies, but not our souls, and we will forever be separated from our brothers, the very brothers we had hoped to avenge," Johnny said.

Charlie opened the Bible and read a portion of a verse. "Vengeance is mine, I will repay, sayeth the Lord."

Bill felt goose flesh on his arms and trembling in his heart. He put out his hands to his brother and to Johnny. The three bandits knelt as one and begged God for His forgiveness...

...and for His mercy.

They went to bed. Bill and Charlie tossed and turned. Johnny made no effort to sleep. He stayed up and wrote a letter to Christine. Everything told him it was a wasted effort, but he clung to a small hope that Hawk might have it delivered to her after his death. The letter was more like a poem. Johnny titled it, *One More Time*.

One More Time

I've been blessed with true forgiveness
I've been finding peace of mind
I've been hoping I could hold you one more time
I've been feeling lonesome feelings
I've been crying late at night
I've been dreaming I could hold you one more time
One more night to spend together
One more chance to make things right,
One more way to say 'I love you'

Before I face the morning light
See the gallows, they are building,
Soon the noose will hold me tight,
I'd been praying, that I'd see you
One more time...before I die.

Johnny wrote the last word, then fell into a fitful sleep. He dreamed he was drowning in a dark river flowing through a desolate canyon. He heard other voices – a droning, dirge-like chorus of others who had made their choices – bad choices – long ago.

No matter how hard he tried, Johnny could not find the surface. He was drowning...drowning in a river of lost souls...drowning in a river of fire.

§§

Hawk served the boys a big breakfast. He didn't want them to run out of energy during the day's festivities, which included a gauntlet and a public hanging. Yes, a gauntlet. It had been Hawk's idea, and the judge and mayor thought it was brilliant. Let the citizens enjoy a little vengeance. Nothing too severe. No whips or clubs would be allowed but punching and kicking would be encouraged.

Pinkertons would precede and follow the prisoners and control the level of punishment. Hawk would not let them die before they reached the hanging tree. He wanted to kill them with his own hands.

§§

The Raiders had not been spotted. Most of Lawrence was getting ready for the hanging. Even the farmers were all in town. No one missed a hanging, let alone three hangings at one time. They were fascinated by the idea of the gauntlet. Many remembered the Lawrence Massacre like it was yesterday, and they wanted revenge.

They were so focused on getting in their licks and watching the trio swing, they paid no attention to anything on the outskirts of town. So, the reconstituted Quantrill's Raiders rode into Lawrence undetected...

...just as they had twelve years before.

§§

"Are you ready, boys?" Hawk asked. "You're in for a little surprise. Something I call 'collective justice.' Today is the day of vengeance, first for the town, then for me."

"How would that be a surprise?" Bill asked. "We already know you're going to hang us."

"Walk outside, boys, and see for yourselves."

It was a mile from the jail to the hanging tree. People of all ages had formed in two long rows along the route. They wore expressions of ravenous expectation.

"Boys, I think it's only fair that prisoners know what they will be facing. The good citizens of Lawrence are gathered to repay you for what you did to their town twelve years ago. One hundred fifty good men and boys died at your hands. Today, you get to meet the families. Every person along this line has the opportunity to hit you once – no clubs, no whips, and no deadly weapons. If it gets too much, I'll stop it – not for your sake but for mine. No one gets to kill you but me."

"So, you're going to make us run the gauntlet," Johnny said. "I don't think that's been done for several hundred years."

"I'm impressed by your knowledge of history, son. Such a waste. You had so much potential. Yes, the gauntlet has fallen out of favor, but I've always been known as a renaissance man, and today the tradition is reborn in my hands. Shall we proceed, boys? Your public awaits."

The boys began their slow march to the tree. They were punched, kicked, spit on, scratched, and even bitten once. Between assaults, they were mocked, especially Johnny.

"It's The Badman!"

"Look at The Badman."

"He doesn't look so tough now."

Three-quarters of the distance to the tree, Hawk almost stopped it, but Johnny, Charlie, and Bill were not going to give him any satisfaction by falling or asking for quarter. They focused on the tree like it was the only source of water in a desert and kept moving.

When they made it to the tree, they were beaten, bleeding, bruised, and swollen. A soldier walked forward with three horses. Other soldiers lifted the condemned onto the horses. The horses were led to the hanging tree, where three nooses were slung from the oak's sturdiest branch. Hawk remembered where his boy had been years ago. Johnny's noose was placed there. Johnny was in the middle, with Charlie on his left, and Bill to his right. The Pinkertons cinched the nooses around the condemned men's necks.

Hawk cleared his throat and began the speech he had spent hours perfecting.

"Good citizens of Lawrence, vengeance is ours today! Twelve years ago, these bloodthirsty criminals were part of a group known as Quantrill's Raiders who murdered many of our good men and boys including my own son, Julius Hawk, Jr. These three men hanged my boy on the very tree behind me. The Good Book says the ground is cursed where innocent blood is shed. My son's blood cries up still for vengeance. The only way to remove this curse is to shed the blood of the guilty on the exact same spot. That is why I have chosen to bring them back here to be hanged on—"

Before Hawk could utter another word, a murmur crescendoed through the crowd. It grew to a rolling chorus, a wave of shock and fear that crashed into Hawk's ears. Even as he heard the words, he refused to believe them.

"It's Jesse and Frank James. They just robbed the bank! They killed three men, and they're riding this way!"

The crowd scattered and left Hawk and his Pinkertons alone with their prisoners. Miles fired at Hawk first, but he missed. Hawk ducked behind Charlie's horse. Cole and Jake began to pick off the Pinkertons one by one. Hawk fired his pistol at the invaders, but Jake kept him pinned down with a steady barrage.

Miles, Bowie knife in hand, started to climb the tree. He was going to cut the ropes. If the horses bolted before he could help them dismount, they would be all right. Johnny, Bill, and Charlie could ride anything, even without using their hands.

Miles extended the knife toward the first rope when pain tore through his left thigh. As he fell, he saw the Derringer in Hawk's hand. Miles crawled behind Bill's horse and prayed the gunfire would not cause the animals to bolt.

With a shout for cover fire, Victoria booted her horse's flank and rode toward Miles.

Jake started to yell, realized it was useless, and recommenced firing. Victoria swooped past Miles. She bent to the side of the animal and while at full gallop flipped a pistol to her brother-in-law. Hawk fired at her, but the shot sailed wide.

A memory flashed through Hawk's mind: William Quantrill slashing his spurs across the horse on which his young son sat. Hawk stayed low and crawled towards Johnny's horse. The animal was beginning to get a little twitchy. It would not take much encouragement to make it panic.

From her vantage point, Christine discerned Hawk's intent. She flicked the reins to Midnight's sides.

"Hyah!" she yelled. Midnight galloped towards the tree.

Hawk was zeroed in on Johnny's horse. He did not see The Raven riding across the open ground. He knew he could not reach the animal – the gunfire was too steady. So, he raised his hands and stood.

"Don't shoot," he said. "I surrender. Don't shoot."

Jake almost pulled the trigger. Better to end it all now. But he'd never shot a defenseless man before – and he would not start now. His ethics weren't situational.

The second Jake lowered his weapon, Hawk ripped off his hat and slapped the rump on which Johnny sat. The horse snorted in protest and broke into a gallop.

Hawk looked up, expecting to see Johnny's broken neck. He saw something altogether different. Hawk hadn't seen Christine. While Hawk was behind the tree, Christine had positioned Midnight adjacent to Johnny's horse, close enough for her to cut the lynch rope with the knife. To do so, she stood tall in the stirrups and leaned out toward the rope while calming Johnny's fidgety horse. She had cut the last strand just as the horse bolted forward, and Johnny had fallen to the ground, neck bruised but unbroken.

When the horse bolted, Christine, leaning against it, lost her balance, dropped the knife, and threw out her hands. She caught hold of a tree limb, hung for a second, then dropped. When Hawk looked up, he saw her atop Johnny – both on the ground – both relatively unscathed.

"No!" Hawk yelled.

He raised the Derringer to shoot Johnny, but gunfire forced him back behind the tree. Hawk crawled over and grabbed Johnny by the feet, dragging him face down toward the cornfield, the same cornfield from which Hawk had watched his son hang.

Jake and Cole hesitated to shoot for fear of hitting Johnny or Christine. Christine was holding onto Johnny for dear life, clinging to him with all her strength, when Hawk's right boot landed square against her jaw and caused her to lose her grip. Christine began to cry. Hawk dragged Johnny's weakened body into the cornfield.

Miles tried to rise. "Miles, you've been shot," Victoria said.

"I'll be all right. I've got to save my boy."

Struggling, he got up. Blood trickled from his left leg. Miles and Christine followed Hawk. Jake and Cole cut Bill and Charlie down, The brothers collapsed to the ground, exhausted and barely breathing, but still alive. Victoria tended to their wounds.

Suddenly, Frank and Jesse rode up, having made a substantial withdrawal from the bank. Jesse saw Miles and Christine. Jesse and Frank dismounted and ran over to help. Miles called to them.

"Boys, they're somewhere in that cornfield. We've got to hurry. Frank and Jessie, we'll be on this side. You go to the other. We'll search row by row until we find them. Hawk's got a gun, so be careful."

§§

Hawk dropped Johnny with a righthanded haymaker. The gauntlet had weakened Johnny. When they'd put him on the horse, he had no more will to fight – no more desire to live.

Then, Hawk kicked Christine.

A spark of anger ignited within him and grew into a roiling, uncontrollable rage. Hawk had to die.

Johnny head-butted Hawk and swung blind. Hawk sliced the air with his knife. Johnny blocked with his forearms, but the emotional surge he had experienced was losing ground to the reality of battered fatigue.

Hawk brought the knife from above, a savage, descending strike intended as a death blow. Johnny caught the Pinkerton's wrist and fell backwards. Hawk placed his chest on the butt of the knife and leaned against it. All Johnny could see was the savage blade inching ever closer. He felt the steel scrape against his Adam's apple.

Hawk and Johnny were rolling across the rows; the sound of their struggle gave away their location. Jesse pulled his pistol. He was trying to get a bead on Hawk. Just as he aimed, though, Johnny lurched hard to one side. His move knocked Hawk off but placed his body between Jesse's gun and the Pinkerton. Exhausted, Johnny tried to stand.

Hawk picked up a rock and slammed it into Johnny's temple. Johnny groaned and collapsed. He moaned on the ground, bleeding from the blow. He was not quite unconscious. Hawk sat behind Johnny and laid his knife across Johnny's throat.

"I walk out of here right now or Mr. Badman dies. I'll slit his throat, ear to ear," Hawk said.

Jesse used his bank robber voice, the one designed to strike fear into his victims. "This is Jesse James, Hawk."

It worked. Hawk felt his knees weaken a little. Jesse kept shouting. "You harm Johnny, and I'll make you pay."

Desperation settled in Hawk's mind – the understanding he was very close to death. His mind searched for a solution.

He needed a diversion. He reached into his hip pocket and extracted a flask. He flipped the cork from the top and poured whiskey over Johnny's bare head and shoulders. He tossed the flask behind him. It trailed a stream of whiskey as it flew through the air. He rummaged through his jacket pocket. He brought out a sulfur-tipped match. The whiskey woke Johnny up. He saw Hawk lift up the match, high enough for all to see.

"I'll set him on fire," Hawk said. "You may kill me, but he'll live the rest of his days in a very special type of misery."

Johnny discerned Hawk's intentions. He had to do something fast, but what?

Hawk saw Miles moving through the corn stalks.

"Stop, preacher man." His voice was coarse and strained – the insanity of fear had seized his mind. "I'll turn your boy into a human torch."

He flicked his thumbnail across the top of the match. The end sizzled, then burst into flame.

Miles froze.

Christine gasped.

Now or never. Johnny summoned all his remaining strength and threw his elbow back and caught Hawk across the nose. The Pinkerton fell back. Caught off guard, he dropped the match as he fell. It landed near the whiskey flask. The dried corn was a tinderbox, and the fire began to spread through the field.

"Roll, Johnny, roll!" Miles yelled. He fired a haphazard shot at Hawk and ran towards his son,

Christine by his side.

Johnny rolled away from the flames, toward Miles and Christine, who were standing near the field's edge. Billowing smoke soon made vision nearly impossible. Miles and Christine heard Johnny's voice. They ran toward the sound and reached Johnny at the same time – where they also found Hawk. He had hold of Johnny's foot and was dragging him back towards the flames.

As tongues of fire licked at his shoulders, Hawk cried out with a guttural moan. "Burn, Badman, you're gonna burn! Forever!" The timbre of Hawk's voice suddenly changed from a resonant baritone to a shrill, high-pitched cackle – the sound of madness.

Miles and Christine grabbed Johnny's upper torso and pulled with all their might. Miles raised his leg and delivered a savage kick to Hawk's mouth. Hawk lost his grip; Miles and Christine pulled Johnny out of the field, away from the flames. Miles cut the rope cuffs, freeing Johnny's hands, and Christine tended to Johnny's wounds.

Recovering from Miles' kick and fueled by adrenaline, Hawk rolled to the Derringer, grabbed it, and shuttled through the flames, face down, still in pursuit. His coat was aflame. He reached the edge of the field, raised up, drew, cocked the Derringer, and looked for Johnny. He spotted him.

Perfect, he's walking back to the tree. That's where

he needs to die – where Hawk, Jr. died. That will remove the curse.

He pulled the trigger. There was nothing but a dull click.

No ammunition.

With Johnny braced between them, Christine and Miles staggered from the conflagration. They gently dragged him towards the tree that had been intended as his execution site. He leaned back against the oak while Christine tended to his wounds. He had some cuts and bruises from the gauntlet and his fight with Hawk. He also had a few small blisters on his arms from the fire. Thankfully, the burns weren't too bad. With time and a little Cherokee medicine, Johnny would heal up just fine.

The field was consumed by flames. The small group stared as fiery fingers reached toward the sun.

"He's gone, Johnny," Miles said. "And I think that's a nice preview of where his soul is headed."

Johnny leaned against the oak. "Would have rather killed him myself, but it'll have to do. Let's go."

They helped him up. He was about to mount Midnight and ride away. Johnny turned to his friends and loved ones. His back was turned to the corn.

"Thanks," he said. "I never would have—"

Christine's scream interrupted.

"Johnny, behind you!"

A fiery specter staggered from the blazing cornfield. Knife in hand, Hawk rushed towards Johnny's exposed back like a demon from the pits of everlasting fire. Johnny's hand flew to a saddle holster where he always kept a Navy Colt loaded and ready for action. He drew, whirled, and fired.

Blam! *Blam*! Two shots, in rapid succession, one almost on top of the other. The first tore through Hawk's heart – the second ripped through his forehead and out the back of his skull. Hawk's burning body collapsed as the skin melted away from the bone.

Johnny looked skyward.

"Now you can rest, Gene," he said.

Christine hoisted herself up onto Midnight, in front of Johnny, taking the reins. She turned and kissed him gently on his bruised cheek. Johnny winced but smiled.

"We've got to move," Miles said. "They'll be coming for us." He said a short prayer, and the battered and bruised contingent rode towards Mount Oread to rendezvous with the raiders.

§§

"Hey Badman, Frank and I are going to ride with Cole for a spell. Hear tell there's this bank up in Minnesota that's just ripe for the picking, and it's owned by some Yankee. Care to join us?" Jesse asked. "We sure could use that gun of yours."

Johnny looked at Christine and Miles, then back at

Jesse.

"That's Johnny from now on. And no, I don't guess I will. I've got a wedding to go to."

"Whose is that?" Jesse asked. He winked at Christine.

"My own," Johnny said.

"I see," said Jesse. He looked at Christine, then back at Johnny. "You know what? I can't say as I blame you."

Johnny watched them ride away somehow knowing he would never see them again this side of the Jordan.

§§

Johnny felt his father staring at him. They had not spoken much. With all the blood on his hands, and all the sins in his heart, Johnny couldn't look him in the eye. Then he thought of his precious mama.

"Pa, thanks for coming. I've been so lost." He paused. "How's Mama?"

"Son, she died, several years ago now," Miles said. His voice was wistful but not bitter. "On her deathbed she told me to head west and find her lost son, to preach the Gospel, and see that he was baptized. I think it's time to finish what we started all those years ago in the Paint Rock River."

Johnny could see his mother's face and hear her voice – the sweet sound that would never grace his ears again. And Johnny Collins cried.

"There's no salvation for the Badman, Pa. I've got

thirty-seven notches on my guns, not counting Hawk. I bear the mark of Cain, and, like you preached many years ago, it won't wash off."

"I was wrong, Johnny. Sometimes it does," Miles said. "Moses once killed a man, but God chose Moses to deliver the Israelites from bondage in Egypt. Saul of Tarsus laid his cloak to the stoning of Stephen, but God selected Saul to preach the Gospel to the Gentiles. King David sent Uriah the Hittite to the front lines, but Nathan the Prophet made it clear that David's sins were taken away."

The horses plodded along.

"Johnny, I've never told you this before, but I killed my share of men back in the Mexican War, and I've killed a few since, in self-defense when I felt it was necessary to protect myself or the ones I love. There's not a sin you have committed that cannot be forgiven, and there's no stain on your soul that cannot be removed."

Johnny listened to his father. Well-versed in the Bible, which he still read every night, Johnny was very familiar with the Bible characters referenced by Miles and their life stories. With respect to his own story, Johnny had always assumed he was beyond redemption, haunted by the guilt he felt for young Hawk's death. Johnny began to see a glimmer of hope flickering in a remote cavern of his mind.

"Well, I'll tell you what, Pa, you keep preachin' and I'll keep listenin' all the way to California. What do you say?"

"Let's ride," Miles said.

"California, here we come," Christine said.

"Can I tag along?" Victoria asked. She smiled at Miles. "I always found you Collins boys so handsome."

"Of course," Miles said, with a twinkle in his eye.

§§

Jake, Bill, and Charlie rode with them as far as Dallas and stayed for the wedding. Miles served as the preacher and best man. Victoria was the matron of honor. Miles looked around and found another preacher to preside over his wedding to Victoria. Jake stood with him. Jake, Bill, and Charlie were homesick, and they returned to Cross Hollows to be with Naomi. Johnny and Christine rode west with Miles and Victoria through New Mexico Territory and Arizona Territory toward California.

Miles must have preached at least a hundred different sermons by the time they reached Arizona. Johnny loved them all, but one in particular. He listened as Miles opened his Bible to Luke.

"There was a man who had two sons. The younger one said to his father, 'Father, give me my share of the estate.' So, he divided his property between them."

Johnny had known the Parable of the Prodigal Son

for as long as he could remember. He listened in rapt attention.

"...[he] squandered his wealth in wild living. After he had spent everything, there was a severe famine in that whole country, and he began to be in need. So, he went and hired himself out to a citizen of that country, who sent him to his fields to feed pigs. He longed to fill his stomach with the pods that the pigs were eating, but no one gave him anything."

The next line speared Johnny's heart.

"He came to his senses."

Yes, Johnny thought. *He came to his senses. Have I? And if I have, will it matter?*

"... 'I will set out and go back to my father and say to him: Father, I have sinned against heaven and against you. I am no longer worthy to be called your son; make me like one of your hired servants.' So, he got up and went to his father."

He left home, Johnny thought. *He squandered his fortune. He sullied his family's good name. And still he was drawn back home.*

"...*But when he was yet a great way off,* his father saw him and was filled with compassion for him; he ran to his son, threw his arms around him and kissed him. The son said to him, 'Father, I have sinned against heaven and against you. I am no longer worthy to be called your son.' But the father said to his servants, 'Quick! Bring the best robe and

415

put it on him. Put a ring on his finger and sandals on his feet. Bring the fattened calf and kill it. Let's have a feast... For this son of mine was dead and is alive again; he was lost and is found.' So, they began to celebrate."

The son came home.

There was no condemnation...

...only a celebration of a father's never ending love.

When the sermon was over, Johnny walked over to Miles.

"All right, Pa. Don't say another word. I've heard enough."

Miles studied him, concerned his son might be leaving again. But one look at Johnny's face told him otherwise.

"Pa, I'm ready. I want to be baptized."

Miles smiled from ear to ear.

"Me too, Miles," Christine said.

"Might as well make it three," Victoria said.

"I didn't realize I was preaching to you girls, too."

"For every prodigal son, there's a prodigal daughter," Victoria said. She tossed her hair and laughed.

"Only one problem, though, Pa, we're in the middle of Arizona. Where are we going to find any water?"

"Well, son, I spoke with an old Hopi trader in the last town who told me about a canyon. At the bottom of that canyon is a river, and somewhere along it is a pool that would be perfect for our purposes. It's a few miles from here."

"We were headed there the whole time, weren't we?" Johnny asked.

Miles' face beamed with love, joy, and satisfaction. "I kept hoping you'd come around," he said.

§§

They stood on the rim of the Grand Canyon and looked down. "I bet that Indian is still laughing at us," Johnny said. "How deep is this canyon?"

"He said it wouldn't be easy," Miles said. "But nothing's been easy with you since you were seventeen, son, so why should this be any different?"

"Well, I don't think it would be very smart to get killed before I got baptized. Maybe we should find another river."

"Where's your courage, Johnny? I thought they called you The Badman?"

They looked up to find Miles' new friend, the Hopi trader, riding up with two younger braves and two strings of donkeys, three to a string.

Miles turned to face Johnny and grinned.

"Relax, son, you didn't think I was going to guide us down there, did you? These men know how and where to go."

The old Hopi stayed with the horses; the braves led them down into the canyon. They mounted the burros and began their descent. Many hours later they were at the river. Their guides led them to a travertine pool near a place they referred to as *sipapu*. According to Hopi myth, human life began there.

Miles and Johnny waded into the pool, their reflections on the water. Miles led the way. Waist deep, Miles turned around to face Johnny as he had in Paint Rock years before.

"Son, do you believe with all of your heart, soul, and mind that Jesus Christ is the Son of God?"

"Yes sir, I do."

"Then I now baptize you in the name of the Father, the Son, and the Holy Spirit, for the remission of your sins."

Miles placed one arm behind Johnny's back, and his opposite hand over Johnny's nose, and thrust him backward down into the pool. Johnny rose up from the water, rejoicing. All of his sins were washed away, including the mark of Cain.

He was now free from sin and death, raised to walk in newness of life. He felt an indescribable joy and peace he had never experienced in his lifetime. True cleansing. Eternal salvation. He wanted others to feel this way. There was no better feeling on Earth.

"To new beginnings," Miles said.

He shook Johnny's hand and wrapped his arms around him with a bear hug that seemed as strong as any

Johnny remembered.

Johnny offered a prayer of thanksgiving to God for His wonderful grace, for allowing him to find his way home. He now realized that home was not a house made by human hands, nor was it the homestead or village where he had grown up. Home was wherever God was. It had been a long, arduous journey, but this time, Johnny was home to stay.

§§

After Miles baptized Christine and Victoria, he saw Johnny looking for his black suit and pistols. Johnny had been in his long johns for the baptism.

"There's one other thing, son," Miles said.

"What's that?"

"Do you remember, growing up, how you used to say you wanted to be a preacher someday, somewhere in the West?"

"Yes, sir."

"Has that desire ever truly changed?"

"No, sir."

"I didn't think it had. Life just got in the way?"

"Yes, sir."

"Well, there's nothing stopping you now. Saul started preaching right after Ananias baptized him. And he was a bit of a prodigal son too, I'd say. Didn't stay that way, though. Became a force for God."

"What are you saying, Pa?"

419

Miles removed his preacher man's frockcoat and handed it to Johnny along with the Collins Family Bible.

"You'll need a different garment now, son. That black suit doesn't fit you anymore."

"But Pa, I've never preached a sermon."

"Johnny, your whole life's been a sermon. You are a trophy of the Lord, evidence of His power. If The Badman can be saved, then anyone can. You can be a preacher to the outlaws, the misfits, the outcasts, the dark wanderers and wayfarers of this world for you have been one yourself. You speak their language. You, my son, will be a prodigal preacher man, just like me."

"Pa, what is it you did?"

"Son, it's not important who I was, or what I did, but who I am today. Forgetting what is behind me, I press on to the goal. There is no future in your past. You must put it behind you and move on. You can never go back to the outlaw you once were."

"Now Johnny, you've surrendered to God's authority. You've been pardoned. You're free, but not to live as you used to live. Sin shall not be your master now that Christ has set you free. You were bought at a price. You were ransomed. You belong to God now. So, walk in the light and flee from the darkness. I love you, son. You and Christine be safe out there, and preach the Gospel, in season and out of season, wherever you go."

§§

Miles and Victoria bade farewell to Johnny and Christine. California would have to wait. They were homesick. It was a long way to Cross Hollows, but with any luck they'd be back in time for harvest. He wondered where Johnny would go and what he would do. The West was a rough place, but Johnny had pluck, so he would survive.

Christine was twenty-nine years old and beautiful, still young enough to have children. Miles might be a grandpa soon. He said a prayer of thanksgiving to God for saving his lost son.

Victoria smiled, ready for new adventures with Miles. After Cross Hollows, what would they do, and where would they go? She had all kinds of plans, audacious, bold, and exciting, and she always got what she wanted, including Miles. Those Collins boys were oh so handsome.

Christine sang beautiful love songs to Johnny as they rode through the West. At night they slept by the warm campfire, holding each other, loving each other, making up for lost time. All rage gone, only love remained. Johnny Collins had been worth the wait. True love always is. She felt the new life forming inside her and smiled, glowing with expectation.

§§

Johnny donned the preacher man's frockcoat, excited to begin his new journey in the Wild West, a lawless frontier with many lost souls drowning in sin. The West was where men often ran from their past and their dark shadows. They went to reinvent themselves, to be born again, to find new life – and one such man was Johnny Collins.

In his former life, he had been The Badman, the fastest, deadliest gunfighter the Civil War had ever seen, and the Wild West had ever known, but The Badman was dead. Johnny Collins was back. Reborn, revitalized, and reinvented, Johnny was now a prodigal preacher man, wielding a double-edged sword, searching for lost souls adrift in a fallen world.

Ascending the canyon trail to the plateau above, Johnny found the old Hopi and exchanged his burro for Midnight, his magnificent black stallion, constant companion, and faithful friend. Johnny placed the Collins Family Bible in a saddle bag. He swung into the saddle, hands on the reins, Christine behind him, her arms wrapped around his chest.

Johnny Collins would walk in newness of life. His pistols would remain in their holsters, and the Sharps in its scabbard. Resolved never to kill again, Johnny was determined to be a man of love and peace, practicing what he preached. How long would the Wild West let him stay that way?

EPILOGUE

The reader might fairly wonder how I came to write the rest of Johnny's story, specifically those events transpiring after our fateful encounter on Dunvale's train and those months directly following. I acquired much of the information for this book during those initial sessions. He told me about his young life, from his growing up through the hanging of young Hawk and his leaving the Civil War. He also described various train robberies and gunfights preceding our encounter. Additionally, I was allowed to witness several robberies firsthand, so as to get a flavor of their planning and execution.

One day, though, The Badman simply disappeared. Years passed. He did, however, occasionally deliver messages, letting me know how he was, that he was still alive, and that he was not yet ready to authorize publication. He refused to provide any further details about his most recent exploits, so there were significant gaps in my knowledge of his history.

Along with the rest of the public, I read of The Badman's capture in the newspaper by his nemesis, Julius Hawk, and of his scheduled execution. The newspaper described his capture, as well as the methods and tactics used by Hawk to apprehend the world's most notorious outlaw.

Upon reading the article, I traveled with all haste to Lawrence to try to meet with The Badman one more time before his hanging, after which all stories would forever be lost.

Once I arrived, I met with Hawk on the pretense of writing his biography. I assured him the book would present him in a most favorable light and cement his place in history as a vaunted fighter of crime. I asked for access to the notorious Badman, so I could tell the public how my negative conclusions concerning the outlaw were based on firsthand impressions, not secondhand accounts. I assured him that anything the Badman said would be either ridiculed or ignored altogether.

Agreeing to my terms, Hawk arranged for a guard to escort me to the jail. I was allowed to spend an evening with The Badman but was warned that he should be considered dangerous and any risks attendant to the meeting would be mine to assume. I was a bit apprehensive, not knowing whether The Badman would remember me, as I had gained a few pounds over the intervening years.

Entering the cell, I was relieved to see a look of recognition in The Badman's eyes. In fact, it appeared as though he were struggling not to smile. I sat across from him, and, after the guard had returned to his station, we had a long conversation, which lasted throughout the evening. He recounted his activities since our last meeting including his description of the events surrounding his capture. I was sorrowed by his sad reunion with Christine. To find his true love still alive after all those years, and then to be sentenced to die without its consummation seemed unbearably tragic.

Surprisingly, The Badman spent much time discussing spiritual matters. He was filled with remorse for the sins he had committed on Earth. He was ashamed of the blood on his hands. He expressed his deepest remorse for the death of Julius Hawk, Jr., for which he felt a profound guilt.

He instructed me to attend the hanging and to secure his personal effects. These included the letter he had written to Christine from jail and the bloodstained locket he had bought for her years before. After the hanging I was free to publish the book. As I got up to leave, he slipped me the letter he'd written to Christine. On my way out, I bribed a guard and left the jail with the letter and the locket in my pocket.

I bought a ticket to the hanging. I witnessed the

improbable rescue. I heard Hawk's speech and the commotion caused by the bank robbery and hid behind a tree during the gunshots that ensued. When the gunfire ceased, I walked toward what would have been the hanging tree, where I saw The Badman embracing a beautiful woman with raven hair. They were about to mount the black stallion I had first seen those many years ago. I walked over, in time to see The Badman shoot Hawk.

As they were about to mount up, I handed the locket and the letter to The Badman.

"Here you go. I bought them from your guard."

The Badman smiled and clutched them in his hand. Then he gave them to Christine, whose eyes were misty. They asked me where I was going. I told them I had no plans, as my client yet lived, and his story was ongoing.

"Well, you'd better come with us, so you can write about my escape and what happens next," The Badman said.

I rode with Johnny, Christine, and the rest of their companions through Texas, New Mexico Territory, and on into Arizona Territory. When I last saw The Badman, he and Christine were riding west together.

In our final conversation Johnny asked me to publish this story now, and not to wait until his death. He expressed his hope that wandering and lost children might read this tale and realize they can go home again, even if they've traveled far away from everything they have known or been taught. I asked Johnny where he would go and what he would do. Johnny told me he intended to preach the Gospel of Jesus Christ to all who would listen.

I was instructed to send a copy of the book to Johnny at some future date, once he and Christine established their new abode. He will not hide his notorious history but will use it to help others realize that their past is neither their present nor their future. It can be overcome. If The Badman can be saved, so can anyone.

Johnny desires to wield the double-edged sword of God's Word as proficiently as the guns he used to fire. He feels the divine instructions of life can conquer any instrument of death. Johnny has resolved never to kill again, but to live at peace with all people, loving everyone, even his enemies. The Badman has died.

A new man lives...

...saved by the grace of God.

THE END

ACKNOWLEDGEMENTS

I acknowledge Jesus Christ as the Son of God. He came to seek and save the lost. He died as a ransom for many.

Thanks to my wonderful wife Tonya, my daughters, Lindsey and Lauren, my parents, Dr. Miles and Mary Eckert, my sister Angela, my brother-in-law Craig, and anyone else who has in any way supported or encouraged me in the writing of this book.

Thanks to Art Fogartie, my talented editor, for helping me bring this story to life, Mo Raad for his beautiful artwork and cover design, and all of my team at The Paper House for their hard work in helping publish this novel.

ABOUT THE AUTHOR

Ron Eckert resides in Texas with his beautiful wife Tonya. He is an author, composer, singer, songwriter, and attorney. He once served as Ector County Judge in Odessa, Texas, where he was born and raised.

CPSIA information can be obtained
at www.ICGtesting.com
Printed in the USA
JSHW030012020722
27570JS00001B/3